I0549185

Sentinel's Choice

Michael E. Witzgall

SENTINEL'S CHOICE is a work of fiction. Names, characters, places, and incidents are either products of the author's imagination or are used fictitiously. Any resemblance to actual persons, living or dead, business establishments, events, or locales is entirely coincidental.

Copyright © 2013 by Michael E. Witzgall

Sentinel's Choice
First Edition
First printing 2013

All rights reserved. Published in the United States of America by CME Publishing, P.O. Box 4628, Cedar Hill, Texas 75106-4628.

No part of this book may be used or reproduced in any manner whatsoever without written permission, except in the case of brief quotations embodied in critical articles and reviews.

For information, contact Charlie-Mike Enterprises (972) 291-7809

Cover design by Michael Canales
Formatting by Polgarus Studio

For Shelly Lynn and P.J. who refused to let me give up.
Jon & Rose Owen and all the Palmer Alaska PD gang
(I miss ya'll like crazy).
Tactical (SWAT) Sergeant Lynn Heathman – R.I.P. my brother.
For all the badge numbers, especially those of SWAT.
And to the Blue Eyed Warrior who has my six – I am now and shall always
be your friend!

*The measure of a Warrior is not in just the way he lives,
but also in the way he chooses to die!*

ACKNOWLEDGMENTS

What an interesting journey writing this book has been! I must admit that, like most new writers, I had absolutely no idea just how difficult and painstaking this project would become. The hours I spent typing and then retyping a single sentence or paragraph grew beyond count. I've come to realize that my publicist, P.J. Nunn's favorite expression is: "Nope, you can do better." I've also come to realize that each time I hear those words I've grown closer to going postal.

With the above paragraph in mind, I would like to thank Ms. P.J. Nunn for keeping me on track and for pushing me when I needed a not so delicate nudge. My wife Shelly Lynn deserves a great deal of credit for her encouragement and patience – especially when I felt like trashing the entire idea. Being married to me is no easy thing, I add a new definition to "For better and for worse."

I want to express a special word of thanks to LaRee Bryant, Kim West, Fred Witzgall, Juston Coffman and Robbie Cross for reading and editing the first five drafts of this book.

I would be remiss if I did not thank my brothers and sisters of the badge. Not for helping with this book, but for helping me to be here today. On one cold and wet winter night, I had to put out an "Assist Officer." I was in serious trouble. There might have been snow, ice and sleet coming down; but when the bullets were flying and I needed help... it also rained blue!

And finally, I want to thank Gunnery Sargent Kay M. Joy, USMC. Gunny Joy took the boy out of me and made me into the Warrior I am today. Years after boot camp, I ran into him at Camp Pendleton. I asked him if he spent so much time with all Marine recruits, his answer floored me: "Only the ones I felt worthy of the Eagle, Globe and Anchor." Semper Fi, Gunny!

CHARACTERS

Anne & Tomas LaFleet: Sht. Renee LaFleet's parents.

Carl Kothner, Catholic Priest, aide to Father Michael Leopole, Dallas Tx.

Carmen Hansen, Doctor: Forensic Pathologist, Dallas County Medical Examiner

Daniel "Tex" Beers, Sergeant: Dallas Police Department, CAPERS/Homicide Unit, "A" Squad Supervisor – Detective.

Emil "Rocky" Connor, Sergeant: Dallas Police Department, Public Integrity Unit – Detective.

Harold Wong, Deputy Chief of Police: Dallas Police Department, Crimes Against Persons (CAPERS) Division.

Hershel Gaspar, Doctor: Forensic Psychologist (Criminal Profiler), FBI, Dallas Texas.

Ian Web, Staff Writer, Dallas Tribune

James Garret, Officer: Dallas Police Department, Special Investigator for the Chief of Police.

Jon Hill, Corporal: Dallas Police Department, CAPERS/Homicide Unit, "A" Squad – Detective.

Michael Leopole, Monsignor: Catholic Priest, Dallas Tx.

Rachel Saxen, Lieutenant: Dallas Police Department, CAPERS/Homicide Unit – Commander.

Renee Lynn LaFleet, 1st Lieutenant: Commander of 2nd Platoon (Moniker Copenhagen Six), Alpha Company, 1st Battalion, 2nd Force Reconnaissance, 2nd Marine Division, Later: Sergeant: Dallas Police Department, CAPERS/Homicide Unit, "A" Squad – Detective.

Richard Shannon, Lieutenant: Naval Special Warfare Group 1: SEAL Team 1, Commander, 1st Platoon (Moniker Blue Steel). Later: Catholic Priest.

Steven Burt, Sergeant: Dallas Police Department, Public Integrity Unit – Detective.

Thomas Nolan, Officer: Dallas Police Department, Special Investigator for the Chief of Police.

Todd Miller, Corporal: Dallas Police Department, CAPERS/Homicide Unit, "A" Squad – Detective.

William Smyth III: Chief of Police, Dallas Texas.

The Cotton Bowl
Dallas Texas

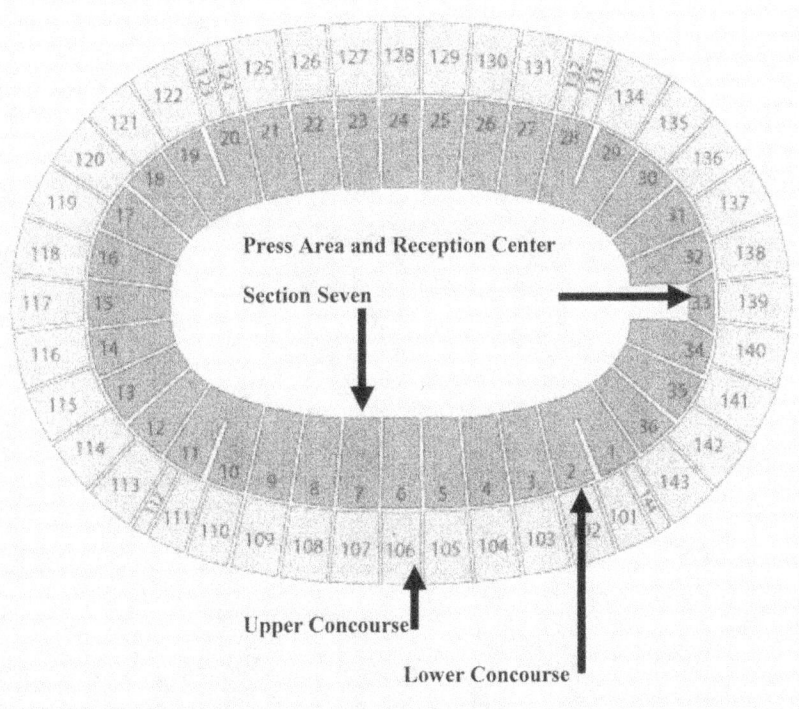

Press Area and Reception Center

Section Seven

Upper Concourse

Lower Concourse

... And in those days, the Land was troubled. There was corruption in high places. There was violence and anarchy in the streets.

A few courageous spirits answered the challenge. They opposed the violent, confronted the unjust, and protected the innocent.

Criticized by many and thanked by few, they remained faithful. They were lonely Sentinels, standing vigil in the whirlwinds of chaos.

But one day, the Land was healed. Peace and order were restored. Justice reigned.

The Sentinels were rewarded with their rightful place in the Halls of Honor...

From: The Chronicles of Ancient America
Fredrick L. Witzgall

PROLOGUE

Present day.

Dear Granddad: It's been a lousy two weeks. Here I am your former U.S. Marine turned cop grandson, Sergeant Renee "Ren" LaFleet, stuck in a hospital bed at the Southwestern University Medical Hospital in Dallas, Texas. My body is trashed (again) from two back to back fist fights (which I think I won, though I really don't feel that way), several gunshot wounds, falling head first down a long flight of stairs and then allowing myself to nearly bleed to death. I mean, for crying out-loud, I have two black eyes, my left forearm and wrist are fractured, my nose is broken, a couple of ribs are busted; but worst of all (as if it could get any worse), three of the bullets shattered my left knee and the upper fibula and tibia. Within a few days of the shooting, a life-threatening infection set in and my left leg was amputated above the knee two days ago. If this is what a victory looks like, I'd hate to see a defeat.

I wish I could make some way-cool macho comment about how messed up the bad guy looks, but the truth is we cheated. I tried to shoot him… missed; but at least I tried. And then someone else, doing a much better job than I did, shot him several times. Being well-ventilated, he died. Not the damn slow, agonizing death I wished he would have suffered, but in this case, dead is dead. And I am thankful for it. Anyway, I got credit for the kill and some shiny medals as a reward, but I really shouldn't have.

1

Who was the bad guy? Someone I knew. Or perhaps I should say someone that I thought I knew. But isn't that the way it always goes? Don't national statistics show that 68% of all murder victims know their assailants? He and I had known each other for a while; therefore, my sense of betrayal is pretty overwhelming at the moment. Crap! Just when you think you know a person, they turn out to be a prolific serial killer.

I guess I'm still in shock about the chain of events that led up to this mess. Or maybe the morphine is clouding my judgment. Either way, I've started writing this story at the end. At this moment you know that the good guys (including me) survive and the bad guy was killed. What I've left out is that there's a trail of dead bodies that led up to this point – bodies that were once good people and bodies that were once evil people. With that in mind, I'll start over at the beginning, which was in Iraq in 1998. This tale is not about my years in the Marine Corps, though for a while you might think so. Please bear with me. It will all come together at the end. Boy Scouts Honor.

CHAPTER 1

Iraq, December 1998.

Using zodiac inflatable boats we inserted near the small southern port city of Umm Qsar, Iraq. America wasn't at war with Iraq, at least not yet, so we shouldn't have been there. My sixteen-man, Marine Force Recon platoon was cold, wet and sweating – all at the same time. The distance to our designated objective required that we move at a hard pace if we were going to meet our guide and be on site by first light. Of course this really sucked because it meant that we had no choice other than to keep moving. Changing into dry socks would have been absolutely orgasmic at this moment; however, we were behind schedule and couldn't spare the time.

Since I was the team leader, the now screwed- up mission was, technically speaking, my fault. But in my own defense, our maps and satellite pictures didn't show the two kilometers deep and six kilometers wide marsh that we walked into less than a hundred meters from the shore. We couldn't go around it (it would have taken far too much time – or so we believed) so we had to go through it. Yep, darn near right up the middle. And three hours later we emerged on the far side wet, cold and covered in mud. Not to mention exhausted. That was the down side. The up side was that, though we didn't know it at the time, coming out of the marsh so far behind schedule probably saved a few of our lives.

As soon as my team was clear of the marsh, we began searching for our native guide. While the team did the search, I checked the Global Positioning System (or GPS) to verify our location. Nothing else had been going right, so maybe we were in the wrong location for the link up. As I was making my final GPS checks, my assistant team leader, Gunnery Sergeant O.W. Roberts, moved up to me, knelt, and in a low stage whisper, "Boss, we found a burned-out warming fire and a few small empty food cans. There are footprints, *lots of footprints*, that lead off to the north but that's about it. We could send an element to follow the tracks, but we're bad on time as it is."

Shaking my head, I whispered back, "No, we need to get moving. The guide was a nice idea, but we have the objective coordinates anyway. I'm not sure about all the footprints around here, though – maybe some nomads came through and scared the guide off. Either way, we're not compromised so we don't break radio silence. Do me a favor and use your compass to verify our directional heading with the GPS and then let's move out."

Roberts took out his compass and asked, "You still don't trust the high tech GPS navigational equipment our Marine Corps blessed us with?"

Smiling, I shot back, "No, and because it was built by the lowest bidder, neither should you."

Two minutes later we were moving again. I wasn't terribly worried about an ambush because our route would only slightly parallel the footprints we had found and the terrain was relatively flat with small rolling dunes. Also, with our night vision equipment (NVE) we would see someone approaching us long before *they* saw us. These factors, trivial though they may seem, meant that we could really push the pace and hopefully make up some lost time. Besides, the quicker we got to where we needed to go, the sooner I could get the mud chafing my crotch cleaned out. Yeah, I know, we are the special forces of the Marine Corps. We are supreme athletes and resistant to pain. But after walking in thigh deep muck and slime for three hours, I swear getting bit in the crotch by an angry dog would hurt a lot less.

4 hours later.

We had just paused to take another GPS reading when Sergeant Joseph Palen, my pointman, signaled me to come up to his position. "Lieutenant, we got our forward scout element hauling ass back to us. I picked 'em up on the NVE's about 400 meters out when they crested a small dune. They flashed lasers, so I'm positive on the identification; but they are *really* beating feet back to us."

As I activated my own NVE, I asked, "Are they being chased?"

"It doesn't look that way, sir."

I scanned the area in all directions but saw only my scout team still about 200 meters away and closing with reckless abandon. My team was already in a tight 360' degree perimeter, so finding the Gunny was easy. "Gunnery Sergeant Roberts, get the team spread out in a linear defense facing our direction of travel. Our scouts are coming in fast. Every third man flash lasers – give them something to home in on."

Roberts whispered sharply, "Aye-aye, sir."

As the team took up positions, I turned back to Palen and asked, "Are the scouts still clear of pursuit?"

Palen scanned the area behind the running scouts and replied, "Sir, their six o'clock is still clear."

Less than 30 seconds later, my scout element, Sergeant Tom Anderson and Sergeant Jose Guera, passed through our defensive line. Both men now knelt next to me and the Gunny trying to explain what had caused them to abandon their scouting mission and rush back to the team. Instead of talking articulately, they were mumbling between gasps of breath. Look, jogging in sand when wearing running shoes and gym shorts is difficult at best; but running hard in sand in combat gear (boots, ammo, weapons, water and field pack) is an absolute killer. All I could do was wait an extra few tense seconds for them to stop sucking wind and talk to me. When the moment was right, I said, "Mister Anderson, please report."

Taking one more deep breath, Anderson said, "Sir, we were about a half a kilometer out when we saw signs that a large group of people, maybe a hundred or more, had cut across our path heading west. We quickly backtracked east for a hundred meters and concluded that this was the same bunch that made the tracks at the marsh. We then followed the tracks west and it wasn't long before we found 'em. They're well dispersed, dug-in and set up in an L-shaped ambush – just waiting."

"Alright, we're burned," I said. "Gunny, turn the patrol around and let's get out of Dodge."

Before I'd finished issuing orders, Guera spoke up, "But that's just it Lieutenant, their formation is facing the wrong way to *ambush us*. Even if they were facing our direction, they're still several hundred meters off our path and the terrain favors us getting by unnoticed."

Looking Roberts in the eyes, I asked, "Ok, what do you think, Gunny?"

Roberts was quiet for several seconds, thinking. When he replied his voice was filled with concern. "Sir, Saddam's militias are very poorly trained, but they aren't stupid. If we can sneak by them, we can continue our mission, but if we're caught, help is a long way off *and* we'd be sorely outnumbered. Also, if we need help, the request has to work its way up the flag pole and that could take time we don't have. But Boss, I think there's a more important issue here. If those militia guys aren't here to ambush us, then who are they after?"

His question made me stop in my tracks. "If they're not after us… That must mean… Crap! Don't Navy and Marine commanders ever talk to each other? Staff Sergeant Johnson, break radio silence and contact command – ask those boneheads if we have friendlies operating in our area! If so, get their radio frequencies and call signs."

Staff Sergeant Todd Johnson didn't answer because he was already on the radio to command before I finished my sentence. That's one of the great things about working in special operations – the men are highly intelligent and stay in these units for years. While the mortality rate can be high, voluntary unit turnover is extremely low, which goes to explain how we can practically read each other's minds. Staff Sergeant Johnson was great at this. He was third in command of this platoon – if the Gunny and I bought the farm (or a piece of the farm) the surviving platoon members would be well led by him.

Snapping me back to reality was a sudden, loud explosion and heavy gunfire to our northwest. Based on the amount of noise coming from that location, no doubt about it, someone was getting lit up pretty bad.

Johnson said, "Sir, command says there's a twelve man Navy SEAL team in this area. I'm switching over to their radio frequencies now and attempting to make contact. "Blue Steel, Blue Steel, this is Copenhagen do you read, over? Blue Steel, Blue Steel, *this-is-Copenhagen* do you read, over?" Nothing but radio static answered Johnson's third and forth repeated calls. Looking up at me Johnson stated, "Sir, negative contact with Blue Steel."

Turning to me, Roberts said, "Sir, either Blue Steel's radio is down or their communications are being jammed – either way they're getting doodled."

I quickly began issuing orders. "Alright Gunny, we're the cavalry. At a fast, *safe* pace we're at least ten minutes from the SEALs. Get Anderson and Guera to lead us in behind the militia. Tell those two to stop short at a decent position of cover and keep their eyes peeled for rear sentries. With any luck, we can trap the militia in between us and Blue Steel. And Johnson, contact command and brief them; also keep trying Blue Steel."

Moving out, the Gunny and Johnson responded in unison with a quick, "Aye-aye, sir."

As we moved closer to the fight, the noise got louder. I heard the distinct crack of U.S weaponry, indicating that the SEALs had obviously recovered from the initial shock of the ambush and were giving as good as they were getting. *Go Team*!

As we continued on, Johnson came up to my position and said, "Still no contact with Blue Steel, sir. Also, we now have negative contact with command. I think some Iraqi army turd must have purchased Russian radio-jamming equipment."

I said, "Great. The only piece of Russian equipment that actually works, and we're getting boned by it. Drift back and brief the Gunny. Also, tell him that just before we move into our final assault positions, we'll need to talk. Then hustle back up here." With a half-assed mock salute, Johnson moved out.

Ten minutes later we halted. Gunny Roberts and I bellied up a dune to look at the militia's positions. "The SEALs return gunfire is still heavy, sir. Means our Navy boys are still in the fight. But they can't be good on ammo or casualties."

I replied, "Yeah Gunny, that's what I was thinking, too. Radio's still down so there's no way to let the SEAL team know we're here. We'll deploy the platoon along this dune just behind the militia."

Looking at that the dune and the militia positions, Gunny Roberts said, "This is only about fifty meters out – that's darn close, sir. But I guess there's nothing else for it. One minute before we start shooting, I'll have our snipers picking off targets of opportunity. That should add to the confusion. Also, I'll set the anti-personnel mines aiming north. If the militia tries to break contact and run that direction, we'll nail 'em in the ass. Sir, I'm sure you realize that the militia may have radioed for help and it will be full light soon – all meaning we don't have time for much fighting."

Glancing around at the terrain I realized what Roberts was talking about. If the militia had help coming, we would lose the cover of darkness *and* be trapped along with the SEAL team. Looking Roberts in the eyes, I answered, "I understand. Ok, one last thing Gunny, if we get in position and see that the bad guys have overrun the SEALs and killed them off, we don't attack. We move out and continue our mission. The platoon won't like it, but they…"

Cutting me off, Gunnery Sergeant Roberts said, "They're professionals, sir. They'll do their jobs. You're right, they won't like it, but they *will understand!* And so would the SEALs."

Nodding my head and realizing the Gunny couldn't see the gesture in the darkness, I stated, "I stand corrected Gunny. Get the lads in place – green star flare signals the attack. I'll give you three minutes to get the mines and snipers in place. I'll fire the flare in five minutes. Good luck and good hunting."

Smiling, Gunnery Sergeant Roberts replied, "You too, sir. Try not to get yourself killed."

Some people not involved in the military might question why we took the time to talk and plan. Even though every second is precious, a poorly planned and executed rescue is worse than no rescue at all. Maybe we *should have* planned longer, but I don't think it would have helped. Because about the time we started shooting, the Iraqi militia had some of their own Calvary show-up. What should have been a well timed, slam-dunk on Saddam's boys, turned into an absolute Charlie-Foxtrot. That's military speak for a Cluster F... ok, you can guess what the "F" stands for. I'm not above using profanity, but I think it's a little early in this story to drop the F-bomb. Besides, it's used at the end of this story where it really has meaning.

Anyway, within seconds we had a platoon of Iraqi soldiers – that's roughly 32 guys – mixed in with my platoon duking-it-out, playing king of the sand dune. The SEALs, not knowing we were there to help, picked that same moment to charge the Iraqi militia. The SEALs were busted up pretty bad and figured they were going die if they stayed put, so they might as well go for broke. Logical thinking... and it's what any true warrior would do. I should have expected as much, but everything was happening so fast and had become such a brawl that trying to make sense of it was useless. Unless it was at pointblank range, no-body including the Iraqis, could do much shooting for fear of hitting a comrade. The SEALs were, for the most part, running out of ammo which kept them from shooting us by mistake. My troops are experts in hand-to-hand combat (as are the SEALs) but it didn't really matter because all the martial arts training in the world doesn't help in a knock down drag-out brutal slugfest!

I ran dead on into my first adversary with a down field tackle that would have made any football coach proud. As we fell to the ground, I drove my bayonet up into his chest. I rolled off him and started to stand when I was immediately slammed back to the ground. I felt a knife slide off the back of my neck and bite into my upper right shoulder. I rolled violently away from my assailant, pulled my handgun and fired two shots directly into his stomach as he dove on top of me. He lay on the ground screaming and clutching his guts while I got up and ran deeper into the fight looking for my men. Somewhere along the way, I recovered my rifle (I still wonder if it had been there the whole time hanging from its sling on my back). I stopped to fix my bayonet onto the end of it and was glad I did because the next Iraqi I faced a second later had done the same thing. We circled one another and then clashed several times. Jumping toward me he attempted to jab me in the chest; I blocked his jab and ruthlessly slammed the butt of my rifle into his head shattering his skull. He was dead, or close to it, before he hit the ground.

All around me I could see men fighting and dying. I saw Gunny Roberts straddling a man, plunging his bayonet into him over and over again. In the ravine where they had been trapped, I could see the SEALs carrying several of their wounded teammates while still fighting and attempting to break contact. There was a sudden inexplicable moment of silence in the battle, so I screamed, *"Navy SEALs, Marine Recon fight toward us!"* And for the love of God they did!

If you've never seen a special operations team conduct a coordinated assault movement, it is a thing of wondrous beauty and lethality. The SEALs are absolute masters of such tactics – but no matter how good this team was, they remained in desperate need of help.

Only a few of my boys were still engaged in hand- to-hand. Those that weren't, were now shooting at the Iraqis that were falling back from our little sand dune. What I should have done then was put my platoon in a hasty perimeter; what I actually did defies common sense. Looking back on the whole thing, I'm not sure why, but I started fighting toward the SEALs. Maybe it's because I could see that they were struggling to carry their wounded and fight at the same time. Maybe it was because I could see from my vantage point that they were sorely outnumbered, surrounded and still fighting hand- to-hand. Or maybe it's because I'm an idiot with a death wish (I don't think so, though I've heard stranger explanations for what I did). Anyway, I attacked toward the SEALs. Strangely enough, my little one-man assault took the militia by complete surprise.

Firing my rifle as I moved, I hit three Iraqis in the back, killing them instantly. I would have kept firing, however, I was now out of ammo with no time to reload, something I probably should have thought about before playing hero. Suddenly I was back fighting hand- to-hand. The first guy that came at me got a bayonet blade in his face and fell off to the side. The second, third and fourth men also died though I can't tell you how. At some point my bayonet broke off and I resorted to swinging my rifle like a club. And then the SEALs were all around me, killing more Iraqis with knives, feet and hands. I grabbed one of the SEAL wounded and carried him to free up his team-mates so they could fight unencumbered. Honestly, I was too out of gas and couldn't fight anymore anyway. I carried the wounded man up the dune and began yelling for my platoon and the SEALs to form a perimeter around the seriously wounded.

We could see forty or fifty Iraqis about a hundred meters off gathering for another go at us. As the perimeter quickly formed I counted heads. My platoon was missing five including Gunnery Sergeant Roberts. I had three seriously wounded. The SEALs numbered twelve with four seriously wounded and out of the fight. They also had two men out running around looking for the jamming station. Those two might be dead already or too wounded to come back and fight. Hells bells, we were all wounded; but worse still, we were all very low on ammunition and hand grenades. While contemplating our next move, I heard a slurred, weak voice, come from the middle of the perimeter

"Excuse me lad, are you in charge of the Marines?" The question came from the SEAL that I had carried in.

"I am. My name's Lieutenant LaFleet. And you would be?"

With a faint grin and holding out a bloody hand to shake mine, he replied, "Lieutenant Shannon. I'm the commander of this SEAL team. And before I forget, thanks for coming for us. I'm not sure how much longer we would have lasted."

Kneeling and taking his hand in mine, I said, "You're welcome, sir. But I'm afraid we're not out of this mess yet. Communications with command was down when all this started. Staff Sergeant Johnson, my radioman, is trying to reestablish a link, but no luck at the moment."

Not letting go of my hand, Lieutenant Shannon informed me, "Just before the crap hit the fan we lost communications with command, too. I immediately sent out two of my boys to find the radio jamming site. If it's Russian-made, it's truck mounted and it has to be close since the range on their equipment is bad. Look, we both know I out-rank you; but I'm in no condition to lead and my number two is out of the fight also. You have the command."

"Aye-aye sir, I have the command" I said. I watched a moment longer as Lieutenant Shannon drifted off in a morphine stupor. Though I shouldn't have been, I was amazed at his strength to fight off the morphine long enough to talk to me. Mental and physical toughness – well beyond that of civilian understanding, is inherent to the U.S. Special Forces, especially the Navy Seals. Anyway, thinking he was asleep, I went to check my command.

It was almost an hour later when someone on the perimeter yelled, "Sir! They're making a move."

"Alright people, heads up. Mark your targets. No full automatic fire," I yelled.

The perimeter responded with a resounding "Aye-aye sir!"

I felt a shiver go down my spine. There is nothing more dangerous in this world than ticked-off American fighting men and women. I was thoroughly convinced that we were going die in about five minutes. But I could guarantee one thing: we might be all dead in five minutes flat, but for four minutes and fifty-nine seconds of those five minutes the Iraqis were going be in a living hell. Smiling at my own bravado, I moved to the middle where I could maintain command and also react to any breaches in our thin perimeter.

It wasn't long before the gunfire grew intense. Screams of pain and death echoed off the dunes. Gunpowder smoke choked the air, making it difficult to breathe. I began to hear yells for more ammunition. Ammunition magazines were passed to those that needed it, but that wouldn't last long. It couldn't. We were just too short on ammo. I saw the first Iraqi breach our perimeter and ran to meet him. I slammed my rifle butt into his teeth, knocking him unconscious.

Attempting to run past me, several more Iraqis tried to breach our lines. I tackled one of them and we began a wrestling match that ended only when one of us was dead. Somehow, I had gotten on top and was hammering his face with my fist when I felt a searing pain in my right side. I looked down and saw that a knife was lodged just under my ribs. I was still staring at the knife when I was grabbed from behind in a neck lock. Some sorry bastard was trying to strangle me. Worse, he was succeeding! As the lights started to go out in my head, I heard a strange noise and the person killing me fell off to the side, obviously dead. The guy whose face I had been beating and who I was still sitting on was either dead or out cold, so I rolled to the ground, gasping for air. I heard fighting next to me so I turned my head to see who had saved me. To my utter amazement my savior was the SEAL team commander Lieutenant Shannon! Lieutenant Shannon? That man was messed up bad, doped on morphine and here he was fighting hand to hand with cold, brutal efficiency. He finished off the two men he was fighting and fell to the ground next to me.

As the fight raged all around us, he panted, "How you doing Lieutenant?"

I answered, "I'm… I'm not sure sir. We'd better get back to the middle." I rolled over and started to crawl toward the middle of the perimeter. I looked back to see if Lieutenant Shannon was coming. He wasn't. He had passed out from the pain or blood loss or the morphine. Not that it mattered. I grabbed the neck of his uniform shirt and began dragging him.

As we made it back to the middle, I found that my perimeter, not large to begin with, was so small that we were literally on top of the seriously wounded whose numbers had grown drastically. We had repelled several assault waves. The next one would be our last. I didn't bother to ask about ammo. I could see men holding knives and empty rifles with bayonets attached. A few had picked up enemy weapons, but there were not enough within reach to make a difference. I could see the Iraqis moving and wished

I could say something gallant or inspirational (not that anyone would know – the words would have died with us). So all I said was, "It's been an honor, guys. When they crest the dune, we'll abandon the perimeter and attack. Leave the wounded here; we won't be coming back."

The Iraqis wouldn't take prisoners – in anger, they would shoot the wounded where they lay. But at least we wouldn't torture our guys by dragging them around. When the moment was right and the Iraqis were just over the crest, I shouted, "Charge!"

Suddenly there was a bright flash and an explosion to our direct front that knocked us off our feet. One of the anti-personnel mines had gone off, launching over 3000 tiny pellets that swept the Iraqis from the dune. Within seconds, the other mines blew killing the remaining Iraqis as they attempted to flee. And just like that, as quickly as it had started, the battle was over.

I was not sure what had happened or why we had survived. Unsteady on my feet, I dropped to my knees looking around, trying to sort things out. There was absolute silence… a silence so profound that it was deafening. I hadn't survived unscathed. No one had. I had the original knife wound in my shoulder; somehow my back got laid open like a fillet; there was a bullet wound in my right thigh; and the knife was still sticking out of my side. I also had a deep jagged three-inch gash on my left cheek that frothed every time I breathed.

But I had survived and was almost giddy about it. I felt arms around me and someone gently pushing me to the ground. It was Gunnery Sergeant Roberts and he was saying, "I blew the mines, sir. I was cut off and couldn't get back to the perimeter so I stayed low and waited. Now lie down. It's over with. We got communications back up and helicopters are on their way in to extract us. You've done very well, Lieutenant. I'm proud of you."

I felt the sting of a needle going into my arm and the pain slowly started to ease. In the distance I could vaguely hear the sweet sounds of helicopters coming toward us.

U.S. Army Hospital
Kuwait

Hours or days later I woke up in Kuwait with my commander, Colonel Fredrick Davies standing over me talking (more like arguing) with a Navy doctor. Davies said, "I want him and the rest of his platoon *and the SEALs* on the next flight to Landstuhl Army hospital."

I could see that the doctor was a lowly Navy Lieutenant (equal to a Marine Captain like Lieutenant Shannon – if I forgot to mention it, that's why Shannon outranked me) and well below the rank of Davies.

"I can't do that, sir. Our protocol specifically states that they *all* have to go to Saudi Arabia then to a hospital ship for the trip home – that's if they live that long," the doctor stated with a smirk on his face.

Look, most U.S. Navy doctors are the best and I owe my life to them, but this guy was a jackass. I was also wondering what he meant by "if they live that long." Suddenly, living seemed very important to me and I tried to sit up and hit the prick in the face. Seeing I was awake and had heard this exchange, the doctor suddenly looked pale. Colonel Davies' face was a brilliant color of furious red. Cool… the old man wouldn't let me die at the hands of Doctor Ass-face. He gently pushed me back down on to the bed and said, "he's not talking about you, son. Several of the SEALs may not make it, though."

As my eyes began to tear up, I had to ask, "Sir, what about my platoon?"

Looking stricken, Colonel Davies cleared his throat, "Counting you and Gunny Roberts, there were only seven survivors from your platoon of sixteen. I'm sorry, son."

I shut my eyes and let the medications take me away.

Landstuhl Regional Medical Center
U.S. Army Hospital
Landstuhl, Germany

I guess Colonel Davies won the argument because when I woke up again, I was in a hospital room in Germany. I was foggy from the drugs, but

I immediately recognized Lieutenant Shannon in the next bed looking at me.

Seeing that I was finally awake, Shannon asked, "You've been in and out for several days, Lieutenant. What do you remember?"

In choppy sentences (it really hurt to talk with the stitches in my face), I told him I remembered the battle, how it ended, and then about what happened in Kuwait with Colonel Davies and that idiot doctor. Everything since Kuwait was a blur.

"Sir, I know about my platoon. Colonel Davies told me. How did your team fare? And what happened to begin with?"

Several long moments passed and I began to think Lieutenant Shannon wasn't going to answer my question. As I waited wondering if I should let the question go, I studied him. I already knew he was tall, maybe 6'2 or 6'3 and highly athletic – as all SEALs are. He had a scar that started from the corner of his right eye, moved along the temple and then disappeared into his jet black hair. But what caught my attention most, was when he looked over at me. He had the bluest eyes I have ever seen…

Glancing over at me, Shannon took a deep breath and answered my questions, "Out of my twelve man team there are only five left counting me."

Shannon paused again. Then as his jaw clinched in obvious pain and sorrow, he continued, "It was supposed to be a soft intelligence gathering mission. All we had to do was go in and photograph some warehouses in the middle of nowhere that the UN inspectors thought were suspicious. Our guide – we had used him before – tried to lead us into a trap. We spotted the trap early, but got pinned down. Then we started taking casualties and couldn't break contact. That's where you found us. Screwed and beaten blue."

As he finished the story, a faint tear ran down Shannon's cheek. I guess even Superman has weak moments.

Shifting my body to try and get comfortable, I stated, "Sir, our story is about the same. We were supposed to meet a local guide to take *us* to an antiaircraft missile site. Because we were about three hours late from crossing an uncharted marsh, we missed the hook-up time and the guide left. I think we were supposed to be ambushed too. Both our teams were set up. It would have been a real big deal in Iraq to bag two American special operations teams."

We said nothing else that night and eventually I drifted back to sleep.

One Day Later

My eyes popped open at noon the following day. I was hungry, thirsty, and had to go whiz like a race horse. There was an empty handheld urinal on a table right next to the bed and, discarding any degree of modesty (as if a Marine would have any) I swung my legs out of bed, stood up and emptied my bladder into the urinal.

From behind a drawn curtain that separated our beds, I heard Shannon's voice, "Feeling better, Marine? I was starting to wonder if you were going to wake up today. Your father has been here. Looks just like you. It was pretty funny when he showed up – him being an Army Brigadier General. The hospital commander almost killed himself trying to kiss your dad's butt."

Shannon pulled the curtain open and saw the confusion on my face as I looked around for my old man. Lieutenant Shannon continued, "Sorry Lieutenant, I didn't mean to confuse you. I'm probably not making much sense. I'm still a little doped up, too. Your dad went to take a nap. He'll be back in a few hours."

Slowly climbing back into my hospital bed, I ask, "So my dad is here and upsetting people? That sounds about right. My mom isn't here too is she?"

Shannon shook his no, saying "If she is, I haven't seen her."

I said, "My Mom is a beautiful lady. Highly intelligent, but if she was here, you would've heard her ripping the doctors a part long before you ever saw her, sir!"

Smiling at that remark, Shannon replied, "Let's drop the "sir," shall we? As you know, I'm Lieutenant Shannon. My first name is Richard. My close friends, and that includes you, call me Rick or Rich; but for obvious reasons, please don't call me Dick."

Chuckling softly (laughing hurt too much), I said, "My friends, including you, call me Ren. And before you ask, please prepare yourself because it's short for Renee Lynn."

"Oh sweet Jesus! A jarhead with a chick's name. Tell me your name isn't spelled like a girl? This is just so… poetic! I know your parents love you or else your Dad wouldn't be here in Germany. But why did they give you a girl's name?"

Shaking my head slowly, I answered, "It's spelled like a girl would. My Dad's two best friends in Vietnam were Renee – spelled like a chick's name – Mario and Lynn Heathman. They saved his life at the cost of their own. So there ya have it. I got stuck with a girl's name that a man can be proud of."

Smiling, Rick said, "Well, with that in mind, I'll not tease you about it again. I wouldn't want to offend your father."

"What about you, sir, I mean Rick? I thought you were dead and then there you were fighting next to me. After saving me, you went out again and I had to drag you back to the perimeter. After that I didn't have time to check on you. Besides, I thought we were all dead meat."

Looking thoughtful, Shannon replied, "Yeah, I know most of what happened. Gunny Roberts – who's been here checking on you day in and day out – briefed me. He could see us fighting, but he was wounded and cut off and couldn't make it to the perimeter."

Recalling such details was like looking through a fog. Forcing myself to concentrate, I said, "Early on, I saw him fighting it out with a rag-head. I lost sight of him after that. I guess… I guess, I thought he was dead."

Giving me a moment to collect my thoughts, Shannon continued, "He waited and blew the mines when he thought it appropriate. That saved the day. Well that and *your actions* under combat conditions."

Trying to dredge up the memories was now becoming almost painful. "After the mines detonated, I vaguely remember talking to him. Or, at least I think I remember doing that. I don't think I did anything special, Rick. I just led as best I could. Even with my best efforts, our teams died out there. I almost feel… guilty that I lived."

Nodding that he understood my meaning, Shannon said, "Me too. I'm not sure why I was spared when so many good men died. This was supposed to be my last deployment as a team commander anyway. I've resigned my commission and I'm going back to school when I get out".

We spent the next few weeks rooming together as we healed. Eventually we got shipped out to Bethesda Naval Hospital in Maryland where we went through months of grueling rehab. Our friendship grew daily as we struggled to overcome the pain of our injuries. We pushed each other and even at times competed against one another to reach higher goals of fitness. In spite of the pain, it was one of the highest points of my life.

Also, based on the testimony of the surviving SEALs and Marines – especially Rick and Gunny Roberts, I was awarded our nation's second highest military medal for heroism, the Navy Cross. Yes, this was an incredible time in my life, but it also became one of the lowest points. The day after the award was pinned on my chest by Colonel Davies and my Dad, I made captain *and* I found out that I would be leaving the military. But unlike Rick, mine wasn't voluntary. It was due to the President's Military Reduction in Forces (also known as the Great Clinton Purge of 1998). A lot of good military people got the boot during the purge. I was just one of many.

I know I went on for awhile about the fighting in Iraq. It was essential to this story that you understand what Rick and I had been through together and why he is so important to me. Anyway, that's how I met Father Richard Shannon - brother, priest and assassin.

CHAPTER 2

Nicaragua 2009

Sitting on a log in the village square as the sun began to come up, Father Reese took a deep breath and looked around at the piss poor living conditions that he was now forced to endure. He had been doing well in Houston, Texas when the media broke the scandal. He believed that none of it was his fault. The children all knew what they were doing and had asked for it. *The authorities* said that he was just another pedophile preying on the weak and innocent. What tripe! He knew in his heart that he was teaching the children – both boys and girls – about life. About sex. No lasting harm had come to any of the little ingrates. The parents had run first to the media, not the police. That was their mistake because it all took time. Then that idiot reporter had called the Monsignor to ask for their side of the story. This alerted his superiors and gave them the opportunity to get him out of the country before an arrest could be made. Angry now, he thought about the Church. Oh yes, they had moved him to this dung-hole almost overnight; but it was so wrong. The village had no running water, no indoor plumbing and almost no children to mentor. Frustrated, Reese shouted, "This is so unfair!"

Caught up in his own self-pity, Father Reese didn't notice as a stranger dressed in military camouflage stepped out of the jungle and stealthily moved up behind Father Reese and said, "Turn around."

Surprised at the voice, he spun around and faced the man that had intruded on his thoughts. Snapping, Reese ask, "What do you want? If you're lost, there's a dirt road over that way. Follow it and you should hit civilization in a week or two. Now leave me be."

Shaking his head, the stranger said, "What I want *is* you. Father James Lee Reese, you have been found guilty of crimes against humanity and the sentence you have been given is death." Quicker than a man can blink, the stranger un-holstered a silenced .22 automatic handgun and fired three shots perfectly grouped between the eyes of Father Reese. "You're wrong Reese. You weren't sent here as punishment. You were sent here to be punished. May God forgive you of your sins." As silently as he had come, Father Richard Shannon moved back into the jungle.

Argentina 2010

Head down crying and praying for forgiveness, Father Raul Valdez sat in the front pew of his small inner city church thinking to himself that for ten years he had resisted the temptations that had tormented him his entire life. Why had it happened again? After so long, why had he betrayed those that loved and trusted him? He had worked so hard to atone for the wrong-doings of his past. He looked down at the small handgun next to him and knew that he didn't have the courage to use it. That would damn his soul to hell and, though he felt he deserved it, he just couldn't pull the trigger. Nor would the police in this predominantly Catholic country arrest him. The stories would never make the newspapers or television. It would all be covered up. There would be no justice for the lives that he had ruined, now or in the future. Still weeping, he heard the front door to the sanctuary open and someone walking up to him very quietly, almost cat-like. A soft respectful voice, said "Father Valdez, do you know who I am?"

Valdez looked up and said, "Not who you are, my son – but I do know why you are here and I thank you and God for it. I've prayed so hard. But it will happen again, I know that now. *It must stop!*"

Father Valdez then shut his eyes and began to pray again. In quick succession the three shots fired from the suppressed .22 caliber handgun echoed slightly off the walls of the empty sanctuary. Three small bullets entered Father Valdez's brain killing him instantly and as the body slid to the floor, the shooter said, "Forgive me, Father Valdez." Stepping out from the pew, he knelt and crossed himself. Silently praying for the soul of Father Raul Valdez, Father Richard Shannon walked out of the building into the cold dark night.

CHAPTER 3

Dallas Texas, Friday, 8 February

Father Robert Lanton had parked his little Kia Rio on Jefferson St. hoping that it was far enough away from his destination that it would not be recognized. Knowing in his heart that he should not have been there, he stared at Maria Gonzalas's house for almost two hours wanting, and at the same time not wanting, to knock on her door. He fantasized what it would be like to hold her – to love her. And of course for her to love him back.

"This is foolish," he muttered to himself and in that moment he made his decision. Monday morning he would ask for a transfer. If it meant coming clean about his infatuation with Maria, then so be it. He was a priest, and a good priest at that. He truly loved the vocation that had chosen him and he would not betray it. Feeling at peace for the first time in months, Father Lanton turned his collar up against the cold damp air as he began the last short walk of his life.

Saturday 9 February

It was a dark and stormy night (really), and it happened all at once; lighting flashed, my cell phone started ringing and my hundred and ten pound coonhound, Danner, pounced on my chest seeking refuge from the storm. Pushing him off me, I looked at the clock as I reached for the cell phone. It was Saturday, three o'clock in the morning. That meant I had been in bed less than an hour and there had been no time for the dreams to start. Thank God. Opening my phone I mumbled, "Let me guess, there's been another murder in Dallas. Am I right?"

My immediate supervisor and partner, Sergeant Danny "Tex" Beers laughed and said, "Damn you're good! I've trained you well, young Jedi. Get dressed. I'll be by the house in thirty minutes to pick you up." He hung up without saying good-bye or I love you. God, I hate it when he does that. It makes me feel so cheap!

Launching my 5'10, two hundred and ten pound body out of bed I staggered toward the shower for a quick rinse. Drying off, I glanced at the mirror to see if I needed a shave. Nope, still good. Even if I did need one, I would have passed. Shaving for me is a lengthy ordeal with that nasty scar on my mug (the one the Iraqi camel jockey gave me). Physically, I hadn't changed much since I had left the Corps. I think being an avid martial artist, runner, swimmer and weight-lifter helps a lot. The battle-scars on my body were pretty nasty and though they had long since healed over, I was still very aware of them.

Psychologically, I've changed a lot in the last decade. From time to time, I have horrible nightmares from combat and from law enforcement (occasionally mixed together at the same time, lucky me). My attitude about people had depreciated significantly over the years; but being a cop does that to you. It's tough not to become jaded in this line of work. Let's face it, cops don't see the best parts of our society and, like any bad wound, it leaves a scar. Trouble is, these scars are on the soul.

I quickly got dressed and put coffee on. I've always thought coffee tasted a lot like mud, but with the hours a homicide cop puts in – especially in Dallas, Texas – you practically live on the stuff. I've been a cop for over ten years and with Crimes Against Persons (CAPERs), Homicide section, for two years and, in spite of the shitty hours, I was really enjoying it. I suspect this was because Tex, a Vietnam vintage jarhead getting close to retirement, is as warped in his sense of humor as I am. This made work fun. But making things even better, we worked for a great Lieutenant, Rachel "Mom" Saxen. Saxen had been my sergeant back when I was a patrol officer working at the Southeast substation. On one occasion, I screwed up awfully bad (while trying to do the right thing) and should have ended up at Internal Affairs with days off and a letter of reprimand. She took care of me and protected my career. So it's an understatement to say that I am fiercely loyal to her.

Also, though I would never admit to anyone. Not even to Tex or Rick, I've had a crush on her for years. Rachel looks a lot like the actress Uma Thurman. She is a tall, big boned but not heavy set, athletic Norwegian gal with thick blond hair, blue-green eyes and a smile that lights up a room. Is she beautiful? That depends on what you're looking for. To me, yes, but I'm the one with the crush. Just so you know, even if she were inclined to – which she isn't – we couldn't date because she's my Lieutenant and it would royally cause problems with fraternization.

Exactly thirty minutes later, Tex honked the car horn and I began shutting down the house. Danner looked at me like I was a traitor for leaving him during a thunder storm. "Sorry old buddy, duty calls. Anybody tries to break in, rip his throat out. You know what to do with the body." I knelt down and hugged him, he licked my face good-bye and then I was out the door running through the rain with two cups of coffee in my hand. Giving one to Tex, I sat down and buckled in. As Tex pulled out of the driveway he asked, "Danner upset about the storm?"

"Yeah, he really hates this kind of weather. Just as you called, he jumped into bed on top of me trying to hide."

Laughing, Tex said, "I've seen that stupid mutt track the most vicious felons through woods and swamps in worse weather than this and never stop to worry about it. Why does this crap suddenly bother him?"

I answered, "I have no idea. Maybe it's because he has nothing else to occupy his mind during a storm." Trying to stifle a yawn, I changed subjects and asked, "Ok Tex, we *just* finished a case not four hours ago. So, why us and what have we got?

Tex replied "Well, it's us because Mom called me and I called you. And it's a dead Catholic priest by the name of Father Robert Lanton."

Staring out the side window, I asked, "How do we know who the victim is? I think I know that name though. Didn't he work for one of our volunteer chaplains, Father Michael Leopole?"

Tex said, "Yeah, his name sounds familiar but I got nothing. Mom's going to meet us at the crime scene. Says there's some information she needs to pass on that may be pertinent to this investigation. I guess there was a witness that named the victim." Sipping from his cup he grimaced and coughed out, "Great Buddha's balls you make a lousy cup of coffee. Every Marine ever born knows how to make good coffee except you! It's our life's blood. Damn it son, what did they teach *you*?"

Giving him my best Dirty Harry stare I said, "To kill people, you ungrateful punk!" We burst out laughing. I admit it wasn't *that* funny of a joke, but stress and fatigue will do that to a person.

As we drove on I asked, "What about our other cases? You and I are so buried right now we can't solve much of anything let alone take on a new case." In general, recruiting had fallen off for law enforcement across America. Specifically speaking, the Dallas Police department was almost three hundred officers short. In response to this, the Chief of Police (William Smyth III) had cut CAPERs by almost twenty five percent and SWAT by almost fifty percent. The former detectives and SWAT officers got sent back to patrol. Granted, patrol is always desperately short-handed, however, the Chief could have shut down his less imperative 'feel good' programs such as the costly and ineffective community policing store fronts. Even better, he could have cut top heavy bureaucratic positions before taking veteran officers out of CAPERS or SWAT.

Mom had saved both Tex and I from being sent back to patrol – especially me. Technically, when I made Sergeant, I should have been sent back, but somehow I had gotten to stay. Which means either I am a very good detective (I'm not, but Tex is and we're a great team) or none of the Chiefs at the substations wanted me. That's always possible, but not very likely (they're too short handed). Of course the trade off is a horrendous case load.

Tex replied, "I know Mom's already catching hell from Assistant Chief Wong. All the other squads are just as buried – including the ones on duty right now. So I guess it's just our turn to get buggered… again. Hope you didn't have any weekend plans."

Snickering I said, "No plans and if I had a name like 'Chief Harold 'Harry' Wong' I'd have a sex overhaul, get married and change my name. Either that, or become a porn star."

Coming off I-35 onto Beckley Avenue we continued north until we came to Jefferson Street where we turned west. As we approached the nine hundred-block, two full blocks from where the crime scene was, we could see media trucks packing the street and patrol cars parked in the distance with the overheads still flashing red and blue. Tex said, "Looks like a long walk. There's Mom standing by that squad car and … Oh piss up a rope, Wong's standing next to her. Wonder why he's here?"

I shrugged my shoulders, "Let's park over there and go find out. Whatever it is, it can't be good."

Wong was of Mandarin Chinese ancestry and a practicing Buddhist. He is short, pudgy and looked terrible in a uniform. He is disliked by almost everyone in the police department with the exception of the Chief of Police. Personally, I can take him or leave him (mostly leave) because the truth is, I can't seem to read him. He can be rude and abrupt and then turn right around and be incredibly compassionate and understanding. He also has the most annoying habit of always being right. I don't mean he *thinks* he always right, I mean he *is* always right. We mortals find that type of thing irritating. He does have redeeming qualities; the man is a brilliant detective. Also, Wong works hard to make sure his detectives have whatever they need to get the job done. To that end, as long as we get results, he's known to turn a blind eye at things other Chiefs would have a fit over. If he wasn't such a prick (and always right) he would be a great Chief to work for.

We got out of the car, straightened our suits and ties – yes, we still wear suits and ties to crime scenes – and walked over to where Mom and Chief Wong were waiting. I said, "Good morning sir, ma'am. We got here as…"

Chief Wong cut me off saying, "You were called in at 2:58 am! It took you almost an hour to get here. With this incessant rain, we'll be lucky if the evidence is not washed away. Get started as soon as your Lieutenant briefs you." He spun around to leave and walked right into a patrol car push-bumper.

To keep from laughing out loud, I looked at Mom and saw the expression on her face and I almost lost it. In a low voice, I muttered, "If there is a God, I hope he made that hurt."

Mom faked a cough to cover her reaction. To help her efforts, Tex intervened, "Sorry Ma'am, we got here as fast as we could. Interstate 35 was backed up pretty bad with a 7X (a wreck with injuries). Why was his majesty here anyway?"

Lieutenant Saxen looked over her shoulder to locate Wong and quietly said, "He's already getting heat from Chief Smyth. The murder is only about two hours old and the Chief of Police wants it solved yesterday. About every ten minutes Smyth is calling Wong for progress reports."

I said, "I understand what is going on between Wong and Smyth, but why the *interest* from the Chief of Police to begin with?" Normally the Chief of Police, known to rank and file of the Dallas Police Department (sarcastically) as 'Mr. Personality,' stays in his office and refuses to mingle with his officers.

My opinion of him is a bit different. I had fought the Chief several times at Karate tournaments and had my clock cleaned by him. I'm great in hand to hand fighting where there are no rules except survival; tournament fighting with points and referees still eludes me. Even though the Chief had beaten me, he was gracious in victory and, the few times I saw him lose, gracious in defeat. After our matches he gave me some helpful training and fighting advice. Last year, after a good friend was killed in the line of duty, the Chief and I talked for several hours at an orphanage while we helped lay tile and paint. Overall, I really liked the guy. Unfortunately, most of his officers have long since given up trying to get to know him.

Mom said, "To answer your question, Ren, you know that Chief Smyth is Catholic and he knew the dead priest. Smyth demanded that I put you and Tex, who, because he is your partner and is therefore guilty by association, on this case. Not that it should matter, but the Chief of Police believes that you're Catholic, albeit back-slidden, and he asked specifically that you be assigned this case."

Stunned, I looked at her, "Ah, Lieutenant, ma'am, I am Catholic, but in name only. Anything I know about Catholicism I got out of a World Religions class in college. Oh, and the brother of my heart, Richard Shannon, is a Catholic Priest, but that's…Wait a minute! You know this because you met Rick over the holidays."

Taking a deep breath Lieutenant Saxen said, "You've done some volunteer work with two of the department's Chaplains, Father Leopole and his aide Father Kothner over at St. Thomas's, right? And you've helped them and the Chief over at Buckner Orphanage many times, and you…"

Not meaning to (I should have kept my mouth shut), I cut her off saying, "Helping an eighty-five year old priest and his aide with painting and laying tile doesn't make me very Catholic!"

Mom's eyes flashed angry, "I'm going to talk *real* slow and use small words Ren, so that even *you* will understand what I am about to say. The Chief of Police wants a detective on this case that has a Catholic background. We do not have such a detective in CAPERs at this time. Therefore, I would have to bring back from patrol a former detective that does. Remember Detective John Lasoya? He would be the only choice I have. He is at the North Central substation working as the deep night patrol sergeant. I would have to do a one for one trade. Meaning: *you* for *him*. Between the two of you, I prefer you. I cannot stand his whiny, high-pitched voice. Do you now grasp the situation *Patrol Sergeant* La Fleet?"

Realizing that Mom was trying to protect me again, I said, "Yes ma'am, I do, and might I add what a delightful color of lip gloss you have on this morning."

Rolling her eyes, she turned to Tex, "Sergeant Beers, please take the village idiot with you and start working the crime scene before Wong gets another burr up his ass and starts chewing on mine."

"Yes Ma'am, and I'll have the idiot flogged for being obtuse."

As Tex grabbed my arm and pulled me away, I quickly scanned the area and noted that Chief Wong had the media busy. Good, no cameras or microphones were pointing my way so I started whispering my own version of a Hail Mary, "Hail Rachel, blessed are you among all Lieutenants. Blessed be your colorful fruit of the looms." For this I got slapped in the back of the head, as Tex mumbled something about me burning in hell.

Game faces on. As the cold rain continued to pummel us, Tex and I moved over to the crime scene access point and gave the patrol officer our names and badge numbers for record. The crime scene, lit up by street lights and store front marquees, was circled by yellow police tape that the heavy rains had pushed nearly to the ground. Following our standard routine, Tex and I stood at the access point and stared at the victim from about twenty-five feet away. He was laying there on his back, arms stretched out sideways and legs crossed in what appeared to be crucifixion pose. I turned and asked the patrol officer who had taken our information if he was the responding officer.

"Yes, Detective, I was," he said. Referring to his whip-out book, "My element is 467 and I got the call at 2:30. I marked out here at 2:31. My beat's down along Camp Wisdom but we're real short people tonight, so I was up in this area answering a shots fired call over on Davis St. When I pulled up I could see the victim where he is now – in the middle of the street and positioned the way you see him – I immediately called for backup and an ambulance. I then exited my car and, from this access point, I walked directly to the body. I could see several bullet holes to his head. I reached down and touched his neck checking for a pulse. Finding none, I called for a shooting team (CAPER's, Crime Scene Response and the Medical Examiner). The ambulance got here at 2:33 and, using the same path to enter and exit the crime scene, I escorted one paramedic in to again check for a pulse. My backup arrived and put up the tape while I was with the paramedic. I have the paramedic and the backup's element number, names and badge numbers for you."

"Any questions, Tex?" I asked.

Shaking his head, Tex continued to study the crime scene.

Turning to the officer, I said, "Excellent report, officer. Would you make a copy of your notes for me please? I'll get them from you in a while." That last part is standard operating procedures for the investigation, but both Tex and I believe it's essential to treat patrol officers like they count. Patrol officers are not, and I emphasize the word *not*, stupid. They are well trained and serve as the backbone of law enforcement. They work long shifts and get little or no recognition for their herculean efforts. Because of Hollywood's misguided and foolish influence, the public sees detectives as the heroes of law enforcement. But let me ask you this: If that is true, why do we hear so frequently about patrol officers dying in the line of duty, but seldom a detective? Sorry, I go off on a tangent like this from time to time.

Tex and I didn't walk directly up to the corpse – we rarely do. The technique we prefer is to follow the tape line around the crime scene first. This serves two purposes: It gives us a look from different angles at the body, and it allows us to search the outlying ground for evidence. As we complete each spiral lap, we slowly collapse our circles closer in. Eventually this technique puts us at the body where, almost forty-five minutes later, we now stood.

Kneeling next to the body, Tex got out a small recorder and began his assessment. "No shell casings that we can see. There are what appears to be three small holes in a quarter group at the right temporal area of the head just above the jaw line. Can't say for sure until the autopsy is done, but those holes look fairly small. Of course that may be because the skin has folded back over the wound; however, something around a .22 or a .380 caliber would be my guess. Also, it looks like there are no exit wounds. That may support the small caliber bullet theory. There are no burns or puckering that indicates a contact wound, nor is there any visible tattooing. This indicates that the rounds may have been fired at a relatively close range I'd give it three to five feet. In this rain, any soot would have been washed away already." Looking up at me, "Your turn, Ren."

Tex handed the recorder to me and I knelt next to the body saying, "The victim's white male. Approximate age... 40 to 50 years. I am still unclear as to who made the identification." I looked at Tex who just shrugged. Continuing on I said, "I concur with Detective Beers concerning the type of rounds used and the range from which they were fired. The fact that we found no shell casings may indicate that the spent cartridges were recovered by the suspect or it may mean that a low caliber revolver was used. The clothing has been obviously neatened. This body appears to have been arranged in a symbolic position of crucifixion. The arms are slightly up and straight out forming a 'T' and the legs are somewhat bent and crossed at the ankles and feet. There are visible stab wounds on the palms of the hands – which are displayed open palms up. It appears that an edged or spiked weapon was driven through the legs just above the ankles. There is a lack of blood that might indicate this was done postmortem. The victim's eyes are open, as is the mouth, albeit slightly. As we made our approach to the body, I noticed a faint odor that I associate with spent or burnt gunpowder. Because of the rain, there are only slight traces (at least to the naked eye) of blood that sprayed out from the head wounds. There is a rain-diluted puddle of blood under the victim's head."

Taking back the recorder, Tex and I exited the crime scene and spoke for a few minutes discussing our gut feelings about what the scene told us. Gathering our thoughts, we watched as the Crime Scene Response (CSR) guys and the Medical Examiner (ME) began processing the crime scene. After about ten minutes, we went over to where Lieutenant Saxen and Chief Wong were waiting. Stopping to think for a moment, Tex cleared his throat and began a detailed explanation of our preliminary findings. When Tex had finished we all stood in silence digesting the information.

Finally Chief Wong asked, "What is your gut telling you, Detective LaFleet?"

Wiping the rain from my face, I answered, "Sir, I am basing my opinion on the belief that the suspect used an automatic handgun. First, the victim was not robbed. His wallet, watch and ring are still there. Second, the casings being absent from the crime scene shows a deliberate plan to avoid apprehension. Third, the small quarter-sized grouping of the bullet holes put in the head of a moving target indicates excellent marksmanship capabilities."

The Chief interrupted me, "Why do you think the victim was moving and not standing still talking to his murderer?"

"Sir, I base that on the location of the wounds. The holes were well grouped on the temporal area of the head. Had the suspect and victim been talking to one another, I believe the wounds would have been to the front and not as well grouped if he tried to defend himself or look away. Personally sir, I don't think the victim knew what hit him."

Nodding, Chief Wong stared at me for a long few seconds and then said, "Very well, continue."

"Yes sir. Ah, fourth, the location and the time of the attack would also reduce the possibility of witnesses and apprehension. Fifth, Chief I'm a little shaky with this part, but the suspect took the time to arrange the body in a religious pose. I am not sure what a psychologist would tell us this means – other than the standard 'he's taunting you' response. But the assailant *did* know he or she had the time. Based on this information, we believe that Father Robert Lanton was assassinated and not randomly murdered."

Chief Wong stated, "I agree. I'll notify Chief Smyth and hopefully he won't nag you during the course of this investigation. Lieutenant, this case takes precedence, so have these two pass off all of their critical cases to the other detectives in your unit. Chaplain Leopole and his aide will meet you at your office at 7:00 this morning. After you meet with him, type up your notes and then go home and get some sleep. Even with us begging to make this a rush job, nothing will be back from CSR or the ME for several days. So rest while you can, I want you two on top of your game. And Detective LaFleet, you got your wish. There is a God, and yes, walking into that damn bumper hurt – a lot. I hope you are satisfied."

Shit! What a way to start a day.

CHAPTER 4

Police Headquarters / CAPERS

For the first few minutes the drive to the office was quiet as we contemplated what we had just seen and what we had to do next. Death is never a pleasant sight, not even when it's expected, but when a person is murdered the victim suffers a continued level of assault and indignity until the investigation is completed. Why? Because we have to know everything about the victim and the life they've led. Through the investigation we usually end up knowing a victim's deepest, darkest secrets. Sometimes those secrets are pertinent to solving the crime and other times they're not. Either way, we know. It's the one part of the job I truly hate.

Breaking the silence Tex said, "Father Robert Lanton was accused of sexually assaulting a sixteen year old female about five years ago. Turned out the alleged victim was actually twenty-one at the time. She had tried the same stunt at several other churches – different faiths – in north Texas and Oklahoma. I guess she was trying to cash in on some of these clergy molestations law suits. Anyway, it went to court and Father Lanton was completely exonerated. For awhile his life was turned completely upside down. It was pretty obvious from the get-go that the guy was innocent – at least to the cops – not the media. I think the only reason it went to trial was that the old District Attorney wanted to prove he was tough on this issue. He really got egg on his face."

Nodding in agreement, I put in my own opinion, "That's probably one of the many reasons he's not our District Attorney any longer. Do we know what happened to the alleged victim?"

Tex replied, "Last I heard she was in the state hospital up in Wichita Falls. There are two things that I distinctly recall about the investigation and the trial. One is that she made death threats against Lanton and the other is that she was a real nut job."

Looking at Tex I chuckled saying, "No way. It can't be this easy, can it?"

"Rarely," Tex retorted, "but sometimes we get lucky. You know, if I just remembered all this, you can bet Wong thought of it three hours ago. That little turd has a phenomenal memory."

We pulled into the parking lot at the new police headquarters building on Lamar Street and Tex smiled at the ease with which he had found a parking space near the building. "What a difference things are around here. Parking here is great! You go on up, I've got to hit the men's room," Tex said as we walked through the main doors.

The department occupied this building in 2005, so it's new, relatively speaking. Many buildings owned and used by the City of Dallas are fairly old and quite dilapidated. With our city government, at thirty years, a building is seen only as broken in, instead of just permanently broken and not worth repairing. This explains why police headquarters had stayed at 106 South Harwood for over fifty years; which was long after the department had critically out grown the location. That's where Ruby shot Oswald just after the Kennedy assassination in 1963. The building was almost eight years old when that happened. I've been with the department for ten years and I can remember hearing officers complain about the old headquarters facilities. How cramped conditions were, about ceiling tiles falling on their heads, how the air conditioner and heating system did not work when needed, about toilets overflowing flooding other floors and the parking situation as being beyond frustrating. Tex would know, he had been a detective for almost twenty-five years, so when he smiles about the parking or getting to take a dump in clean functional bathroom with air conditioning or heating, I understand his joy is real.

I got to my desk, plopped down in my seat and then immediately got back up and made Tex and me cups of coffee. Five minutes later, yawning and looking haggard, Tex joined me. "I am really getting too old for all this late night / early morning stuff," Tex groaned as he sat down and asked me, "How are you feeling?"

I answered, "I'm good, but now that we're sitting down it's going to hit me pretty fast. The chaplains are supposed to be here in another hour. What do you say we transcribe our notes while it's quiet?"

Typing close to seventy words a minute Tex finished in about five minutes. I hunt and peck so Tex had a second and then a third cup of coffee while he waited for me. Trying to lend a hand, Tex had bought me one of those learning to type software programs last Christmas… It didn't help. I had just finished proofing my notes when Chief Wong, heading straight toward his office like his ass was on fire. Talking over his shoulder, "I need to see you two, *now*." He didn't even look back to see if we had heard him. *Our god commands and we cometh!*

Getting up, both Tex and I looked at one another and shrugged. As we walked into Wong's office he began talking as he was rummaging around in his file cabinet

"Detective Beers as I am sure you recall, Father Lanton had serious legal trouble several years ago. He was exonerated. The 'victim' – and I use that term only as an identifier – was Ms. Suzy Baker. She is still locked up at the state hospital in Wichita Falls Texas."

Shit, I knew it was too good to work for us.

Wong was saying, "I knew that you would be hoping that she was the murderer, so to keep you from blowing off any real leads," (*Damn it, now he's reading our minds*) "I made the call to the hospital and she's still there, heavily medicated and under lock and key. So forget her. There is something else however that may have bearing on this case." He handed us two sheets of paper that he had just pulled out of the file cabinet, "We got these from Interpol starting in 2005. There are about a dozen more from various countries in my files that you should have read long before now. All of them, including the two you are looking at, have the same modus operandi as our shooter this morning. Small caliber, three shots to the head, well grouped, all religious figures – specifically catholic priests, lay ministers and nuns. All suspected or confirmed pedophiles. No real witnesses, but there are a few people that claim to have heard the conversation between the assassin and the victims. The only difference is that shell casings were found at most of the other crime scenes and none of the bodies were posed."

Raising my hand – *God that's so high school* – I asked, "Sir, do we know anything about the background of these victims?"

Chief Wong shook his head no and said, "No we don't. Interpol might, but they're not volunteering any information. I've already made a few calls and tried. But as luck would have it, Detectives, I went to the FBI National Academy with Inspector Hector Villa from Argentina. He is now the director of homicide investigations for the Argentinean Federal Police. If anyone has the dirt on the victim in 2010 it will be him. It's about four hours' time difference. That would make it noon there. I'll give it another hour then I'll call him. Meantime Chaplains Leopole and Kothner are here."

Tex and I got up to leave when Wong started talking again. "There's one more thing. LaFleet, I'm sure you've wondered why I fought to keep you here after you made sergeant. By general orders and departmental policy, you should have been sent back to patrol – at least for awhile. Here's the deal. Every now and then a high profile case comes along that requires detectives that not only work very well together, but also detectives that have some rank, seniority, and more importantly, enough maturity to handle the investigation. Guarding against this day, I've kept your entire squad from being reassigned as promotions have come. Gentlemen, I am afraid this one is going to get very nasty before it's over. Best not fail or we will all be back in patrol working deep nights."

Great! 37% of all homicide cases are never solved and our careers as detectives are riding on this one.

Chapter 5

CAPERS (Conference Room)

Father Michael Leopole and his aide, Father Karl Kothner, were a study in contrast to one another. Father Leopole had the look of an aged Olympian. He is about 6'4, handsome, straight shouldered and moves with the grace and self confidence of a warrior priest resurrected from ancient times. His height and demeanor reminds me a lot of Rick Shannon and the actor Sam Elliot (raspy voice included). In his day, Father Mike would have been a formidable opponent. Even now I could picture him carrying a sword and fighting as a Knight's Templar.

Father Kothner, on the other hand, is 36, about 5'8, very athletic in appearance, but not self assured. Strange for the national Shorin-ryu karate champion that he is. Whereas Father Leopole smiled a lot, Father Kothner seems to have a permanent look of sadness etched on his face. He comes across as if he is uncomfortable having to deal with people outside his own faith. But before I give you the wrong impression about Father Karl, let me explain that he and I have known each other since my rookie years and I consider him a good friend. He roped me into volunteering at the orphanage, painting and putting in tile. Also, when time and scheduling allow, we run, do some karate training (sometimes with Chief Smyth) and pump weights together. After my first shooting as a police officer, he and I talked about it and he provided gentle guidance and prayer. Even though

I'm a hardened combat veteran, that shooting was different. For starters it was an American trying to kill me, not some foreign national and worse, it was suicide by cop. You know, where a shooter can't take his own life, so he makes a cop do it for him? It's the most cowardly thing a person can do to another human. Anyway, Rick was out of the country and Father Karl was there. Trust me when I say that Father Karl helped me a great deal.

Father Mike has been a volunteer chaplain for the Dallas Police Department for almost twenty years and Father Karl, to the best of my knowledge, at least eleven years - maybe more. Both had been through the citizen's police academy and both had concealed weapons permits issued through the state of Texas. I know that's a little different than the stereo-typical image of a meek and mild priest, but neither of these men fit that bill.

Tex and I walked over to Father Leopole and, extending my hand, "Hi Father Mike. How goes the war against sin?" It was an old joke between us; however, the situation for our meeting negated his normally cheerful mood.

Shaking my hand and smiling to take the edge off his reply, he responded, "I suspect about as good as your war on crime – all things considered."

Turning to Father Kothner and shaking his hand I nodded in agreement. "I'm not sure if ya'll have met my partner Detective Danny 'Tex' Beers? Danny, this is Father Michael 'Mike' Leopole and Father Karl Kothner."

As Tex was shaking hands he stated, "Gentlemen, I am truly sorry for the circumstances of this meeting."

We moved down the hall to a conference room where we could talk undisturbed. Sitting down, we were all quiet for a moment. Then Tex said, "There are standard questions that we have to ask as a matter of protocol. We do this to eliminate both of you as suspects. With that in mind…"

Red faced, Father Kothner cut him off, sputtering, "We came down here to help and you start to immediately look at us as…"

Father Mike put up his hand and stopped Kothner in mid-sentence saying, "Karl, these detectives have a very difficult job ahead of them and yes, we are here to help; but they have questions that they *must a*sk us first. You know what their procedures are."

Looking sad rather than chagrined Kothner said, "Yes sir, my apologies. Ren, Tex, I am very sorry. I guess that I'm still in a state of shock by all this. Robert was my friend, confidant and more importantly, a mentor and role model when I first entered seminary."

To ease the situation, Tex answer back, "We do understand, Father Karl. No offense was taken. We'll try to get through this part quickly so we can focus our efforts on finding the killer. Father Mike, would you start by telling us where and what you were doing last night?"

As an investigative technique we always separate and question witnesses and suspects. Doing that, we often catch inconsistencies or outright lies that we can further exploit. But in this case, neither man is a witness or a suspect – not even a person of interest, so we opted to keep them together for now.

Father Mike answered, "I made several social calls on members of my congregation until about 9 pm. Karl was, of course, with me. We got back to our residence – we live in the Kessler Park area – at around 9:15. I studied and meditated until 10 pm, showered and went to bed. That's my normal routine. I'll provide you with a list of families we visited. I got a phone call somewhere around 1 am from one of my families going through a crisis. We talked for about forty-five minutes. Then I prayed and went back to bed. I'll provide that name too. I got the call from Chief Smyth about Robert around 4 or 5 am. Anyway, I gave up on sleep and stayed up."

Taking notes, Tex said, "Thank you Father Mike. Father Kothner same question please."

Taking a deep breath first, Kothner replied, "After we got back to our residence, I read for an hour. I showered and went to bed. But at around midnight or later I was still awake and feeling fidgety so I decided that I would go for a long run. I can draw you a map of the course I took, it's about 10 miles. During my run I passed a couple of newspaper guys loading a newspaper-stand in front of the gas station at Hampton and W. Illinois Ave. Later I passed a police squad car sitting idling on the south end of the Wynnewood Village shopping center; it looked like they were doing paperwork on the car computer. They saw me and waved. I'm not sure what time I got home again. I showered and went to bed. Father Leopole woke me up later and told me about Robert being murdered. I didn't go back to sleep."

Father Mike said, "While I was on the phone, I heard Karl leave the house for his run. He doesn't sleep well so that is a fairly common occurrence."

"Ok, enough of this line of questioning. We'll check all this out." Tex stated. "Father Karl, I'm sorry to have upset you but we have to ask. Let's talk about Father Lanton. Do either of ya'll know if he had any enemies that would wish him harmed?"

Father Mike answered, "Just that young lady that made the false allegations against him several years ago. She threatened to kill him."

I said, "We've checked that lead and she's hospitalized up in Wichita Falls. She has been for several years now."

Father Karl looked surprised to hear this and said, "I thought she was out now. Robert told me months ago that she was up for release. He said that he was worried that she would do something stupid and come after him."

Tex said, "I've got to ask this, so please don't become angry. Was Father Lanton ever accused of inappropriate conduct with anyone else?"

Wringing his hands, Father Karl answered, "If you're asking if he was a pedophile, the answer is no! But he did tell me, more than once, that he had trouble with celibacy. Not that I believe he had broken his vows. Yet I think it was on his mind a lot. I know for a fact that there was a young lady he was infatuated with, though I don't know her name."

Father Mike informed us, "The celibacy issue is a very difficult thing for some priests. I can only imagine Robert was no different."

I asked, "Was anyone in his congregation upset with him?"

Both men looked ill at ease, forcing Father Mike to explain, "There are always people in a congregation that disagree with an occasional sermon – sometimes rather heatedly. And from time to time a person gets upset over a stance that the church has taken on a political or social issue. I'm not naïve, but enough to murder a man? I doubt it. Besides, Father Lanton very rarely conducted mass. Public speaking was not his strong point, but he was an incredible scribe and activities manager."

"Anything else that ya'll can think of? Did he have any hobbies?" Tex asked.

Father Mike said, "He loved to coach boxing at a private club, but I am unsure where the club might be. Other than boxing, he was very passionate about football."

Running out of questions, we had Kothner draw his running map and Leopole make his visitation list (including the name of the family with the crisis). After another few minutes of casual talk the two priests left. Tex and I stayed in the conference room discussing the conversation and some of the answers we had received.

I started off, "My first impression is that I don't believe either man is involved. While the run Father Karl took literally encircled the crime scene, it will be easy to check out his story with the officers that saw him. If they marked out for paperwork – as they are supposed to do – dispatch will have the exact time they were sitting there when he passed by. If they didn't mark out, which is more than likely the case, dispatcher GPS will have their location pin pointed and how long they were stationary. It's just more of a hassle to get GPS information. The newspaper guys should be easy to check since they deliver around the same time every morning. I'll ask a patrol supervisor over at the Southwest substation to run this down. Father Mike is easier still with that 1 am phone call."

Tex agreed, but looked pensive, saying, "Both alibis seem pretty solid. But I don't think Father Karl was completely honest about Lanton and his issues with celibacy. I wonder if there was more to it than he was willing to say. Ren, you know these two, I mean I've seen them around, but you actually know them. Would they lie to cover each other?"

I said, "Tex, I think that Father Karl was visually nervous or shaken about this whole thing. And I agree that there is more to the Lanton celibacy thing than what we were told. As a far as lying to cover each other, I just don't think so."

Interrupting the discussion, Chief Wong walked in and began talking. "I've just gotten off the phone with Inspector Hector Villa in Argentina. Because he didn't feel safe using his office phone he went home and called me back from there. He informed me that the murdered priest, Father Raul Valdez, had a single history of accusations of molestation – though none in the last ten years before his death. The accusations were never seriously investigated. In his country, victims of this type of crime and nature are rarely believed over the word of a priest. Oddly enough, during the murder investigation, a copy of a letter turned up that Valdez had sent to the Vatican begging to be reassigned to a remote location for 'committing unspeakable sins.' Those were the exact words in the letter. Anyway, the letter was dated six months before he was murdered. He took out a two hundred and fifty thousand dollar life insurance policy that became effective one week before his murder. The beneficiaries were several children in his parish."

CHAPTER 6

Chief Wong's Office / CAPERS

We finished up our paperwork and back-briefed Wong on our interview with the chaplains. Mom walked in and caught the tail end of the back-brief. She looked worn out and ready to go home (it was her Saturday too).

When we finished, Mom said, "I got some 'fill in the blank' stuff. One of the cars, a Kia Rio, parked close to the crime scene belonged to Lanton. So either he was returning to his car or he was just leaving it when he was hit. I checked 911 Services and they got the call about Lanton at 2:29 am from a payphone at the corner of Beckley and Jefferson. That's about seven blocks east of the crime scene. On the way in I went by that location. There are no cameras or lights on the payphone and the handset has been yanked off." Turning to me she said, "Ren, the caller identified Lanton by name and occupation. The dispatcher knew Lanton from church and when the responding patrol element requested CAPERS, she put a call in to Smyth who also attends her church. She violated about a dozen general orders, but that solves that little mystery. I'll send someone over to listen to the tape, but a supervisor over at dispatch said the caller must have put something over the handset because the voice was muffled."

At this point, I was feeling brain dead from a lack of sleep and couldn't think of anything to say or a question to ask. Glancing at Tex, Mom and Chief Wong, they looked like I felt. I knew that we were missing something important, but we just stood there blinking our eyes trying to connect the dots. Lest you think we're all wimps that can't handle missing a little sleep, let me explain. Before we got the call for *this* murder we (and that includes Mom and even Chief Wong to a lesser extent) had completed a kickass investigation that started last Tuesday. By Friday evening, after working without sleep for over seventy two hours, we had solved a major who-done-it and arrested the perpetrator. We were paying for that now.

Mom was still talking and I had zoned out (Oops). "Father Lanton was murdered on the far west end of the Jefferson business zone. There's houses and apartments one street over on both the north and south sides. Later today Detectives Miller and Hill are going to canvas those neighborhoods to see if anything was heard or seen at the time of the shooting. Also, Miller and Hill are going to search Lanton's residence. That's all I got for now."

Then it clicked and I asked, "Ma'am, what did you say about the caller?"

Mom recited what she had said, then gave me a puzzled look, clenched her teeth and slapped her forehead in disgust. "How did all that go over my head?" she asked.

I answered, "Don't feel bad, Ma'am. There's an old saying 'sleep deprivation is a weapon' and I'm thinking we are all getting our butts kicked by it. Chief, I think based on the information about the caller using Lanton's name and title we can eliminate any thoughts of it being a random murder. It also means that the suspect had either followed Lanton to that location or knew that he was going to be there at some point in time. Both concepts show a high degree of familiarity with Lanton."

Chief Wong looked at the three of us and said, "I'll pass all this on to the detectives working the neighborhoods. Lieutenant, make sure the team searching Lanton's residence looks for anything that might tell us why he was out there at such an odd hour. Then I want you three go home and get some sleep. I'm heading over to Chief Smyth's office for the hourly up date. After that, I'll be at home hopefully sleeping too. Be back here Monday morning and be ready to work. No screwing off."

The trip home was very quiet – at least for awhile. It was my turn to drive and I was focused on trying to keep the car between the pretty white lines. To show moral support, Tex was trying to stay awake by constantly flipping stations on the car radio.

Obviously bored with the radio, Tex leaned back in his seat and said, "I hate to admit it, Ren, but the Chief is right. This case could get very nasty, especially if our murder is related to all the others. The media would have field day with an international serial killer."

Keeping my eyes on the road, I asked, "So you want me to call the FBI now? Maybe they'll send one of those high-speed low-drag serial-killer investigative teams that all the TV shows are about these days." Of course my question was meant to be sarcastic.

Laughing, Tex responded, "Nope! You know as well as I do that Hoover's fair haired children are like vampires, once you invite them into your house, you can never get rid of them."

Before someone gets their underwear in a knot, let me tell you that I believe the contemporary FBI does a lot of good stuff. The men and women of the FBI are very hard working people and excellent investigators within the *confines* of their areas of expertise; however, they are not super cops as shown on TV. Most will never deal with a momma and papa fight (unless they're involved), search a warehouse in the middle of a cold winter night with a gunman inside, walk in on a murder in progress, be shot at or take a human life. What I am talking about is street experience and most Special Agents of the FBI have none at all (unless they were cops before they became agents). That's not their job – it's mine (and people like me).

Also, people should always keep in mind that the FBI has a less than flawless history – no law enforcement agency does. It was the FBI that rounded up Japanese, German and Italian Americans during WWII and put them in internment camps. During the McCarthy era it was the FBI that destroyed lives, careers and families all because someone 'thought' their neighbor might be a homosexual, a socialist or a communist spy. McCarthyism gave the FBI a free hand to do whatever it pleased and they willfully abused that power. Throughout those years, much like the Spanish Inquisition, the FBI was noted for using strong arm tactics (torture) to extract confessions of guilt. Like I said, the FBI does a lot of good stuff now days, but they also have a very dark and troubling past. A past I believe they could just as easily revert back to with enough incentive.

Refocusing my attention, I asked, "Do you really think these murders are related? I mean Interpol sends these teletypes across the entire world. How hard would it be for someone to get one and decide killing a priest with three bullets to the head is a good idea?"

"Not very," Tex replied. "Still, I don't believe in coincidences. With the exception of the posing and the lack of shell casings, all of these cases are far too similar to dismiss out of hand. I wish Interpol was more forthcoming. It was lucky that Wong had a connection down in Argentina or else we wouldn't have shit to connect all this."

Pulling into my drive way, I asked, "but Tex, what do we really have other than one dead priest with celibacy issues murdered by someone that either he knew or knew him?

Rubbing his palm across his eyes, Tex answered, "Ren, until we hear from the ME we haven't got shit. Seriously, I'm not sure what to think."

I said, "Well, no sense thinking about for now. Ok, are you good to drive home? You can sleep on my couch or in one of the guest bedrooms if you want to."

Tex answered, "And have to deal with that frigging mutt of yours? That damn dog snores louder than my wife's mother and that, my friend, is saying something. I'm good – it's only another fifteen minutes down the road. I'll pick you up Monday at the usual time."

Waving as Tex drove off, I unlocked my front door and walked in. Danner, who was lying on the couch, opted not to get up. He did however have the decency to wag his tail in greeting. Walking over, I plopped down on the floor and began rubbing his ears. "Sorry I bailed on you during a storm. Are you ticked off at me, old buddy? You would not believe the case I'm on now. Real bad deal. I know you're probably bored to tears but I have got to get some sleep. I'll take you on a long run later, I promise."

A doctor would probably tell you that talking to a dog like it's human isn't healthy. But Danner is a good listener, never complains and is better company than most people I know. I got up and walked to the bed room, kicked off my clothes, showered and lay down. As I drifted off to sleep, I felt Danner jump on the bed and curl up next to me. And there we slept, the exhausted warrior and his faithful guardian.

I woke up about five hours later feeling confused. Was it six in the morning or six in the evening? Judging by the light coming through the windows it could be either. Danner was still lying next to me but I could tell by the way he smelled (like outside) that he had been in and out of the dog-door all day. From my bed I could see the light on the answering machine blinking. I must have been comatose not to hear the phone. I staggered over and pressed the play button. The machine blurted out 'you have four new messages:

'Message number one:' Hi honey it's your mother. I saw you and Tex on the morning news standing over another dead body. The news reporter said it was about 4 am. So I guess your day began when someone else's day ended." Giggling my mother continued saying, "Sorry that was a really bad joke. But it's nice to know you have such great job security! Dad's gone fishing, he'll lie about his catch later. We love you... call us." My parents... Since Dad's retirement, his whole outlook on life was much more relaxed. He spends a lot of time fishing. My mother was, well, my mother. She has always had a very sick sense of humor. No doubt that's where I got it.

'Message number two:' "Hey, it's me. It's one o'clock we were supposed to get lunch. Call me!" Oh crap, it was Carmen my on-again off-again girl friend. She was very nice, very pretty, very possessive and very high maintenance.

'Message number three:' "Where are you? You're not answering your cell – call me!" Alright... I'll call. Just let me wake up a little.

'Message number four:' "I talked to your partner's wife. Pat said you and Tex were out on a case all night. You could have called, but once again you didn't. You know what? Call me when you aren't married to your damn job. Until then, just leave me alone." This time she slammed the phone down. It looks like she's my off-again girl friend. I'm not sure why I kept going out with her because the truth is, she's a royal pain in the ass. Plus she flunked the Danner test. When she comes over he goes into the back room and won't socialize with her. Period! For a Black and Tan Coonhound, that is a major insult. It's like you or me flipping someone the bird at church. Oh well, it's a package deal. Love me, love my hound dog.

An hour later Danner and I were out running. It was pitch dark out, but who cares? There was just enough ambient light to see the trail we like to take. I've always loved long distance running; however my body type – thick – isn't really geared toward extreme distances. Because of this, I generally keep my runs at three to five miles but no further. Sometimes Tex and I will run together which is not one of my most favorite things to do. Tex is about six feet tall but his body frame, which is quite lanky, is conducive to long, fast runs. To him a short run is ten miles at a six minute pace. Danner loves running with him. Traitor!

I think we were at mile number three when my cell phone rang. It was Tex. "Hey where are you?" he asked.

Trying to catch my breath, I managed to puff out a reply of "I'm out running at the old nature center. What's up?"

CHAPTER 7

District Attorney's Office,
Harris County (Houston) Texas.

11 am Monday 5 February.
Four days before the death of Father Robert Lanton.

District Attorney Samuel R. Wetz sat behind his desk with his head in his hands. Torn between crying or smashing something, he was utterly livid and felt paralyzed by his anger. How in God's good name was he going to explain to the citizens of Houston, Texas how his office had lost this case? It wasn't that he was afraid the loss would impact his re-election chances. Wetz was one of the good guys that cared very little about politics. No, the anger he felt was because a monster is free despite his best efforts to put it in jail for the rest of its natural life.

There was a soft knock on his door. Wetz said, "Please come in."

The door opened slowly and Lead Prosecutor Thomas Ruddy walked in. As he took a seat, he asked, "You pissed at me, boss?"

Wetz slowly shook his head saying, "No Tom, certainly not. The cards were against us. Is there any chance that there are other victims out there that we don't know about? Victim's that we could build another case with?"

Tom answered, saying, "If there are, they're not coming forward either out of loyalty to the church or fear. Fear of what, I don't know; but…" Shrugging, he let the sentence die.

Wetz said, "We made a mistake by putting Randy Waton on the stand, didn't we?" Seeing the hurt look on Tom's face, he quickly added, "That was my call Tom, not yours. Even though the boy has special needs, he's far from slow or stupid. I honestly thought he could handle it. And for the most part he did, but when he got confused, it made him look like a liar. It was *very* effective counsel by Grayson Riggs. All the other evidence was circumstantial and without a solid witness or another victim to testify, we were dead."

Emotionally, Tom said, "Boss, why didn't the other victims come forward? We made sure anyone possibly involved understood that in the State of Texas, there is no statute of limitations on this crime. Why was it left up to an eighteen year old Down Syndrome kid to get this thing to trial?

Wetz said, "Tom, I don't know. You know as well as I do what some of the victims have told us. Father Cedric Redcliff is extremely charismatic and he made them fear spiritual retaliation." The desk phone rang softly and Wetz was tempted to let it ring, but knew he couldn't. "Yes! Oh? All right, send him up." Hanging the phone up Wetz said "Grayson Riggs is here."

Waiting in silence both Wetz and Ruddy were almost startled when Riggs walked into the room without knocking. "Gentlemen, thank you for seeing me," he said. "I know that emotions are running high right now." Taking a deep breath and exhaling slowly, he went on, "You may not believe this, but I'm as sickened by my client's freedom as you are, maybe more so because I helped free him!"

Staring at Riggs for several long moments, Wetz said, "Yes, Grayson, I believe you are. Please sit down."

"Thank you, Sam. Tom, you did a great job of tearing my game plan to pieces."

Tom said, "Yeah, until I put the boy on the stand."

Riggs fired right back, "Tom, putting the boy on the stand was not a mistake. I would have done it, too! He did fine until he got confused and as God is my witness, that wasn't my intent."

Riggs looked at Wetz and said, "Sam, you and I have crossed swords several dozen times in the last thirty years. Some times I've won and sometimes I've lost. But Sam, you have to know that I do not believe it's ever ethical or appropriate to belittle or humiliate a victim – especially a special needs child!"

Wetz said, "Grayson calm down. No one here is accusing you of doing something inappropriate or unethical."

Looking embarrassed at his own outburst, Riggs said, "Damn me. I came here to hopefully help sort things out and I get all emotional. How childish, you have my apologies. So what questions about my *former* client can I answer for you – without breaking confidentiality, of course."

Without pause, Tom asked, "Sir, you're not a public defender, so who paid your client's bill?"

Riggs thought for a moment and replied, "Tom you may not believe this, but I honestly don't know. I was contacted by phone requesting information about my services for this case. Two days later a cashier's check covering my retaining fees and services arrived at my office. I've been hired by vague sources before, but not quite like this. After the verdict was read this morning, another Cashier's check arrived via FedEx covering the final amount owed to me."

Wetz asked, "Grayson, do you think the Catholic Church could have paid the bill?"

Riggs said, "It's always possible I suppose, but to what end? Even though statistics have shown that about 4% of clergymen of *all faiths* do such heinous crimes, the reputation of the Catholic Church seems to have suffered the most. Point being, why would they pay for his defense? If the media found out, there would be yet another more damaging scandal."

Wetz asked, "In your opinion, Grayson, where did we go wrong in our strategy?"

Riggs replied, "I'm not entirely convinced you did something wrong, Sam. I honestly thought that I was getting spanked pretty bad in there. No, I do not think your strategy was off, I think it all boiled down to Randy Waton losing focus and becoming confused. And I have a very strong idea how that happened." Both Wetz and Ruddy immediately perked up as Riggs continued, "You couldn't see from your angle, but during the course of my cross examination Randy periodically made eye contact with Father Redcliff. At some point, their eyes locked and Randy didn't break contact until he was dismissed."

Tom said, "Are you saying Redcliff hypnotized the boy?"

Riggs answered, "No. From what little I know about hypnosis that would be impossible. No, Tom, what I think is that Randy suffered from the fight or flight syndrome. In that physiological and psychological state several things happen to a person all at once; heart beat goes from normal to up around 160 to 200 beats a minute, there's heightened visual capability to the point of tunnel vision, auditory exclusion, dry mouth, an inability to concentrate, severe sweating and even urination and/or defecation. I think this is what happened when Randy locked eyes with Redcliff. He was so terrified that all he could think of was escaping what he knew to be a monster. Quite frankly, I was very impressed that he didn't do just that!"

Wetz said, "Grayson, is there anything else you can tell us about Redcliff?"

Thinking for a moment and then shaking his head as if he had just made a crucial decision, Riggs said, "Many defending attorneys, me included, don't like surprises during the course of a trial. Hypothetically speaking, in cases where there could be such problems, the attorney might have his client list all possible surprises. Depending on the arrogance of the client, this list might even include other victims not known to the police."

Wetz sat silently for several long seconds trying to think how best to frame his next question. Speaking haltingly, Wetz asked, "Hypothetically speaking, Grayson, based on Redcliff's arrogance and propensity to… boast about his crimes, …do you believe that there are more victims out there – victims that we could build a case with?"

Suddenly standing up and stretching, Riggs said, "Hypothetically speaking, I'm sure of it. Gentlemen, I've got an appointment in less than an hour and then I have to be in Dallas tonight for a meeting tomorrow, so I had better leave." Turning toward the door, Riggs paused and said, "One thing you might consider, if Redcliff is to be charged with another crime, you had best hurry. He is being transferred to a station in Honduras sometime in the next few months. If you do arrest him again, I will not be defending him because I'm sure I'll have the flu that month. Good day."

Watching Riggs walk out of the office Tom said, "For a defending attorney, he really is a good guy, isn't he, boss?"

Wetz didn't answer because he was staring at a piece of folded notebook paper sitting on the same seat that Riggs had occupied. "Tom, would you be so kind as to hand me that piece of folded paper?" Taking the paper from Tom's slightly shaking hand, Wetz unfolded it and began to read. "Holy shit Tom, call in your team, our investigators, the Chief of Police and the police detectives that worked the original case. We have a lot of work to do and not much time to do it."

Hyatt Regency, down town Houston, 6 pm that same day.

Seated in the far back corner of the hotel bar, Father Richard Shannon sat sipping a rum and Coke, reflecting on the trial that he had watched for the last month. While it had not been a surprise, especially after the only victim's testimony had gone down in flames, the verdict was a pathetic let down and spoke volumes about America's legal system, where the rights of the accused are greater than that of the victim. Shannon believed that rape (known in Texas as Aggravated Sexual Assault) of a child should carry the death penalty option. It was mind blowing to him that a person could rape a child and not get the death penalty, let alone life behind bars without parole.

Knowing that there was no advantage to musing about the way things should be as opposed to how they really are, Shannon decided to concentrate on the issue at hand. Father Cedric Redcliff was going to die either here in Houston or in Tegucigalpa, Honduras. If Shannon had it his way, he would follow Redcliff to Honduras and pop the sick bastard there. The Honduran police would investigate to some extent, but they wouldn't give it the effort Houston police would. Even a twisted person like Redcliff would get a fair investigation from the cops whether he deserved it or not. The trouble was Redcliff would not be sent to Honduras for several months – there were a lot of innocent children whose lives he could destroy in those few months. Chances were he would escape to Honduras before those new crimes were ever reported. No. It was best to get this over with before Redcliff could hurt someone else. Besides, it was why his masters had paid for Redcliff's defense. Keeping that sick pig out of jail gave Shannon easy access to him. With his decision made, he left the bar and went to his room to catch a few hours sleep.

2 am, 6 February (*Three days before the death of Father Robert Lanton*)

Father Cedric Redcliff was restless in his new found freedom. He couldn't sleep but at the same time he didn't dare venture forth from his rented house. After the verdict was read, his lawyer had him taken home. There was no chance for interviews with the media (which was something he craved), he had been snatched out of the court room, stuffed into the backseat of a car and told to lie down on the seat. When he tried to make conversation with the driver he was told to keep his "nasty mouth shut." After he got home, the driver searched the house, handed him an envelope and left without saying a word. He'd forgotten to open the envelope so, giving up on sleep, he got out of bed and retrieved it from the kitchen table. Opening it, he began to read the short letter inside:

'Dear Sir, my services have been paid for in full. Today's verdict concludes our relationship. Please do not, under any circumstances, contact me.' It was signed by Grayson Riggs. What a pisser, Redcliff thought, then laughed. Oh well, he didn't like the sanctimonious jerk very much anyway. Tossing the letter in the trash he walked into his living room, grabbed the remote and turned on the television. And there on CNN was his smiling face. The commentator was saying, "In a surprise verdict today, Father Cedric Redcliff, an accused pedophile, was found not guilty of molesting a special needs teenager. There were as many as twenty more possible allegations against Father Redcliff, however, other potential victims refused to cooperate with the investigation." The picture shifted to live footage of the verdict being read, and then swung and panned the crowd's angry reaction to the verdict. Had Redcliff kept the volume on his television low, he might have heard his front door open, then gently shut.

Father Shannon had no problem slipping by the two police officers sitting in their squad car in front of Redcliff's residence. It was plain to him that either the police department was protecting this animal from revenge, which he seriously doubted, or they were making damn sure he couldn't leave his house without their knowledge. Regardless, they were parked at the wrong angle to see Shannon silently defeat the lock on Redcliff's front door. Stepping inside, Shannon froze, listening. Had Redcliff been asleep, night sounds would have been all Shannon heard – snoring, coughing and maybe tossing and turning in bed. Instead he could hear the television blaring in the living room and then suddenly go off.

Shannon dropped to a knee and sat back, heel to butt, making his form and outline as small as possible. If Redcliff walked past, his peripheral vision would sweep over the top of Shannon where he knelt low to the ground. There was no doubt in Shannon's mind that he could, with his hands or feet, quickly dispatch Redcliff to hell. But with each moment of physical contact, Locard's Exchange Principle would come into play. In other words, forensic evidence would be left behind. The mark of a great assassin was to leave no trace of his coming, presence or passing, only of his actions. Shannon held his position for several minutes, patiently waiting.

To the casual, observer it would have looked as if Shannon had fallen asleep, so still was he. Slowly, he unfolded into a fighting stance that resembled a cat ready to pounce. Then, after freezing for another minute, he began to walk toward Redcliff's bedroom taking a step every ten or fifteen seconds. Step – heel toe, listen. Step – heel toe, listen. It took him almost five minutes to move from the front door, down the hall to the bedroom where Redcliff was now hopefully sleeping with the bedroom light still on. Shannon paused just outside the door and listened to Redcliff's deep steady breathing. Shannon pondered how easy it would be to step into the room without warning and kill this beast. Yet there were rules that Shannon felt must be followed. This creature that had once belonged to God must know and understand why he was dying this night. With that thought in mind, Shannon took the silenced .22 caliber automatic handgun from its holster and stepped into the room. "Father Cedric Redcliff, wake up!" Shannon commanded in a low but firm voice.

Shannon watched as Redcliff came awake in an instant.

Staring at the handgun, Redcliff shouted "What do you want? I'm a priest… I have no money or jewelry."

Shannon said, "No Father Redcliff, I'm not here to steal from you. You have been found guilty of…"

Cutting Shannon off, Redcliff sobbed, "No, no you've got it all wrong. I was found innocent… not guilty! I've done nothing wrong. I'm innocent!"

Staring at Redcliff, Shannon thought, '*So this was the monster. This piece of offal had spread terror into the hearts of those least capable of defending themselves.*' Disgusted, Shannon said, "Father Cedric Redcliff, it is true that you were found not guilty in a secular court, but you are far from innocent. You have been found guilty of crimes against humanity *by your peers*! You have been sentenced to die for these crimes."

In disgust, Shannon fired his handgun three times in rapid succession. Almost simultaneously there were brilliant flashes of white light, a bizarre popping noise as each bullet shattered Redcliff's skull and entered his brain and then, at the last, a gurgling noise that came from Redcliff's throat. Moments later Father Cedric Redcliff was dead.

Watching as Redcliff breathed his last, Shannon began to pray. Not for the soul of Redcliff as he knew he should, but for his own soul. Because Father Richard Shannon knew that had it been left up to him, he would not have permitted this creature to die so quickly.

6 pm, 6 February.

The Joule in downtown Dallas was one of the best five star hotels in the city. To Mr. Grayson Riggs, Attorney at Law, the only thing that could have made his stay more enjoyable would have been if his wife could have joined him. As he changed clothes, he thought it was probably better that she had not made this trip since the meeting went on far longer than he had anticipated. Mumbling to himself, "I wonder how much longer that idiot would have talked? Thank the Lord we ran out of time or we'd still be there. Next time, I'll fake a heart attack or something. Even a ride in an ambulance would have been more fun than listening to that fool drone on."

Sitting down on the edge of the bed, Riggs turned on the television hoping to catch the afternoon sports scores on ESPN. Whoever had occupied the room before him had been watching CNN and the face of Father Cedric Redcliff came into view as the screen cleared. In anger Riggs burst out, "Damn it, I can't get away from this guy!" He started to continue his ranting but then caught what the commentator was saying, "…was found dead this morning, shot through the head, an apparent victim of murder. Police are not giving specific details at this time, however, they have said that Redcliff was found by a work associate around nine this morning." Riggs had lost interest in the sports scores and turned off the television. Thinking for a moment he picked up his cell phone and called Sam Wetz.

"Yes ma'am, this is Grayson Riggs. Is the District Attorney in?" After being put on hold for only a few seconds Wetz picked up.

"Grayson, I guess you've heard the news?"

"Yes, Sam, just now on CNN. I'm still in Dallas. Are there any suspects, I mean other than the entire population of the city of Houston or the state of Texas?"

Wetz's reply was slow in coming, "Yes, Grayson, there is. We've arrested Randy Waton. He was found less than two blocks from the crime scene unconscious laying in some bushes. He looked like he'd been out there all night and there was blood on his clothing. The point of entry to Redcliff's residence was a back window that had been smashed out, not in. Randy has what look to be deep glass cuts on his arms and waist. It'll be a day or two before the tests come back. Until then, he's being held as an adult at the county hospital for medical observation. In light of things, that was the best I could do."

Riggs asked in a quiet voice, "What do you think, Sam? I find it very hard to believe that boy is capable of murder."

Wetz agreed, saying, "Me too, Grayson. Look, his family hasn't got shit for money and I don't want to leave this to a poorly paid and over-worked public defender; however, I think you being involved might be construed as a conflict of interest. What I'm asking is, do you know anyone that could help?"

Riggs immediately replied, "Yes, Sam, I know a great lawyer that would do this pro bono. She goes by the name of Jessie Hardin. She practices law in Galveston, but owes her mom and dad – that would be me and Sara – some big favors, you know, like paying for law school. I'll call her right away. Just be warned, she's not nice like me, she's going kick ya'll in the ass!"

Wetz replied, "I certainly hope so." Hanging up the phone Sam Wetz smiled for the first time that day.

4 hours later.

Maybe it was guilt about setting a person like Redcliff free or maybe it was how hurt Randy Waton had to have been over the verdict, but three hours later Riggs still felt unsettled about the whole situation. On impulse, Riggs decided to check out of the hotel and head back to Houston even though he was not sure how he could help. Still, going back seemed like the right thing to do. Thinking out-loud as he walked out to his car, Riggs said, "If nothing else, I can give Jessie all my notes including the police reports and victim's medical reports. That will help her understand what that fiend did to Randy. No worries about confidentiality, since the asshole is dead."

Riggs tossed his suitcase into the back seat and fired up the engine on his 1980 Mercedes Benz 450SL. Turning north onto Main Street, he picked up Interstate 45 southbound. Thinking about the death of Cedric Redcliff and the boy arrested for his murder, Grayson Riggs only occasionally glanced at his rearview mirror. So focused on this new turn of events Riggs failed to notice that he was being followed.

Interstate 45 is never empty of traffic, but around midnight on a drizzly winter night, traffic certainly slows down. After nearly two hours behind the wheel, Riggs was beginning to doubt how smart his decision to make the drive home was. His eyes were heavy and his colon and bladder were on overload. There were plenty of gas stations along this route, but they all looked to be closed. The last decent truck stop had been in Corsicana where he gassed up and pounded down a hamburger with a very large coke. Huntsville was still another five miles down the road so when he spotted a rest area with toilets, he pulled over. As soon as his Benz came to a stop in front of the building, Riggs bailed out not even stopping long enough to lock the doors on his prized car. Running toward the toilets he thought, *Screw it. If someone takes it I'll buy a new one. Better that than fouling my pants.*

Fifteen minutes later, Riggs came out of the bathroom feeling sorry for the next person to walk in there. *I ought to leave a letter of apology tacked to the door,* he thought. Chuckling to himself, he began walking toward his Benz when he noticed a small, dark colored sedan parked next to his car with its headlights on. It hadn't been there when he pulled in, he was sure of that. As he walked closer he realized that the car was empty and still had its motor running. *That's odd. Maybe they had to hit the toilet like I did and went to the ladies restroom on the other side of the building,* he mused. He debated waiting to make sure the person, most likely a woman, was okay. If nothing else, someone should watch her car until she returned. Walking around to his driver's side door he decided he would at least sit down and stay warm until she returned.

As he reached for the door handle a noise behind Riggs startled him and he spun around to face a man pointing a gun at his head. The man seemed tall, well built and was dressed in black clothing with the white collar of a clergymen. Taking a breath to settle his nerves, Riggs said, "Goodness Father, you spooked the fire out of me. It's dark here and quite desolate so I can understand the gun, but could you lower it, sir?"

The priest said nothing in response.

Fearing what this encounter might mean, Riggs began to immediately size up the man and, to his dismay, realized that even on a good day he could not possibly take this man in a fight. "Sir, my name is Grayson Riggs. I am on my way home to my wife. I have money and credit cards – all of which you can have, just please lower the gun."

After a moment, in a tired monotone voice, the priest said, "Mr. Grayson Riggs, you have been found guilty of aiding and abetting in crimes against humanity. For this you are sentenced to die." Three shots were fired in quick secession dropping Riggs to the ground. Holstering his gun, the priest first searched the ground for his shell casings. Finding all three, he then looked at Riggs and saw no intake of breath. Saying a prayer for the deceased, he put on black gloves and began to position the body.

2 Miles North of the Rest Stop.

"Man I love this job," Tony Ellis said to his dog lying on the seat next to him. Ellis and his wife Angie had been a big-rig truck team for almost thirty years. In fact they met at the Texaco truck stop off of Interstate 35 in Waco Texas shortly after he had returned from Vietnam in 1972. At the time, he was driving for a local company and she was working at the truck stop running the cash register. Six months later they were married and with the help of the Veterans Administration they purchased their first 18-wheeler. Always together, they had seen the country several times over and now, both in their late 50's, they were starting to talk about retiring. The trouble was, even though diesel prices had soared and the economy was tight, they still loved the business.

Half asleep Angie mumbled from the cabin bed, "Honey, I have got to get to a bathroom."

With a smirk on his face Tony said, "Babes, can't you use the cabin toilet?" Their new truck cabin had not only a bed; it also had a toilet and shower, a small kitchen and living room.

Dislodging Ram-boo, their Beagle, from the seat where she slept, Angie sat down saying, "Nope, not for what I've got to do. And besides, I need to stretch a little."

"And here I was blaming Ram-boo for farting up the cabin. I told you not to eat the liver and cabbage back in Dallas. Don't anyone light a match, the cabin will explode." Laughing at his own joke he continued on saying, "Ok, Babes, there's a rest stop coming up with toilets. It's the one just north of Huntsville. That ok?"

Looking at her husband of nearly forty years she grinned saying, "That'll be fine, Mister I-never-fart."

Seconds later Tony had to slow the truck and blast his air horn to clear the highway of deer. 'Sorry Babes, wouldn't want to hit one of those guys in our new truck. I'll get you to that outhouse now."

Less than a minute later they pulled into the rest stop. The truck came to a halt shy of the bathrooms by about 50 yards – Tony and Angie had long since learned that to park in front of something meant risking being parked in by rude car drivers. "Whew, there ya go honey. Guess I'll use the bathroom while we're here, too. You go first and I'll walk Ram-boo. God knows she's probably ready for it."

Angie quickly climbed down and headed for the ladies room. Climbing out of the cabin Tony stood there taking a few deep breaths enjoying the cool night air. Still in the cabin, Ram-boo began to whine. Reaching up and grabbing her with both hands Ellis said, "Oops, sorry little girl, bet you've got to go, too." Setting her down, he clipped on her leash and walked her over to the grass only vaguely noticing the Mercedes sitting in front of the bathroom building. A few minutes later Ram-boo had finished her business and, pulling Tony behind her, began a tour of the rest stop grounds. Suddenly she stopped, raised her nose in the air and began sniffing in deep breathes.

"What is it girl, smell something fun?" said Tony as he looked around to see if Angie was out yet. Not seeing Angie he decided to let Ram-boo get some exercise and follow her nose for a few minutes. "Girl, if it's a dead critter by the road don't you dare roll in it." Unexpectedly Ram-boo bayed and without any warning took off running almost pulling the leash from his hand. "Damn girl, slow down!" Tony yelled as she pulled him straight for the Mercedes Benz.

Angie intercepted them asking, "What's up with her?" As all three of them rounded the front of the car they saw a body lying in a pool of blood.

Pulling the dog back, Tony said, "Babes, take Ram-boo to the truck, call 911, and get my medical bag. And bring the camera, too." It wasn't because of some morbid desire to save these memories. No, Tony knew that the man might be dead and that this was a crime scene. The moment he walked up to check for a pulse he might disturb or destroy valuable evidence. And if the guy wasn't dead, the same thing applied, especially when the ambulance crew showed to haul him away.

After calling 911 Angie quickly returned and, handing him the medical bag, she began taking pictures as fast as she could. Slowly Tony moved up to the body and knelt studying the wound as he had been taught to do in his days as a combat Navy corpsman. Tony extended his stethoscope and placed it on the man's neck over the carotid artery listening for a pulse.

"Ok, Babes, the dude still has a heartbeat." Taking off the stethoscope, Tony put thin latex gloves on and opened one of the man's eyes. Shining a pen light into the eye he said, "Pupils are somewhat dilated but still responsive." Gently he ran his hand over the man's face and head. "Babes, he's bleeding from the ears, nose and what looks to be two or three small head wounds – probably small caliber bullets. Look how the skin and scalp are puffed out in these lines. Those are the paths of the bullets that didn't penetrate the skull. They followed the skull under the scalp and exited back here on the side where he is bleeding from. I saw this a few times in Nam. The third wound has a small lump. I'm guessing, but I think this bullet got stuck in the skull. Babes, hand me the C-collar and get the cold-pacs from the freezer. What kills most people with head trauma is the secondary injury when the brain swells. Maybe we can keep that from happening with the cold-pacs."

After Tony put the C-collar on his patient he placed the cold-pacs on the forehead, sides and under the neck of the man. He carefully moved the man's arms to his side, grabbed a disposable blanket from his bag, opened it and covered him. In the distance Tony and Angie heard the sirens of the ambulance and police squad cars approaching them.

1 hour later.

For the last hour both Tony and Angie Ellis had been sitting at two separate picnic tables either staring at each other or watching as the crime scene was processed. They had been questioned quickly only once and then told to sit quiet. Neither had been allowed to get a drink of water or use the bathroom. Two police officers had been posted to make sure that they didn't escape.

Escape to where Tony wasn't sure, they had his truck parked in. Shaking his head in frustration, he suddenly stood up and stated, "Damn it, I need to take a leak." Tony watched as his guards put their hands on their duty weapons and faced him. Seeing this, Tony said, "Boys ya'll can draw those hog-legs and shoot me if ya want, but it'll have to wait until I get back from the bathroom." Not waiting for permission or escort, Tony walked to the bathroom to relieve himself.

Coming out a few minutes later he noticed that the guards were gone and that Angie was talking to one of the detectives from the Walker County Sheriff's office. Seeing him approach, the detective said, "Mr. Ellis, Mrs. Ellis, I sincerely apologize for keeping ya'll here like this. I know that ya'll have been questioned once already, but this time I'd like you to walk us through how ya'll came to be here and how you found the victim." Three hours later they were finally done with the walk through and questioning. The detective seemed astonished, and thrilled to boot, that Angie had gotten pictures of the crime scene before it was disturbed by the paramedics or when Tony started first aide. Looking at the pictures that Angie had downloaded on his lap top, the detective asked, "And to you his body position didn't look natural, it looked posed?"

Tony replied, "Sir I was a corpsman in Nam and I've seen hundreds of wounded Marines and at least that many dead. No sir, I have never seen a person fall like that. It's like he was being crucified or something."

Just before they got back on the road the detective came over to the truck smiling saying, "Good news! The victim, Mr. Grayson Riggs, is going to make it. The doctor said to tell ya'll that you saved the man's life. He's in a drug induced coma for a few days, but putting those cold-pacs around his head was brilliant. It kept the swelling under control until surgery. They removed a small bullet – as you suspected lodged in the skull. There were some bone fragments they had to remove from just on the inside of the skull. Anyway, barring any serious complications, he should make a full recovery."

Shaking hands with the detective, Tony and Angie Ellis loaded back up and hit the road. Tony looked at Angie and with a shit-eating grin on his face, said, "We saved a man's life today, Babes. It really makes all that crap I went through in Nam worthwhile. That's really something, isn't it?"

Glancing over at her husband, Angie pretended not to see the tear run down her husband's cheek. Reaching out and taking his hand, Angie replied, "It sure is!"

CHAPTER 8

Dallas Nature Center (Present Day)

I slowed my running pace to a near walk to listen to what Tex was trying to tell me. Tex replied, "I got a call from the office. Some stuff came in on the teletype from Harris County and from Huntsville. Our murderer has been a very busy boy. Can ya guess what he's done?"

Too winded to care overly much, I said, "Ok Tex, I'll play your silly ass guessing game. What has the murderer done? Killed another priest?"

Tex answered, "Yep. And not just any priest. He killed that serial pedophile Cedric Redcliff. He's the one that got a not guilty verdict last week. All the details match up with our shooter as well as the others from Interpol."

I was walking now, much to the disgust of Danner, who wanted to keep running and to hell with the wimp holding his leash. "Tex, there's a problem with this. Lanton never hurt anyone that we know of. Why do I get the feeling there's more?"

Tex said, "That's because *there is more*. Just outside of Huntsville Wednesday night someone, probably our killer, tried to whack Redcliff's attorney at a highway rest stop. Put three bullets in his head and then posed him like Lanton. Only none of the bullets penetrated his skull and he's alive. He's in a medically induced coma, but he's expected to make it. With any luck, he might be able to identify our shooter. Also, the investigators recovered all three bullets. They're really flattened out so, other than telling us that the bullets are .22 caliber, they'll not be much help."

Checking my watch, I noticed that it was already going on eight. "All right Tex, now what? Do I need to shower up and get dressed for work or what?"

"No" he answered, "but why don't you and Carmen meet me and Pat for a late dinner at Chili's in Cedar Hill around 9:30? Mom said she would meet us, too. We can discuss the case and stuff our faces, all at the same time."

"Sounds like a plan, only Carmen has dumped me again. So unless they'll let Danner in at Chili's, it'll just be me. See ya soon." Closing the phone I looked down at Danner and said "We've got an extra half hour, little black dog, and you're not fast enough to keep up with me!" I took off at the hardest sprint I could manage. As Danner blew by me, he licked my hand in thanks... or maybe he was mocking the slow guy.

Home

The old Dallas Nature Center was only about a fifteen minute drive back to my house on Mt. Lebanon Road in Cedar Hill. I live in a 1970's, four bedroom, Ranch style house surrounded by ten acres of wooded land. Before you think that I'm some spoiled, only child, rich kid, let me tell you I'm not - rich I mean. As for me being spoiled, my grandfather (on my mother's side) spoiled me horribly when my dad was gone on various tours of duty overseas. The old guy taught me how to work hard, play sports, manage money and woo the pretty girls. Hence why I'm still single – granddad was great at everything except dealing with grand mom and their six daughters. He once said that he loved to hang out with me because his house had far too much estrogen in it. There were times he told me he wasn't sure if he wanted to scream in frustration or secretly put on a dress and paint his toe nails red.

I turned off Mt. Lebanon road into the drive way and headed for the house almost a hundred yards away. As I approached, I could see a dark blue Dodge Caliber sitting in front of the house. It was a rental – had to be.

No one in his right mind would put such cheap tires on what should have been a nice looking car. The only person in the world that would visit me (and use a rental car) was Rick Shannon. I pulled up beside the Caliber and tapped the horn on my old full sized Bronco to let him know I was back. As I opened the car door Danner bolted past me, ran around to the dog door at the back of the house and went in. As I opened the front door I could hear Rick laughing in the living room. I started to ask what was so funny but as I walked into the living room, I saw Rick stretched out on the couch with Danner on top of him licking his face. "Well that explains what's so funny. How are ya?" I asked.

Still laughing Rick answered, "I was fine until this stinky mutt pounced on me! I figured you two were out running, so I took a short nap. That is until I was brutally attacked by this fierce hell-hound." Gently rolling Danner off him, Rick stood up, hugged me and said. "Good to see you, little brother. How's business?"

I said, "Maybe you haven't heard, but crime is kicking our asses. Still, it beats being out of work." Rick laughed but it sounded… strained?

Rick was thirty-eight (two years older than me) and still looked every bit the Navy Seal; yet there was a distinct tiredness in his bearing that I'd never seen before. Not even after the fight in Iraq. Rick's parents were deceased, had been since his first year at Annapolis (car wreck) and he had no other family, so he considered me his little brother and this his home. I felt the same way. He came and went as his duties required but he generally came home at least once every month. This time Rick hadn't been home in almost a year. During that time I'd hardly spoken to him by phone and he only infrequently answered my emails. Maybe what I was sensing was work related.

His job within the church was a bit like mine. He investigated criminal activity and violations of church doctrine done by people (priest, nuns and laymen) within the Catholic church or aimed at the Catholic church by people outside the faith. While I am unsure exactly *what* crimes he investigates, I do know that he reports his findings to a council of Cardinal's bishops within the Roman Curia. They in turn report his investigative conclusions directly to the Pope. It had to be very stressful and although I wasn't sure what was up now, the brother of my heart looked like a man carrying a heavy burden.

"Is there anything to eat around here? I'm starved." Rick grabbed my arm and pulled me toward the kitchen.

Nodding my head, I said, "There's plenty of food in the fridge, but I'm supposed to meet Tex, Pat and Mom at Chili's in about a half hour. It's a working dinner, but if you'd like to come along, you'd be more than welcome."

Rick thought for a second and said, "If you don't think I'd be in the way I would love to." Smiling he continued on saying, "Of course I'll spring for every one's dinner, broke public servants that you people are."

"Hey, I may be a poorly paid public slave, but as you well know, my family has money – ah, even if I do not!" My family comes from very old money made during the rum-runner years.

One of my great-great grand sires retired from the Navy as a Ship's Captain and then turned around and made a fortune running naval blockades with illegal booze during prohibition. Each generation thereafter has invested well to the point that we are now comfortable, though not filthy rich. I won't see a dime of family money until dad and mom pass away or I get married. When that happens a very substantial trust fund kicks in. With granddad's teaching on my side, looks like I'll have to wait till my folks are gone. Or maybe I should kiss and make up with Carmen. Naw, too much trouble!

With an unsympathetic voice, Rick said, "I don't see a wife around here or even a girlfriend so Carmen must have dumped you again. This means that there's not a potential marriage in the wings that would help activate your trust fund. And I know for a fact that your Mother and Father are still alive since I just got off the phone with them not an hour ago. So I guess you are indeed broke and I am indeed picking up the tab."

"Ok Rick, I'll let you flaunt your hard earned divinely blessed wealth, but if we break your expense account at the Vatican Bank and Trust, it's your own fault! I'm going to take a shower – I stink."

Rick pulled his shirt up to his nose and sniffed. "Whew, I'm gonna shower too. I smell like a coonhound." Danner looked up at Rick with an expression of, "What did you expect?"

As only military trained people can accomplish, less than eight minutes later Rick and I, showered and changed, were on the way to Chili's. Staring out the side window of the Bronco, Rick said, "Cedar Hill has really grown in the last few years. Looks like this'll be a good place to retire to when you're done with Dallas. Hey, I forgot to tell you, the house looks great. The new tile in my room and bathroom really makes a difference – Thanks."

I said, "No worries. I had Lieutenant Saxen pick out the colors. She has a knack for that type of thing." After riding in silence for a couple of seconds I finally asked, "What's wrong Rick?

Not even trying to fake ignorance to my question, Rick replied, "I'm very tired, Ren. It's been a roller-coaster five years for the Mother Church. There's been one scandal after another – some deserved and some not deserved. Since I was last home, I've been in a dozen countries investigating such a wide variety of crimes and severe doctrinal infractions that it's taken a toll on me. As you know, I spent the last month in Houston watching the Redcliff trial. During that entire ordeal, I couldn't come home because I was stuck interviewing his lesser known victims on the weekends."

Rick had grown mildly agitated as he talked. "Ren, fifteen minutes after that trial started, I knew with certainty that he was guilty, but he still walked. God forgive us all, what he did to that Down syndrome boy was an abomination. It just kills me that these monsters are able to beat such crimes and it hurts the image of the Church so much."

"Rick, please don't take this wrong. You and I both know that statistics show that all faiths, religions and occupations have suffered the same problems with pedophiles in the ranks. Hells bells even law enforcement and the military has had a share. But I think what's caused such embarrassment for ya'll is there's a misperception, promoted by the media, that the Catholic Church protects these bastards and even endorses the practice."

Taking a deep breath, Rick said, "And I agree. I'll say this to you and no one else, but I believe we, the Catholic Church, helped to influence that misperception by trying to 'cure these people' rather than put them down like the sick animals they are."

Rick has never been a pacifist. Nor has he ever shied away from expressing his support for the death penalty for the most heinous crimes, but the angry passion in his voice took me by surprise. Rick must have sensed my shock because he lightened up and changed the subject.

"Ren, to be honest with you, I was coming home anyway. I've been ordered to look into Father Lanton's death. I hope that doesn't upset you."

Chuckling I said, "First, no it does not upset me, and second, I would have been surprised if you hadn't been sent."

About a year and half ago Fort Worth, Texas (our neighboring city) had a Catholic nun murdered by some gang members. 'Eastside Loco's' was the name of the gang. They had been involved in numerous murders across the Dallas - Fort Worth Metroplex region. As I recall, the good sister's murder was very brutal and Rick had been sent in to investigate for the Church.

"Rick, I just wish I had something to tell you. There are some new developments that may have bearing on this case; but it's too early to tell. That's what this working dinner is about."

Chili's Cedar Hill

Less than a minute later we were walking through the door at Chili's. As I had expected we were fashionably early. I've never been able to figure out how I stay in a state of perpetual earliness. In spite of Chief Wong's accusation that Tex and I were late to Lanton's crime scene last night (we weren't, but try telling him that) even when I'm trying to be late – I'm early.

Rather than wait for the others to arrive, Rick and I pulled a couple of tables together and we both sat next to one another with our backs to the wall. This might have looked strange to someone who's not a cop or a combat veteran, but it's the way we're hard wired to think. Everything and everyone unknown to us is a potential threat so we sit with our backs to the wall where no one can sneak up on us and/or where we can watch the door. Don't believe me? Next time you eat out, if there are cops in the restaurant watch the ones who are forced to sit with their backs to the door (or a crowd). They may be eating but they're not relaxed.

Rick and I had just ordered a pitcher of beer when Tex and his wife Doctor Patricia Beers, MD, PhD. walked in holding hands. Tex is tall and lanky and Pat is short and plump. I have to admit they look really good together. They've been married for over thirty years, raised four boys (all proud members of the Marine Corps) and they are as in love today as they must have been when they first got married.

A recently retired Clinical Psychologist, Pat had worked at Parkland County Hospital for twenty-five years. She's never worn a badge and gun but I know for a fact that she takes no shit off of anyone, especially me. Of course she simply adores Rick. She views him as the perfect gentlemen. Spare me!

Sitting down across from us, Pat reached over the table and took my beer daring me to say something. I didn't because I know better. Taking a long slow sip she smiled, "Hmmm, *that's really good!* Ren are you going to have some beer tonight?"

Both Tex and Rick thought this highly amusing. Deciding that dishonor was the better part of valor, I refilled Pat's glass and said, "Why yes, Pat. I'll be having a beer as soon as the waiter brings us some more glasses. Until then, please don't wait to enjoy yours."

About that time Lieutenant Saxen walked in the door wearing cowboy boots, blue jeans, and a semi-tight black turtle neck sweater. I was staring and didn't realize that the others were watching me and snickering about me staring at her. Ah Shit. Why couldn't Mom have shown up wearing canvas coveralls, hair in a bun and no makeup? This was going to be a very difficult night for me, and hearing Rick, Pat and Tex making fun of me wasn't going to help.

"Honey, do something. Why doesn't Ren ask her out? You know he wants to! He looks like a little lost puppy." Pat said in a loud stage whisper.

Tex replied equally as loud, "Pat, I can teach him how to be a great detective; but his love life is a lost cause. His grandfather's influence is just too strong!"

Smiling, Rick just shrugged saying, "Don't look at me I'm celibate."

Mom walked over and greeted Rick and Pat like long lost family. Tex got a professional smile and a slight head shake and all I got was a glance as Rachel took a seat at the far end of the table. Yep, this was going to be a long ass night.

Over dinner we talked about everything except the murder case which was the proverbial elephant in the room. We finally finished our meals and Mom ordered coffee for us all. She then said, "Rick, I figured at some point you'd be here to look into the murder of Father Robert Lanton. So the earlier you're involved in our investigation the better. To that end, I've already talked to Chief Wong and Chief Smyth, who, without any reluctance, gave their permission for you to sit in on any briefings that might help you complete your investigation. And Pat, like your husband, you've got a keen analytical mind so feel free to give us your input."

Shooting me a strange look, she said, "Ren just try to keep up with the adult conversation if you can."

Ouch! What was that all about?

Taking a sip of coffee, Mom passed out the crime scene photos and continued on, saying "As ya'll may or may not know, there have been some interesting events that might be tied to this case. Before I get into that, the autopsy for Father Lanton is not back yet. All we have from CSR at this time are these crime scene photos. The search of Lanton's residence turned up nothing; however, Detectives Miller and Hill have asked to hit it again. They were disturbed about every ten to fifteen minutes by Chief Smyth's office calling for an update. Then two 'Special Investigators' from the Chief's office showed up at Lanton's place and really got in their way. Finally Miller contacted Wong who came out and yanked a knot in some asses. Anyway, by then it was so late in the day and they still needed to start canvassing the neighborhood. Miller and Hill decided to start fresh tomorrow morning – hence why Hill and Miller opted out of joining us for dinner. So are there any questions about where we are at from that approach?"

I asked, "Ma'am, just who and what are these 'Special Investigators' and why are they inferring with this case?"

With a ticked-off look on her face, Mom answered, "Ren, I'm not sure and neither is Wong. Wong suspects that they were pulled out of the Public Integrity Unit or Internal Affairs and are reporting directly to Smyth. We all knew that Smyth could possibly cause problems for us because of his affiliation with Lanton and the Catholic Church; but as for why he's doing it, Ren, we just don't know."

Rick cleared his throat and said, "Rachel, I might be able to shed some light on this; however, please keep in mind that this is pure speculation and I have nothing to back it up. Anyway, because of all the church related scandals many Catholics are feeling falsely persecuted by society in general and specifically by the media. By all accounts, your Chief of Police is very devout and has even worked as a Lay Minister at times. I believe that Smyth may be trying to protect the Catholic Church from yet another media blitz."

Having nothing to contribute, I sat listening to the 'adult conversation' and thinking about some of the scandals the Catholic Church had suffered in recent history. Maybe I'm bit biased because of my high regard for Rick, but I think *some* of what has influenced public opinion against the church has occurred as a result of the media censoring information. Case in point: One source of contention came when it was discovered that *some bishops* knew about sexual abuse allegations against priest. None of this diminishes the evil nature of this crime; however, for years the media has run detailed stories about 'pedophile priests,' yet the media has glossed over mentioning pedophiles found in other religions and faiths. I can almost understand a devout person like Chief Smyth wanting to protect his faith from more scandal.

Exasperated, Mom asked, "Rick, doesn't he understand that by his interference, he may end up creating a greater scandal for the Church and the Department?"

Rick started to reply when Mom, holding up her hands in a gesture of surrender, said, "Sorry Rick, I guess that was a rhetorical question. And it came out much more abrupt than I meant for it to. I understand that you're speculating. Tex, you had something?"

"Yes Ma'am, as you know, Ren and I talked to Father's Leopole and Kothner early this morning. Father Kothner mentioned to us that he believed Father Lanton was infatuated with a young lady in his congregation. Anything turn up on that?"

Mom shook her head no. "Hill and Miller got doodled on that too and for the same reasons. They'd just begun to canvass the neighborhood when they bumped into the 'Special Investigators' again. Not wanting to knock on the same doors so soon, they called it a day."

Looking at us, Mom summed it up. "We haven't got crap right now, guys. So let's talk about what we know has occurred down south in Houston and Huntsville." Collecting her thoughts for a moment she continued on. "The notorious Father Cedric Redcliff was found not guilty in court last Tuesday morning. Wednesday morning he was found murdered at his residence. He was in bed when he was shot three times in the head. He was DRT (dead right there). With the exception of the body not being posed – Pat I've got some questions for you about that in a moment – and three shell casings being found, it looks like the same perpetrator who killed Lanton. Arrested was Randy Waton, age eight-teen. He was the last known victim of Redcliff and he's a special needs child with Down syndrome. There is strong evidence that he was in the house and that he smashed a window to get out – not in."

I asked, "So how did he get in and why did he go out through a window and not back out the way he came?"

Mom answered saying, "No one knows right now but his lawyer is willing to have him talk to the police; however, she wants it to be a onetime deal to keep from further traumatizing him. That's going to happen Monday late afternoon. Tex, I want you and Ren down there for it. Afterward I want ya'll to head up to Huntsville."

Rick said, "Rachel, I heard on the news that Redcliff had been killed. I also heard that his lawyer had been shot. Is that true?"

Mom replied, "Yes, Rick, it is. That's why Tex and Ren are gonna hit Huntsville too. He's expected to recover and has been, up until today, in a medically induced coma. His body was posed like Lanton. Pat, this brings us to you. What do you think of the posing of the victims?

Looking at the crime scene photo's, Pat answered, "The school book answer would be that the perpetrator is very narcissistic and this is an in-your-face taunt. Nothing more. However, I would disagree. Look at the way the legs overlap only at the ankles and feet. The legs are slightly up and bent toward the left, the arms are out forming a 'T', both hands are open with palms up, the head is slightly chin down to the left. The eyes are open as is the mouth but only just. This indicates a lot of attention to detail like he has studied a painting of the crucifixion of Jesus and tried to imitate it. Don't be surprised when the autopsy comes back if the victim has a post mortem stab wound on one side or the other. Along with the wounds in the hands and lower legs - a wound on the side would complete the symbolic crucifixion."

Pat stopped and slowly pushed the pictures from her. Taking a deep breath she continued, "Your perpetrator is punishing his victims because of a perceived belief that these people have sinned specifically against his religion. That's why he kills them in the first place. After he kills them, he then poses the victim in a symbolic crucifixion because he views the crucifixion as a horrible means of death. A death that is so horrific that his victims' wrong doings are cleansed and forgiven. Why he recovers his shell casings I don't know. Maybe he's keeping souvenirs or trophies."

I said, "Pat, we've got Lanton and the attorney down in Huntsville with bodies posed and no casings. But we also have teletypes from all over the world with virtually the same MO except for the posing and the casings. Is he just getting sicker, more bold or what?"

Shaking her head Pat said, "No, Ren – none of that. If it is the same person, and I am highly skeptical, those victims he poses meet some type of criteria. Maybe, and this is a guess, he believes their sins can be forgiven so he takes time and effort to pose them; whereas the non-posed victims are beyond redemption and not worth his effort. That's a guess, Ren. What I truly believe is the person that killed Lanton and shot the lawyer are the same. The person that killed Redcliff and is also mentioned in those teletypes is a different person entirely. In other words you are dealing with two separate killers."

Later That Same Night
The Arena - Fort Worth Convention Center.

Reverend Alexander Joshua was wrapping up his sermon to a sellout crowd of over 13,000 people. Looking around at his dedicated followers, in a fabricated, hoarse voice he said "Let us pray, my children. Oh Lord, forgive us of our sins. We all fall short of your magnificent glory. Especially me Lord your humble and battered servant." Crying now, "And Lord you know how much good this ministry does, not just in America but all over the world. We feed the hungry in dozens of countries and we've housed the poor all across this land. And, and our doctors, Lord, have treated and healed the sick in your name." Yelling and crying, "But Lord you know I, I am a sinner with no true talent and I just can't keep it all going without the blessings and financial support of those here. Please Lord, give this poor ministry a financial blessing so that we can continue your work. Lay a horrible burden down upon those that won't open their hearts and wallets to support your will. Amen!"

It was the shortest prayer of the night Joshua thought. But what the hell, they had passed the plate at least three other times during this sermon alone. Listening to the choir drone on and on with the closing hymns, Joshua slowly moved back to the podium. Ten minutes later, a small computer screen built into the wood stand beeped and the final tithe numbers began to appear. They had collected close to fifty grand during this show. Counting admission of twenty-five dollars a person it looked like they would make roughly $375 thousand dollars. Cheap SOB's, that's less than average for this area, Joshua thought heatedly. Calming himself, he mumbled, "Oh well, add that to the other eight shows in the last two weeks and those numbers look a damn sight better." But it was still not what he had expected out of the last show.

To everyone except his devout followers, Joshua was a sham artist. His real name was Alex Jones and he was a former Vegas hustler who had failed at everything he ever tried. His one true talent was that of a master con-artist. He had found religion (but not Jesus) at a tent revival one late night after some whoring and a three day drunk. As he stood on the makeshift stage, he began confessing his laundry list of failings and sins. As he did so, he noticed how the people in the crowd were shouting at him to preach-on and the more graphic he got the more they yelled and carried on. It was in this moment of illumination that Alex Jones found his niche in life and a way to make money... lots of wonderful money! Within a few short years Jones was a multimillionaire several times over. With the exception of his overhead (that included a mansion, several cars, prostitutes, drugs, occasional bribes, lawyer fees and hush money), he kept the money he made during his shows. There were no charities, medical doctors, schools, or homeless missions that ever saw a dime from him.

Walking off stage as the crowd applauded, Joshua decided that there would be no encore tonight. "Let those tight-wad low-rent thieves rot in hell," he said to no one in particular. Looking at his ten thousand dollar Rolex he saw that it was already close to nine o'clock. He seriously wanted a back rub from one of the little doxies that hung out in the bar of his five-star hotel. If he waited much longer they would all be gone or he would end up with a real skank like last night. Exiting the back stage elevator into the parking garage, the first thing that Joshua noticed was that there were no security guards keeping tabs on the parking garage like there usually were. That was odd but not completely unexpected. Must be out checking another area, he thought. Then he saw his limo parked and running some distance away and forgot about the missing security guards.

"Dumb shit knows I'm coming down and doesn't bother to move the car closer – that's what I get for hiring my white-trash brother." As he approached the car he could see that the driver door was open and that his brother was lying on the ground next to it.

"Johnny, Jesus H. Christ, if you're stoned again……" Hearing a voice behind him Joshua turned around thinking that the missing security guards had finally shown up.

Ten minutes later.

Bending over the body of Alexander Joshua, Father Karl Kothner reached down and checked for a pulse. Since Grayson Riggs had survived being shot it was worth checking; even if it was obvious that both men were dead. Riggs was a mistake that would not happen again, Kothner was sure of it. Being very cautious not to disturb the carefully posed bodies of Joshua and his brother, Kothner surveyed the area looking for any signs of evidence of that he had been here. Then stepping away from the bodies he began to recite a prayer for the dead. As he finished the prayer, he noticed the damp cold of the night and slipped his hands into the deep pockets of his black overcoat. As he did so, his fingers gently touched the automatic handgun he carried.

2:30 AM. Sunday Morning, 10 February.

I was dreaming that Uma Thurman – or maybe it was Rachel, was about to finally kiss me when in the deep recesses of my mind I heard the phone ringing. As I reluctantly – *and I mean reluctantly*! – came awake, I reached for the phone thinking that Uma or Rachel had been saved by the bell. Damn it I couldn't even score in my dreams!

"Yeah, what is it?" I didn't say it harshly; but I was really foggy and miffed at having my sleep interrupted.

"Ren, it's Lieutenant Saxen. Ah, it's Rachel."

Before I could control my mouth I said, "Yes Ma'am, I'm well aware of your first name. What's up?" Great! Way to go Ren. If she wasn't pissed off before, she will be now.

"Ren, *sorry for waking you,* but I just got a call from Chief Wong. There's been a double homicide at the Fort Worth Convention Center. That television evangelist Alexander Joshua and his brother both got popped, three to the head. Also, both bodies were posed."

Mom seemed very uncomfortable talking to me and I wasn't sure why.

As I sat up and tried to clear my head I asked, "Ah, Lieutenant, what would you like Tex and I to do? By the time we got over there the crime scene would be shut down and the detectives don't need us bothering them while they do their initial paperwork."

She replied, "No. There's no need for ya'll to go out there. Actually I didn't want you to be surprised when you saw it in the morning paper – if it's in the paper. Or on the news! I mean if it makes the news. I mean when it makes the news. Anyway, Chief Wong has scheduled a meeting at 8:30 Monday morning with the Fort Worth detectives and us. I just wanted to give you a heads up." Mom paused for a moment and then said, "Listen Ren about dinner last night, I… Never mind, I've got to go, bye."

Before I could finish saying, "Thanks for the heads up" she was already gone.

Rubbing my hand over my face I looked at the ceiling and tried figure out what had just happened. It was very uncharacteristic for Mom to act so unfocused. It was also uncharacteristic for her to treat me like crap. During dinner last night she had laughed and talked to everyone else; but other than to answer my questions about the case, Mom had blatantly ignored me. The few times she did say something to me it was in the form of a slam, jokingly, yet a slam nevertheless. Rachel is one of my most favorite people and to have been treated like dog meat by her really confused me.

Rolling over I tried to go back to sleep. About ten minutes later I heard Rick pull into the drive-way. As I drifted off to sleep I was thinking that Rick must have gone for one of his midnight marathon drives. Even a dedicated man of God can suffer from the long term effects of combat.

CHAPTER 9

5:00 AM Monday, 11 February

I got out of bed at four forty-five and found Rick waiting to join me for a fast three mile run with Danner. We quickly stretched and headed toward the back gate of my property. Once through the gate we ran down an old game trail, crossed over a fallen barbwire fence and entered the property of Mt. Lebanon Baptist Encampment. The encampment has over 600 acres of land much of which is heavily wooded with old dirt roads and tons of trails. It's the cross country runner's dream. The old Dallas nature center was great for some variation in my training, but Danner and I loved the encampment.

Rick let me set the pace and after about a half mile he asked, "Mind if I attend the meeting this morning? I have to hook up with Leopole and Kothner later today, so there's no way I can head down to Houston with you."

Drawing a quick breath, I said, "No worries – Mom may be ticked at me but she still loves you. Wong has already opened the door for you, so I think it's rather expected that you'll be there. Rick, what do you think is going on with these murders and the attempted murder in Huntsville?"

'Ren, I'll answer your question about the case in a moment. What I want to know is why Mom... Rachel, is on your ass? Last night I thought she was going to claw your eyes out. You two have been if not good friends, then certainly professional ones since you first met. So what gives?"

We ran on another few minutes, before I answered, "Rick, I seriously don't know. We were fine the other night at the Lanton crime scene. Last night at dinner was something new. She called me around two this morning to tell me about a double homicide over in Fort Worth. She started to say something about dinner, but hung up suddenly rather than finish her thought."

"All right, Ren, I'll let it go for now. Anyway, I went for a drive last night and heard about the murders in Fort Worth on the radio. The victim was that sham evangelist Alexander Joshua. His brother was the other victim. Think they're connected with our cases? "

Glancing back over my shoulder, I said, "Yeah, by all appearances they are. And I'm sorry, Rick. I meant to mention this new development to you. I forgot about it until we starting talking about Rachel. Okay, since we are back on the case, what's your opinion?"

Forming his thoughts, Rick didn't answer right away. "I think Pat's right, you're dealing two separate killers. Redcliff and the killings being investigated by Interpol is one killer. The second killer is the one who did the attorney, Lanton and Joshua and his brother." Rick stopped talking as we hit a series of small but harshly inclined hills. After we crested the last hill, he continued saying, "The first group are, as near we can tell because Interpol isn't cooperating, pedophiles that have beaten the wrap or have never been prosecuted. The second group is religious people or people connected to the religious community such as the attorney or Joshua's brother, that the killer believes have done something wrong."

Thinking about this for a while I said, "Ok, if all this is true, then why is the MO so close on each shooting? Is it possible that we're dealing with a single psychotic shooter with what he or she views as two separate missions? Kill the religious-based pedophile and kill anyone that has brought shame to the Christian community like Joshua? That would explain the relative uniqueness of the MO with slight twist for the non-pedophile victims."

Rick replied, "That's one theory, Ren, and I don't think we should discounted it. But then why Lanton, the attorney and Joshua's brother? It can't be the wrong place at the wrong time; because to kill Father Lanton and attempt to murder the attorney, the shooter would've had to actively hunt them down. Also, how many of these serial killers can travel internationally?"

After taking a deep breath I said, "Rick I agree – two separate shooters like Pat said; but, we can't discard the possibility of a single shooter. And while I've said the MO's are very close in appearances, there are some startling differences. No, it's two shooters."

Without saying another word we continued running until we completed the three mile loop – not in record time but certainly faster than normal. Just like always, Rick and I had pushed each other to reach a higher level of fitness. Gasping for air as we came back through the gate we sprinted the last hundred yards and then went into a slow jog and finally a walk. Looking at Rick I said, "Good run. Are you going to ride with Tex and I or follow later?"

Rick answered, "I'll have to take my own car. I'm meeting Leopole and Kothner after you head out for Houston."

Thinking about what Rick and I had talked about during the run, I went in the house to feed Danner, shower and change for work. Rick stayed outside and started his lengthy Navy SEAL calisthenics routine. After several hundred push-ups, sit-ups, pull-ups, flutter kicks, and a few runs through our home made obstacle course, Rick finally came in for a cup coffee and to shower up.

At 7AM sharp Tex was pulling into the drive way to pick me up.

7:45 AM Monday, 11 February.
Police Headquarters / CAPERS

Tex and I were seated and ready for the big meeting roughly forty-five minutes early. Like me, Tex is always terminally early. I think it's the Marine in us. Being early comes in handy because it usually means we get the best seats. Of course it can also produce problems like at funerals when they haven't even brought the casket in yet. Last time that happened, Tex and I were at his great Aunt Martha's funeral and of course we were seated over an hour before the service was to begin. We had great seats and everything was just fine until they wheeled the casket in, opened the lid and started arranging Aunt Martha's body. Suddenly all I could think about was Jonathan Maberry's books Zombie CSU and Patient Zero (great books if you are into Zombies – like me) and I started to snicker. I leaned over and made the mistake of telling Tex, who busted out laughing – we were both thinking about old Aunt Martha coming back to life and grabbing one of the morticians for dinner! Tex was heir to Martha's rather large estate; but it didn't matter. We were asked to leave and not come back. Talk about awkward.

I started to lean over and remind Tex about Aunt Martha and how hurt I thought she would have been to know that her beloved nephew had missed her funeral. Suddenly Rachel and Chief Wong walked into the briefing room and I decided not to make Tex laugh – that would have been poor form – this being a homicide investigation and all.

Rick came in a moment later followed by the other two members of our section, Detectives Miller and Hill. Todd Miller is tall, olive skilled, chunky and looks a lot like TV's Captain Kangaroo; but with a military haircut and much younger. Todd is very shy, talks slow and comes across like an uneducated good-old-boy. Just the opposite is true; however, it's a persona he has mastered and more than one criminal has fallen for it.

In contrast Jon Hill is smallish. He's unassuming, maybe 5'6, has a slight build, is laid back and is very hard to anger. Unlike many of his peers (me included) Jon is highly educated (two Master Degrees and a PhD. – why is he a cop? Who cares, I'm just glad he is). Best of all, like most cops, Jon has a wonderful sense of humor about the job. Both men are great to work with; however, of the two, I liked Jon the best. We had worked together a few times during our patrol days in South Dallas and we had really gotten into some shit. I always knew that no matter what happened - Jon had my back. The biggest mistake criminals make about Jon? He may be small and unassuming like a mouse, but let me tell you, that mouse has sharp teeth!

A few minutes later, Detectives J.T Harrison and Rosa Hudson from Fort Worth walked in looking unhappy. I didn't have time to speculate on this because right behind them were two men and a woman that I had never met before, but based on their demeanor I knew that they were Special Agents of the FBI. I heard Tex mumble, "Great, who invited the vampires?"

Looking over at Chief Wong and Lieutenant Saxen it was easy to tell that they were as equally displeased to see the Feds as everyone else. Last to arrive were two officers from CSR and the representative from the Dallas County Medical Examiner, Dr. Carmen – yes *that* Carmen – Hansen.

After everybody had taken seats, Chief Wong stood up and began introductions. Once that was completed Tex (as lead investigator for the case) was called to the podium. Using a power point presentation, Tex led us through a thorough briefing of our current findings. As he concluded his presentation, he said, "We believe that the murderer of Father Robert Lanton, Rev. Alexander Joshua and his brother, Johnny Jones to be the same person. At this time, we are unsure if there is a connection to the shootings down in Huntsville and Houston; however, based on what we're hearing, which is by no means conclusive, there is a very strong possibility that they're connected."

The lead detective for Fort Worth, Rosa Hudson, followed Tex with an equally in depth briefing. The problem was, neither agency had crap. There were two things that Hudson did say that really caught our attention. The first was that just before the murders were committed an entry/door alarm had been set off in a secured part of the convention center. This drew the security guards away from the parking garage for almost thirty minutes. The second was that the cameras in the parking garage had been disabled approximately five minutes after the alarm was set off. Nothing elaborate – they were just smashed. One of these things happening could be chalked up to a coincidence; but certainly not both. To a homicide detective, it shows a great deal of planning, knowledge of the location (of when and where to strike), an understanding of the victim's life style, habits and activities, and that the murderer was not working alone. In short, it was a well planned execution with military perfection. Thinking about Father Lanton, if the suspects had studied him with same such dedication, the poor, innocent bastard never stood a chance.

Next to speak was my ex-girlfriend, Carmen. "Good morning. Because of the similarities in these cases, this briefing will also contain information provided to me by Dr. Willis Booth at the Tarrant County /Fort Worth ME's office. This report will also contain the forensic information provided by CSR. All right, all three of our victims were killed with a small caliber handgun. CSR has confirmed that even though the bullets are pretty flattened out they are intact. This indicates hollow-point ammunition was used rather than ball. Based on weight and size, it's fairly safe to say that the weapon is a .22 caliber. In all three murders the bullets have given us very little forensics – again because the bullets were so flattened out. Victim number one, Father Lanton..."

And on she went for another forty-five minutes detailing the findings of the autopsies, CSR's findings and her own personal conclusions. "I intentionally saved this for last, ladies and gentlemen, because I believe it ties some of these cases together. During the autopsies we found a post mortem knife wound."

As the pictures of the wounds flashed up on the screen, I leaned over to Tex and whispered, "Pat was right."

Staring at the screen, Tex nodded his head slowly and said, "I'm sure she'll be thrilled. Wonder what else she pegged?"

Carmen continued saying, "Each wound is approximately 5.08 centimeters long and .508 centimeters wide – that's about 2 inches by .3 inches. The depth of the wound in each case is roughly 20.32 centimeters or about eight inches deep. Based on the jagged edges at the top of the wound, I would say that this was a combat fighting knife. As you can see the knife entered just below the rib cage near the sternum on the right side and was driven up at an angle into the heart. The location and angle of the wound may indicate that the perpetrator is left handed or ambidextrous."

The screen went blank and Carmen stated, "That's all I have for now, folks. As more information comes in, I'll let you know. Are there any questions?" Quickly scanning the crowd and not seeing any hands raised, Carmen nodded to Chief Wong and then sat down.

Chief Wong stood up to introduce the last speaker. "The Chief of Police has asked the FBI to review our cases. To that end, as ya'll know, the FBI has developed profiles on serial killers. These profiles have been very helpful in the apprehension of more than one active and non-active serial murderer. Chief William Smyth has requested that the FBI put together a profile on this killer. Even though there is some doubt as to whether or not these cases meet the 'serial killer standards' set forth by the FBI, Dr. Hershel Gaspar on loan from the Behavioral Science division at Quantico, has consented to assist us. Doc, you have the floor."

If I could stereo-type what a person from the much applauded FBI Behavioral Science division looks like, it would be Dr. Gaspar. He's handsome to the point of being delicate and feminine, well dressed, fairly tall, thin but not skinny, dark hair graying at the temples, wore glasses and acted holier-than-thou. At his first words, every cop in the room got pissed off – including the two *real* Special Agents that had escorted this pencil-necked geek to our offices.

"Yes, well, that's Doctor, not Doc, not Sir or Mister – it's Doctor. One deserves the title after one spends so much time earning it, don't you all agree?" Exhaling audibly and rather theatrically, he said, "Wong is correct. There is doubt if this meets our standards; however, *I* believe that this situation is a single serial murderer; not two murderers, as one less astute might think. We have multiple murders, including international murders, that all fit into strongly related patterns. I'll not overwhelm you with the clinical terminology – which would be lost on you anyway – but please keep in mind that patterns are what profiles are based on, and the FBI has studied thousands of cases to formulate our profiles."

I yawned and quietly wished I could block out Doctor Gaspar's voice. We had heard this drivel before and it never helps. Why? Here's the deal with these goofy serial killer 'profiles' everyone *outside* of law enforcement is so hyped about. Criminal profiles are supposed to give the investigator a *tool to use* to catch the killer. It is just another tool – profiles are not a cure all! The profile focuses on what significant traits and similarities there are between different killers and the killer being investigated. Trouble is, most profiles are like horoscopes; they are too general and can be applied or dismissed in any given situation. Worse, the profiles are often wrong. For example, most serial killers are profiled as having been sexually abused as children. However, one of our most notorious killers, Jeffrey Dahmer, had a very normal up-bringing with a loving family. Also, if profiles are so useful, then why can't they be used to catch serial rapists, serial burglars, serial robbers or the everyday common murderer?

Gaspar was saying, "For instance, the type of victim, location of the crime or an abduction, injuries to the victim (anti, pari and post mortem), tools and weapons of the crime and how the body is disposed of – all play into the profile of the suspect. We at the FBI…"

Leaning over next to Tex, I whispered, "Some religion is missing their messiah."

Tex smiled and whispered back, "How can he be the messiah when Wong is? This guy is such a condescending ass-bite."

We both turned our attention back to good old *Doc* Gaspar who was saying, "So, based on all the information provided to the FBI here is the profile that I believe will, if you *pay attention* and use it as you should, help you locals (*said like he had a mouth full of shit*) to arrest this murderer."

Jon mumbled, "Here we go, sports fans" just loud enough for the detectives to hear. I looked over at the Special Agents who both had their heads in their hands. Either they were asleep or they don't buy this bullshit either.

"Your killer is a single, dark or tan skinned male with no outstanding features. He has no job; but he does have a degree of inherited wealth. His non-distinguishing looks allow him to travel unnoticed. He was sexually abused (*told ya!*) multiple times by a priest or clergymen as a young man. Abused, of course, is a relative term because the sex, in this case, was consensual; however, he is not a homosexual (*Really? So, how many times can a man have consensual sex with another man and still not be gay?*). He is now 18 to 36 years of age, still wets his bed, he is poorly educated; though not from a lack of opportunity. He has no significant achievements in his life to speak of. He is socially inept. He has been shunned by females because of his looks and he no doubt suffers from a Micropenis condition. Therefore, the crimes he commits are done for sexual gratification. As with most serial killers, masturbation was his original means of release (at least five times a day); but somehow, probably by torturing small animals, he discovered a means of achieving a more satisfying orgasm – physically and psychologically – and that is of course murder. The victims are complete strangers to him. He picks them because they resemble the person or persons he has had sex with and he is trying to relive those moments. He will not have a history of reported mental illness. There is no, and I must emphasize this, *No* religious reasoning associated with or assigned to these murders. He attends church, revivals and even prayer meetings; but he is more than likely an atheist. The posing of our victims is a taunt. That's all I have. Thank you."

Herr Dock-tor didn't take questions as he headed out the door with Carmen hot on his heals with an adoring look on her face (*Huh?*). Looking frustrated and embarrassed, the other two Special Agents quickly grabbed their coats and prepared to take off after him. Before they left, one stopped at the door and said, "Sorry. I wish I could say that he is not always like this, but I would be lying to you. We're looking at the Interpol stuff, I'll be in touch."

We all just sat there for a few seconds in idle speculation trying to make sense of what we had just been told. Finally Jon broke the ice saying, "So let me make sure I understand this. What we are looking for is a wealthy, single, ugly male, age 18 to 36, wets his bed, sociably inept, tortures small animals, has had homosexual experiences but is not a homosexual, is rejected by women, has a very small penis and whacks-off five times a day. Well, these crimes are solved. Ren, are you going to come peacefully or do we need to call the SWAT team out here?"

As expected, everyone – including me – busted out laughing. Leave it to Jon to knock one out of the ballpark! Even though it was at my expense, I really enjoyed watching Mom laugh too. Jesus, when that gal smiles, the entire world lights up.

Still chuckling, Chief Wong adjourned the meeting with promises of cooperation and communications, should any of us come up with anything new.

CHAPTER 10

District Attorney's Office
Harris County, Houston Texas.

As soon as the meeting had ended, Tex and I headed down to Houston. No matter how you cut it, it was at least a three to four hour drive. By mutual agreement, we gave talking about the case a rest. That's a major problem with homicide detectives – actually any cop worth his badge – we get so involved that we fixate on the job. When that happens the case becomes all consuming and we tend to ignore our friends and family (the really important stuff). The divorce rate in law enforcement is very bad. In your investigative units it is absolutely horrendous.

I've known more than one talented detective to leave CAPERS in an effort to save his marriage. Unfortunately, even leaving law enforcement altogether rarely saves the marriage. Why? Because as I've told you, at some point in our careers we become damaged goods! Here's the scoop: We very rarely get to deal with decent people. When we do, they have usually been the victims of a crime and quite often take it out on us. I've had victims scream at me, spit in my face and then cry in my arms as we've stood over the body of their dead child. We understand. But after years of this psychological abuse, the chinks in our armor start to show. Couple this with all that we see from *criminals* – the hatred and anger, the lying, the total disregard for human life – and after a while we lose the one thing that is most important to us; our belief that what we are doing counts for something.

As we got closer to Houston, our conversation began to focus on not just our case, but also on the Fort Worth shootings, Riggs and Redcliff. We had already dismissed the profile material supplied by the FBI as not being applicable. Pat's profile of our suspect (suspects?) was in my opinion more likely to prove beneficial. I think a clinical psychologist that worked for a county of close to three million people for over twenty-five years has pretty much seen it all. Whereas these FBI PhD. 'Profilers' have studied serial killers form the safety of their desk by piggybacking off the research of people like Pat.

"Tex, I think we both know that the Waton kid is not our shooter. But I really want to hear from him what he found in that house."

Tex replied, "Yeah, me too. I wonder if the boy saw something that might help us. Maybe Riggs did too."

Thirty minutes later Tex and I were seated in the Harris County District Attorney's office cooling our heels waiting for Randy Waton and his attorney. The District Attorney, Sam Wertz, and one of his prosecutors, Tom Ruddy, were waiting with us, but other than exchanging names and pleasantries, none of us were doing much talking yet. After several minutes of strained silence, Wertz said, "Gentlemen, I apologize for our not be more friendly. I assure you that it's not personal. I think what we, Tom and I, as well as others that have worked on this case are in fear that there is indeed a serial killer active in Texas. You know the way the media will play this thing up and the panic and distractions they will cause, like they did with the Beltway Sniper attacks in Washington D.C."

In October of 2002 two black males, John Allen Muhammad and Lee Boyd Malvo killed 10 people and seriously wounded 3 more in random sniper attacks. These attacks were designed to throw-off the police. Muhammad's final target was to kill his ex-wife. The televised news media as well as the newspapers published misinformation provided by FBI profilers about the attackers. Reporters kept insisting – actually force feeding the public – that the shootings were an act of domestic terrorism committed by a single, angry, white male. Leads supplied by the public to law enforcement reflected what the media had put out, which served to distract law enforcement efforts. Remember, every lead, factual or not, must be followed to a logical conclusion.

Nodding my head yes, I said, "We understand, sir. And we're afraid that you might be right. Though three of our shootings up north look like the Riggs shooting, the Redcliff shooting stands alone here in the US; but matches at least one of the Interpol shootings in Argentina."

Tex said, "Based on the FBI profile there is only one shooter. We have another profile that makes it two shooters. The second profile seems more likely to us."

With a sick look on his face, Wertz knew he had to ask, "Is it possible that we have two shooters working together? The reason I say this is when this meeting was arranged, I talked to Chief Wong and then pulled up the Interpol reports. I contacted Interpol and because of my status as a DA, I was able to get *some* information that regular law enforcement could not." Pausing for a moment to consider his next words, Wertz went on, "In the international cases, spanning the last 10 years, all of the victims in the reports had prior histories of serious sexual offenses such as pedophilia and aggravated sexual assault. All of the offenders were priests, nuns or lay ministers of the Catholic Church. All had the same MO's that match Redcliff's."

Tex and I hadn't had the chance to review the Interpol material. In all honesty, we had thought that maybe a few of the cases like the one in Argentina *might* look the same; but certainly not all. Shit! Looking rather chagrined, Tex confessed as much.

However Wertz wasn't done. "There's something else you two need to know that might have bearing on your cases. Six years ago we had two ministers – both men beaten to death. Then five years ago we had a female minister beaten to death. All three had had accusations of religious impropriety cast against them within their faiths, Baptist, Lutheran and Episcopalian. Things like supporting homosexual clergy, gay marriages, abortion and divorce. The stories made the newspapers but not for long.

None of these people had any criminal dealings with law enforcement. For the most part they were pillars of the community. The autopsy report for each one was about the same: Massive internal injuries and dozens of broken bones throughout the entire body. All three were killed at night between the hours of ten and three in the morning. Also the bodies were posed like the victims in your cases and they all had post mortem knife wounds in their sides. The posing and the wounds is what triggered our memories. If you look at the photo of the first victim the posing is very obscure and not very sensational, the second victim the posing is more refined but we still didn't think much of it because people can fall that way; however, by the third victim, the positioning of the body in a crucifixion pose is very obvious – which made us go back and look at the other two. Of course the biggest clue was that they were all Christian ministers and had controversial beliefs."

As Wertz was talking he handed me the crime scene photos and autopsy reports. The third victim, Lutheran Pastor Karyn Avery, was beaten beyond recognition. Looking at a family photo taken six months before the murder, I saw a strikingly beautiful woman surrounded by her equally beautiful children. The comparison almost sickened me.

Tex asked, "What were they beaten with?"

Wertz replied, "Bruise impressions, bone fractures and break patterns indicate that the victims were beaten with some type of thin wood or steel rod. Some of the injuries indicate a closed fist."

As we continued to study the pictures, Tex asked me, "I've seen a shit load of people beaten to death – but this looks different. Almost surgical. Ren, you're big into the martial arts, what are we looking at here?"

I said, "Tex, let me ask Mr. Wertz this question first. Sir, I seem to recall reading in the paper that Pastor Avery's husband had been charged with the murder; but it never went to trial. I mean no disrespect, but the fact that you're showing us these pictures tells me that you have some doubt as to this man's guilt. Is he a martial artist or does he have military combat training?"

Tom Ruddy, who up until this moment had not spoken, replied in a confrontational tone. "No military or martial arts training. But what makes you think he *isn't* guilty? How dare you two come in here and question our ability to do our jobs... Who in hell do you think you are?"

Rather than get into a heated exchange and say or do something I might regret later (like punch this idiot in the nose), I stared at Ruddy with as much intensity as I could generate. I started to reply when Wertz intervened saying, "Tom knock-it-off! Nothing the detective said was inappropriate. Detectives, I keep finding myself apologizing. Tensions are running very high right now. We've had numerous scandals come out of the police forensics lab – meaning that hundreds of cases will have to go to retrial or be dumped. We lost the Redcliff case and then he was murdered. The defending attorney, Grayson Riggs was almost murdered. Now these and the Interpol cases seem to be related. It just goes on and on. So please, let's all calm down. Tom, you owe these gentlemen an apology."

Still looking angry, Ruddy said, "My outburst was uncalled for. I apologize."

Yeah sure... Whatever you say asshole!

Addressing Tex, I said, "To answer your question, this reeks of a very well trained martial artist or a guy that has some advanced military hand to hand combat training." Looking directly at Ruddy, I asked, "Is Mr. Avery right or left handed?"

Pausing to think, he said "He's right handed – why is that important?"

Handing him the pictures of the victims, I said, "Look at the severe bruising on the right side of each of the victim's necks. See how the bruise is most brilliant on the lower mastoid muscle of the neck at the trapezius junction?"

Ruddy and Wertz began intensely studying the pictures. After a few minutes, Wertz looked up and said, "Ok. I see what you are talking about. What of it?"

"I'm no forensic pathologist," I continued, "but I don't believe a rod did this. That blow is called a *shutō-uchi* or a knife hand strike, better known to laymen as a karate chop. A strike to the neck in that region stuns a person for several seconds or more. If delivered with enough expertise, power and focus the clavicle can be smashed rendering the arm on that side useless. Change the angle of the strike just slightly or attack from the rear, and the neck can be broken. If this had been a rod, then the bruise would have been equally represented; however in this case the bruise tapers off. And you're right, Tex. The shuō -uchi is a *very surgical or precise* hit. Any martial arts beginner can use it, but to use it this effectively shows a great deal of mastery. If Avery is right handed, the bruise should be on the left side of the victim's neck, not on the right side. This might mean that the murderer is either left handed or ambidextrous."

Ruddy interrupted me saying, "What if the assailant did attack from behind? That would put the bruise on the left side."

I answered, "That's a good question; however you still have the bruising tapering off in the wrong direction. I didn't read the autopsy report, but I bet each victim's clavicles are busted clean through, aren't they?"

Ruddy looked pale and nodded his head.

Looking at Wertz, I said, "Had the suspect attacked from behind, the scapula would have been fractured or crushed. I don't know who your suspect is, but I would hate to meet the son of a bitch in a dark alley."

Before Ruddy and Wertz could say anything, Randy Waton and his attorney Jessie Hardin showed up.

Randy Waton

After making introductions we all took seats with the exception Randy who politely but firmly declined. As with many Down syndrome people, Randy was mentally retarded. Albeit, in his case, mildly so. This made him a little nervous around strange environments and people he didn't know. The fact that he was here spoke volumes about his courage.

Randy was short, stocky and had soft, almost loving brown eyes. But based on his clenching and unclenching of his hands, his breathing and his body posture – I'd say Randy Waton was about to give Wertz and Ruddy a piece of his mind. We didn't have long to wait because as soon as we were seated the lad began tearing them apart by saying, "You promised me! You said he would go to jail and you broke your promise. He hurt people, he hurt everybody and you let-him-go. He hurt my friends!"

Randy's voice was loud, measured and matter of fact, but he wasn't yelling. "Why did you let him go home? He made my Mom and Dad cry!" Ruddy, whose face was now crimson tried to say something but Randy shut him down. "I'm talking now! You talked before. You let a bad man hurt *my family.*"

Wertz looked as if he was about to cry and Ruddy had his head in his hands. And then Randy ran out of steam, or maybe it was anger he ran out of because as quickly as the rebuke had started, it was over. Randy sat down and I noticed something I shall never forget. In Randy Waton's eyes, I no longer saw anger. What I did see was absolute compassion for those two men. With tears running down his face, Randy said, "I'm sorry I was mean to you. Don't be sad."

Jessie Hardin reached out and took Randy's hand and asked, "Randy are you all right, now? Randy took several deep breaths and said yes. Jessie continued saying, "These two detectives are from Dallas and they would like to talk to you about what you saw the other night. Will that be all right?"

Randy looked at Tex and I and smiled saying, "Yeah, that would be okay."

I introduced myself again and said, "Randy, we know that Redcliff is dead and that you didn't hurt him. But we were wondering how you got into his house?"

Randy looked nervously at Jessie, who smiled and said, "Go ahead Randy – you're not in any trouble."

Randy said, "I walked from my house and hid in the bushes across the street from *his* house. I fell asleep waiting. It must have been a long time cause my clothes were wet and I was cold. It was real dark, too. I started to leave and I saw a man walk up to the front door. He unlocked the door and went in. The police car sitting outside in the street was facing the other way and didn't see the man. After a few minutes, the man left. I watched how he walked up to the house and did it the same way. The policemen never saw me. I went inside and snuck into *his* room. I was gonna make him say he was sorry. But there was blood all over the bed and wall and I got scared and ran to the window and fell out of it. I ran and ran and then I hid in some bushes. I was really scared and I hurt my arms when I fell through the window. I fell asleep again. And a policeman woke me up and took me to the doctor."

Tex said, "Randy, that's really a rough night. I know it was dark, but can you tell us what the man who went in the house looked like?"

Randy answered, saying, "Not his face cause he wasn't looking at me. But there's a street light and when he left I saw his clothes. He looked like *him* at church."

At first none of us understood what Randy meant. Suddenly Tex sat up and asked, "Randy, do you mean that he was dressed like a priest, like Redcliff at church on Sunday?"

Randy shrugged, smiled and said, "Duh, yeah that's what I said."

After another thirty minutes of talking, we got ready to leave. Jessie told us that her father, Grayson Riggs, was resting comfortably and could take visitors, but only for short periods of time. We thanked everyone and as we prepared to leave, Randy hugged us both good-bye. There was something else that I should point out about Randy's reprimand of Wertz and Ruddy and that's this: Not once did he mention the hurt and pain that Redcliff had caused him. His anger was over the hurt of others – his family and friends. As Tex and I drove off, I contemplated this fact and came to the conclusion that Randy Waton was the bravest person I'll ever know.

1200 Block Swiss Ave. Dallas Texas

As soon as the meeting had adjourned, detectives Hill and Miller headed over to Father Robert Lanton's house on Swiss Avenue. As they approached Lanton's house, they saw a car parked on the street sitting in front of the residence. Hill's patrol instincts kicked in and he pulled over about a hundred feet from the other car. "Shit! That can't be Lanton's next of kin. They live out of state and won't be here until tomorrow. Todd, I've got some binoculars in my bag behind you. Can you get the license plate off that car? I'll call it in."

Reaching for the binoculars, Miller said, "Maybe estate robbers? That happens a lot these days." Estate robbers added insult to the loss of a friend or loved one. Criminals read the obituaries in the newspaper and on the day of the funeral – when no one is around – burglarize the home of the deceased, stealing anything of value.

Putting the binoculars to his eyes, Miller took a moment to focus the lenses. Looking at the plate he said, "Jon we have a problem. That's a city vehicle. Call Wong and tell him what we have and ask for a team from the Public Integrity Unit to get out here ASAP. Also tell him we'll stay off the radio in case we are being monitored."

Less than a half hour later, a car pulled up next to Hill and Miller, rolled down the window and handed them a cell phone, then drove off. Less than ten seconds later, the phone rang. Answering it, Hill said, "Hello, this is Detective Jon Hill, CAPERS."

The voice on the other end said, "Jon, it's Steve Burt, PIU. Wong has already explained what is going on. We'll set up on this and follow them when they leave. I'll call you…"

Jon interrupted saying, "Steve looks like they're coming out now. Those are the two 'Special Investigators' from Chief Smyth's office. Can't tell what they have but they're carrying something – maybe a computer and a box."

Burt said, "Special Investigators – what the hell is that and what division are they assigned to? Never mind that for now, we're in position to cold trail them. After they pull off, wait five minutes then you can go ahead and search the house. Stay safe old buddy!" Burt hung up.

Hill and Miller watched impotently as the two special investigators loaded their car and left. After waiting the requested five minutes, they walked into Lanton's house. The place had been ransacked. The furniture was flipped, cushions were sliced open, drawers were emptied with the contents scattered on the floor and clothing was strung everywhere.

Miller said, "Jesus, what a mess. Looks like the sphincter twins had a good time in here. Think there is anything left for us to find?"

Smiling, Hill said, "Yep. The fact that they tore this place apart and carried out a box and a computer tells me that they didn't find everything they were looking for – whatever that might be."

Miller looked around and, pointing at a large empty store box, said, "Jon, that computer was brand new. Look at the key board and monitor, both have the clear protective tape still on. So the computer is useless."

Hill walked over to the book shelf and said, "Todd, I think that box the twins were carrying had books in it. Look at the first book shelf. The dust outlines shows that several books are missing. I looked at those the other day. They were all were text books with personal hand written notes at the sides and between the columns of each page. Right now I would hazard a guess that we're looking for a book or a series of books."

Jon's eyes met Todd's and at the same time they said, "Diaries!"

Huntsville Memorial Hospital

Grayson Riggs was eating an early dinner when Tex and I walked into his room. For a guy that had been shot and left for dead, Riggs looked pretty darn fit. Looking up he said, "Ah, you must be LaFleet and Beers from Dallas. My daughter called and said you were on the way."

Pushing his tray away, he said, "God that food is nasty. That bland hospital shit is all they'll give me. Don't suppose either of you has a pizza hidden on you?"

Laughing Tex said, "No sir, we don't. But I reckon we could find you some if it's that important."

Shaking his head no, Riggs replied, "Best not. With my luck my wife would walk in and all three of us would be up shit creek."

I immediately liked Riggs. As near as I could tell, he's in his early sixties and obviously pumps iron – a lot! He also has some serious cauliflower ear, which is the mark of an old wrestler. I asked, "So what weight class did you wrestle?"

Reaching up and touching his left ear, he said, "In high school I wrestled at 157. In college I couldn't suck weight down that far so I wrestled at 174.

You've got the mark of the beast (talking about my own cauliflower ear) how about you?"

I answered, "In high school I went 168 and in college I wrestled 197. Fortunately for me, my coach was not supportive of cutting weight. He liked for us to be lean but not starving."

Riggs said, "I should've been so lucky. I starved my ass off all through school. I would like to keep talking wrestling, but I know ya'll didn't come all this way for that. So what questions do you two have for me?"

Since I had inadvertently established the rapport with Riggs, Tex gave me the lead. I said, "Mr. Riggs, my partner and I have looked over the police report given to us by the Huntsville police department. That report is very well done and quite thorough. And the pictures taken by the Ellis's were better than most professional crime scene photos. What we're hoping for is that you'll talk to us about whatever you remember starting with when you left the hotel in Dallas."

For the next hour Riggs told his story with as much detail as he could recall. "I got to the rest stop and hauled butt to the bathroom. When I came out I saw a small dark colored car parked next mine, empty with the motor running. I decided to wait for whoever the car belonged to. It was cold so I was going to… to wait in my car. Then I heard a voice behind me and I turned around…" Riggs sat there trying to recall what happened next. "I haven't told this part to anyone yet. I just remembered it. The man was dressed like a priest. He said that I'd been found guilty of something… For that I had to die. He had a gun – I don't know what caliber but it was an automatic with a silencer attached. And then I felt several slaps to my forehead. I fell to the ground and felt my body being moved around. I could see and hear; but I couldn't move or talk. Strange, I remember him reading scripture and then I actually remember hearing an 18 wheeler blast its horn in the distance. Then I heard a car door slam and a car burn off pretty fast. That's when I think I passed out because I woke here a few days later."

I said, "Mr. Riggs, I know you're getting tired. And I'll stop asking questions any time you want. Can you in any way remember what he looked like?"

Riggs thought for moment and said, "We were both standing in the parking lot on level ground. I'm 5'11 but he seemed taller. He was also broad in the shoulders like a wrestler or a boxer. He had very short hair – almost a military cut. He was holding the gun in his right hand while he talked...... but switched it just before he shot. I'm sorry, that's all I can remember."

I looked at Tex who said, "Mr. Riggs, we'll let you alone now, sir. We'll let Huntsville know they need to talk to you again to update their report. You can decide on when and where. But I suspect they'll want to talk sooner rather than later."

Riggs said, "Leave me your cards boys. If I think of anything else I'll buzz 'ya. Oh, Detective LaFleet, my daughter thinks you're hot. She said too bad you live in Dallas, if you ever move to the Galveston area, look her up."

Great! A beautiful gal thinks I'm hot and I live 400 miles from her. Is there something about my face that has ticked God off?

1200 Block Swiss Ave. Dallas Texas

It was a full hour later when Miller shouted, "Bingo! Look what ace detective Miller has found, kudos for the big guy! Geez Jon, how many times did we look here?" 'Here' was a small sliding panel that the missing books on the first shelf had concealed. Behind the panel was an empty space where a small fire-safe had once been hidden. Reaching into the space, Miller extracted a thick leather bound book with the name Father Robert Lanton engraved on the front.

Hill came over and said, "Todd, I think we've found what we came for. Let's tuck that diary in your shirt in case we're being watched. I want them to think we're leaving empty handed."

Miller shut the panel carefully and then put the diary under his shirt. Tucking his clothing back into place, he put his coat on and said, "I guess we'll know what the diary says soon enough. But I've got to wonder what a priest might have written that is so darn important."

As they were headed for the door, the phone given to them by PIU rang. "Jon Hill, CAPERS."

It was Steve Burt. "Jon, we lost them on I35 south bound at Camp Wisdom. Including mine, we had three cars trailing them. We were almost past Camp Wisdom when they shot across three lanes of traffic and took the exit. I'm not sure how, but we got burned. I'm sorry, dude."

Jon replied, "Understood, Steve. Can you meet us at our office in the morning around ten? We've got paperwork to get done tonight, so we can't visit now."

Comprehending that Jon meant that they had found something, Burt said, "Yeah, we'll be there at ten."

Walking out the door to the car, Miller asked, "Parked about two blocks north of us is a car that looks city owned. Do you see it?"

Hill stopped and knelt down and tied his shoe. "I see it. Keep the book hidden. Call Chief Wong and let him know what's happening. See if he can send a back up unit from the Central Substation to escort us to the office. Also see if you can get the phone number of Father Leopole or Kothner. Let's get someone over here to clean this mess up before Lanton's family gets here."

CHAPTER 11

Home

Tex dropped me off at the house around 8 PM. Rick still wasn't home, so I changed clothes and headed over to the new 24 Hour Fitness gym in Cedar Hill. This was one of the few truly 24 hour gyms in the Dallas/Fort Worth Metroplex. It had come in handy more than once, with my shitty hours. I was knocking out a quick lifting routine when Rick walked in, plopped down on a bench next to me and said, "Hey there! What a *perfectly lousy* day I've had. How was yours?"

In between my lifting sets I outlined to him the entire day's conversations. Rick was quiet for a moment and stated, "So what we have is a killer that dresses like a priest, is possibly left handed or ambidextrous, maybe a martial artist or a military trained fighter, is evolving his kill technique from hands to shooting, is an excellent marksman, passes sentence before shooting and has perfected his signature of posing his victims over *several* years. Did I leave anything out?"

I answered, "Nope that about covers it. So, what made your day *lousy?*"

Rick replied, "Nothing new. That's why it was lousy. I felt like I was running in circles."

Pausing for a moment, Rick continued, "There is one thing. I think you might want to talk with Father Karl again. He told me he wasn't as... as forth coming with you as he felt he should have been. Ren, he didn't lie to you, but there is some embarrassing – at least to him – background he'll be forced to disclose to you. He's willing to do so because he feels it might help the investigation"

'Ok. I'll handle the interview carefully. You know me, Mister Diplomacy."

Rick laughed and said, "Maybe Tex better talk to him."

Rick left and I finished up my workout and headed back to the house. I had scheduled an early sparring session at the police academy and I wanted to get some sleep. If I was well rested, maybe I wouldn't get my ass whipped so badly. Or if I did, at least I would be awake for it.

As I drove home from the gym, something a bit odd occurred to me. In every police investigation, there is information that we withhold from the public. We have to do this for several reasons. One is that *some people* in the media have absolutely no level of discretion when it comes to what they report. They'll contact a family before us to avoid getting 'scooped' by other news agencies. The second reason is that when too much information is released, we get copy-cat crimes. This, of course, confuses and slows down the investigation. And the third reason is that every crime has little nuances that are specific *only* to that crime. No matter how minuscule those nuances may be, they help us to focus on the correct suspect.

In my conversation with Rick, he made a comment about our murderer sentencing the victim before killing them. We had just found that out today from Grayson Riggs and I couldn't remember telling Rick about it. Strange; but then again I was very tired. Maybe I did say something.

9:00 PM. Cedar Hill Texas, City Recreational Center.

Reverend Randal Whitehouse felt demoralized. Looking around at the near empty banquet room there were less than twenty people in a facility that should have held close to three hundred. Whitehouse had spent years building a youth ministry only to have it swept away almost overnight. Reverend Whitehouse was truly an innocent man; but the accusations of impropriety with a very young teenage girl had been pounced on by a story-thirsty media. Like Richard Jewell who had been falsely accused by the media in the 1996 Atlanta Olympic bombings, the Reverend's entire life was in shambles. His bank accounts had mysteriously been drained, the inside of his house had been ransacked and the outside had ethnic slurs spray painted on the walls. His car had been set on fire, his lawn salted and some poor soul had even dug up his sewer line and crushed the pipes. But the worst came when he sent his wife and children away for safety sake. As he hugged his wife of twenty years good-bye, he saw doubt in her eyes. Above everything else, that broke his heart.

For the last five years his annual 'Kids Success' banquets had standing room only. *No! Best not to harp on that right now*, Whitehouse thought. Thanks to the hard work of the Cedar Hill police department, he would soon be exonerated. Through much overtime work, those officers had discovered that the accusations (given anonymously to several news channels) had come from a young girl mixed up in a local South Dallas gang.

Gang members had attempted to extort money from his ministry and the accusations were done as reprisal to his refusal. Tomorrow's leading news stories would clear his name. The lawyers from three of the local news channels had already contacted him asking if he would be willing to take an out of court settlement. The irony was that the Reverend didn't believe in law suits, but he wasn't going to be stupid either. The money they were offering would help rebuild his ministry. Until then all he could do was pray for those that had so deeply hurt him. Taking a deep breath, Reverend Whitehouse decided to take a long walk around Bradford Park when he left the banquet hall. He needed some time to clear his head and meditate before he went home to an empty house.

2 hours later. Bradford Park, Cedar Hill, Texas.

Father Mike Leopole scanned the area and then looked at Father Kothner who was kneeling over the body of Reverend Randal Whitehouse. Sliding his handgun back into its holster Leopole asked, "Dead?"

Father Kothner nodded yes and then realized that in the dark Leopole would not be able to see the gesture. Kothner replied, "Yes he is... very much so."

Crossing himself, Leopole asked, "Father Shannon?"

Kothner took a deep breath and looking around for potential witnesses, answered, "Yeah, we need to bring him in."

Tuesday, 12 February
7:00 AM Dallas Police Academy

Father Karl and I had been going at each other off and on for about an hour. We would spar, take a break while he showed me how and why I had screwed up and then spar again. Karl was a great instructor and though I had a tendency to end these sessions looking like a used punching bag, I really enjoyed them. That is, up until today.

Karl and I were in the middle of a takedown series when Chief Smyth walked in and began warming up. He never talks very much to begin with and today he seemed... quiet, distracted, and angry all at once. The Chief usually fights Karl first, then me. Except when teaching, there is little sense training against someone below your own skill level. However, this time as the Chief bowed in, he faced me. This relegated Father Karl – who outranked us both in Shorin-ryu – to the lesser position of referee (where I should have been). This may seem trivial; nevertheless, in the martial arts it is a major breach of etiquette.

I only had a moment to glance at Karl who had a very worried look on his face. The fight was on just as I set in a fight stance, and in that moment, I sensed that this was a very dangerous situation for me. A good fighter never backs up, so I immediately began to circle, hoping to keep Smyth off of me. Instinctively, I wanted to revert to my combat training, but that degree of ruthlessness and brutality was not allowed in 'tournament fighting.' This put me at a disadvantage because I was fighting the *chief of police* (my boss) and my instincts at the same time. In other words, the chief could go balls to the wall and I couldn't (leastwise, not here and not under these specific circumstances).

Smyth threw three lighting quick punches. I blocked the first two but caught a harsh blow by the third. That hit landed right on the scar on my cheek and stung like crazy. We wear very thin 'fighting gloves' that are designed to protect the hand – not the person on the receiving end of the punch. Other than a mouth piece, that's all the protection we use. In training, unless otherwise agreed upon, it's up to the fighters to protect each other from harm. At this moment Smyth did not seem inclined to care about protecting me because as he finished that third punch, he tried to take my head off with a spinning heel hook kick. I dropped to the ground under the kick and swept Smyth's leg out from under him. He landed hard but was up again in a heartbeat.

I wasn't so quick, and as I rolled to regain my feet, Smyth was on me – Karl was yelling 'teishi' (stop) over and over – but Smyth kept coming with a stomping attack that could have crushed my skull or broken bones if he had connected with me. For only a second, Karl managed to step between us giving me time to make my feet and, without pause, I launched an attacked. With a series of punches and kicks that slammed into Smyth's body and face, I drove him back. Then suddenly he ducked, side stepped into and past me, and threw a vicious *illegal* punch that nailed me in the left kidney. I could have blocked the hit by spinning into Smyth and slamming my elbow into his face; but that too would have been an illegal strike which could be fatal to the recipient. Dropping to my knees, I became completely debilitated with a searing pain that choked off my breathing. Smyth grabbed my throat and whispered close to my ear, "Now you know the difference between street fighting and tournament fighting, young detective!"

And then Karl was between us, yelling for Smyth to stand down. Smyth said something to Father Karl who responded with an angry, "Back off!"

Staring at Karl for several tense seconds, suddenly the fire left Smyth's eyes and he let go of my throat and left the room. As he walked out, the Chief of Police had s strange sorrowful look on his face.

Helping me to my feet, Father Karl asked, "There's a reason that kidney strikes are forbidden in tournament fighting. Sweet Mary, Ren, are you all right?"

I was still fighting the pain and the need to vomit but I managed to croak out, "I think I'm ok. I'll be peeing blood for a month though. Do you have any idea what just happened?"

Father Karl answered slowly saying, "I'm not sure. But Ren if it ever happens again, screw the rules and go with your combat training. It could mean your life."

Fighting back nausea, I asked, "What did he say to you there at the last?"

Looking very uncomfortable, Kothner replied, "He said this lesson isn't over."

As I grabbed a nearby trash can and began to puke my toe nails up, it struck me that the entire fight had lasted less than twenty seconds.

Dallas Police Headquarters / CAPERS

An hour later I was at the office feeling really pale and not just a little shaky. I had rinsed off at the academy and Father Karl had to help me get dressed. Father Karl had also wrapped my waist and ribs for support (that's all you can do for such an injury); anyway the wrapping helped but I still felt like shit.

A few minutes later Mom, Tex, Jon and Todd all came out of Chief Wong's office looking rather angry. Not moving from my desk I said, "Morning. What's up?"

Mom stopped in front of my desk and said, "While you were out playing the Karate Kid, we were getting our collective asses chewed on by Chief Smyth." Mom went on to explain that Smyth had phoned Wong and demanded that the four of them come into the office. Once all were present, Smyth told them over the speakerphone that he was getting some extreme heat from the mayor and city council over the lack of progress on the Lanton case. Mom ended the explanation with, "Smyth threatened to transfer us all out of CAPERS if we didn't get some results pronto."

Mom was talking and I glanced at Tex. I realized that he was studying my face with a look of concern on his. When Mom stopped speaking, Tex asked, "Ren, you look like crap. Are you sick?"

Keeping as still as I could, I answered, "Not sick. But I think we all need to go back into Wong's office and talk. While ya'll got an ass chewing from Smyth, he gave me an ass kicking." Looking at the distance from my desk to Wong's office (probably twenty feet or less) I hoped that Chief Wong might consider coming out here for our meeting.

As I related the story to the team, the tension in the room had risen tenfold. When I finished Tex, Jon and Todd had looks of disbelief on their faces. Mom and Chief Wong were obviously furious. Chief Wong said, "I'm the only one that is allowed to beat my detectives!" Looking over at me, Wong continued, "LaFleet, you could piss off a saint on one of your good days. But I doubt very seriously if you had this one coming. What did Father Kothner have to say about it?"

I answered, "He was as shocked as I was and just as clueless. He'll be by later today to talk to me, if you need a firsthand account of what happened. Sir, the Chief looked angry when he first came into the room. Maybe he had just had his ass chewed, too."

Chief Wong looked thoughtful, then said, "Kind of early to have had his butt snacked-on by the city manager or mayor. It could have happened late yesterday. Still, I've known Will Smyth since he was a patrol sergeant in Pasadena Texas and what happened today was not the guy I know. Do you need to see a doctor?"

I replied, "No sir. I think I'll be ok." *Especially if I don't move or breath for a while.*

While Tex and I were typing our findings from Houston and Huntsville, Hill and Miller were diligently working on deciphering Father Lanton's diary. When we were all finished with our projects, Tex and I briefed the team on our road trip and then turned the briefing over to Hill and Miller.

Jon said, "As you know, we found Lanton's diary at his residence in a little hidden nook covered by a small sliding panel. Including Chief Wong and the Lieutenant, we four are the only people that have knowledge of this find. I'm sure Steve Burt from Public Integrity and his immediate partner know that we found something, but they have no specific knowledge of what. They'll be here soon and we've been given permission from Chief Wong to bring them up to speed."

Todd picked up where Jon had left off, saying, "Father Lanton was a prolific writer. The diary *we have* is several hundred pages long and is one of several volumes. We derived that from comments that Lanton makes concerning past events having been recorded. Such as statements like *'you may recall what I wrote about these issues on April 10th of '04* – only this particular journal starts in June of '08."

Jon said, "A lot of what Lanton wrote about was simple observations, feelings, poems and prayers. Nothing very earth shattering – in fact, it's all quite innocent. There are three things, however, that did catch our attention. The first was that Father Lanton was struggling with the celibacy requirements of his faith. He mentions a young lady by the name of Maria Gonzalas, who is a member of his congregation. The poor guy had one hell of a crush on this lady. We've tracked down her address and will be talking to her today."

Todd began speaking again. "The second thing to catch our eye was that he has a close friend that he feared had become mentally ill. He never mentions this person by name; but he says and I quote *'my good friend and brother in Christ has continued to show a tragic decline of rational thought.'* There are at least twenty such entries concerning this person. The last thing that we found interesting was the way he talks about his absolute admiration for Father Leopole. Not that Leopole isn't deserving of respect, but the way Lanton felt was almost an adolescent hero worship. He made several references to the *'horrendous responsibility Father Leopole must carry in his heart.'* We're not sure what horrendous responsibility Lanton was referring to. Nor do we understand the context for which it is applied. Is this a horrendous responsibility that has already happened, is happening, or will happen in the future? That's all we got, any questions about all this?"

I asked, "Jon, what specifically were Lanton's duties. I mean we know his normal priestly duties, but did he have other work assigned to him?"

Todd answered, "Actually yes, he was a clerk-typist for Father Leopole. You'll have to ask Rick if that's normal because I don't know jack-shit about Catholicism. It does seem strange that an elderly priest would have both an aide and a scribe."

From the office hallway a voice rang out, "What seems strange? That Ren LaFleet is still a cop on this department or that Jon Hill is not the Chief of Police?"

Looking up I saw the grinning faces of Detective Steve Burt and Emil "Rocky" Connor, PIU. Smiling (laughing hurt too much), I said, "Jesus, what pile of dog crap did you just crawl out from under, Burt? You've got long greasy blond hair, need a serious shave, a bath, and that Old Spice you have on is well...really old!"

Steve Burt and I had gone through the door a hundred times together back in our SWAT days. Nasty looks aside, if I could describe Steve with one word, that word would be *dependable*. Burt was about 5'10, lean to the point of being almost frail, pale looking and spoke with a strong Doc Holiday/Val Kilmer southern accent.

Reaching across my desk as gently as I could, I shook hands with Burt and Conner. "Sorry I'm not standing up to shake hands and welcome you back to real cop work. I took an ass kicking this morning while sparring. What have ya'll been up too?"

As Burt and Conner took seats, Burt replied, "Doing real cop work figuring out who the Special Investigators are for the Chief of Police. And we already know about you getting the crap beat out of you."

Seeing the look on my face, Rocky laughed, and said, "We have our sources. And you know PIU, we're so secretive we don't even know what we're doing."

Rocky Connor was another former SWAT guy. He had been our team 'Breachman' (also known as 'Slammer'). Rocky had played five years of professional football and then abruptly quit. In his words: "I woke up one morning and decided that pro athletes contribute nothing to our society. I wanted to contribute - so, I quit." Rocky is close to 6'8, dark black skinned and carries himself like a very unhappy caged lion. His voice is a deep baritone and sounded like two boulders grinding together, hence the nickname 'Rocky.'

Still speaking, Rocky explained, "Sorry we're late, guys. Steve and I ran into a bit of trouble getting information on Chief Smyth's Special Investigators. I had to call in some favors to get the scoop on these two. Remember those assholes Garret and Nolan? They got fired for taking two suspects down to the Trinity River bottoms and beating them senseless. Well, as you know they didn't go to trial, so guess who got rehired by Smyth about six months ago?"

James Garret and Thomas Nolan had *finally* been fired from the Dallas police department for beating two hooks almost to death on a hot summer night. Over the years Garret and Nolan had been accused of everything from abusing prisoners to delving in organized crime. Allegations against them never seemed to last for very long. In many cases the charges would suddenly disappear, often along with the complainant. That's what happened to the two hooks they got fired over – they disappeared and Garret and Nolan walked free. How they got rehired is anyone's guess; however under Civil Service laws, short of an indictment, it was tough to keep someone from being reinstated. I knew Garret and Nolan pretty well. Because to my embarrassment, they were in my police academy class and I disliked them both very much. They represented what every police officer in America hates – corrupt cops!

Tex asked, "Any chance of getting those two in here for questioning?"

Steve answered, "Here? It's doubtful. There just isn't any reason to call them in." Seeing the expression on Jon's face, Steve quickly added, "Before ya'll balk, I already ran it by legal. They said it would be your word against theirs about ransacking Lanton's house. They would claim they found it that way. Or worse, claim that you two did it to frame them. As far as them carrying off evidence, same deal. Also, if they are secret squirrel special investigators working for the Chief of Police, then technically they had a right to be there 'investigating.' Not sure what they might be investigating, but we need to find out."

Exasperated, I said, "That's so much crap! You mean no one can talk to those two even though they've interfered with this investigation from the start"?

Smiling Rocky said, "We didn't say that they couldn't be talked to. We just said it couldn't happen here. And the truth is, you had better let us handle it."

In his best German accent Steve said, "Vee have our vays of making zeese people talk, Herr LaFleet!"

Even I knew better than to ask what those 'vays' might be. Across the nation, Public Integrity Units had been developed to combat corruption and criminal activity *inside* the ranks of law enforcement and city government. By right of job description, Public Integrity Units are very secretive and often operate in gray areas between police procedure, the law and crime. In other words, these guys frequently work outside the box. They have to, they're investigating people that have badges, a permanent bad attitude, and carry guns! I've always thought that if I left CAPERS, I would like to pull a tour with PIU.

We began to discuss Hill and Miller's diary findings with Steve and Rocky when Chief Wong called Mom into his office. In less than a minute Mom came out with an anxious look on her face. "Ok, guys we have another problem. Cedar Hill police found another body at Bradford Park several hours ago. The Modus Operandi might match the other cases. Maintenance crews found the body and called it in. Crime scene is about done being processed. Tex, you and Ren head out to Cedar Hill and link up with their detectives. I know I don't need to say this, but remember to be forthcoming on our cases. A little cooperation from us could go a long way in solving these murders. Hill, Miller you two talk to Maria Gonzalas – maybe we'll get lucky there."

Even though I was still a little shaky, I could move now without too much pain. Against departmental General Orders, I had taken three or four Hydrocodone (otherwise known as Vicodin) for the pain. It had taken a few long minutes but the medication had finally kicked in and I was feeling a little better. Tex would drive and do almost all of the talking, so as long as we didn't get into a shootout, I would be fine. Of course if I did get into a shooting in my condition Internal Affairs would eat my lunch. I would also be fired and indicted. Still, as shitty as I felt, it was worth the risk.

Ms. Maria Gonzalas

Detectives Hill and Miller walked the short distance from the Lanton crime scene to the Gonzalas residence. In six short blocks the scenery quickly changed from seedy to well kept lawns and houses. Looking around, Hill said, "When I was a teenager, this entire area used to be run down. Looks like Maria Gonzalas lives in one of those houses renovated back in the mid 1990's." Starting in 1991 baby boomers had thought it in vogue to fix up houses in the older parts of South Dallas. Many of the houses and streets were considered historical sites and therefore valued by the City of Dallas. The boomers had spent millions of dollars in an effort to revitalize those few neighborhoods that could be saved.

Unfortunately, neighborhoods not worth reclaiming bordered those few beautifully renovated city blocks. *Those* neighborhoods were left in disrepair and suffered from out of control crime including murders resulting from heavy gang activity. Most people in this area never went outside their homes after dark, it was just too dangerous.

As they climbed the steps onto Maria's large covered porch, someone said, "I was wondering if ya'll were going to be talking to me."

Both detectives stopped suddenly and turned toward where the voice had come from. Buried in a lawn chair and covered with a blanket was Maria Gonzalas. "Sorry, I didn't mean to startle you. I suppose you're here to talk about Rob?"

Not Father Lanton or even Father Robert – just Rob and that suggested a degree of familiarity neither detective had expected to hear. Based on the diary, both detectives believed that the crush was rather one sided.

Hill answered, "Yes ma'am we are. My name is Detective Jon Hill and this is my partner Detective Todd Miller." Showing her his police identification card and badge he continued saying, "We're with the Dallas Police department's homicide unit."

Standing up Maria said, "Let's go inside where it's a little warmer and more private. My neighbor across the street is the local gossip and has caused me no small amount of trouble." With that she walked to the door and went in with Hill and Miller trailing behind her.

Maria insisted on playing the proper hostess and served the two detectives coffee. Studying her while she moved about, Hill surmised that she was about 30. She wore no wedding band and judging by the absence of 'guy stuff' in her house, she probably had never been married and had no serious boy friend. Maria was not beautiful or even pretty – leastwise not physically. As Hill watched her he thought that maybe *handsome* was a good way to describe the full figured lady. Hill glanced at his partner and noticed that Todd was making the same observations, but he was also watching her a little harder than normal. Doing a mental shrug and taking a sip of coffee, Hill said, "Ms. Gonzalas, we know this is a difficult time for you and we are very sorry for the loss of your friend. Please understand that we have to ask some questions which might be very personal about your relationship with Father Lanton. Would you start by telling us where and how you two met?"

Hill had asked the easiest of questions to put Ms. Gonzalas at ease. After all, this was an interview, not an interrogation. Hill sensed that Maria Gonzalas simply needed an opportunity to talk to someone that would be non-judgmental.

Maria replied, "Thank you for your condolences. I had seen him at Church, during mass, many times. Rob and I actually met at a parish fund raiser six months ago. We hit it off right away. We both love… loved pro football. It didn't matter to us who was playing, we would meet at a sports bar and watch the games with other members of the congregation. It was all great fun and very spirited."

Miller asked, "Ms. Gonzalas, when was the last time you had seen or talked to Father Robert?"

Maria's eyes clouded over with tears as she answered, "The night he died he called me. It was around ten or eleven. He asked if he might be allowed to come over… that he had something to talk to me about. I said yes. And I waited. After an hour or so, I looked out the window and saw him there – just standing there shivering with his hands in his pockets looking at my house. I wanted so very bad to ask him to come in. It was so cold and damp. But… But I knew he was struggling and I didn't want to interfere."

Knowing the answer, but needing to hear it, Miller gently asked, "Ms. Gonzalas, what was he struggling with?"

Maria began to openly cry as she replied, "Most men don't give me a second look, let alone a first one. Rob was always very kind to me. I think he wanted to be with me… and I wanted to be with him. But he gave an oath to serve God and remain celibate and that's where it stayed. Nothing happened between us. He never touched me, though I wish that he had!" Taking a deep breath and then smiling Maria looked at Miller and said, "After awhile I watched him walk away and I knew that he would ask to be transferred."

Miller asked, "Did Father Robert have any enemies that you know of?"

Maria shook her head no and then said, "In this area, we're surrounded by a lot of criminal activity. I'm sure ya'll already know that. I think Rob fell victim to one of those gangs that run this area. But there's one thing that I noticed as Rob walked away. He was being watched by another person and, while I can't be sure, I think it was a priest by the name of Father Kothner."

Both detectives abruptly sat up. Hill asked, "We have talked to Father Kothner and he has an alibi, why do you think it was him?"

Maria shrugged and said, "I can't be certain, but he had Father Kothner's build. When Rob left - whoever it was didn't immediately follow, he waited a few minutes talking on his cell phone and the then took off jogging in the opposite direction that Robb went."

After saying good bye to Ms. Gonzalas, Hill and Miller went across the street to the residence of the neighborhood busy-body, Ms. Edith Cox. Cox opened her front door before the detectives had an opportunity to knock. "It's about damn time someone talked to me! Did you know that Mexican across the street comes and goes at all hours? She must be some type of whore because she leaves at midnight and comes home at seven every morning."

Hill replied, "Actually Ma'am she's Spanish not Mexican and she's a Registered Nurse at the Methodist Hospital right up the road."

Looking disappointed Cox said, "Well she probably works as a whore in her free time… you know the way those Mexicans are."

Ignoring the statement, Hill said, "Ma'am, last Friday night a man by the name of Robert Lanton was murdered several streets over. He was last seen standing in front of Ms. Gonzalas's house fairly late in the evening. Did you happen to see or hear anything that night?"

Answering, Cox said, "Have to do your job do I? Yes I saw him and another man standing in *my* yard watching him. They were probably waiting for their turns with her. Newspapers said that your dead boy was a Catholic priest. You know the way those papists are. They breed like rabbits! And those priests are all boy lovers. Guess they got tired of waiting to have sex with her because they both left in different directions a few minutes apart. Can't tell you what they looked like. You'll just have to work harder to find that out. Now tell me what you're going to do about my other neighbors? They keep letting their dogs crap in my yard!"

Telling Ms. Cox that they would talk to the beat officers about her neighbor's dogs, they left as quickly as they could. Glancing back over his shoulder at Ms. Edith Cox who was still standing in the door, Miller said, "I'd like to crap in the old bitch's yard too!"

Chuckling Hill said, "Me, too, but I think that would get us fired."

Miller replied, "Naw, after five minutes with her, Wong would drop his trousers too."

Chapter 12

Headquarters
Cedar Hill Police Department

Traffic wasn't heavy so it took Tex and I only about thirty minutes to get to the new City Hall and police headquarters complex on Uptown Blvd. in Cedar Hill. Tex and I pulled into the parking lot and sat staring at the new building. Because of the color of stone used (rose or light pink) to construct the building, it had quickly become known as the 'Pink Pig,' or the 'Pepto-Bismol' building depending on which officer you talked to. Most times the color was tolerable, but when it rained, like today, the light pink became a brilliant color of pink that would have made *Mary Kay* Ash want to gag.

"Jesus," Tex said, "Do you think that they really knew how bad that stone would look when it rained?"

I shrugged and said, "No way! But staring at that pink and with the Vicodin in me, I suddenly feel very mellow *and* in touch with my feminine side."

Getting out of the car, Tex said, "Well snap out of it, oh sensitive he-man, we've got bad guys to catch."

I exited the car as slowly and as carefully as I could, trying – and failing, not to irritate my injured back and side. I groaned, "God-oh-mighty that hurts! Every time I move wrong it's like getting punched again."

Stopping and waiting for me to catch up Tex asked, "Are you sure you don't need to see a doctor?"

"No," I replied, "I'll be ok in a day or so." *If I don't die first!*

We were met at the door by Cedar Hill detectives Ron Green and Robin Stuart. As we were escorted to a conference room, looking around I said, "Nice digs. Though I think I could live with a different color of stone outside."

Chuckling Stuart said, "Yeah, us too. But that pink does have its advantages. Our officers have suddenly stopped complaining, work stress has significantly lowered and everyone around here seems nice and relaxed these days."

Looking at the walls as we walked down a long hallway, Tex asked, "And these bright yellow walls – who thought that would look good?"

With mock resignation, Stuart replied, "No idea, but we think the city planning committee has absolutely no fashion sense… that or they suddenly went color-blind. Either way, I hate being reminded that I need to pee every fifteen minutes."

Finally reaching our destination, we entered a large room filled with a large table and chairs. Sitting down at the table, Tex said, "If you two don't mind going first, it might save us a lot of time and discussion if these cases are not related."

Left unsaid by Tex, was if the cases *aren't related*, he didn't want to give out too much information. Neither Green nor Stuart was offended by this. In cases likes these what a person doesn't know they can't talk about; therefore case confidentiality can't be blown.

Green said, "No problem. I'll give ya'll the Readers Digest version and we'll go from there if it's necessary. No autopsy is back yet; but I estimate the time of death was last night around midnight. The murder occurred at a small city park surrounded by residential neighborhoods. The victim is Reverend Randal Whitehouse – we had just cleared him of allegations of sexually molesting a young lady. Turned out it was a gang related extortion attempt. He has three bullet wounds well grouped to the head and a knife wound to the right side. There was a great amount of blood from the knife wound indicating that he wasn't dead from the head shots when he was stabbed. Any of this crap sound familiar?"

Gently leaning back in my chair, I said, "Well guys, looks like we're going to be here a while. Tex, I'll call the Fort Worth detectives, if you'll start bringing these guys up to speed on our stuff."

Looking back at Green and Stuart, "One of you might want to see if your supervisors and the Chief of Police want to sit in on this. I am afraid that we are dealing with a serial killer."

Four hours later we were finally wrapping up the discussion. Tex had done his normal thorough job of briefing people with me and the two Fort Worth detectives adding tidbits as we went along.

Green said, "What I don't understand is why the suspect didn't finish off the lawyer with the knife like he did Whitehouse."

I looked at Tex and you could see the wheels turning. He was quiet for a moment, then replied, "Riggs told us that before he passed out he heard a truck horn in the distance. That might have disturbed the killer into fleeing before he could finish things. Lanton, Joshua and his brother all had *post-mortem* stab wounds as did all but one of the victims – Redcliff – in Houston. He had no stab wounds at all. Whitehouse had an *ante or pari-mortem* stab wound and Rigs had no stab wound. With the noted exception of Redcliff *all were posed* – meaning that he poses the victims then uses the knife. Their clothing was not torn or punctured by the knife. So the knife was inserted after the clothing was moved out of the way. Lanton, Joshua and Jones had their clothing straightened *after* the suspect had inserted the knife. The pictures of Whitehouse show that his clothing was not straightened…"

Pausing for a moment and then nodding his head yes, Tex explained, "Which means with Riggs, he never got the chance to use the knife and finish the job. With Whitehouse, he *couldn't* wait for the head wounds to kill, which means he was rushed into stabbing his victim then fleeing before he could complete the routine of straightening the clothes."

Dallas Police Headquarters / CAPERS

After interviewing Maria Gonzalas, Hill and Miller returned to the office and began to go over the information they had obtained. Hill grabbed some coffee, sat down and began working away. Miller on the other hand, sat at his desk with a pensive look on his face.

After typing for several minutes Hill stopped and asked, "You want to talk about it, Todd?" Jon had always thought that while Todd's 'IQ' scores were high enough to make him a smart man, his 'EQ' scores must be off the charts. Todd was the most intuitive officer Jon knew. It was almost unnatural the way Todd could read people's emotions and body language. Jon had always regarded his partner as a more reliable form of a polygraph test. Criminals just could not successfully lie to him. The only problem that Jon felt his partner had is that away from work, the poor guy was so shy he had no social life.

Miller answered after a moment or two, saying, "What do you think makes a woman like Maria go for a man so inaccessible like Lanton? Not meaning to put him down, but I think Maria is beautiful, intelligent; she has a nursing career. She could have any guy she wanted! Yet she goes for a guy that she simply cannot have – that is if he stayed true to his vows."

Surprised at Millers comment, Jon thought '*Maria is handsome, yes, but beautiful? She wasn't ugly by any means… but.* Suddenly realizing what this was really about, Jon said, "My guess is that in spite of the attributes you've so aptly stated, Maria is like a lot of people. She's very lonely. You know partner, Maria isn't a suspect in this investigation. Not even a person of interest. Give it a little time but I think you should ask her out." Jon had to suppress the desire to laugh because Todd sat there looking like a deer caught in the headlights. Yes indeed Jon considered, '*beauty is truly in the eyes of the beholder.*' Jon went back to his work wondering how best to help his partner and Maria hook-up.

1 hour later

Tex and I got back to the office just in time to keep Kothner from having to wait on us. Father Karl seemed a little nervous yet very determined to talk to us. As we sat down, Jon and Todd joined us. Jon hand-signed me that he had something important to discuss before this interview began. Many investigative teams use methods of subtle nonverbal communications. This may seem strange; however, there are times when detectives (especially those undercover) obtain information that they must relay to their partners without tipping off a suspect. Military Special Forces and CIA teams do the same thing. Entire conversations can be held in the field without uttering a word by using the slightest of hand or body movements. This is not the same thing as sign-language used by the deaf or mute where the hands are used in a rapid fire secession spelling out words or using complicated *hand gestures* to converse. In this case, as Jon walked in, we made eye contact and he faintly coughed into his hand twice. This was a signal for me to pay attention.

Jon then sat down, placed his pen on the table with the writing end facing Karl and causally scratched his ear. I glanced at Jon's right hand resting on the table and saw that his middle finger was on top of his index finger. This meant that he had information that he did not want Father Karl to hear. I blinked twice, assuring Jon I had gotten the message. I glanced at Tex who dipped his chin telling me he understood. Jon then extended three fingers indicating that we should excuse ourselves and meet in fifteen minutes.

Why didn't we just excuse ourselves right then and go talk? Because criminals are not stupid – they may be stupid criminals, but they are not stupid people. A detective coming in and saying 'we need to talk' would alert a suspect that something was seriously up. Also, it was just good practice for when we are in the field.

Father Karl cleared his throat and said, "I... ah... want ya'll to know that the last time we met I didn't lie to you, but I wasn't as forth coming with information as I should have been. I omitted some things in an effort to keep Father Lanton's personal life out of the investigation and therefore out of the media. Please let me reiterate that Robert was a good and honest man and he was also a very good priest. As I told you in our first meeting, he was struggling with the issue of celibacy. There is a young lady by the name of Maria Gonzalas. The night that Robert was killed he was ……"

Jon coughed quietly into his hand and out of the corner of my eye I glimpsed his right index finger tapping the tabletop. This meant Father Karl was touching on the information he (Jon) needed to pass to us. Jon then closed his left hand into a fist indicating that we would stay put and forego our meeting if Father Karl kept talking.

Father Karl continued, "…supposed to meet with Ms. Gonzalas at her residence. I know this because Robert told me he was going there. And that's where he was coming from when he was killed."

Jon said, "Father Kothner we have spoken to Ms. Gonzalas and she confirmed what you just told us. She also informed us that Father Lanton never went inside her house. He stayed in her front yard, torn between being with her and being a priest. But then again, you already know all this, don't you Father?"

I sat there stunned at what I was hearing. In the next few seconds we would be putting the cuffs on one of my closest friends. Then, much to my relief, Jon negated that thought, saying, "We also know that when Lanton left, you left in the other direction continuing on your run. That was confirmed by two people. What we want to know is what you were doing there in the first place?"

Father Karl could have denied being there. There are no street lights near the Gonzalas house. Also that night was very overcast and raining, I doubted that Karl's physical features could be seen well. Of course I'm a cop, not a defending attorney so I kept my mouth shut. Not trying to deny this information, Karl said, "Yes I was there. And I was going to tell you so, but you've jumped ahead of the story. Robert called me and told me he was going to see Ms. Gonzalas. He asked that I be there to 'Bear Witness.' I promised that I would be there."

Miller asked, "Father Kothner, would you please explain what this means for us non Catholics?"

Taking a deep breath Kothner began to explain, "Bearing Witness can actually mean several things. In this context it meant that I would bear witness to Robert's actions. If Robert had decided to see Ms. Gonzalas and break his vows, I would have been expected to report the infraction to our superiors. Look at it as personal means of being held accountable for something you *might* do. Keep in mind that Robert did not have to call me – he could have gone there, broken his vows and not spoken of it. Instead he chose to be held accountable."

Miller said, "So you just stood there watching and freezing in the cold weather?"

Smiling, Kothner said, "Yes… that and praying for my friend."

Miller looked down at his note pad and then cautiously asked, "Father, would you tell us what you prayed?"

Leaning back in his chair Father Kothner said, "Normally I would say no. However, I'll answer the question for Robert's sake. My prayer was that Robert would be at peace with whatever course he took."

Tex asked, "No offense, but from what little I know about Catholicism that sounds rather open minded. Father Karl, why exactly did Robert ask you *personally* to be there? You're awfully young in the priesthood. Why didn't he ask another, older, more experienced priest like Father Leopole?"

Looking upset Kothner replied, "There are several reasons why. The first is that Robert trusted me to do the right thing should he have broken his vows." Growing angry, he continued, "The second was that he knew that I would not judge him – no matter how much his actions hurt. And, as God is my witness, it was killing me."

Looking directly at me, Kothner said in a quiet voice, "And the third… is that my job is like Father Shannon's. We investigate such infractions and crimes as they occur inside the Catholic faith."

Miller asked, "Father Karl, what are you not telling us? Is there another reason outside of friendship that his request and possible infraction would hurt you so much?"

Growing angry again and then suddenly looking defeated Kothner said, "Father Lanton… There were those within the Church that did not want to see *me* become a priest. The Church has a very long memory. Robert fought a gallant battle to see that I was given the opportunity to become ordained.

The sins of the father... I... I am the product of an improper relationship between a Catholic priest and a woman in his congregation. I was never allowed to know my father and my mother stuck me in an orphanage before I was one. By the time I was ten I was considered unadoptable. That's when I met Robert. He was coaching boxing and over the years he became like father to me. The only Dad I ever had. I have struggled to emulate him. That's why I was so hurt. I felt betrayed that he might break his vows." The last few sentences were said in nearly a whisper.

I sat there with my side hurting again, feeling emotionally drained. We knew that Father Karl had been watching Lanton. We also knew that he had run off in the opposite direction when they both had left Gonzalas's neighborhood. That didn't mean that Kothner could not have circled back around and killed Lanton. Feelings of anger or betrayal had gotten more than one person murdered, but this just didn't feel right. Then there was the statement made by Grayson Riggs that his assailant was dressed as a priest. Also, there is Karl's martial arts background, he was an ambidextrous fighter and the surgical way the murder victims in Houston had been beaten all pointed circumstantially to him. Studying the faces of my fellow detectives I knew that Father Karl Kothner was now a person of *strong* interest in a lot of murders.

Shit, first I get the living hell beat out of me. Then the guy that pretty much stops my own execution becomes a 'person of interest' in a multi jurisdictional murders (plural, as in more than one) case. My side hurts like crazy – but it's my heart that hurts more. This day just keeps getting better and better.

CHAPTER 13

Wednesday 13 February

I woke up at 6 AM feeling like hammered dog crap. I had had nightmares of Iraq and every time I would jerk awake, I would set my side and back on fire with gut wrenching pain. Those *really bad dreams* don't happen that much – unless I am under a great deal of stress or injured... Or like now, injured *and* highly stressed. It sucks, but what can you do? If a person in law enforcement, the military or firefighters seeks counseling and word gets out (*and word always gets out*), our careers are pretty much done. The bottom line is this: If you don't get help you're screwed (like me right now), if you get help you're screwed, so basically you're just screwed. You learn to deal with it or you don't.

Rick must have gotten up earlier and gone for a run with Danner because my devoted watchdog was gone when I woke up. I hurt so bad that my alarm was still going off when Rick and Danner quietly came into my room. Rick asked, "Hey Ren, are you awake?"

I slowly opened my eyes and said, "Yeah. Been awake off and on most of the night...Life really sucks right now, though."

Rick said, "Father Karl told me what happened yesterday with Smyth. Are you sure you don't need to see a doctor?"

This time I had to think about my response. I was fairly certain that the muscles around my left kidney were only bruised and there wasn't anything a doctor could do about that. I answered, "No, I'm ok. I'll soak in the shower for awhile and take some Vicodin before I get dressed. I'll be fine."

Looking doubtful Rick stated, "Well it's probably for the better because you have a major league problem that you don't even know about yet."

Rick handed me the morning newspaper and as I read the headlines I said, "Oh we are so boned! Maybe calling in sick isn't such a bad idea."

'International Serial Killer Stalks Texas'
Inept law enforcement kept guessing by deranged killer.
By Ian Web
Staff Writer

An anonymous source with the Dallas Police Department has informed this reporter that an international serial killer is on the loose in Texas. Worldwide, this killer has murdered as many as 20 high profile religious figures with questionable backgrounds. In Texas, the killer has murdered at least seven or more people in the last six years. Even though the similarities between the cases should have aroused suspicion with Dallas police investigators, they have refused to acknowledge that a serial killer is prowling our streets. Dr. Hershel Gaspar, an FBI expert in the study of serial killers, stated that the Dallas Police department has been less than receptive to his profiling work. Dr. Gaspar informed me that he had tried to give detectives assigned to investigate these cases the benefit of his assistance; but was rudely and unprofessionally shunned during a meeting this week. Dr. Gaspar further stated...............

I read the rest of the article with a sinking feeling in my stomach. Whoever the anonymous source was, he or she had given up every detail of the Lanton and Alexander murders – including the posing and the knife wounds. It also mentioned Father Kothner as a person of interest. How the hell had that gotten out?

I looked at Rick who had remained silent as I read. Slowly shaking my head, I said, "Rick, I'm not sure how this going to affect this investigation.

You weren't there yesterday during our meeting with him, but as far as Father Karl is concerned, the team agrees that while it simply does not feel right, Karl did have a possible motive to kill Lanton. Also, his lack of cooperation during the first interview casts him in a bad light. We have to consider him a possible suspect."

Rick had a worried look on his face and didn't reply. At a snail's pace, I turned and headed to the bathroom to shower and dress. By the time Tex arrived to pick me up I was moving only slightly better.

Dallas Police Headquarters / CAPERS

As Tex and I entered the office, we saw people sitting at our desks, going through our papers and files. Jon and Todd were leaning up against the far wall watching other people do the same to their desks. Mom was standing off to the side with Chief Wong, both of them looking angry. I could see shadows moving around in their offices, so their spaces were being searched, too. Before we could ask what was going on, one of the people doing the searching told Tex and I to keep our mouths shut and stand up against the wall away from Jon and Todd.

As soon as that jackass opened his mouth to speak, I knew who these clowns were.

In law enforcement the only people this arrogant and disrespectful were detectives assigned to the Internal Affairs Division (IAD).

So what's my problem with IAD? Before I answer that question, let me explain that all police departments *must have* an IAD that investigates departmental policy and procedural violations committed by officers. Without an IAD to rein certain people in, there are just some officers that will run amuck in total disregard of the rules. Now with that said, I will admit that I have (like most officers) a very intense dislike for the IAD. As a rule, IA investigators work hard and do their jobs to the best of their ability; however, no police officer is without sin. Most IA investigators seem to have forgotten that they themselves came from the street and have, during their own careers, violated departmental rules and regulations. No matter how good an officer is, no matter how conscientious an officer tries to be, he or she *will violate* those rules on occasion. The trick is discerning which officers make honest mistakes trying to do their jobs from the officers that can't do their jobs without making mistakes. Unfortunately, rather than even try, IA investigators rarely distinguish between the two. This is what causes the animosity between street officers and IAD. In my opinion there is very little difference between a third grade tattletale, a bet chronic wetter and many IA investigators.

Three Hours Later

As each IA investigator finished the desk search, the CAPERS detective assigned to that desk was taken to a separate rooms to be interviewed. My IA investigator was Kathleen Hamerick. I had known Hamerick back when she was a rookie in patrol. In those days I had thought her to be a fairly good officer, if a little too aggressive at times which, of course, was the card that I would play. We entered the first available vacant office we came to and I gently sat down at a large table. In an effort to dominate and intimidate me, Hamerick remained standing. Staring at me for several seconds (another intimidation trick), she said, "Ren, you know I've got a job to do and friendship aside, I am going to do it."

I answered, "Yes Corporal Hamerick, I know you have a job to do. Just like the time you clocked that dope suspect with your flashlight in violation of general orders." I might as well set the adversarial tempo for this interview right out of the gate. Also, I needed to kick her off balance and let her know that I was not going to be intimated nor dominated by a junior officer. I am sure it is what Tex, Jon and Todd would be doing, too. "Seems to me that he got what, twenty stitches in the head? What do think would have happened had I filed a complaint for excessive force against you?"

Trying to recover a little ground she stated, "That was several years ago and has no bearing on this investigation!"

She was only half correct, but it didn't really matter because I was about to put the blade in (figuratively speaking of course). "Yes it does have bearing, Corporal. It shows that you have a complete disregard for departmental policies *then and now*. You have searched my desk and the personal contents inside the drawers and have also searched my locker all without my permission, my presence or even a warrant."

The locker was a super, wild ass guess, but by the shocked look on her face, I knew I was right. Keeping the momentum, I began to twist my imaginary knife. "And then there's the violation of failing to notify me 24 hours in advance that I was under investigation. You have also failed to tell me what the allegation is and who filed the complaint. Because of those two violations of general orders, you have denied me the opportunity to seek legal or union representation."

I hadn't given her the chance to tell me what the allegations are or who filed the complaint. The reason I did this was to forestall Hamerick's first move which would have been to make me sign a legal document called the 'Garrity Warnings.' Signing that document would obligate me to cooperating with an administrative investigation or risk termination of employment. I needed time to find out who talked to the media; therefore, I had to keep the pressure on and get out of this meeting without writing a statement or signing any paperwork.

I knew that Hamerick was a good officer and very aggressive. But she didn't think fast on her feet. I'd have to hit Hamerick so hard with a counter allegation that she wouldn't know how to respond. The *coup de grace* I gave was short and ugly (but it worked). I said, "Also Corporal, the fact you did fail to inform me of the allegations *before* you searched my desk and locker tells me – as I'm sure it will tell my lawyers – that you and your IAD buddies have no idea what you are looking for. This means that IAD is on a fishing expedition which *violates* Court Law concerning Internal Affairs Investigations and the Law Enforcement Officers' Bill of Rights!"

Standing up and looking her in the eyes, I said, "Quite frankly, I'm not sure what pisses me off more, the newspaper article or you people being here disrupting this high profile investigation. I wonder what the media would do with *this* information?"

As I walked out of the office I turned and said, "One last thing. I am a Sergeant and you are a *Corporal*. In this department we have an established chain of command and rank structure. If you ever again call me by my first name while on duty, I'll file an insubordination charge against you. Am I clear, *Corporal?*" I didn't wait for her to answer – I couldn't, I had to get my butt out of there fast.

The only thing that I had succeeded in doing with Hamerick (other than really ticking her off) was putting her temporarily off balance and buying me some time. She would come after me later with the tenacity of a bull dog. As I walked back into our office area, I saw that the rest of the team at their desks waiting for me. As I mentioned, more than likely they had used some of the same cards that I'd just played. They all knew the same thing that I did; we were in some deep shit.

Tex turned to Lieutenant Saxen and said, "Ma'am, do we know who filed the complaint with IAD? We all know the allegation was an unauthorized release of information to the public – that's a no brainer, but who actually made the complaint?"

Mom answered saying, "The only answer I got when I asked that question was that the complaint came directly from the office of the Chief of Police."

Wow! IAD had really screwed the pooch on this one. Because the Chief of Police must decide punishment for violations this severe, he technically cannot file a complaint against an officer. Chief Wong would've had to make the complaint or even the Assistant Chief of Police, but not Smyth. This *really was* a clear violation of general orders and the Law Enforcement Officers' Bill of Rights. Maybe IAD would *not* be back anytime soon.

Mom was saying, "All right guys, I know that no one here talked to the press. So the question is, who did?"

I asked, "Ma'am, is it possible that Dr. Gaspar leaked the story? In the article he seemed pretty pissed at us."

Mom replied, "Possible, but not likely, Ren. The FBI would neuter an agent for volunteering the specifics of a case. While Gaspar's a jerk and a prick he isn't stupid."

I wasn't so sure about that. Still, in spite of what Mom had just said, I knew she would be calling the FBI and reading them the riot act over what Gaspar *had* said.

Rubbing his temples, Chief Wong said, "Hill, you've got a buddy at the department's Police Information Office. Contact him and see what he knows. Tex, make a call to IAD and talk to your old patrol partner. Find out what this was really about. IAD is a pain in ass, but they know better than to start an investigation with what little they had. Ren, call Steve Burt and ask him to come by, please. PIU needs to know what just happened. When he gets here, bring him up to speed. Miller, call Hansen at the ME's office and make sure she knows we didn't release this crap to the media. Just so ya'll know, I'll be at the District Attorney's office letting them know we didn't talk."

We should have been working our murder case. Instead, we spent the rest of the day making calls and following false leads to find out where the media leak had occurred. Jon's call to Police Information was fruitless. They were as angry and baffled as we were. The officers assigned to the Police Information office are very well trained and take a lot of pride in their jobs. They wouldn't release the details of an ongoing investigation without sanitizing the information first.

Tex's old partner was assigned to the late shift at IAD. He informed Tex (out of school, of course – he was one of the good IA investigators) that the IAD head honcho, Chief Winn, had gotten reamed by Smyth about the newspaper article and ordered him to open an internal investigation. While this answered the question of why IAD had come here half-cocked, we still didn't know where the leak came from. I talked to Steve Burt and Rocky Connor at PIU. Steve said that they were working on something for us and that they would come by tomorrow morning.

It was after six when the team called it a night. The events of today had been a terrible distraction and the only thing we would accomplish by staying late would be to aggravate ourselves and each other. We're a great team, make no mistake about it, but even great teams have their limits and we were hitting ours. This was the fifth day of this case and even though we were working hard (excluding today), we had nothing significant to show for our efforts. Making things more frustrating, the reporter, Ian Webb had even managed to slip in the idea (promoted by Television shows like CSI) that a homicide case that isn't cracked within seventy-two hours of the murder isn't going to be solved. Of course that's a load of garbage but people, even police officers, believe that crap. The problem is, while I may enjoy picking that type of stuff apart, we can't escape the fact that we *were on day five*. Our killer had struck again just yesterday in Cedar Hill. Most serial killers had 'cooling off periods' some as long as ten or more years. Our guy (or gal) had no obvious pattern.

Jon Hill had summed it up the best when he said, "The only thing consistent about when our serial killer strikes, is that he seems to be consistently inconsistent and maybe that's the pattern."

Jesus, just thinking about it made me dizzy.

Tex dropped me off at the house and after loving on Danner for a few minutes, I went inside to shower up. Because of the injury I was still several days away from being able to work out. Even though I was feeling a lot better, I knew that one screw up could really set me back. Heading to my room I saw a note from Rick telling me that he was going to be staying with Father Leopole for the next week while he investigated Lanton's relationship with church members. Crap, I really didn't want to eat alone, so I showered up and headed over to Chili's for a quick meal and a beer. I would still be eating by myself, but at least I would be surrounded by people.

Chili's Cedar Hill

I found a table in the bar area and took a seat. Even though I didn't hang out here, I knew the lead bartender, most of the waiters and waitresses as well as the evening bar room clientele. A fair number of the customers (fairly drunk by now) knew I was a cop so they gave me a wide berth. I had just ordered my dinner when I saw Mom (Lieutenant Saxen) walk in and head my direction.

I stood up and said, "Good evening Ma'am, ah, I mean Rachel – care to join me?" Even off duty it was difficult for me to call her by her first name.

Rachel replied, "Sure I'm not intruding?"

I looked around and shrugged saying, "Rick's with Father Leopole tonight and this place won't let Danner in the door – so it's just me."

Smiling slightly Rachel said, "Nice to know I rate between a celibate priest and a dog."

Oh shit! I said, "Rachel that is *not* what I meant. Of course you're welcome to join me."

Grabbing the menu she sat down and began to read. After a minute of uncomfortable silence Rachel blurted out, "In two months, I leave CAPERS for an assignment with the Family Violence Unit. I've been with CAPERS a year longer than most lieutenants get to stay."

Rachel had said all this so fast I had to do a replay in my mind to understand what she'd told me. Finally as it sank in I asked, "Other than the case we're stuck with, is this why you've been on edge?"

Rachel replied, "On edge? What makes you *think* I've been on edge?"

I knew I should keep my mouth shut and wave off answering that question but I couldn't. For the last week she'd used me as her whipping post and I was tired of it. "Yes, you've been on edge or at least acting that way! Every time I turn around you've hammered me with put-downs, dirty looks and last week at dinner here at Chili's you didn't say ten civil words to me. What have I done to deserve this?"

Standing up Rachel said, "Other than the fact that you're an immature, dimwitted, arrogant asshole – I guess you've done nothing!"

I could have said a thousand other things at that moment but all that came out of my mouth was, "I'm not dimwitted."

Rachel spun around and headed for the door. Were those tears I saw in her eyes?

An hour later I was still sitting there trying to figure out what had just happened between Rachel and I. Suddenly the bartender, Janice, sat down next to me. Janice was fifty something years old and treated most cops that came into her bar like the kids she never had. Janice has lived a very hard, fast, life and it showed. She'd been married five or six times, smoked and, like most bartenders, she drank a lot. But that's what you saw on the outside. On the inside she had an absolute heart of gold. Over the years Janice had become a Dear Abby of sorts to dozens of police officers like me.

She had one golden rule: Whatever you said to her stayed with her – she would never break a confidence.

I looked up at her and said, "Hey, babe. I really upset Rachel... again. This whole last week has been tough and I can't figure out what I am doing wrong to make her so angry."

Janice took a long drag off her cigarette and then said, "Honey, you haven't done anything wrong. I know Rachel told you that she was transferring to another unit soon. Which means Renee, you're no longer safe."

She saw the question mark in my eyes and said, "Renee, sometimes you really are dimwitted. I'll spell it out for you dearest – while she is your Lieutenant you couldn't ask her out. She could like you and you could like her, but it couldn't go any further. Now it's anybody's ball game and she's scared."

Janice stood up and kissed me on the cheek and then said, "Renee, the day she transfers, you need to call her. Don't blow this chance to have something good in your life."

10:00 PM (that same night)
Southern Methodist University, Dallas Texas
McFarlin Auditorium

Rabbi Abraham Ezra took a deep breath and smiled. His presentation 'Contemporary Affects of the First Crusades' had been very well received tonight and in spite of his own worries that the presentation focused a bit too much on the corruption of the Catholic Church in 1096 AD, no one in the audience had seemed offended. One of three attending Catholic priest, Father Richard Shannon, had asked several good questions about Pope Urban II and his motivations behind the crusades. Ezra chuckled thinking about Father Shannon and the feisty – but never mean spirited – historical debates that they had shared in the past. Though they were of different religions and therefore maintained vastly dissimilar theological perspectives on historical events, he considered Shannon a friend and an excellent world-history sparring partner.

By the time Ezra had finished answering questions it was late and sleeting. For personal safety reasons, he hated being the last person to leave the building; but the parking lot was well lit and he wasn't parked very far from the doors. Muttering out loud he said, "Looks safe enough. Besides, only an idiot like me and the abominable snowman would be out on a night like this." Concentrating on walking to avoid falling on the now slick pavement, Ezra never heard his murderer walk up behind him.

Chapter 14

Thursday, 14 February

This time I was more than thankful when the phone rang at three in the morning. I had only thought that last night's dreams were bad. Tonight I had what I consider to be the worst of the worst. In my dream, actually my night-terror, I was back on the damnable sand dune in Iraq fighting the same Iraqi's in hand to hand combat. I've always wondered how many times I must kill the same enemy. How many times must I drive my bayonet into a body, taking the life of a man I had never met? And for Christ's sake, how many times do I have to watch my Marines die? I don't believe war is a sin (read the Old Testament if you disagree), but I do believe that great sin occurs during war. Maybe the nightmares are God's way of reminding us of this fact.

Before someone thinks that I'm just another suffering-basket-case military vet or cop, I'm not. There are very few people like me that want or need pity. A little understanding would be nice from time to time. However, with all the psycho-babble being preached from the medical community on Post Traumatic Stress Disorder (PTSD) it seems that 40% of all Americans suffer from this ailment. Point is, if everybody is special – then nobody is special. So why would anybody care about the Warriors in American society?

I'm not dismissing the psychological impact that a traumatic event, like a car wreck or being a victim of a brutal crime, can have on a person. I'm just not sure how the doctors can lump a car wreck victim in with a soldier that's been in sustained combat for days or weeks; or a cop that has just been forced to shoot and kill a person or the firefighter that survives an explosion that kills everyone around him. But lump them together, they do. Personally, I think that the doctors should remove all cops, firefighters and military people from the PTSD categorization. In WWI the doctors called psychological trauma 'Shell Shock' or 'Battle Fatigue.' Neither of those are a pretty clinical title like PTSD; but for us *Warriors*, they're much more accurate and therefore they should be used. Besides, we've earned the distinction so I think we should have it.

Glad to be awake, I reached for the phone and said, "Yeah, Tex, what's up?"

Tex replied with a sober, "Hey, partner. We've got another killing, this time at an SMU parking lot. The victim is a Jewish Rabbi by the name of Abraham Ezra. Sergeant Mark Smith's team is handling it; but based on what he was able to give me over the phone the Modus Operandi looks the same. Chief Wong wants us at the morning debrief."

I must have been quiet for a moment because Tex asked, "Ren, did you get all that?"

I answered, "Yeah, Tex, I was just wondering what this poor guy did to get whacked."

"The only person that can answer that question right now is the bastard that pulled the trigger. Maybe Smith's team will come up something we've missed," said Tex in a weary tone.

I fired back, "Doubtful. Smith's team is good; but so are we and we haven't missed anything. We just need a break."

"You're right, thanks for reminding me. One last thing… Look, you sounded like shit when you answered the phone. Level with me partner, are the dreams back? The really bad ones?"

I could have tried to lie but Tex was a combat veteran and would've seen through it, so I said, "Yeah… it was pretty bad tonight. They started again just the other night. Damn sheets are soaking wet."

Knowing not to push too hard, Tex said, "Okay pal…. why don't you talk to Pat? God knows she helped me with my Nam baggage."

Tex had made the offer more than once. I knew that Dr. Pat Beers was a very skilled psychologist. More importantly, she wasn't affiliated with the City of Dallas. After several long seconds of silence, I said, "If you think it will help."

Sounding more than just a little relieved, Tex replied, "I'll tell Pat. She'll want to talk to you as soon as possible. I know you haven't had much sleep, but why don't you go for a run? That always seems to help."

Less than fifteen minutes later Danner and I ran through the back gate at a near sprint. With each stride my back and side screamed with pain. It didn't matter. I needed to feel alive and running was my way of doing it.

Deep Ellum
Dallas Texas
5 AM

The late night poker game had just ended with Garret and Nolan losing about three grand apiece. To most cops losing that much money in something as insignificant as a poker game was unthinkable. However, to Garret and Nolan, the benefits outweighed the loss. Now that they worked in the Chief's office, they would quickly earn the money back with the selling of a few tidbits of classified information. Having advanced knowledge of where and when things – like dope and vice raids – are going to happen in the city made them valued commodities. Organized crime in Dallas wasn't big but what there was of it, paid very well. So while the booze and drugs were free as were most of the women at these clandestine parties, the most important aspect of attending such events were the 'social contacts' Garret and Nolan made. These contacts had kept them both out of prison several times over – knowledge cuts both ways.

After belching loudly as they walked to their car, Garret asked, "So we lost about what, six grand?"

Nolan replied, "Not sure. I think that sounds about right, though. We'll recover at least that much plus about double that again with the current information we have up for bid."

Garret said, "Yeah, Smyth's fear of liability and his micromanagement style of leadership has helped us."

Chuckling, Nolan said, "Everything passes through his office for approval."

At the beginning and end of each week the commanders of every division and bureau in the Dallas police department are required to email the Chief of Police a detailed overview of the progress of current police activities including all investigations. Because more than one commander in the last five years had been reassigned for failing to comply with this mandate, the overviews now looked a lot like doctorial dissertations with names, dates and times listed. This made for easy pickings for Garret and Nolan. In the old days, they would have had to develop dirt on officers assigned to critical units and then extort information from them. Nowadays, they just walked in and fired up the Chief's desktop computer – they had long since broken the password protection codes – and then pretty much took information as they pleased and sold it to the highest bidders.

Wiping fatigue from his eyes, Garret said, "Deep Ellum is really quiet this time of morning. I've got to take a leak. I'll be bac…"

Suddenly lifted completely off the ground and then slammed into the hood of his car, Garret grunted then lost control of his bladder. Nolan turned to see what the ruckus was when an arm shot across his neck and then clamped down cutting off blood flow to his brain. Within a second, Nolan dropped into unconsciousness across the hood opposite to Garret. As quickly as it had happened, the pressure on his neck was gone and Nolan slowly regained his senses. When he opened his eyes Nolan felt the cold steel of a gun barrel pressed against his ear, and simultaneously a hand reaching into his clothing removing his handgun from its concealed belt holster.

Nolan listened as the magazine was ejected and then cringed when he heard his gun tossed to the muddy ground.

In a slow southern drawl, Detective Steve Burt whispered into Nolan's ear, "Listen sunshine, you and your ugly friend are in deep shit with us. Unfortunately for us, we don't have time to worry about you right now – maybe later. At this moment, what we want to know is who released the information to the media on the Lanton case?"

Foolishly, more angry than scared, Nolan replied, "Piss off assholes!"

"Well now that's just the wrong answer, precious."

Nolan watched, stunned, as Garret was jerked away from the car hood and then, head first, smashed back down again three times in rapid secession. Nolan heard Garret's nose break and nearly vomited as blood began spewing from Garret's nose.

"Your friend is having a terrible morning, so you want to try again, Buttercup, before your morning goes to shit, too?"

Like most bullies, when they're confronted by a superior predator, Nolan knew when to give up and said, "The information came from Smyth himself. We were there when he was talking to the reporter Ian Webb – I swear to God! He said it would make CAPERS work harder!"

Pressing Nolan's face harder against the hood, Burt said, "Ok dearest, one last question. The stuff you took from Lanton's house, where is it?"

Whimpering, Nolan answered, "Sitting on the floor of the Chiefs office – piled up in a corner."

Smiling, Burt said, "We don't have time for you right now – but we'll be back to collect the garbage. In the meantime *do not interfere with CAPERS again.*" Stepping away from Nolan, Burt said, "Now, be a sweetheart and stay put for a sixty count. Partner, you ready to go?"

Releasing Garret to fall unconscious to the ground, Conner walked around the car and grabbed Nolan by the back of the belt and the scruff of his neck. Conner replied, "Just a second."

With a feral grin on his face, Conner quickly lifted and then hammered Nolan three times face first onto the hood of the car. Blood spurted from Nolan's own nose and mouth. Connor said, "Ok, now I'm ready to go."

Dropping a dazed Nolan back onto the hood, Steve Burt and Rocky Conner walked off talking. Looking a bit chagrined, Connor said, "Sorry about that, Steve. You know how I like things to be symmetrical. Now they match."

Quietly laughing, Burt said, "As long as you're happy big guy, I'm happy too!"

Walking quietly for a moment, Connor said, "Back in 1992, Dallas had a major scandal with two officers nicknamed Cruiser and Bruiser. I don't remember their real names. What they were doing was taking money from dope dealers in exchange for information on when SWAT was gonna hit a narcotics raid. For nearly a year SWAT would raid a dope house only to find it vacant. No rhyme or reason as to why the dopers had fled. I talked to some of our SWAT buddies and the same thing is going on again. Methinks Garret and Nolan are the new Cruiser and Bruiser."

Burt said, "I agree but there's a problem. These two shit-birds work directly for the Chief of Police. This almost makes them off limits. Look, the Chief of Police is a bit different, but he's always struck me as a fair and honest, by the book guy. I can't believe that he would intentionally protect those two. We need to run this by our boss and, if he agrees, I think we need to give up this information to Chief Wong, too. Besides, we also have the answer as to who made the press release. You know, after touching that asshole, I feel like I need to take a shower."

Watching Burt out of the corner of his eye, Connor replied, "Jesus Steve, if that's what it takes to get you to shower we need to make a daily appointment with those two!"

7:45 AM Dallas Police Headquarters / CAPERS

I made it back to the house with just enough time to shower, get dressed and feed Danner before Tex picked me up. We got to the office just a few minutes before Sgt. Smith and his team started the briefing.

Sipping coffee, Tex said, "Pat wants to see you Saturday morning at 11:00. She'll meet you at her Cedar Hill clinic. She said to bring her a Starbucks coffee; light on the sugar and heavy on the cream. Said you would be there about two maybe three hours. I'll come by around 10:30 and take Danner for a run at Mount Lebanon."

I sighed heavily, and said, "Thanks Tex. Last night was a real bitch and…"

Before I could finish my sentence Jon Hill, Todd Miller, Mom and Chief Wong walked in together and sat down. Mom gave me a hard look and said, "Are you alright?"

As I started to answer, Tex spoke up, "He's fine, Lieutenant. The moron got up way before the sun and ran too far and too hard. With a very sore back and side to boot – tell me Ren, are you still whizzing blood?"

I knew what Tex was doing and I loved him for it (in a guy sort of way). By redirecting the question, Tex had taken the focus off the shell shock and put it on me running while injured.

Mom looked dubious at best but said, "Fine. Ren if you're still hurting by Monday I want you to see a doctor."

Tex said, "Already taken care of Ma'am. He's seeing a doctor Saturday morning. I made the appointment myself."

After several more minutes of idle conversation, Sgt. Smith and his team began briefing us on the latest shooting. "Our victim is named Rabbi Abraham Ezra. White male, 56 years of age. The shooting occurred in the parking lot outside the McFarlin Auditorium on the SMU campus sometime between the hours of ten and midnight. The body was found by SMU campus police officers at five minutes past midnight. We were contacted and arrived on scene at one in the morning."

Sergeant Smith is an excellent supervisor and runs a good team of investigators, but his monotone voice was enough to put even the worst hyperactive child (namely me) to sleep.

Burning my tongue as I took a large sip of coffee, I refocused my attention as Smith was saying, "At first glance, the elements of the crime look the same as what ya'll are dealing with on the Lanton case; however, my team and I have some serious doubts that this is the same shooter."

Suddenly I was wide awake and hanging on every word Smith said. "After we got the call, I pulled the file on Lanton and the corresponding cases. As a side-note, Lieutenant Saxen, I think all the other supervisors in CAPERS need to read up on what Sergeant Beer's team is dealing with. It would have saved me some time this morning had I been more familiar with the other cases from the start. Anyway, the reasons we do not believe our shooters are the same person is as follows: First, while the victim was shot three times in the head, the bullet pattern is scattered, not well grouped. Contrary to *the other* cases, this shows a lack of expertise with the weapon. Second, the rounds struck Ezra in the back of the head, not the front or side of the head as in the other cases. Third, it appears that the caliber of handgun used was much higher – the front of Ezra's head was nearly blown off with the exit wounds. And fourth; the posing and postmortem knife wound both appeared to be haphazard at best. Also, the knife was inserted *through* the clothing not under the clothing. Points three and four indicate the shooter might be squeamish about touching a dead body. Tex, your shooter does not seem to have that phobia."

After a moment, Tex said, "Mark the Modus Operandi in all of these cases is slightly different. This could be accidental and based on exterior factors like time and opportunity. What if this *is* our shooter and he is *intentionally* changing his Modus Operandi just enough to screw with us?"

No one has ever said that a serial killer had to be stupid. In fact, the truth is just the opposite. While it is not a hard fast rule, many serial killers are highly intelligent men and women that integrate well into society. These types of predators have to be intelligent – at least on a primal level – to avoid getting caught and to lure and trap new victims. The FBI places these killers into three categories – Organized, Disorganized and Mixed. Some killers change from being organized to disorganized, as their need progresses. At the start, these killers will carry out careful and methodical (organized) murders, but become careless and impulsive (disorganized) as their blood lust takes over their lives.

This is fairly common knowledge with homicide teams so I asked, "Is it possible the killer is losing control and shifting from an organized killer to a disorganized killer? The more impulsive this person gets, the more likely he is to make a mistake."

Sergeant Smith shrugged and said, "Ren, you and Tex may be right; however, based on the media doodling us with that article, I think what my team is dealing with is a copy cat."

Shifting a little uncomfortably on his feet Smith continued saying, "Ren, there's one more detail. We looked at the lecture attendee list and your friend Father Shannon was on it. He isn't a suspect of course, but maybe he saw someone or something that might help. We would like to talk to him ASAP."

I wasn't surprised that Rick was there. Rick and I both are members of every historical society in this region. When Rick is in town we are constantly going to historical lectures and conferences together. Rick and I had even tried a Civil War reenactment club once. We got asked not to come back because right in the middle of a major engagement we got the giggles when my musket misfired and covered my face in black soot making me look like a Vaudeville actor (*How I love ya, How I love ya Mamieee*).

Anyway, I would have been with him last night if it had not been for the Lanton case. I said, "Mark, I'll call him as soon as we're done here. Maybe he saw something and we'll get lucky." Left unsaid but in the back of my mind was Rick telling me about the suspect 'sentencing' his victims before shooting them. I still wasn't sure that I had mentioned that to him.

After the meeting broke up, I sat at my desk thinking about Rick and what I hoped to be nothing but coincidences. Growing frustrated after losing track several times, I grabbed a pen and paper and began to make a list: One, Rick had been in Houston during the Redcliff trial and murder. Two, he had been on the road supposedly to Dallas when Riggs was shot. Three, Rick showed up at our house less than twenty four hours after Lanton was killed. The drive from Houston to Dallas wasn't very far; so being at the house that quickly was no great feat. What I could not set aside, is Rick not conducting a follow-up investigation in the murder of Redcliff. Rick is too good of an investigator to ignore the murder of a priest (even a monster like Redcliff) – unless he wanted to distance himself from the crime. Four, he was out very late the night Joshua and his brother were killed. Five, Rick was staying with Leopole and Kothner the night Whitehouse was killed.

All this was interesting – but circumstantial at best. I felt a knot in my stomach the size of a large rock. Rick was certainly capable of killing – in his prior life he had been the ultimate apex killer. But he had set that life aside.

Circumstantial in no way was conclusive proof. But people had been convicted with just a little bit more information and no bodies. In our case, we had lots of information *and* the ability to tie it all together, but no clear suspect to put the murders on. We also have bodies in abundance giving new definition to the meaning of Habeas Corpus (yes *judge, we can bring you the body. Exactly which one would you like to see?*) Crap! And wasn't Father Kothner still a person of interest? Reaching for the phone, I called Rick's cell and ended up leaving a message for him to call me.

Waiting until the office cleared for lunch, I walked over and checked Chief Wong's office door. Normally Wong always locked the door behind him; but today he had been running late to a meeting and had apparently forgotten. Acting like I knew what I was doing (just in case someone got back from lunch early), I causally walked into the Chief's office and went to the cabinet where the Interpol cases were filed. The file cabinet was ancient and the locks had long since become nonfunctional so I didn't have to worry about tossing the locks. I quickly looked back over my shoulder and opened the cabinet. Taking the Interpol folder directly to the copy machine I made copies of all the case notifications in the file and then quickly returned the folder to the cabinet. Could I have done all this by simply asking the Chief to see the file? Yes, probably, but I might have had to tell him why before I was ready and there was something I had to check before I said anything to anyone.

CHAPTER 15

1:30 PM Dallas Police Headquarters / CAPERS

I spent the rest of lunch on my personal laptop pulling up archived email Rick had sent to me during his overseas travels. I'm not sure why I save every email I get – I just do. In Rick's case, I rarely knew exactly what he was doing in his duties, but I almost always knew where he was at any given time. I had the Interpol reports spread out on my desk and cross referenced the dates and locations of the murders with the emails. They matched up perfectly. In most situations when something like this was discovered, there was a euphoric feeling attached to the discovery. Something like this meant the case might very well be cracked. Instead of euphoria, I felt sick to my stomach... Very sick to my stomach!

It was well after lunch when Burt and Connor walked in and asked to have a meeting with Mom and the team. Thirty minutes later we all sat with our mouths hanging open after hearing what Burt and Connor had to say.

Hill asked, "Steve, is it possible that Nolan was lying?"

Burt replied, "Sure, but I seriously doubt it. He and Garret were in no position to lie."

Mom said, "Okay... I'm not going to ask exactly what that means, Detective Burt. None of this makes any sense. Why would the Chief of

Police compromise a murder investigation that he wants us to solve immediately?"

Frustrated, Miller said, "Ma'am, are we sure the Chief wants this solved? I mean every time we turn around he does something that seems to thwart our efforts – including threatening to transfer us if we don't solve the case. And let's not forget Ren getting his ass beat!"

Attempting to break the tension, Hill popped off with, "I must confess that I really enjoyed your pain and discomfort Ren – and I wished it had lasted a little longer but I agree with Todd. What exactly is going on here?"

I heard the team laughing at Jon's joke but I just sat there thinking. I knew I had to clue everyone in on my discovery. I wished like crazy that I could have run this by Tex first. He might be able to find flaws in my research that would exclude Rick from our investigation. There just wasn't time. It was several long seconds before I realized that everyone in the room was looking at me.

I said, "I ah... I might have something. I don't know what's up with the Chief. Or Garret and Nolan for that matter, but..."

It took a good solid hour to lay out what I had discovered. Repeating the research I had already done, Mom had me print up all the old emails I had archived from Rick. We then took the Interpol reports, put them out in order by date and then matched them to the emails. We also did an overlay of the times and dates Rick was in Houston with the murder report of Father Redcliff.

I didn't notice when Wong returned from his meeting. I looked up and suddenly he was there. He and I locked eyes. Sputtering, I said, "Chief, I ah... I went into your office and..."

Before I could finish Chief Wong held up his hand and said, "I understand Ren. I know it won't happen again. So let's just drop it."

That's what I meant when I said that as long as we got results Wong would let things go that most Chiefs would have a fit over. Besides, I'm sure Chief Wong knew that what I'd discovered was punishment enough.

As we continued to work, Wong took a few minutes to gather his thoughts, then said, "I can't speak on the Houston or the Interpol cases, though the correlation of that data from those cases is very convincing, if circumstantial. However, assigning Lanton, Whitehouse, Alexander, Jones and now Ezra to Father Shannon – I just don't know. But we don't have anything better other than Kothner. So here's what I want done. Detectives Burt and Connor, I know we should turn this over to the Criminal Investigations Division; but, I don't like the idea of involving yet another investigative team in this current mess. We can't regain the initiative here by turning the leg work over to someone else. Anyway, I spoke to your boss at lunch during our weekly Commanders meeting and he's good with you two working for me for the duration of this investigation. I want you two to find and then follow Father Shannon. LaFleet, where's Shannon staying?"

I had to stop and think for a moment, then answered, "Rick left me a note yesterday. He's staying with Leopole and Kothner for a week while he interviews members of Lanton's congregation."

Wong said, "Good. That should at least make finding him a bit easier. Detectives Hill and Miller, I want you two to follow Kothner. If Kothner and Shannon leave together, Burt, you and Connor have lead. Beers since you're the team supervisor, you and LaFleet follow Burt and offer support should they require it. We won't be able to keep this type of surveillance up for very long. Assuming that the Ezra murder might be a copy cat, it's been since Monday that our murderer last struck in Cedar Hill. Point is, we're due. If we don't turn anything following these guys tonight, we'll bring in some extra help from Criminal Investigations. One last thing, Detective LaFleet, I know that Father Shannon and you are very close friends and that you have a long history with him dating back to your military days. What can you tell us about Father Shannon's military background and skills?"

How do you tell your friends and fellow police officers that there is not a person in the room (with the exception of me – and that's when I am healthy) that could possibly take Rick in a no-holds barred fight? That their only hope of survival is to shoot and kill him before he got physically close or in handgun range? They simply could not understand the level of skill, brutality and violence that Rick and I could unleash. I felt the best way to handle this question was to start at the beginning when Rick and I first met.

Only Tex knew the full story and though I hated dredging up those memories, my team needed to know what they might be facing.

When I finished speaking, Chief Wong asked, "Detective, please understand that I have to ask. Can you remain objective in this investigation?"

I looked around the room before answering. I wasn't sure if I saw doubt or pity in the eyes of my peers. "Yes sir, I'll be fine. If it gets to be a problem, you have my word, I'll speak up."

What else could I have said? Rick was the brother of my heart and I owed him a debt beyond life. If he had become sick and needed to be stopped, then I should be a part of his arrest or his death. I would be the one that put him down.

Everyone started walking toward the door when I blurted out, "Chief there's one more thing."

Stopping and turning to look at me Wong gestured that I should keep talking.

"Sir, from the start we've been trying to figure out why Chief Smyth has been so involved with this investigation. At first, we thought he was trying to push it along to get the murder solved to avoid media attention on the Catholic church. Hence his frustration with me and the butt kicking I took when we had no immediate results. But what if he… what if he suspected all along that the killer was another priest like Rick or Kothner? What if he was doing everything possible to screw up the investigation to avoid a scandal?"

Shaking his head no, Wong said, "How would he have reached that conclusion? And the timing is off. We just now included Father Shannon as a person of interest. I understand what you are saying detective; however,…" Shrugging his shoulders Wong stopped talking.

Somewhat heatedly, Burt said, "Chief, I hate to agree with Ren. But how Chief Smyth knows what we are thinking isn't hard to figure out – at least where Kothner is concerned. By policy the Chief of Police gets constant updates from all division and bureau commanders *including* you, sir. The son of a bitch knows every detail of this investigation through those updates. Also, he has a very strong investigative background himself, so knowing what we're going to do next would be easy to figure out, plan for and negate."

Without pause, Hill immediately interjected, "This theory, if true, could explain a lot. Back when he thought Lanton was just a random murder, the Chief of Police wanted a good investigative team with *someone on the team* with close ties to the Catholic church – like us with Ren. And though the timing is off with Ren getting injured – he got hurt earlier the same day we began to consider Kothner a person of interest; there is a strong possibility that when Nolan and Garret ransacked Lanton's house they found the other diaries we suspect Lanton kept."

Miller said, "And if those diaries included the same information about a close friend '*showing a tragic decline of rational thought*' or if he actually used Kothner's name, then the Chief would have certainly pieced this crap together."

Chief Wong said, "Okay. I'm still not a hundred percent convinced you're right. Too many if's. But a lot of what you've said makes sense, especially with that press release coming from the Chief's office. If this theory is correct, I'll be talking to the District Attorney very soon."

The meeting finally ended and we all headed to our homes to get personal items that we would need during the surveillance.

4:00 PM. The residence of Father Michael Leopole.

Father Mike Leopole thought for a moment, then said, "Rick, the fact that Renee needs to talk to you immediately, tells me that they've tied you to the location of Ezra's murder. If they've done their work, and we know that at least young Renee might be able to piece things together – including your travels, you might now be a person of interest, if not a suspect."

In a subdued tone Rick replied, "Quite frankly, I would've been surprised if Ren hadn't begun to put it together. I've watched for years as people dismissed him as a big dumb jock. What they fail to understand is just how intelligent the guy is. Anyway, how much he has figured out is anyone's guess but from here on out we walk a hazardous path. After Cedric

Redcliff, I should have left the States for a few months but Father Lanton needed our attention."

Listening to the conversation, Father Kothner interjected, "Not that I don't appreciate you being here Rick but we could have handled Lanton ourselves. Father Mike, we could simply shut down and return to Rome for a period of time. Especially you, Rick, you have no ties to this area other than your friendship with Renee."

All three men sat quietly for several minutes. Finally breaking the silence, Father Leopole said, "Yes, we could leave but our mission here is far too important to just give up." Putting up his hand to forestall Karl's retort, Leopole continued saying, "I know that you're not advocating us quitting our mission, Karl – just backing off for awhile. Unfortunately, we simply cannot let things continue as they are. People's lives and souls are at stake."

5:00 PM Kessler Park

Surveillance duty sucks ass. Hollywood makes sitting in a car watching people (or a house) look glamorous and cool but the truth is just the opposite. The car is always cramped; your partner always has gas or halitosis (sometimes both); you've always got to pee and worst of all, it's simply boring as hell!

We parked a block from Leopole and Kothner's residence. Hill and Miller set up at the far end of the block with Conner and Burt stationed two blocks over to the south. Tex kept the engine running and the heater going on low. The weather had really gotten nasty again so we had the car windows only three or four inches down instead of all the way down. That's an old patrol trick that allows us to stay semi-warm but also allows us to hear outside noises. Back in the 1960's and 1970's more than one officer had been murdered while writing a report or sleeping in his or her patrol car with the windows rolled up and the 'good-time' radio on.

Officers are now trained to keep their heads on a swivel looking for people trying to sneak up on the car. Civilians often get upset when they approach a patrol car and have an officer demand that they stay back – usually in a very loud harsh voice. What the citizen doesn't know is that, if the officer is smart, he also has his duty weapon out and is, quite literally, ready for a gun fight. People don't realize that a suspect shooting into a car is like shooting fish in a barrel.

Anyway, safety habits learned on patrol die hard, hence the reason Tex and I had the heater running and we were drinking hot coffee to stay warm. Of course the down side to all this hot coffee is that we would eventually have to take a bathroom break – probably at the most inopportune moment.

Tex was watching the house and I was working a cross-word puzzle book for beginners. I have always held a secret hope that someday I would graduate to a higher level of crossword puzzle proficiency but I think God enjoys watching me struggle too much to grant that desire. Looking at my crossword puzzle, I said, "Damn, it doesn't fit."

Not even taking the time to glance over at me, Tex said, "Ok. I know I'm going to regret this, but I'll ask - what doesn't fit?"

I answered, "I need an eleven letter word for fantasy and Uma Thurman doesn't fit – only ten letters."

Shaking his head Tex said, "Put her middle initial 'K' in between her first name and her last name and it will work."

Filling in the boxes, I said, "Cool, it fits! How did you know that?"

Shrugging and yawning at the same time, Tex replied, "You have to know that kind of useless shit when you're a lead investigator."

There are people that would think, based on our joking around and casual attitude, that we are not taking the situation with Rick and Kothner seriously. Not true. Cops see so much bad stuff that we learn the best way to deal with it - is not to deal with it. Meaning we cover up our emotions with childish, sardonic humor, drugs, alcohol or sex. Sex would be my first choice but since I rarely if ever score, I am forced to resort to childish, sardonic humor to hide my emotions (*chew on that one, Doctor Phil*). Plainly put, I just didn't want to think about Rick being a murderer right now – so any conversation off that subject was okay with me.

Rolling his eyes, Tex said, "What is it about Uma Thurman that you like so much? If she got on an elevator with you, you wouldn't even recognize her!"

Putting on a look of mock-sorrow, I said, "You're right Tex. I wouldn't recognize her... I mean she's changed so much since I *dumped* her!" Laughing at my own little joke, I said, "She looked awesome in the movie the 'Producers' and then she looked like a hot psycho scary monster woman in 'Kill Bill.' So I guess you're right. I wouldn't recognize her. Anyway, I just like the name Uma."

Tex said, "And the fact that she looks like Lieutenant Rachel Saxen is just a minor coincidence?"

Damn it, any conversation *but* that one! Trying to keep the frustration out of my voice, I asked, "Is it that obvious?"

Chuckling, Tex said, "To everyone but you and her. Look, you know she transfers soon to the Family Violence Unit. Do us all a favor and ask her out once she transfers."

Taking a deep breath and exhaling slowly, I said, "Janice over at Chili's said pretty much the same thing."

Tex replied "You should listen to Janice. She's counseled more cops than any ten family counselors I know. Pat says Janice has the truest heart for people she's ever seen."

Shifting to get comfortable in his seat, Tex said, "We've beaten around the bush enough. Ren, I know this thing with Shannon is kicking your ass. And I'm sorry for what may happen with all this. I keeping hoping that we're dead wrong but even though the evidence is circumstantial, *it is compelling*. And you saw those pictures of victims beaten to death down in Houston. Based on my Nam experience, I know that as a Navy SEAL, he's fully capable of sowing death in a hellish manner. Still, I just can't believe that the Rick Shannon we know is capable of *wanton murder*."

I looked at Tex and tried to reply but I had to keep fighting back the tightness in my throat. Finally I managed to say, "I don't know what to think. Rick has seemed very tired and distracted since he got back into town; but I..."

Seeing movement at the front of Leopole's house, I grabbed the radio handset and said, "CAPERS-133 to CAPERS-139 and Union-449. The two subjects and a third person – Father Michael Leopole have exited the residence."

Tex fed me information as he watched them through binoculars. I repeated the information saying, "They've gotten in three separate vehicles. Union-449, your target vehicle is a dark blue Dodge Caliber license Texas 436Jack-Mary-Paul, that's 436JMP. CAPERS-139, your target vehicle is a black Nissan Xterra license Texas 552X-ray-George-Henry, that's 552XGH. Union-449, your target vehicle has turned south and is now headed your way. CAPERS-139, you should have visual on your target vehicle by now. Union 449, we'll slowly catch up and are going to cold trail (follow at a distance) you."

Connor replied, "Union-449 to CAPERS-133, 10-4, we have a visual on our target vehicle. I'll call directions. It's getting pretty dark outside, Burt says you can close with us."

After Tex had read the plates to me he dropped the binoculars and began to drive.

Miller came on the radio and said, "CAPERS-139 to CAPERS-133, 10-4, we also have a visual on our target vehicle. He's just passed our position and appears to be heading for I-30 west bound. We've turned around and are closing with him."

I responded saying, "10-4 CAPERS-139. Unless it is an emergency, we'll stay in contact by cell. Good Luck. Union-449 we have you in sight."

Communicating via radio takes a lot of time, practice and forethought. When a rookie officer first hits the streets he spends a lot of time asking his Field Training Officer (FTO) to translate what was said over the radio. Over the years it does get easier, but even veteran officers sometimes have to ask for clarification. That's why our radio communication is kept short and to the point – too much verbiage and the listener loses the information. Also, the radio is literally our life-line should we need emergency assistance so you don't want to tie up the radio with a lot of nonsensical chatter.

Northbound Interstate 35.

Traffic was thick but not horrendous, so the last forty-five minutes of driving had been uneventful. The target vehicle, driven by Father Rick Shannon, had progressed at a steady pace northbound on I-35. When Shannon's signal light came on indicating that he was leaving the highway, Connor pressed the radio handset call button and said, "Union-449 to CAPERS-133 unless he turns off , it looks like he's heading to the University of North Texas campus. His driving continues to be smooth and steady, so I don't believe we've been burned. CAPERS-133, do you have any idea where he might be heading?"

Listening to Connor I looked at Tex and said, "Don't count on us not being burned. Unless he has his head up his ass, Rick is far too skilled not to have noticed a tail."

Tex agreed. I put the mike to my mouth and spoke, "10-4, my guess would be Willis Library – it's in the middle of the campus. Once every few months he meets with leaders from several other Christian faiths to discuss interfaith cooperation. We're pulling off and parking on Avenue C, ya'll follow him in. We'll let Channel five (Northwest Patrol Division) dispatch know where we are as well as the Denton and University police."

Tex and I pulled into a small parking lot and began our wait. I really wanted to move in where I could see Rick; however, one car following him would not necessarily catch his attention if we had not already been burned, but two cars mirroring his every move most certainly would.

6:00 PM Willis Library, University of North Texas, Denton Texas

As Father Shannon exited his car, Burt and Connor parked at the far end of the lot. Close enough to see Shannon by binoculars; but far enough away to avoid being spotted. Or at least they thought.

Father Shannon took the cell phone from his coat pocket and hit speed dial. When the phones connected, Shannon stopped walking and spoke quietly. "I've arrived at my target location. As you surmised, I was followed, as I believe Father Karl was."

Listening to the voice on the other end, Shannon continued his walk toward the doors of the library as Father Leopole said, "Well, there isn't much to be done about that now. Continue on with your assignment. The chairwoman for your meeting tonight is extremely controversial of late. She's far too vocal to be ignored. He probably already knows; however, I'll contact Karl and alert him – he should be at his assigned location by now. I've got about another ten minutes of driving before I get to my possible target. Call me when you're done."

Closing his phone Shannon walked into the building.

5:40 PM Radisson Dallas Central Hotel

"In a rush as usual – I should have been here all day," Father Kothner mused as he pulled into the parking lot at the Radisson hotel. As he got out of his car his cell phone buzzed. "Yes Father?" he said as he quickly walked toward the hotel entrance.

Leopole replied, "Just as we thought. Shannon was followed and since you're also a person of interest, you most likely were, too. Keep your eyes open and call me as soon as you're done. Also, don't forget to kill the hotel cameras for maintenance. You have the business security code and password. Tell them to keep it shut down for 48 hours."

Not stopping to spot where his tail had parked, Father Kothner entered the hotel lobby as he dialed the number to American Hotel Security Systems.

Radisson Dallas Central Hotel Conference Room

Retired Bishop George St. John was tired after a full day of activities and speeches. Though not a homosexual himself, he had been an advocate within the Episcopal Church for gay rights for over thirty years. Sometimes he felt as if the battle was being won and then at other times he thought otherwise. Tonight was one of those 'otherwise' times. The crowd had been attentive and even receptive to a point; but there was just no changing the minds and hearts of some people.

"Today 'I'm feeling all of my sixty years" St. John thought to himself as he prepared to make his closing presentation.

Two hours later St. John had shaken the hands of the last of well-wishers, packed up his laptop and then sat down for a moment to catch his breath before he headed for his car. He had contemplated spending the night at the Radisson but it was only a forty-five minute drive back to his house in Duncanville. Why spend all that money?

Sipping the last bit of water from his glass, St. John heard footsteps behind him. Expecting to see one of his many friends that had attended the conference, St. John was startled when he stood up, turned around and came face to face with a man dressed in priestly garb pointing a gun at him.

Father Kothner had stayed hidden in the back of the room listening patiently to the short speeches without being noticed. The subject was, fundamentally speaking, against everything he believed in. A few of the speakers were so graphic in their presentations about AIDS and HIV that Kothner wished he could leave. Kothner wasn't a bigot and really didn't care if another person was gay, but did these presentations have to include graphic safe sex practices and tips? Kothner realized the information and presentations were no worse than safe sex lectures given to heterosexual college students. Still the subject matter was… just so damn disturbing to a conservative priest like him.

After two long hours, the conference was over and the room finally emptied. Watching as St. John gathered his belongings and then sat down, Kothner slipped out of his hiding place and moved into a position where he could intercept St. John before he left the large conference room. Kothner had decided not to engage St. John out in the parking lot as originally planned – especially with the police watching him. The conference room was going to be his only opportunity unless he followed St. John home. And of course that wouldn't work for the same reasons. *"No,"* Kothner thought, *"it has to be here"*.

CAPERS-139

Seeing dozens of people leave the hotel at the same time, Hill and Miller surmised that the conference was over. "What do you want to do next, Jon?" Miller asked as he tried stretching his legs in the cramped car.

Having gone inside the hotel, Hill had found out about the conference and about the keynote speaker, George St. John. "Todd, I have to believe that Kothner is here to kill St. John. If you consider that all the other victims have been high profile, controversial, religious people, it makes some sense. I think we need to make contact immediately with St. John and escort him home. We can have patrol in Duncanville provide some security at his house. Kothner will split if he sees us before we can make the arrest. Check your handheld radio, we're in the Central Station area if we need help, that's Channel one."

Both men got out of the car and walked quickly into the hotel lobby heading for the conference room. They had just entered into the hallway leading to the conference room when three muffled shots rang out. Pausing only long enough to draw their duty weapons from beneath their jackets, Hill and Miller began to run.

One minute earlier inside the conference room

Kothner slowly walked along the far wall until he was parallel with St. John who was still seated, sipping ice water. The lights in the room had been turned down low during the last presentation and, for whatever reason, not turned back up.

"*Good,*" thought Kothner, "*this will shadow my movement should someone enter the room before I make contact with St. John. If someone does come in, I can drop down and use the tables to hide.*" Making ready to advance on St. John, Kothner heard the conference room door suddenly open. Looking away from St. John toward the door Kothner saw another priest enter the room and walk down to St. John. The priest pulled a handgun from a concealed holster at his waist and pointed it at St. John who was standing up and turning around to speak to the man.

Running toward the other priest, Kothner pulled his silenced .22 caliber handgun. "*Jesus wept*" he thought, "*this isn't the way it's supposed to happen!*"

The priest, hearing Kothner's running footsteps, turned and fired three times hitting Kothner in the right shoulder, right side and right leg. It's a myth that a bullet that weighs only an ounce can knock a man backward. Not understanding this law of physics, the priest held his position and started to fire a fourth time as Kothner's momentum carried him into a bone jarring impact with the assailant. As they collided, Kothner, knowing that he was seriously wounded and might lose conciseness quickly, did two things almost simultaneously.

First, he lashed out with a lighting quick strike hitting the gunman in the throat as they fell to the ground. The second thing he did was slide his own handgun far under the curtained stage. With any luck at all the police would fail to thoroughly search under the stage and Leopole or Shannon would retrieve the weapon later.

Falling onto his stomach, Kothner rolled over and saw that the priest was slowly getting to his feet, clutching his throat with his right hand and holding the gun in his left. Walking over to Kothner the man yelled, "This is God's work! You should not have interfered and for your interference you must die along with that other sinful bastard!"

Watching as his murderer raised the gun, Kothner wondered if St. John had survived. Kothner put his forearm across his eyes and began praying as he lost consciousness.

Hill and Miller reached the conference room. Hill pulled open the door as Miller button hooked through the opening. Hill did a cross over right behind Miller. A shoulder width apart and perfectly aligned, both men moved toward the front of the room in a tactical walk with knees slightly bent and weapons up. Going from a lighted hall way to a darkened room meant neither Hill nor Miller had time to acquire night vision. While they were not completely night-blind, Hill and Miller were struggling to see specific details. As they continued to move they could vaguely make out someone, probably Kothner, holding a gun standing over a body lying on the floor near a small stage. As they closed with the priest Miller began yelling verbal commands "Police officers, Kothner, drop the gun!"

Hearing the commands, the priest turned and made the last mistake of his life.

In law enforcement there is a rule of street survival known as 'lag time.' This rule says that an armed suspect (with a gun pointed at police or not) can turn and fire his weapon before an officer can identify the threat. So, when Hill and Miller saw the priest start to turn toward them, they immediately began firing their weapons as they continued to advance toward him.

Half a dozen rounds hit the man in the chest and face, dropping him to the ground. Hill scanned the room looking for other threats as Miller held his gun on the dead or dying man. Still covering the downed suspect, Miller reached for his radio with his free hand. Pressing the key he said, "CAPERS-139."

A moment later a female voice came back, "CAPERS-139 you're on Channel one. What's up?"

Taking a deep breath to calm the adrenalin rush, Miller said, "Yes Ma'am. We're in the conference room at the Radisson Hotel, 6060 N Central Expressway. My partner and I have been involved in a police shooting. We're good. Suspect is low sick (critically wounded), and might be 27 (dead). We have another wounded person needing immediate medical care. We need two, I say again two, ambulances. We also need a shooting team – CAPERS, IAD, CSR and probably the ME. We would also like legal representatives from the Dallas Police Association."

"10-4 CAPERS-139, ambulances are moving as is backup and a shooting team. And you guys are okay, right?"

Miller looked at Hill who shook his head yes and then said, "Yes Ma'am we're fine."

Still covering the suspect, Miller asked Hill to check the suspect for a pulse. Holstering his weapon, Hill approached the man who was lying on his side face down almost in a fetal position. First locating where the suspect's gun was in relationship to his body, making sure it was well out of the suspect's reach, Hill reached down and checked for pulse at the neck.

"Todd, he's 27."

Hill got up and moved over to St. John. Seeing the man's chest slowly move up and down Hill said, "This one's still alive." Reaching down and moving the man's arm from his face Hill stared for a moment and said, "Holy shit, Todd, this is Kothner! Who the hell is that?"

Miller quickly holstered his weapon and, on hands and knees, leaned forward to look at the dead man's face. "Christ Jon, don't tell me we killed St. John?"

Hearing a soft voice from under a table, both officers jumped to their feet and spun around re-drawing their weapons. "No officers, I'm St. John. I don't know who either of these men are, but that man saved my life."

CHAPTER 16

7:50 PM University of North Texas

Looking at nothing in particular as I stared out the car window, I said, "Tex, these meetings usually last three hours or more. Why don't we break off and hit a bathroom, get coffee and then relieve Burt and Connor so they can do the same?"

Nodding his head Tex said, "Yeah, it's probably a good idea to do all that before it gets any later. Besides, I really do have to take a whiz."

"I'll let Burt and Connor know what we're doing." But as I reached for the handset Northwest dispatch came on the radio.

"CAPERS-133 switch to Channel one, please."

I keyed the handset and replied, "10-4, CAPERS-133 is switching to Channel one." Turning the radio dial to Channel one (also known as the Central Patrol division) I said, "CAPERS-133 is on Channel one."

Central dispatch immediately responded, "CAPERS-133, CAPERS-139 is at the Radisson Dallas Central Hotel, 6060 N. Central Expressway. CAPERS-139 has been involved in a police shooting. Both officers are good. Suspect is 27 and there's another victim that's low sick at the shooting location. Ambulances and a shooting team are in route."

Keying the radio I said, "10-4. Please show us in route to that location."

Before I could even finish the sentence, my cell phone rang – it was Burt and Connor. Opening the phone I inquired, "Ya'll hear the news?"

164

Connor responded, "Yeah we got it. What does Tex want us to do?"

"Hang on a second, Rocky, I'll put 'ya on speaker phone and we can discuss it." I looked at Tex with raised eyebrows and said, "They need instructions."

Tex answered saying, "Rocky, you and Steve stay on Shannon. Follow Shannon – he may head home or he may head to the Radisson once he finds out about Kothner. When you know what he's doing, call me or Ren if we don't call you first. It looks as if our murderer really was Kothner. If Miller and Todd bagged him, there's no reason to stay on Shannon; however, this whole deal is so screwed up we'll stay with what we know for now. We'll be at the Radisson until late. When you leave Shannon, I may ask you to join us there or at the office. IAD and CAPERS are going to want statements from all of us about the surveillance. The sooner we get that done, the sooner we can wrap this case up and go home."

I closed the phone and sat quietly for several minutes as Tex pulled out onto I35 southbound. "Holy shit, Tex. It was Kothner all along."

I wasn't sure if I should be relieved that it wasn't Rick or upset that it was Kothner. I kept running all the murders over in my head and kept coming up with nothing but confusion. In frustration I stated, "Tex, I want it to be Kothner because I don't want the murderer to be Rick. But what about Interpol and the overseas murders? What about Rick being in Houston when Redcliff bought it?"

As Tex drove he sat listening to me ramble on. Finally he said, "Everything we have on Rick is circumstantial and, like you, I want Rick to be innocent. But I agree. None of this makes any sense. Shit!"

Keeping our thoughts to ourselves, we drove in silence the rest of trip.

8:35 PM
Radisson Dallas Central Hotel

Forty-five minutes, a major traffic jam and a lot of agitation later, we pulled into the Radisson parking lot. Media vehicles were parked everywhere and camera crews were filming even though no information had been released. The ambulances had long since left and the M.E. as well as the CSR had beaten us here. Both an indication of how long it had taken us to make the short drive.

As we made our way past the hotel lobby and into the conference room, we could see Sergeant Mark Smith talking to Jon Hill off to one side of the room and one of Smith's team members talking to Todd Miller on the other side of the room. Both Miller and Hill looked relaxed – which was actually a good sign. In law enforcement when a shooting was bad, meaning possibly not justifiable, the tension at the scene was thick enough to cut with a knife. In this case, Jon actually smiled at something Mark had said. Both Hill and Miller had attorney's, (judging by the expensive clothing and professional demeanor) standing next to them. Provided by the Dallas Police Association, better known as the DPA, the attorney's wouldn't interfere with the questioning unless one of them felt that the officer was in danger of saying or writing something that might be construed as criminally self-incriminating. If that occurred, the lawyer would stop the questioning immediately.

Mom and Chief Wong were talking by the door, apparently waiting for us to show-up, and standing off to the far side of the room were four IAD investigators looking like hungry vultures.

Seeing that we had finally arrived, Sergeant Smith immediately called everyone together. "All right, here's what we're going to do. CRS and the M.E. are about done and waiting for us to do our walk-through before they transport the body. To that end, since we have two officers involved in this shooting, I'll allow the following: two IAD investigators, Sergeant Beers as the officers' immediate supervisor, Lieutenant Saxen and Sergeant LaFleet as companion officers for Hill and Miller, and of course, the officers' attorneys.

"Chief Wong will be present as the head of the CAPERS division. I will remind everyone that you may ask a question for clarification, but you will not be allowed to press the officers on any particular detail or issue." Staring directly at the IAD investigators Smith asked, "Am I clear on this point?"

Looking thoroughly pissed off, the IAD investigators nodded in agreement.

Smith continued, "Two more issues I need to mention. One, CSR reported to me that the hotel security cameras are not functioning. The hotel staff has no idea why. American Hotel Security Systems informed us that the shutdown was authorized around 5:41 today. Its system was killed allegedly for maintenance. Whoever called it in had all the necessary passwords and codes. And two, this crime scene is part of a much larger homicide investigation with multiple victims. We're not sure if the suspect in this case is the original shooter or if this is a copy cat. Let's get started."

Because I've been involved in more than one police shooting, walking through this type of setting is *always* a little disconcerting for me. I keep thinking that if not for the grace of God there go I… again! Jon and Todd have been through a life altering event. At this moment, an hour or two after the confrontation, they're coming down off the adrenaline rush and their heads are slowly starting to clear. This is one of the greatest reasons officers should demand to have an attorney present in such situations – to keep them (the officers) from saying something really stupid before the effects of the fight or flight syndrome wears off. More than one officer has literally talked his way into an indictment by running his mouth after a deadly force confrontation.

As we moved outside to begin retracing Jon and Todd's actions, I stole a glance at my two friends. Both suddenly looked very pale, tired and a little nervous. Yep, the adrenaline was gone.

It took a while as we worked our way back inside and slowly approached the body. Sergeant Smith and his team were doing a great job of asking good, solid, pertinent questions that kept Jon and Todd talking but also relaxed and off the defense. Twice, Smith had been forced to shut the IAD investigators down from an antagonistic line of questioning. On the third IAD infraction, Wong threatened to boot their asses out of the room if they didn't layoff. I guess coming from a Chief and not a mere Sergeant, the threat carried more weight because the IAD guys immediately shut-up and moved to the back of the group where they belonged. Was the Chief overly harsh? Maybe so. But IAD is responsible for finding *administrative* violations of policy and procedure – not criminal violations. By general orders they have to be here but I reemphasize that they're not criminal investigators. We all knew IAD would get their shot at Jon and Todd later and that it wouldn't be pretty – it never is.

As we continued moving toward the body, Jon was saying, "… and failing to obey Miller's verbal commands, the suspect, who we believed to be Father Karl Kothner, stood up with a handgun, possibly a 9mm in his left hand – it looked like he was clutching his throat with his right hand. He stood up and began to turn and raise the weapon toward us and, fearing for our lives, we fired on the suspect. To the best of my recollection, I fired three times; hitting the suspect in the chest twice and the face once."

Todd immediately interjected, "And, to the best of my recollection, fearing for our lives, I also fired three times hitting the suspect in the chest and face."

I know all this sounds rather clunky and as if both officers are reading from a script. That's partially true. An officer involved in a deadly force confrontation must be able to articulate why he fired his duty weapon. In this explanation, it's essential that the officer cover crucial points such as what the threat was and why he perceived the situation to be a threat. The key to a justifiable shooting is the phrase, "I was in fear for my life," or for the life of another person. This may seem rather Mickey Mouse but you have to remember that law enforcement in America is the only occupation that's sanctioned to take human life without the justification of war, medical reasoning, or the approval of a judge and jury. In exchange for this trust, cops are held to a much higher standard than the average citizen. It has to be this way because *your* life depends on it.

We were finally at the body. The ME, my former lover Dr. Carmen Hansen, had waited patiently (*something she is not known for*) while we did the walk through. As we gathered around the corpse, she asked that the lights, which had been left down low to give us the feel for what Jon and Todd had experienced, be turned up.

Carmen began abruptly by saying, "My findings at this time are only preliminary. We have a deceased male, approximate age is thirty to forty years." Speaking and reaching down at the same time she pulled the sheet off the suspect. Carmen or the CSR team had rolled the body onto its back for pictures and identification. I looked down expecting to see Father Kothner and was shocked to see the face of a total stranger.

I looked at Tex who was looking at me with the same comical 'what in hell' expression. I then looked at Mom and Chief Wong. Both had their mouths slightly open and a look of absolute confusion on their faces. It would have been hysterical had the circumstances been different. When we first arrived none of us had been allowed to talk to Jon or Todd, nor had we looked at the body before the walk through started.

Interrupting Carmen, I blurted out, "Who is this?"

Carmen, not understanding the confusion, thought I had asked her a valid question. "His name is Rico Salavar, TCIC (Texas Crime Information Center) and a county check has him listed as a severely emotionally disturbed person. I called Parkland County Hospital and they verified that he has a long history of paranoia and religious delusions.

With his teeth clenched, Chief Wong then asked, "And where is our person of interest Father Kothner?"

Miller looking rather chagrined answered saying, "I'm sorry Chief. We didn't get the opportunity to tell anyone that Kothner was shot by this man as he saved Bishop George St. John's life."

Looking *really ticked* off, Chief Wong asked, "And who exactly is Bishop George St. John?"

Jon and Todd took a collective deep breath and began to explain.

Talk about a break down in communications! The irony is that the break down was self induced by overly restrictive departmental policy that states: "the officer involved (in a police shooting) will talk to no one about the incident with the exception of his/her legal representative and the assigned criminal investigators."

Like I said, the whole thing would have been funny if not for the circumstances. And while I was sincerely thankful that Jon and Todd were okay, I was also secretly enjoying someone other than me being the center of Chief Wongs' wrath.

Jon and Todd were wrapping up their explanations when reality hit home. If the dead guy was really our killer – which meant Karl was not – then I had one friend in the hospital in critical condition and other friends that didn't know about the first friend's situation. Jesus!

As nonchalantly as I could, I slowly backed out of the conference room until I was in the hall. Once I was out the door and around the corner I opened my cell phone and called Father Mike Leopole. I didn't dare call Rick – not until Chief Wong officially said Rick was no longer a person of interest. However, calling Leopole was another story – still, I would need to be careful with what I said. Anyway, Father Mike must've had me on caller ID because he answered on the first ring saying, "Yes Ren, how can I help you?"

I quickly and quietly blurted out as much information as I possibly could about Kothner, asked him to let Rick know and then began answering what few questions I could for him. While I spoke to Father Leopole, I sensed that someone had quietly approached me from behind and was obviously trying to listen to my part of the conversation. As I ended the call to Leopole I pressed the 'record message' button on my cell phone. I am not technologically savvy. In fact, I suck when it comes to using any new, high-tech gadgetry. But I had had my antiquated cell phone for almost eight years and given enough time and opportunity even a Techno-Neanderthal like me can figure out some of the basics.

Taking a quick deep breath I turned around and came face to face with the IAD investigators who had not been allowed to attend the walk through. No doubt these two clowns were seriously upset about that and looking for a fight to prove their collective manhood. Also, while these were different IAD investigators from those that had invaded our offices earlier in the week, nobody likes it when their team gets humiliated. So in addition to everything else going on today, our little encounter could get extra-personal; which, in my humble opinion, is absolutely outstanding! Why? Because it means these Bozo's would be operating on emotions rather than logic. The tough thing will be in exploiting that weakness.

To that end, before they could open their mouths I said, "Gentlemen, I am not accustomed to having people eavesdrop on my conversations."

This not only caught Mutt and Jeff completely off guard; it also put them on the defensive and heightened their ire. Stammering a reply, "I'm Detective Jackson and this Detective Lee. We're from IAD and this is an ongoing criminal investigation *(really, no shit Sherlock?)*. Who did you just call and give information to? Did you call the media or your lover, Father Shannon?"

Excuse me, my what? I could have de-escalated this whole encounter by admitting that I had called Leopole because he was Kothner's registered next of kin (Wong would back me on this even though I hadn't asked permission); but the insinuation that Rick and I were gay lovers was far too good to let go. In Texas, being gay is not a criminal offense but this *is* the Bible belt and reputations have been destroyed by that type of accusation and bigotry. Besides, I'm pretty sure we're not gay. Anyway, this was going to be a lot easier than I had thought.

With as much false anger as I could generate, I replied, "Detective Jackson, who I called is really none of your business *(did I just intentionally put a lisp into that sentence?)*. Also, I do not appreciate your crude comments about Father Shannon and me."

Thinking they had me bent over a barrel *(sorry, poor choice of analogies)* Jackson's partner just couldn't control his mouth.

Lee said, "Listen to me fag. You and your butt-buddy priest have been on our radar for years. We've always suspected that you two sick bastards were humping each other. You make me sick!"

Jackson chimed in with, "Ya know queer-bait, Hitler had the right idea."

I can hear people muttering 'typical cops' or 'give a guy a badge and gun and...' The thing is, very few police officers in America really have this type of attitude. *All people*, regardless of profession, race, creed, gender or color can be, at times, prejudice or bigots. Law enforcement is one of the few occupations that will spend millions of dollars each year training officers against such idiotic beliefs. Most police recruits that have discriminative attitudes are screened out in the academies. Granted, some racists/bigots/sexists still become cops and go on to tarnish the reputations of all police officers. Or, they learn early in their careers that *they* are the minority and had best keep this crap to themselves. Trust me, I'm not defending what just happened. I'm just not entirely certain that Jackson and Lee really think like this or if they're trying to push my buttons to make me fly off the handle. More than likely it's the button option.

Anyway, they failed, which automatically means, I won. Taking a couple of steps back and reaching into my jacket breast pocket for the cell phone, I said, "Some people are just born stupid." Shaking my head in disbelief I pressed the replay button on the cell phone and watched as both IAD pukes lost all color in their faces.

The recording is like the valuable Monopoly 'get out of jail free card' and I'd figure out what to do with it later.

CHAPTER 17

4:50 AM, Friday 15ʰ February
Dallas Police Headquarters / CAPERS

We'd been ordered by the Chief of Police to stay at CAPERS after we finished writing our statements. We would have stayed anyway and waited for Hill and Miller (just like the military, we don't leave our guys to suffer alone) but being *ordered* to do so was a bit out of the ordinary and unsettling.

It was going on five in the morning when Jon and Todd finally joined us. After the walk through at the Radisson, they'd been escorted here to make their written statements. By necessity, Jon and Todd were kept secluded (at CAPERS) until the investigators had *thoroughly* questioned them. This has to happen and cannot be avoided. Technically, after finishing with CAPERS, Jon and Todd were to be put on administrative leave for a minimum of four or five days. That 'down time' is supposed to help let the officer get his shit together and clear his head after a shooting. Unfortunately, it never really seems to work out that way – especially in Dallas, Texas. The entire system is designed under the pretense of helping the officer cope with a traumatic incident; however in reality, the system is geared to assist the investigation. Sadly, this screw job started the minute they pulled their triggers.

Here's what really happens. After a shooting an officer can request to have a companion officer assigned to him. This is permitted allegedly as a show of solidarity; however, the involved officer and the companion cannot talk about the shooting – which of course is the one thing on the shooter's mind. Sometime today (its Friday now), Jon and Todd will have to go the weapons range and qualify with the 'temporary handguns' they were issued because their duty weapons have been confiscated for forensic testing.

Once finished at the range, an emotionally exhausted Jon and Todd will have to report to IAD to make their statements. This is what IAD strives for – they want the officer tired and off balance in hopes that they will catch the officer in a lie or at least an inconsistency that can be exploited. After several long hours at IAD (being threatened, sometimes yelled at, denied rest breaks and generally treated like dirt), they might get time to rest before being called back in for more questioning. In between IAD bouts, they'll be hounded 24/7 by the media who has been given (by an anonymous source) their names, addresses and phone numbers. Somewhere around the fourth or fifth day, both officers will have to see the departmental shrink before being allowed to return to work. Here's the bottom line: If the city really cared about Jon and Todd's emotional welfare, the departmental shrink would be, next to CAPERS, the first person they would be required to talk to… Not the last.

Hill and Miller sat down in a couple of empty seats near the back wall and began waiting with us. Looking at every one sitting around the room staring at the walls, the floor or a blank computer monitor, I think we were all feeling a little dazed. Nothing in the last week had happened the way we had expected things to go. In our hearts, we wanted this damn case to be over with; nevertheless, deep down I think we all believed that Hill and Miller had confronted and killed the copy cat – not the original serial murderer.

Like many other well-known serial killers, ours might suddenly stop killing for a few days or even a few years. If that happened the trails would go cold and we would have nothing until he decided, for whatever reason, to kill again. I wanted to say something about this but looking at the team, I knew that I would only be verbalizing everyone else's thoughts.

As I got up to get some coffee, Burt and Conner walked in looking the way we all felt. Connor immediately walked over to Jon and Todd and shook their hands saying, "Glad you guys are okay. I know you can't talk about it, but if you need anything please call me."

Burt waved at Jon and Todd and said, "Me too, guys. Glad you're okay"

Burt then stated, "Chief Wong, Lieutenant Saxen, I've got an update on Kothner if ya'll want to hear it."

Chief Wong nodded yes and Burt continued, saying, "As requested by Tex we stayed on Shannon and followed him to Parkland hospital. Evidently it was a real close thing for Kothner. The bullet that entered his shoulder ricocheted off the bone and came to rest a quarter inch from the heart. He was in surgery for about the last eight hours. Barring any complications, Kothner will make a full recovery. Just FYI, Shannon and the old priest, Leopole, never knew we were there. We hung out on the next floor up until Kothner was out of surgery. Once we got his condition we came back here."

Lieutenant Saxen asked, "Ren, what time did you notify Kothner's next of kin?"

I couldn't remember off hand so I checked the call history on my cell phone and said, "I called Father Leopole at 10:47, Ma'am."

Looking at Burt, she asked, "And what time did Shannon actually leave his meeting?"

Burt immediately replied, "He left at approximately 10:48, Lieutenant. And when he did, he was hauling ass."

Mom was quiet for a moment then said, "Shannon was the first person Leopole called. Both Kothner and Shannon went to meetings – do we know what meeting Shannon attended?"

Connor answered, "Yes Ma'am. Based on what Ren said, Shannon is a part of a religious discussion group that meets at UNT on occasion. Once Shannon had gone into the Willis Library for the meeting, I went inside and asked a cute little librarian's assistant a few questions about the meeting. She didn't know much about the content discussed there, but she did tell me that the chairwoman is a nondenominational pastor by the name of Dr. Glenda Towers. I looked her up on the internet and found that she's thirty-eight, a former Navy Chaplin, single, no children and lives in the Grand Prairie area. She heads a huge church in Arlington and has been in the papers a lot in the last year or two.

"When Mel Gibson's movie the Passion came out, she was real vocal about being against it and led several protests. But there are two other things she is most known for. First, she doesn't believe an all loving benevolent God would commit a soul to hell. Second, she's been extremely argumentative about women not being allowed as leaders in many Christian faiths. She's written numerous articles and thesis papers about both subjects. These views have made her subject to media attacks by the more conventional religious faiths, especially the Catholic Church."

Leaning back in his chair and staring at the ceiling, Tex said, "She and St. John both fit the victim profile. We know that all of our victims have been high profile religious figures that have done something or believe something controversial. The word controversial is of course rather subjective. In this case it means against standard mainstream Christian beliefs. Father Lanton doesn't fit any of this. He *could not* have been murdered because of an emotional affair with Maria Gonzalas."

Nodding her head, Lieutenant Saxen said, "I agree. Had that been the reason, I think Maria would have been murdered too. Just like Alexander Joshua's brother who, in the killer's mind at least, was guilty by association. So whoever murdered Lanton either knew that he hadn't touched Maria Gonzalas, or didn't know of his relationship with her."

Thinking about what Mom had just said, I asked, "Is it possible that we're looking at this wrong? I mean, we've concluded that Kothner interrupted the killer, but what if the copy cat interrupted Kothner?"

Jon asked, "I know Todd and I are not supposed to talk about the shooting, but is it possible that Kothner, Shannon and Leopole are involved in these murders and acting as a team?"

I glanced at Chief Wong. Like Tex, he was leaning back in a chair. But unlike Tex, the Chief had his eyes shut. It has been a long few days, so I thought he'd fallen asleep.

Suddenly, he stood up and exclaimed, "If Kothner is the murderer, he should have been armed but another weapon wasn't found. Because things were so obvious, I doubt if the place was *that* well searched. If this was the copy cat Hill and Miller bagged, and our murderer is not Kothner, then our original perp will strike again very soon. I doubt very seriously there will be a cooling off period."

This conversation came to a sudden end because the Chief of the Dallas Police Department, William Smyth, chose that moment to walk into our office. Out of respect for his rank and position, and maybe the person, we all popped to our feet.

Chief Smyth smiled and said, "Please everyone sit back down. I know how tired each of you must be." Looking directly at Jon and Todd he continued on saying, "Detectives Hill and Miller, thank you for doing your duty last night. I thank God for your safety."

Chief Smyth paused for a moment to consider his next words and then said, "I want to apologize for my harsh words and yes, even my harsh conduct, over the last few days. Detective LaFleet please forgive me for injuring you during our sparring match – it was completely uncalled for. I hope each of you understand why this case was so... emotional for me."

Listening to Chief Smyth's apology, I felt a range of emotions. One part of me wanted to be angry at him over the injury he had caused me. Another part of me wanted to believe that he had been an emotional mess due to the loss of Father Lanton. As I've already said, I honestly believe the Chief is a stand-up guy.

Chief Smyth continued, "I know there's a belief that this shooting could have been a copy cat. I took the liberty to review yours and Sgt. Smiths' case files and, if you compare the dead suspect with the FBI profile, I honestly think this was our serial killer. It's only by God's grace that Father Kothner and then Hill and Miller were there to stop that maniac from killing the Episcopal Bishop. I really feel that it's over now and we can all get some much needed rest. I've asked Sgt. Smith's team to run down any loose leads. Other than that, this case is closed."

Turning to Chief Wong, Smyth said, "Harry, I talked to Chief Winn over at IAD and convinced him to let Hill and Miller knock out their IAD statements right now if they're up to it. The rest of you can make your IAD statements next week *when you have time.* I also told Winn any follow up questions for Hill and Miller will wait until next week. As soon as they're done with IAD, I want everyone – including you Harry – to go home and get some rest. There's nothing on your desk that can't wait until Monday morning."

Turning back to us Smyth said, "Lord bless you all and keep you safe." With that blessing, Chief Smyth left.

Chief Wong was standing there looking angry, confused and hurt. To an outsider, Smyth's visit may have seemed to be the 'right thing to do' in light of the circumstances (him kicking the shit out of me and everyone else getting their asses chewed on); however, what really just happened – apology aside – was that Smyth had just steam rolled over one of his division commanders. More importantly, he had done it to one of his longest standing friends and a staunch ally of over twenty years. Smyth and Wong had known each other since they were Sergeants (Wong here in Dallas and Smyth a sergeant down in Pasadena, Texas near Houston). In fact, it was Wong who'd convinced Smyth to apply for the Chief's job here in Dallas when the position suddenly came open after the resignation of his predecessor.

Prick or not, Wong is the chief of CAPERS, not Smyth. Smyth had taken the 'liberty' to review case files for an ongoing investigation (with numerous victims) and then, without consulting Wong, decided that, based on the FBI profile of the killer, these cases were closed. Problem is CAPERS has two investigative teams (ours and Smiths), a Lieutenant and a deputy chief that think otherwise.

Obviously trying to calm himself, Wong said, "Listen everyone. We've been ordered home to rest and that is exactly what we're going to do. I'm going to make sure that the conference room at the Radisson is not released until Smith's team has tied up all the 'loose ends.' Smith will also be talking to Kothner when he wakes up – I want everyone else to stay away from Parkland Hospital. This way we won't be violating a direct order from Chief Smyth to close the case."

Turning to Tex and I, Wong said, "Sergeant Beers, after you and La Fleet get some rest, I'm sure that Smith, whose team is very busy, would appreciate it if you two go by the Radisson to check the crime scene security. While you're there, I want you and Ren to search that room from top to bottom. If Kothner is the killer, there will be a weapon. If Kothner is not our killer, then I must reemphasize, the murderer will strike again very soon."

As we all stood up, Mom said, "No sense all of you waiting for Jon and Todd to get done at IAD. Chief, I'll hang here in case they start getting reamed and need some help. I'll let Smith know not to release the conference room and I'll have him call the detectives in Cedar Hill, Fort Worth, Houston and Huntsville and let them know what's up and what we're thinking. Let's all plan to meet at Chili's for dinner Saturday around eight pm. Chief, if you're not busy you and the wife are invited. Burt, Connor, you guys, too. Ren, why don't you invite your mother and father? We haven't seen them in a while."

5 AM
Parkland Community Hospital

"We're keeping him heavily anesthetized until sometime early afternoon. After that, he'll be moved out of ICU and into a private room. Quite frankly, gentlemen, your friend should be dead. I think the only thing that saved him was his physical conditioning. Anyway, barring any severe complications like infection, he should make a full recovery. You both may go into ICU and stay with him; however, he isn't going to be cognizant and able to talk until either late tonight or tomorrow morning. Personally, I think both of you should go home and get some sleep. The nurses in ICU will call you if there are any changes. Do you have any questions?"

Father Michael Leopole looked at Doctor Ralph Gordon and said, "No doctor, I can't think of anything. Thank you for all your efforts and for saving our brother's life."

After Doctor Gordon had left the waiting room, Father Leopole sat back down and with his head in his hands asked, "Rick, how did this happen and where are we with this situation?"

After several seconds of quiet reflection, Rick responded, "Mike, I'm not sure what the story is in its entirety but here's what I've been able to find out. Karl was brought in unconscious and in critical condition – so the detectives have not been able to question him. Unfortunately, that means that we can't talk to him either. St. John was also brought here by ambulance, treated and released around ten last night. He wasn't wounded but did require some minor medical attention for high blood pressure. I guess seeing another man shot triggered it. After the detectives got done with him, I was able to talk to him just briefly and from what little I was able to gather, one second St. John was alone and the next second the fight was on. St. John made no mention of Karl having a gun. He was allowed to go home around eleven."

Father Leopole said, "Karl didn't use his weapon to defend himself. Maybe he didn't have time or maybe he realized what would happen if he used a silenced .22. Having a concealed weapon permit is one thing, having a prohibited weapon is something altogether different. The can of worms that would open up is beyond imagining."

Rick said, "Karl might have left his weapon in his car but I seriously doubt that – he's too well trained. So either the police have it or Karl ditched it somehow. I can't ask Ren, for obvious reasons." Taking a deep breath, Rick continued, "The down side is that the Radisson might still have police processing the crime scene. The up side is that the room will not be released for several days so clean-up crews won't find the weapon anytime soon. Mike, I'm afraid we either wait until Karl wakes up to find out about the gun or I go search for it once the coast is clear. In the meantime, I think we need to get some rest. I'll sit with Karl and catch a nap. Why don't you head home and sleep?"

Standing up, Father Leopole said, "Okay. I'll be back here around three or three-thirty. I'll bring you a change of clothes. After I relieve you, go to the Radisson and search for Karl's gun. Until I get back, try to catch a few hours sleep. If Karl wakes up, call me immediately and I'll come back. I'm really getting too old for all this cloak and dagger stuff."

Chapter 18

8:00 AM Home

I was greeted by Danner when Tex dropped me off at the house. He came sprinting from around the corner of the house with a not so freshly delivered morning newspaper held in his mouth. Kneeling, I hugged him and said, "Bet you're hungry, aren't 'ya, old dog?" I grabbed the newspaper off the ground and Danner and I trudged into the house, him to eat and me to sleep. As Danner gulped his breakfast down – I wonder if he ever tastes anything I feed him – I opened the newspaper to scan the headlines and editorials. What I found was inevitable and not just a little annoying.

'Law Enforcement Kills Serial Killer'
FBI expert says death was unnecessary.
By Ian Web
Staff Writer

Last night at approximately 8:30, detectives from the Dallas Police department's Homicide Division shot and killed Rico Salavar, age 38. Salavar suffered from extreme mental illness and was under investigation for the alleged murders of as many as twenty high profile religious figures worldwide. Earlier in the week, FBI expert Dr. Hershel Gaspar spelled out for the detectives what they should be looking for; but obviously were not. In an interview with Dr. Gaspar he explained exactly what he had said to the Dallas detectives.

"Paraphrased, I told them that the killer was a single, dark or olive-skinned male with no outstanding features. He has no job but he does have a degree of inherited wealth which allows him freedom of movement. His non-distinguishing looks allow him to travel unnoticed. He was sexually abused multiple times by priests or clergymen as a young man. He is now 18 to 36 years of age, still wets his bed, he is poorly educated though not form a lack of opportunity. He has no significant achievements in his life to speak of. He is socially inept and has been shunned by females all his life. The victims are complete strangers to him. He picks them because they resemble the person or persons he has had sex with and he is trying to relive those moments. There is, and I must emphasize this, there is a religious reasoning associated with or assigned to these murders. He attends church, revivals and even prayer meetings – I believe he has a messiah complex. The posing of our victims is not just a taunt – it has deep meaning and is an indication of his pain and his desire to be caught. Also, he has no doubt been institutionalized on more than one occasion."

This reporter checked with Salavar's parents who informed me that Dr. Gaspar was absolutely correct in his assessment of their son. Mr. Juan Salavar, Rico's grieving father, stated that, "had the police done their jobs properly by checking with Parkland Hospital, they would have immediately identified their son as a likely suspect." As the investigation continues………

Disgusted, I rolled the paper up and tossed it into the can with the rest of the garbage. In an effort to cover his own ass, good old Doc Gaspar had changed his profile of our killer just enough to fit Salavar. Of course the FBI would back him because they can't afford to be wrong in front of the media on a profiling issue. It's the FBI's big claim to fame these days. I wonder what they'll say and do if Salavar turns out to be a copycat? I guess it really doesn't matter, even if the original FBI profile had been dead on and even if we'd followed it to the letter, Ian Webb wouldn't have given us a fair shake.

Several years ago, Webb had been a successful investigative reporter for one of the local news channels. Unfortunately for him, he'd been arrested after being caught in the back seat of his car doing the wild thing with an underage, female prostitute. The charges of sexual assault were eventually dropped down to soliciting a prostitute, after his attorney proved to the judge that there was no way for Webb to know that the young lady was not of age. After seeing her picture in the police report, I had to agree. Anyway, the worst of the charges were dropped but not before his peers in the media had a feeding frenzy and his wife divorced him taking half his retirement, a third of his salary and his three kids away. It was enough to almost make me feel sorry for Webb – almost, but not quite. Webb blamed us for all his problems and every time he wrote about a police incident, he drove home this point.

Watching Danner lick his bowl clean I said, "All right, dude, I'm gonna hit the bed until about three. Tex is going to pick me up around four and we're going to do some extra work tonight."

Wagging his tail, Danner licked my hand and then headed to the bedroom. Looks like I'm not the only one that wants a nap. When I'm not around Danner lives a busy life. I'm good friends with the people that work at Mount Lebanon and if what they tell me is true, and I have no reason to doubt them, during the day, Danner spends a great deal of time mooching food from the camp cafeteria, chasing squirrels and generally just hanging out at the office. Chances are last night when the camp offices were closed he'd been on a scent tracking something until the wee hours of the morning. The odd thing is, that no matter what time I finally get home, he's always here waiting for me – must be some kind of doggy intuition. Pushing him to the other side of the bed I laid down, plopped my arm across Danner's chest and drifted off to sleep.

2 PM Parkland Community Hospital

Over the period of an hour, the doctors had gradually brought Father Karl Kothner off the anesthetic and back into a world filled with excruciating pain. As his head slowly cleared, Kothner fought back several bouts of intense nausea. A dozen thoughts flooded his mind all at the same time *"Am I dead? I can't be dead, this hurts too much! Where am I? What happened?"*

From somewhere, Kothner could hear a voice, "Father Kothner, try and open your eyes – if the room is spinning, go ahead and shut them and slowly try again. Take deep breaths, it will help with the nausea."

Gradually opening his eyes, Kothner saw several doctors and nurses hovering over him. "Hey, welcome back to the land of the living! I'm Doctor Ralph Gordon."

Seeing the look of confusion on Kothner's face Gordon said, "You're at Parkland Community Hospital. I don't know all the circumstances, but you were seriously injured. You were in surgery almost all of last night."

Taking slow deep breaths, Kothner mumbled, "Hurts bad."

Gordon said, "I know Father. We're going to help you with that. I want you to relax and drift back to sleep. Don't fight the medication I'm going to give you. When you wake up again you'll be in a private room." Kothner shut his eyes and as the morphine took effect he drifted off to sleep thinking *I need to tell to Father Leopole or Rick about my.........*

2:30 PM Home

I woke up thirty minutes early and just laid there thinking about this last week. Chief Wong had been adamant that if Kothner was not our guy then the real killer would soon strike again, but the questions are, who, where and when? We might not know why our killer targets his victims, but we certainly know the victim's profile. The précis of the entire problem is that murder is one of the only crimes that cops can't stop. That is, not unless we're right there when the bad guy tries to strike.

The myth about putting more police on the streets equals less crime is just that, a lousy myth. No one knows what really influences crime trends, especially violent crimes like murder and sexual assault. Having more officers out patrolling does mean we can answer calls faster and therefore get more boots on the ground looking for bad guys, but as far as actually stopping a murder… no way. Looking at the clock I decided that I had just enough time to take Danner for a short, easy run – he'd like that and it would help me get my thoughts together before this evening's activities. It would also help me loosen up my back a little bit more. Though it still ached, I had stopped peeing blood and had knocked off taking the pain killers.

3 PM Parkland Community Hospital

Father Richard Shannon lightly dozed in the recliner next to the bed where Kothner slept. Shannon rarely allowed himself a deep sleep so when Kothner called his name he was immediately on his feet and at the side of the bed. "How are you doing, Karl?"

Looking around the room, Kothner grimaced as he shifted his weight to get more comfortable. "I think I'm okay, Rick. Not too sure what happened – I mean… I remember some of what happened."

Shannon spent the next few minutes explaining all he knew. As he finished, he asked, "Karl, what happened to your weapon?"

Kothner's answer was disjointed and he was having trouble staying awake. "I remember getting to hotel. Killing cameras and then waiting. I moved down the far right wall. I remember running and falling. I think… shoving my gun under a stage. I knew I couldn't be caught with it if I… was killed. Looks like I screwed this one up pretty bad. I'm sorry."

Shaking his head Shannon said, "No, Karl, you didn't. You had no way of knowing that a copycat would show up. Don't worry, we'll get this guy."

Slowly drifting back to sleep, Kothner said, "We have to…fix…St. John."

As Karl drifted back asleep, Shannon looked at the clock on the wall and decided that phoning Father Leopole now would be a waste of time since he was due back at any moment. Shannon sat back down in the recliner and began to plan his infiltration and search of the Radisson.

4:45 PM. Radisson Dallas Central Hotel

As Tex and I pulled into the parking lot at the Radisson, Tex said, "I'm really out of it. Let's get some coffee in the hotel restaurant before we search the room."

Because I had had a good run with Danner, I was feeling wide awake. Looking at Tex, I could see that he wasn't faring as well. "Sure, Tex. I'm in no hurry."

And I wasn't in a hurry because if we found a gun that we could trace back to Kothner, my day would really be screwed up… not to mention very long. Suddenly, hot coffee and maybe a few things to munch on seemed like an excellent idea.

5:15 PM

Behind the Radisson, Father Shannon waited patiently for an opportunity to make his entry. Dressed in green, multi patterned fatigues' covered by a light green mesh tactical vest, Shannon blended perfectly with a large bush and several trees that surrounded his position. Rolled up in his hand was a large, black overcoat that he would put on once he made entry into the hotel.

There are only a few ways to get into the conference room at the Radisson Hotel. The first option was through the main lobby; however, Shannon decided that he could not risk being seen by hotel staff. Entering directly into the room through the fire exit was out because the moment the door opened, fire alarms would go off. This meant his third and best option was to enter the hotel through the service doors at the back of the building where he now waited. These doors were supposed to remain secured at all times, but maids and cooks notoriously left the doors unlocked or propped open while they were working.

After only a few minutes wait, a maid exited through the service doors carrying several large bags of trash. Certain that the maid would not hear him as she struggled toward the dumpster, Shannon caught the door, slipped inside and quickly moved down the service hallway and past a very busy kitchen without being seen. Within a few more feet, he came to an intersection that would take him out from the service hallway and into the main hallway.

Shannon stopped and donned his over coat, then looked around. With the overcoat on, if he was questioned by hotel staff he could say that he had gotten off the elevators and turned the wrong direction. Glancing up at the ceiling mounted camera, Shannon could easily see that there was no red light on that would indicate it was functioning.

Continuing on, Shannon eventually reached the conference room entrance. Looking at the doors he saw that they were locked and still had yellow police tape tied to each door handle. There was also a small sign taped to the door which read 'Police Crime Scene – Do Not Enter.' After checking the hallway to make sure he was unobserved, Shannon removed a small thin knife from a vest pocket and evenly cut the police tape down the middle letting the tape fall vertical to the door handles. He then gently wedged the blade between the lock tongue and the door frame. With sudden pressure exerted on the knife in a twisting motion, Shannon quietly popped open the door. As he stepped into the conference room, he removed the knife, allowing the door to shut and lock behind him.

At the same time in the Radisson Dallas Central Hotel restaurant

Taking a final sip of coffee Tex slid his chair back from the table and said, "We've put this off for as long as we can. Let's get this over with, Ren."

I stuffed the last bite of my apple pie into my mouth and stood up as I washed it down with a gulp of lukewarm coffee. We could have sat there all night, shooting the bull and avoiding our jobs. In the next few minutes we might find evidence that could link Kothner to many, if not all, of the murders we're dealing with. That is, aside from Rabbi Ezra's murder – we were pretty certain that one belonged to Salavar. If Kothner is arrested, then Rick would, more than likely, be implicated in the Interpol murders. Apart from my feelings of extreme hurt and betrayal by both guys, finding that gun would wrap this case up all nice, neat and tidy – especially if the other crime scene ballistics matched up with the gun.

Tex and I exited the restaurant and walked down the hall to the conference room. I stopped short and said, "Tex, the tape has been cut." I moved quickly to the door and checked the locks. "We need to get a key, pronto."

As Tex walked over and grabbed the wall mounted courtesy phone he said, "Yeah, I guess you're right. Jimmying the lock or kicking the damn doors in would probably upset people around here. I'll call the front desk."

Inside the conference room

As the door shut, Shannon walked over and turned off the room lights. Even though the room wasn't completely blacked out, anyone entering the conference room from the lighted hallway would be partially night blind. Shannon knew that the few seconds it took a person to adjust to the darkness would give him an opportunity to either put up a fight or make good an escape.

Slowly walking toward the stage, Shannon pulled a dozen chairs out from their tables and put them into the walking paths that led to the stage. He then surveyed the room marking the door he would use for a fast exit should he need one. As he reached the small stage, he turned on a small pin light and knelt down on all fours. Lifting the small curtain shroud that surrounded the stage, Shannon shined the light around and there, located at the very back of the stage, was Father Kothner's handgun.

Shannon realized immediately the stage was too low to the ground to crawl under, so seeing the gun and getting the gun were two different problems. Standing up, Shannon lightly grabbed one of the far corners of the stage and gave a short gentle tug, causing the stage to slide easily on the carpet. Having this success, Shannon moved to the opposite corner and tugged again, this time somewhat harder. With a loud grinding noise half the stage moved almost a foot and then collapsed with a loud bang. Deciding that grabbing the gun and making a quick getaway was now his best option, Shannon leapt onto the stage, causing the remaining half to collapse with an even louder bang. As he snatched up the gun and walked to the nearest fire exit, Shannon mumbled, "So much for the stealth and grace of a Navy SEAL – Ren's luck must be rubbing off on me."

Just outside the conference room

The hotel clerk took his own sweet time coming to unlock the doors for us. I'm not sure, but by the way this young man acted, I suspect that the staff here was upset about not having their conference rooms available for use. I started to call the kid on his attitude, when from inside the conference room came a loud crashing noise followed by second crash moments later.

Looking at Tex I said, "Son of a bitch, what was that?"

Grabbing the now unlocked door and yanking it open Tex replied, "I think someone has beaten us here."

Pulling our weapons, we entered the room and were immediately rendered night blind by the sudden darkness. Because of this 'blindness' Tex and I both tripped over several chairs blocking our path. I caught my balance just in time but Tex fell flat on his face with an audible grunt. Never breaking, stride I reached over and pulled Tex back to his feet. As Tex stood back up he said, "Look! By the far wall!"

Squinting, I could see a vague shadow casually walking toward the fire exit at the back corner of the room. I started to give the verbal command of, "Freeze, Police" but as I started to yell, the suspect opened the fire exit, setting off an alarm that drowned me out. Worse still, when the alarm was set off, a million candle strobe light came on, further blinding Tex and I. When we finally cleared the last set of tables, we sprinted toward the door that was still slightly open. I didn't really think we could catch the suspect; however, it would've been considered bad form just to stop our pursuit. Less than a second later I wished that we had.

After slipping out the fire exit, Shannon held the door knob, not allowing the door to completely shut. Quickly reaching into his vest he pulled out a small block of wood trimmed into an acute triangle that would serve as a wedge. Bending down, he set the wedge in place at the bottom of the door and then kicked several times to make sure it was seated. Finishing this, Shannon turned and began walking to where his car was parked.

I didn't bother to slow down or reach for the door knob because the door was - well I thought it was slightly ajar. Of course it wasn't because it was wedged shut. Unfortunately, I didn't know that at the time. This meant that I hit the door at a full sprint, face first. A millisecond later, Tex and I smashed in to each other as the door, acting as a spring board, tossed me back into Tex for what can only be described as a brutal collision. When that happened, Tex was thrown off his feet and slammed into the ground with me mostly on top of him.

We lay there dazed for nearly a full minute. I finally rolled off my partner and asked, "You oaky?"

Laying next me Tex said, "Yeah Ren. Care to explain what happened?"

I looked at the door and said, "My guess is that the door is wedged at the bottom. It's an old special operations trick that we use to keep people from opening doors behind us as we cleared a building."

Tex was quiet for a second and then asked, "I see. And at what point did you realize this?"

Slowly sitting up I grabbed my back as a twinge of horrific pain shot through my body. Grimacing, I answered, "Just about the time I hit the door. Shit Tex, I think my nose is busted again and I hurt my back and kidney again, too."

At some point in the wreck, I'd heard my nose break. If you've never broken your nose let me explain that it sounds terrible (*inside your own head*). Then it slowly begins to hurt – a lot! My eyes teared up and blood dripped from my nostrils.

Looking at me, Tex said, "Yep, it's broken again. It's the least you deserve for what just happened."

With some effort, Tex stood up and moved next to me reaching down and, cupping my nose in his hands, popped it back into place. Taking a step back Tex surveyed his work and said, "There. Good as new. What about the kidney?"

In answer I just shook my head as a wave of nausea passed. My nose might be straight again but I would have two wonderful black eyes and my back and side would hurt like hell for a few days. Looks like I'd be indulging in the pain medications again. Crap!

With help from Tex, I gradually managed to stand up. As I dabbed the tears and blood off my face, I asked, "Now what?"

Looking around at the conference room and at what was left of the crime scene, Tex replied, "Well, first thing we've got to do is cancel the fire alarm (*Dallas Fire and Rescue had to be on the way*). Then, we call Chief Wong and tell him what happened. This crime scene has been processed and the only reason the room hadn't been released was because we wanted to search it again. Frankly, I don't think anyone is going to give a shit about the mess we created. Of course losing that gun, if it ever existed, could cost us later."

Tex was right. Looking around at the room, everything was a mess – but besides my nose and my ego – nothing was broke. Well, the stage *had* collapsed, but that wasn't our doing.

I said, "Ok, that sounds great."

Noting the worried tone of my voice Tex asked, "What is it, Ren?"

Turning back to face Tex, I said, "The suspect we just lost… I couldn't make out his face. But Tex, I know that build and body language. I'm almost certain that it was Rick."

CHAPTER 19

Saturday 8 AM – Home

I would've forgotten about my psych appointment with Pat Beers had Tex not called to remind me. My appointment wasn't until eleven so he could have waited until a decent hour to call, but truth is, I needed the extra time. It took me at least a half hour just to sit up straight on the edge of the bed and there I stayed until my most recent dosage of Vicodin kicked in.

I know it sounds like I use the pain medications all the time and for any reason – I don't. In fact, I've taken more Vicodin in the last week than I have in the last five years. In law enforcement and fire and rescue, there's an old axiom that goes 'there are three kinds of cops and firemen: those that are currently injured, those that have been injured and those that are soon to be injured.' Point being, it's always smart for us to keep some strong pain medications on hand. Besides, studies have shown that people with real pain – as opposed to not so real pain – have less than a 1% addiction rate.

Eventually, I made my way to the bathroom for a hot shower. I must've been in there quite a while because I used up all the hot water in a 50 gallon water heater, letting it soak my back. When I was finally dressed and came out of my bedroom, Tex was in the kitchen making coffee for us. As he had promised, he was going take Danner on one of their marathon runs while I visited with Pat.

Handing me a cup of coffee Tex said, "Jesus, Ren, I hope you feel better than you look right now! You know with those two black eyes you look like a raccoon."

I was too sore to say anything profound so I flipped Tex off. Laughing Tex said, "Seriously, are you good?"

"Yeah, Tex, I'm good. I was too self-medicated to dream last night, so I actually slept some. Getting out of bed was a bitch, but better living through chemistry made it possible."

Tex smiled and said, "Been there *many* times. The medications are a fringe benefit to being married to a doctor – though I do get tired of being told that I'm ill all the time."

Without missing a beat I fired back, "Tex, Pat doesn't tell you that you're ill, she says that you are a sick bastard!"

Grabbing Danner's leash, Tex said, "Semantics! Come on Danner, no sense staying around here and being insulted by a raccoon. Did he bother to tell you just how he got those blacks eyes…………

11:00 AM
The Cedar Hill Family Medical Clinic

As I walked into the clinic Pat met me at the door. Handing her a large cup of Starbucks coffee I said, "Thanks for seeing me today, Pat."

Taking a sip of her coffee she smiled and said, "Yum. Light on the sugar and heavy on the cream! Ya know, Tex is right, you do look like a raccoon with those black eyes." Giggling at her own joke she continued, "Before you and I talk, I want you to meet a couple of people."

We walked down the hallway and into her office where two young men sat talking. When we walked in both men stopped chatting and stood up as Pat made the introductions. "Ren, this is Robert, he's our Internal Medicine guy. He's going do an Ultrasound on your back and kidneys. This other guy is Cody. He's our Eyes, Nose and Throat specialist and he's going to take a look at that broken nose."

Shaking my head, I tried to decline the treatment. "Pat I don't think all this is…"

Pat cut me off saying, "I sincerely disagree. I have a 'City Request for Medical Treatment' form signed by your supervisor – that would be my husband. Specifically stated in that request is that you have the nose and kidney checked out. Anything else that we talk about today is off the record. I'll explain the rest of the rules when you're done with the other doctors."

Getting my face X rayed took just a few minutes and the ultrasound scan lasted about an hour. The big issue with the broken nose was to make sure that I hadn't also damaged the sinuses and that the nose would heal straight. Cody said I was good on both concerns.

Robert, however, was troubled about my left kidney. He said, "You can see a severe hematoma dead center of the left kidney. Also, the ribs are bruised as are the surrounding muscles. I'm surprised that the bruise hasn't come to the surface more. That's probably due to your excellent physical conditioning. You took a hell of hit in the original injury and you're lucky the kidney wasn't ruptured with that trauma. That injury was exacerbated last night. I'll prescribe some pain and anti-inflammatory medications. In the mean time, I want you to be very cautious about infections. Detective, *do not* screw around with any of this. If you get hit again or you get an infection, I'll be visiting you in the hospital."

Robert hadn't said anything about the scars that cover my back, shoulder and side but as I put my shirt back on I could tell he was staring at them with professional curiosity. Not wanting to embarrass Robert I smiled as I said, "Happened back in my Marine Corps days. I got those wounds the same time I got this nasty scar on my face."

Robert's cheeks flushed as he said, "I'm sorry. I didn't mean to stare. My dad was a combat veteran from the Korean War and he had some similar wounds."

We talked for few more minutes about Robert's dad and then I headed to Pat's office.

I found Pat sitting in her office chair with her feet up on her desk reading an old AMA Journal. Tossing the magazine aside she said, "Okay Ren, sit down, it's my turn."

I grabbed a chair (*aren't I supposed to have a couch to lie on?*) and pulled it up to her desk. Once I was apparently comfortable, Pat said, "Ren, here are the rules. One, anything you say in this room is protected by patient/doctor confidentiality. The only reason I'll violate that confidentiality is if I determine that you're a danger to yourself or to others. Then I'm legally and morally obligated to talk to Chief Wong. Two, Tex will not ask me about our conversations during these sessions. Also, Tex will not, under any circumstances reveal that you and I are meeting. Three, I expect complete and total honesty from you and I'll give you complete and total honesty in return. And four, you will agree here and now to meet with me every week for the next six weeks. Saturdays are best for me if they're okay with you. The only reason you may postpone a meeting is if the excuse is duty related. Are you good with these terms?"

I replied, "Yes ma'am, I'm good with it." I was becoming desperate, so what else was I going to say? Because of the pain medications, I had slept last night, but I knew that wouldn't last. Sooner rather than later, the dreams would start again – they always did. Maybe the stress of this case has added to it all making things seem more severe. But even when I have light case loads, I can have a horrible night. Running always helps. It's when I feel closest to God and truly at peace. But 'ya can't run forever... even I know that.

Pat said, "Good deal. We're going to cut out all the Freudian garbage because I don't care how and when you were potty trained, how long your mother nursed you or if your Dad is an asshole – he is, but I love him to death. What I do care about is your life right now. With that said, I'm going to tell what *I* know about you and then you're going to fill in the blanks for me."

Sitting there for the next several hours I was amazed at how much Pat knew about me. Some of the stuff I'm sure Tex had told her – no worries there. Still, there was a great deal of stuff that she just seemed to know. What she didn't know, she coaxed out of me – subtly and at times forcibly. I'm not sure at what point she stopped talking and I started. I told her about my life growing up in a military family. That led to telling her about my granddad and how much I missed him and his wise counsel. I talked about the Corps, my times in combat and what had happened in Iraq, and how I had never forgiven myself for losing so many of my Marines and SEAL's during that bloody fight. And then it was time to stop.

Pat said, "Okay Ren, we've made a good start. Here's what I want you to do. As of today I want you to start keeping a journal. Make the writing in letter format. Like writing to a dear friend, maybe to your granddad? You know that he would never judge you, be angry with you or disappointed in you. I want you write in it every day. I want you to record your most personal thoughts, your fears and your hopes. I want you to write about what you have faith in. When you have a bad night – or a bad day – I want you to write about it in as much detail as you can remember. I also want you to write something about each member of your team. Can you do all this for me?"

I was quiet for several seconds then said, "Yeah, Pat. I can do this."

Hearing this, Pat sat back in her seat and relaxed for the first time in three hours.

Home

I found Danner snoozing on the cold tile in the kitchen. As I walked in, he opened one eye and ever so slightly wagged his tail. Chuckling I said, "So much for greeting me at the door. Tex must have run you hard."

Danner rolled over on to his back just in case I wanted to scratch his chest and tummy. Of course I obliged. What normal human being could resist?

Finishing up the scratching, Danner went outside and I called my mother and father to tell them about the Chili's plans if they cared to attend. Having been married to my dad for almost thirty eight years, my mother, out of necessity as a military officer's wife, had learned to be quite the social butterfly. Name it and the old gal could carry a conversation about it. In her own words she said she would love a "night of intelligent conversation." She also added, "I guess that means I won't be talking to you, Ren honey - sorry." Ouch.

Dad was a bit different. He'd mellowed a great deal since his retirement from the Army; but he immensely disliked large and noisy crowds. In this case, a small group of friends eating dinner together is right down his alley. Besides he thoroughly enjoyed talking to Chief Wong and Tex and he simply adored Rachel Saxen, Pat Beers and Jon Hill's wife, Rose.

Looking at the clock I saw that it was only going on three so I packed up my workout bag and headed to the gym. I knew that I would have to go easy with my back so tender. Still, after talking to Pat, I felt… really good.

24 Hour Fitness – Cedar Hill.

I was right in the middle of my last set when I looked up and saw Rick walking toward me. He had his normal Navy SEAL swagger, but he seemed somewhat apprehensive about talking to me. Setting the weights down, I said, "Hey bro, where 'ya been?"

Giving me a tentative smile, he replied, "Mostly at the hospital with Karl. Father Mike and I are switching off staying there with him. Those black eyes look pretty. Broken nose?"

I answered saying, "Yep. I ran into a wedged door."

Ever so slightly Rick cringed then said, "I would have thought you knew better."

Shaking my head in frustration I replied, "I do. But the adrenaline got the best of me… this time around."

After several seconds of strained silence Rick said, "I went by the house and picked up some clothing and other stuff. I'll be staying with Father Mike and helping with Karl for another week and then I fly out overseas to destinations unknown."

I answered, "Thanks for letting me know. The team is gathering at Chili's tonight for dinner – my mother and father are going to be there if you want to come by."

Rick declined the offer saying, "I appreciate the invite but under the circumstances, I think I'll pass on this one." Rick hesitated for a second and then continued, "Ren, you're right about some things and you're wrong about some things. I promise I'll explain it all to you when I can – if I can. Please don't lose faith in me."

I couldn't meet Rick's eyes so I looked down and said, "You're making it hard to do so, Rick. And no matter the love I have for you, I *will* fulfill my duty."

Rick nodded and stated, "I understand and I would expect no less."

With that, Rick turned and left the gym. Watching him walk away, I wondered if this would be our last conversation as friends and brothers.

Chili's – Cedar Hill.

As expected I arrived at Chili's early and took a seat by myself to think a little. After seeing Rick at the gym, my enthusiasm for the dinner had greatly diminished. At some point, I would have to tell everyone, including my mother and father if they were still there, about my conversation with Rick. Rick had asked me not to lose faith in him. Even if he was innocent of these recent murders here in the Dallas / Fort Worth Metroplex, how was he going to explain the Interpol murders? Not to mention Houston? Being in the same countries when the Interpol murders went down was easy enough to write off as a coincidence: but being in the same cities at the same time of every one of the murders? It was all too much to set aside. Sadly, I knew that my team had already come to the same conclusions.

Two hours later we were finishing up our coffee and desserts. As I had thought they would be, Dad, Wong and Tex were engaged in a discussion about politics. My mother was talking to Rachel, Pat, Rose and Chief Wong's wife, Suzie, about something or another. That left me, Jon and Todd as comfortable bystanders listening and adding our thoughts into both conversations when appropriate. Connor and Burt had called me and begged off, though they were appreciative of the invitation. When Rachel had invited them, we all understood that they wouldn't show. PIU guys are like that. By necessity of their job, they mostly keep to themselves.

As we pushed our plates away, Dad looked around the table and said, "Folks, this has been great. I know that ya'll have business to discuss, so

Anne and I can excuse ourselves and head home, if that would be appropriate."

Chief Wong said, "Only if ya'll want to leave, Tomas. You have a military Criminal Investigations (CID) background and Mrs. La Fleet with your international law background, your combined input will help. Point is, we need a fresh perspective. The case we're discussing has been, against our will, closed by the Chief of Police and……"

Chief Wong's explanation seemed to go on forever, especially with the rest of the team interjecting material from time to time. Eventually we all sat back and my Mother, never one to be shy said, "Holy Shit! Legally speaking, what a freaking bag of worms – domestically *and* internationally." Mother looked at me and asked, "Ren, you know your father and I love Rick very much and we won't pass judgment on him until all the facts are known, but this has to be killing you."

As I nodded she continued saying, "Domestically, you have what, four other municipalities working separate cases that all have the same probable killer? Internationally, there are a dozen or more murders being handled by Interpol with the same probable killer. I'm sure you have a good working relationship with the other cities. When the killer hits again, what about starting a task force? The trick will be keeping the command of the task force away from the FBI."

My Mother has worked with all the federal law enforcement agencies at one time or another and she really does not think too highly of the FBI.

Sounding agitated Chief Wong declared, "Anne, no matter what we do to prevent it, that could happen anyway. The Chief of Police was all too willing to bring in the FBI profiler when these killings first started. I suspect that when this guy hits again, the Chief will call for the FBI to take over the case. After this case is over, assuming I still I have a job, I'll be going to the District Attorney and filing a complaint against the Chief. He's interfered with this case from the get go and friendship aside, I will not tolerate that."

Mother sat there for a second digesting all this, then said, "Harry, I understand your feelings but don't toss the baby out with the wash. I'd recommend that the second this killer strikes again, you head over to the

District Attorney's office and talk to him. If necessary I'll go with you. I've known the District Attorney since I started teaching constitutional law at SMU ten years ago. We need to have him make the City Manager reign in the Chief. Once that's done, crank up a task force. If you don't, you're going to be spread too thin to cover all the bases."

Thinking that normally our team (not to mention Chief Wong and Lieutenant Saxen) would not want to have someone call in markers for us, I decided screw that shit, until this case was solved all the gloves had to come off and if that meant asking my mommy for help, then by God I'll be the first to ask her. My mother is a beautiful lady — tall, slender and very graceful. I love my mother a great deal but let me tell you, she can be quite the bitch when she's working a trial. At military functions she always deferred to my dad; however, I've seen the old gal verbally rip out the throat of more than one defending attorney.

Mother was saying, "Not meaning to change subjects, but as far as Interpol is concerned, I wouldn't signal them yet. They have a really shitty reputation as being less than competent. Back when Tomas was assigned to the Pentagon, I worked for the US Attorney General in Washington D.C. and I found out the hard way that Interpol is a joke. Oh well, what do you expect by an organization run by the French?"

Smiling my Dad exclaimed, "Hey, I happen to be of French ancestry and, even though I hate the French, I take exception to that comment."

Squeezing my dad's hand, Mother said, "I rest my case."

With the mood lightened, I chose this moment to explain about my conversation with Rick at the gym. I hadn't been withholding the information but there just hadn't seemed to be an opportunity to fit it in. As I wrapped up my story, I said, "I'm not exactly sure when Rick is planning to leave the county. But if we're going to make a case on him, we'll have to hurry. Mother, I'm not sure we have the time to not call Interpol or the FBI."

Seeing the hurt in my eyes my Dad asked, "Son, temporarily closed or not, are you sure you are not overly involved in this case?"

Heatedly, I replied, "I'll do my job, Dad. I owe Rick that much." Feeling everyone staring at me I softened my voice and continued on saying, "Sorry, you do have a point, Dad. But look, whether it's Rick or not, we all agree that the guy popped by Jon and Todd was the copy cat. So where does this put us?"

Dad answered, "As with any murder investigation ya'll are reacting to the situation. Somehow you need to get in front of the killer. Are there any real high profile religious speakers coming to town anytime soon? That's where I would set up. Also, see if Bishop St. John and Pastor Glenda Towers will let you follow them around for a while. They may view it as intrusive, but it could literally save their lives."

Dad and I have always gotten along pretty well, mainly because he was always gone when I was growing up. When he was home he worked hard to be a good father which meant he was willing to put up with a lot of adolescent crap from me. Still, it wasn't until I'd served in my first combat action that Dad and I could really talk. Since that first action, we've become close friends – even fishing buddies when work allows me the opportunity. Wonder what he looks like? Just look at me and erase my facial scars, add about twenty pounds and grey hair and that's my father. Handsome devil!

It was close to midnight when we called it quits at Chili's. I'm not sure if we solved anything or even came up with a new game plan, but dad was right about one thing. We desperately needed to get in front of our killer. Meaning, get in front and lay out an ambush and take the bastard down.

Chapter 20

Sunday 11:00 am

1700 Block Clark Rd. Duncanville Texas

Tex and I met at my house around 8 am and went for a long run. On most days off, Tex and I might run together but we wouldn't necessarily hang out after the run. But last night as we were all leaving Chili's, Chief Wong had asked that Tex and I quietly meet with St. John this morning at his residence. The Chief was hoping that after his near brush with death, St. John might be willing to act as bait; or if not as bait, then perhaps he would like some physical protection – especially when we informed him that Salavar was a copycat and not the original. Either way, we wanted to be around if our killer decided to make a play for St. John. It's not that we wanted to intentionally use St. John (*well, maybe just a little*), but we desperately needed a high profile controversial religious figure and he fit the bill. Since the shooting, his name and face – not to mention his cause – had been splashed all over the news. Thanks to the media *our* serial killer had to know about St. John. The question was: would St. John's media enhanced reputation be enough to trigger (*sorry, no pun intended*) a response from our boy?

Tex and I pulled up to St. John's house and I noticed several things at once. There were three newspapers in the drive way, the porch light was on and there was a dog barking for attention in the back yard. I glanced at Tex, shrugged and said, "Maybe St. John went out of town or slept in today."

Getting out of the car he replied, "Yeah, maybe," but his voice sounded doubtful. As we walked slowly across the yard and up to the front door, Tex stated, "Door's slightly open."

We both drew our duty weapons as I gently reached over and opened the glass storm door. From the other side, Tex slowly pushed open the front door as we paused to listen for a moment. Never taking his eyes off the doorway, Tex said, "Partner, I got nothing."

After another few seconds, I quietly responded, "Nothing other than the dog barking outback. I'll lead off."

With only two people to clear a house, no tactics or room clearing techniques we used would be perfect, but sometimes you just can't wait for a SWAT team to show up. Besides, no one was supposed to know we were here. With that in mind, I cautiously stepped into the house and silently moved through a small foyer with Tex at my side. Duty weapons up, Tex and I entered the living room scanning for threats. I visually swept the room a second and third time and then whispered, "Living room is clear, Tex."

After the first scan of the room, Tex had taken several steps backward and turned around to cover a hallway on the right and the kitchen off to the left. Staying focused, Tex uttered, "Jesus it's hot in here, Ren. The thermostat must be set at 100 degrees!"

Coming from the cool air outside, I hadn't noticed the warmth in the house until that moment, but Tex was right. The temperature in the house was stuffy and quite uncomfortable. I wondered if St. John, like my grandfather before he died, was thin skinned and cold all the time.

Continuing my scans, I replied, "Yeah, thank God it's a dry heat! The gas fire place is on full blast, too."

I paused a moment to scan a final time and then said, "Tex, I'll move into the kitchen and clear it. You hold the hallway."

Tex repeated my instructions back to me and then said, "On your movement, partner."

I turned around and quickly moved into the kitchen while Tex stepped over to the hallway entrance and stopped.

The kitchen was small so I practically stepped in and then right back out again. As I joined Tex, I said, "Kitchen's clear, Tex, but the stove is on and the oven door is opened. Hot as hell in there. What do you see?"

Looking down the hallway Tex answered, "We have one door open on the left – looks like a bathroom. There's an open door on the right about five feet past the bathroom; probably an office or a guest bedroom. Also, there's a door at the end of the hallway on the left – a master bedroom would be my guess. The door there is open about ten inches."

"Okay Tex, you move into the bathroom and clear it. I'll stay here and cover the other rooms. When you've finished the bathroom – hold at the door and I'll move into the next room while you hold the hallway and cover the master bedroom door. When I finish the first room, I'll move to the master bedroom door and stop – you step in behind me and cover our six. You got all that?"

Like I said, doing all this with just two officers wasn't a perfect solution. It is slow, awkward and time consuming; however, a lot of officers have been killed blundering around in a house looking for bad guys. So clearing a residence tactically – even with just Tex and I doing it – would give us a margin of safety.

It took less than a minute for us to clear the bathroom, guest bedroom and then setup at the master bedroom door. From behind me I heard Tex taking a deep slow breath. As quietly as I could I said, "Tex, I'm going to push the room door open and then quick peek the room. We'll hold here for a few seconds while we figure out what we've got after I look."

Tex muttered a whispered, "Got it, partner. Do you hear a humming noise coming from the room?"

Listening I held my breath for a second and then replied, "Yeah, I do. It sounds like an electric space heater only louder. I'm setting up to open the door."

The interior walls of a house make for shitty protection should a suspect start shooting at me but it was all I had, so I faced the wall presenting the front of the soft body armor I wore under my clothing. I slowly reached across the door and pushed the door quickly open as I pulled myself back behind the wall. In case a suspect had caught a glimpse of me as I pushed the door open, I knelt down on one knee, leaned sideways into the now open door and quick- peeked the room. To verify what I'd seen, I quick-peeked the room a second time, stood up and said, "We have a problem."

Tex turned around and joined me at the door. For several long seconds we stood staring at the now bloated dead body of Bishop George St. John lying on his bed posed in the manner of the crucifix. Wiping sweat from his face, Tex said, "Well, shit!"

Parkland Hospital
12:15 pm.

Father Richard Shannon sat on the sofa next to the hospital bed where his friend and fellow priest Karl Kothner lay staring at the ceiling. Father Michael Leopole sat in the recliner on the other side of the bed contemplating his team's next move. Looking over at Shannon, Leopole asked, "St. John is dead?"

Shannon nodded yes and then said, "And I've taken care that Pastor Glenda Towers is no longer a concern."

Digesting this for moment, Leopole inquired, "When... for both?"

Shannon answered immediately. "St. John's death was early Friday morning not too long after he got home from the hospital. I took care of Towers before Friday noon."

Rubbing his face in exhaustion, Father Leopole asked, "Is there any chance she'll be found?"

Shannon shook his head no, replying, "Not unless someone gets very lucky."

Leopole nodded and said, "All right, Rick. One last thing. What about the two detectives from PIU: Connor and Burt?"

Shannon replied, "Taken care of also. Last night while Ren's team was at dinner I tracked them down. Things went *very* well."

Leopole sat in silence and then stated, "I'm sorry to hear that. Still, I suppose it couldn't be avoided."

1700 Block Clark Rd. Duncanville Texas

Mindful that we were now dealing with a crime scene, we finished clearing the master bedroom as carefully and as quickly as we could. Tex and I both had to resist the overwhelming temptation to unplug the three space heaters that had been left running full tilt. The temperature in the room had to be pushing over a hundred degrees and was almost stifling. After several minutes the heat got to be too much for us and Tex said, "Ren, let's get outside. That body is going to burst open any second and when it does, the odor is going to be horrible."

As Tex and I stood talking in St. John's front yard I stated, "Hard to tell how long he's been dead. It looks as if he was killed at least four to five days ago. The heat in the house accelerated the process, which I would assume is what the killer wanted to do."

Referring to his notes, Tex said, "St. John was released from the hospital around 10:00 Thursday evening and finished with the detectives around 10:45 pm. So if he left *right after* that and proceeded straight home, he got here around 11:30 to 11:45 pm. That puts his murder any time after 11:45 Thursday night or within about the last sixty hours. That's based on what little we know and the bloating and discoloration of the corpse. Crap, Ren, this is one for the medical examiner to figure out."

Tex and I are good at what we do, but whoever cranked up the heat in the house had thrown us a curve ball. Under normal conditions – meaning without interference from man – bodies decompose in fairly predictable stages and at a fairly predictable pace. Understanding the stages of decomposition helps the M.E. in making an estimation of the time of death, which of course helps us, the detectives, identify or eliminate possible suspects. Alter something, like in our case the room temperature, and these 'predictable stages' can be sped up (with heat) or slowed radically down (with cold).

Think about a piece of uncooked thawed meat. When placed in a cold refrigerator, the meat stays good (meaning edible) for up to a week or more. Take that same piece of meat and put it outside on a hot summer day and in short order the meat begins to rot and stink. While my description is rather overly simplistic, I think it fits.

Nagging at the back of my mind was the fact that there was something that I should find more worrisome than trying to figure out St. John's time of death but I just couldn't reel it in. I started to ask Tex if he had the same feeling when from behind us someone said, "Well now, look at these two lost rookies."

Ok... I didn't know who the voice belonged to, but calling two veteran cops 'rookies' is a major league insult. As I started to tell the jackass that had uttered such sacrilegious drivel to bugger off, I glanced at Tex and discovered he was wearing a shit-eating grin. A little confused (Tex should be as ticked as I was) but not necessarily deterred in my self-righteous indignation, I turned around and came face to face with a living legend of the Dallas Police department.

Chief Detective (back when the department had such a rank) Robert 'Robby' Kincaid had joined the force back in about 1949 after spending ten years in the Marine Corps. In 1990 at the age of sixty-eight he had retired after forty-one years of dedicated service. This guy had seen and pretty much done it all. And yes, in comparison to Kincaid, Tex was a rookie and I was still crapping baby food. Lots of baby food! Also, Kincaid had trained Tex when Tex had first joined the Homicide division. That's how I had recognized the old guy. There were pictures of him and Tex plastered all over the office walls.

Putting out his hand Tex said, "Chief Kincaid, how are you, sir?" As they were shaking hands Tex introduced me, "Chief, this is my partner and fellow Marine, Ren LaFleet."

Chief Kincaid shook my hand and said, "Nice scar on your face, son. Looks like a bayonet got you. I got one just like it from the Japs at Tarawa in 1943."

It was hard to tell with the wrinkles, but sure as shit when I looked more closely, there was a three or four inch white scar on the left side of his face. I replied, "Yes sir, I didn't realize it had happened until much later."

Nodding his head that he could relate, he turned his attention to St. John's house and said, "Tex, I'm glad to see you two boys, but I'm little afraid what your visit might mean. Especially the fact that ya'll did a tactical entry with guns drawn. Sorry, I was watching from my front porch. Anyway, I'm guessing that my buddy George St. John is dead?"

Tex met the old man's eyes and answered, "Yes, Robby, I'm afraid Bishop St. John has been murdered. I'm very sorry."

The three of us were quiet for several seconds as we stared at the house. Kincaid let out an audible shaky sigh then said, "If it helps, George got home around midnight Thursday. He and I shared a drink at my house. I'd caught the news on TV about him almost being killed and waited up for him. We finished talking around two or three Friday morning. He was still pretty shook up and I offered him my couch or a gun. I sure wish he hadn't declined those offers."

I asked, "Chief, you know the drill and what we're looking for. Have you heard or seen anything suspicious since you two shared drinks?"

Kincaid thought for a moment and then said, "Yeah, one thing. We have a very active crime watch program in the subdivision. Meaning, I know my neighbor's cars and they all know mine. I was still up Friday morning around 5 am – couldn't sleep so I went for a walk."

Kincaid stopped talking and looked directly at me for several long seconds and then said, "I think you understand why I can't sleep, son. Anyway, there was a small, dark colored car parked several houses down from George's residence. Looked like a city car or maybe a rental– a Ford Taurus or a Chevy Caprice – that's what caught my attention. All those cars look the same these days and, even with glasses, my eyes aren't as good as they used to be. I'm not sure where he came from, but as I started my walk I saw a man dressed in dark clothing get into that car and drive off. As I said, my eyes aren't that great anymore, but I swear to God he looked like he was dressed like a priest."

My heart skipped a beat as Tex and I looked at each other. I think to divert my attention from the anger and hurt I felt, Tex said, "Ren, we have to contact Duncanville PD. It's their city and technically we aren't supposed to be here. We now have a major jurisdictional problem."

Kincaid looked momentarily confused and then stated, "Shit-fire boys, I forgot that this case was closed by the Chief of Police."

Before I thought it through, I harshly blurted out (as if Kincaid was some type of suspect) "How did you know that, Chief?"

Kincaid chuckled and answered, "Jesus, son, I might be old and half blind but I can still read with my trifocals on. It was in the newspaper Saturday morning."

Sheepishly apologizing, I explained, "Sorry Chief, it's been a real difficult case and I'm pretty worn out."

Patting me on the shoulder in a fatherly gesture, Kincaid replied, "No insult was taken, son – none whatsoever. And Tex, I think I can help with the jurisdiction thing. You remember my grandson, Anthony? He's a homicide sergeant for Duncanville. Had I found George before you, I would have skipped the 911 thing and called him direct. Then being the astute young detective that he is, he would have put the pieces together about the serial killer and called you direct. That would explain why you and your partner are here. I am sure Anthony will run with this. Besides, he still thinks you walk on water, Tex."

Tex replied, "Chief, I appreciate your efforts here. But to make this plan work, we'll need to walk you through the crime scene. I don't mind doing that, but it's pretty gruesome and George was your friend."

Smiling sadly, Kincaid said, "I understand, but let me take care of George and my favorite rookie one last time."

Less than half an hour after we finished the walk through with the Chief, Detective Sergeant Anthony Kincaid pulled up with his investigative team in tow. Getting out of his car Detective Kincaid smiled, winked and said, "Thank you for coming out so quickly, Tex. I apologize for screwing up your weekend. I'm afraid this might have ties to your serial killer. Granddad probably described the crime scene to ya'll – as he did to me on the phone, but since none of us have seen it yet, why don't we all go in and take a look-see?"

Twenty minutes later we all were back outside. Tex was making phone calls while Detective Kincaid was organizing his team and issuing orders. I stood off to the side with Chief Kincaid. After several minutes he looked at me and asked, "Son, are you talking to anyone about not sleeping – about the dreams that ruin your nights?"

Surprised at his directness, I answered, "Yes, Chief, I am. Actually I just started."

Chief Kincaid nodded and said, "That's good. After the Second World War, we didn't have anything like counseling. Remembering the things I saw… the things I was forced to do, it almost destroyed my marriage and my career. Stay with the counseling. Even if you think it isn't helping, stay with it."

Before I could say anything else, Tex walked over with Detective Kincaid.

Tex said, "I just talked to Wong. He's going to ask the Duncanville Chief of Police to allow us involvement in this case. He thinks the best way to do this, and I agree, is to go ahead and form that task force. This way everyone has the same information. He'll have Lieutenant Saxen contact all the other agencies for a meeting first thing in the morning."

Looking directly at me, Tex continued saying, "Ren, based on the information provided to us by Chief Kincaid, Wong wants a warrant issued for Rick's arrest. Also, Pastor Glenda Towers has disappeared."

Son of a Bitch! When we found the body of George St. John, I had forgotten all about Towers. At the same time we were supposed to be interviewing St. John, two detectives from Sergeant Smith's squad were to be speaking with Pastor Glenda Towers. They were hoping to catch her just after she concluded her services for the day. We'd hoped that with any luck at all she would consent to having a security detail as well. With two potential targets covered, we doubled our chances of success. That is, if we had the *right* potential targets covered. Now our collective asses were hanging in the wind and Rick *(that's right, I said Rick! I had to call things as they really were)* had struck not once, but twice.

Less than three hours after the discovery of Bishop George St. John's body, I obtained a murder warrant for the arrest of Father Richard Shannon. Just in time for the six o'clock news.

CHAPTER 21

Parkland Hospital
6th Floor - East Wing
6:02 PM

".... . and there has been a warrant issued for the arrest of this man: Father Richard Shannon for the murder of Bishop George St. John. If true, Gloria, this would be just another black mark on the Catholic Church already suffering from numerous child molestation scandals. This is Angela K. Storm, Channel 19, WFCA News reporting."

Staring at the wall mounted television, Leopole grumbled, "Nice picture, Rick. Next time try to smile."

Shannon replied, "I'll work on changing my dour persona later. Right now I should burn off."

Standing up and putting on his overcoat Shannon continued saying, "Every nurse and doctor on this floor has, at some point in the last few days, seen me here. Not to mention the deputy sheriffs that pull duty here at Parkland."

"Leave now and head to the pick-up point and then the safe house. You'll need the equipment, clothing and money we stored there. If you're compromised there, travel light and stay mobile until I contact you. I'll make the call to have you picked up. This thing is coming to a head very quickly, but if it drags on past another few days, I'll want you to leave the country" said Leopole.

Before Father Richard Shannon walked out of Kothner's hospital room, he paused momentarily just inside the door and looked down the hall where a crowd was gathering. Standing at the nurse's station were six Dallas County Deputy Sheriffs – all turned out in SWAT gear. Thinking out loud, "Well that certainly didn't take long." Shannon did an immediate assessment of the threats he was presented with and where his escape route was in relationship to those threats.

Each man was armed with a M4 Patrol rifle, handgun, asp, Taser, pepper spray and each was wearing heavy body armor over their uniforms. Conspicuously missing were ballistic helmets worn by most teams. Though it was hard to tell with the heavy body armor, three of the six officers looked in excellent shape. Two looked fit but not in great condition and the sixth officer looked as if he would fall over dead if he had to run more than a dozen steps.

The number of officers responding was surprising but Shannon had already planned for this possibility. The problem he faced was that Kothner was in single room on the sixth floor with windows that didn't open. This meant that moving into the hallway was going to be unavoidable. The floor was designed like a giant square with patient rooms on both sides of the hall and the nursing station positioned in the middle of the square. Looking to his right, Shannon saw that the hall, up to the next corner, was clear of patients, visitors and more importantly, police.

Turning to Father Leopole, Shannon said, "Wish me luck, old man," and with that he stepped into the hall and said in a loud voice, "Good evening officers, are you gentlemen looking for me?"

Shannon rolled his eyes as he waited several long seconds before the shock wore off and the officers realized who they were looking at.

One deputy yelled, "Freeze!"

Another yelled, "On the ground."

And a third deputy yelled, "Hands, let me see your hands!"

Shannon shrugged, pivoted to his right and took off in a sprint down the hall. Glancing back to see where the pursuit was, Shannon realized that the officers had just then begun to move. Chuckling, Shannon said, "Oh, for the love of God, no wonder crime is so outrageous."

Shannon slowed to a jog until he was sure that at least four of the deputies were almost on him, then he sprinted full tilt up the hall and around the corner. Just past the corner he came to a sudden stop and slammed his body flat against the near inside wall. Shannon knew that the adrenaline inspired officers would be running so fast that they would fail to slow down and check the corner before they took it. Quietly counting to himself: One thousand one, one thousand two, one thousand three, Shannon stepped out from the wall as the first deputy rounded the corner with a full head of steam. In one smooth fluid motion, Shannon threw out his left arm and clothes-lined the officer just below the neck; but above his body armor. At same time he reached up with his right hand and grabbed the back of the deputy's vest collar and pulled down. This caused the deputy to literally flip backward in the air landing with a horrible thud on the carpeted hallway. Just as the first man hit the ground the other three deputies rounded the corner fast but in a disorganized manner.

Shannon stepped into the middle of them and triple punched the second officer in the face rendering him immediately unconscious. With his head down, the third deputy attempted to tackle Shannon as he stepped quickly back and to the side. As he moved, Shannon struck the deputy with a hammer fist to the back of the head.

Dazed and vomiting, the deputy dropped to his knees, completely out of the fight. The last deputy in this group couldn't make up his mind whether to pull his gun, asp, Taser or pepper spray. Watching this amusing dance of indecision, Shannon was tempted to let this one ride; however, as he started to walk past, the deputy was managing to get his Taser out. Seeing this, Shannon reached up, grabbed the deputy's wrist and bent the Taser back toward the man. With his free hand Shannon struck the deputy in the face with an open palm just hard enough to break his opponent's nose and cause him to let go of the Taser.

"Sorry about this my son," said Shannon as he pulled the Taser's trigger and sent eighty thousand volts into the man.

Dropping the Taser, Shannon stopped and listened for the last two deputies. In an attempt to cut Shannon off from escape, they had run past the nurses' station and into the far hall. Eventually those men would come upon their wounded buddies and hopefully they would halt their pursuit to render aid. Quickly looking at each unconscious or injured deputy to make sure they were all still breathing, Shannon turned and began to run back toward the nurses' station.

Police Headquarters / CAPERS
6:04 PM

Tex and I were sitting at our desk waiting for Mom and Chief Wong to arrive. Jon Hill and Todd Miller might show up, but technically they were still on Administrative Leave. Steve Burt and Rocky Connor had not returned my calls since Friday. This was strange but not necessarily unheard of considering their job descriptions.

Also, Pat Beers had called Tex to tell us that Channel 19 had scooped the story about St. John's murder and then plastered Rick's picture up as the primary suspect in the investigation. The reporter, Ms. Kay Storm, had already been attempting to contact our office for more information. Tex and I knew that it would not be long before an 'anonymous source' (probably at Chief Smyth's office again) would leak information to the media that Rick was also a person of interest in about a dozen other murder investigations nationally *and* worldwide. I sat contemplating what this would mean for Rick when Chief Wong and Lieutenant Saxen walked into the office looking seriously worried.

Wong said, "I just got a call from the County. Shannon is on the sixth floor visiting Kothner. In case this goes bad, I want you two to head over there and help. Our SWAT teams are on location. LaFleet, hook up with the tactical commander and in as much detail as you can, explain to him what he's dealing with. It's a five minute drive to Parkland from here if you run code-three. If you don't have any questions, get moving."

Tex and I grabbed our stuff and bolted for the door. Getting out of this building would take about three minutes (*yes, Tex and I had timed this*) and then running with lights and siren on we would be at Parkland in about eight minutes.

Parkland Hospital
6th Floor - East Wing

Still another fifty feet away, Shannon continued his run toward the stairway at the end of the hall. He was about to pass the first elevator when the doors suddenly slid open and disgorged two more deputies. Both deputies reached for their handguns as Shannon, in a lighting quick move, closed with them.

The first of the two deputies was large and burly and, in Shannon's mind, presented the greatest threat. Grabbing this officer's gun hand in a vice like grip with his left hand, Shannon shoved the weapon back into its holster and at the same time slammed an elbow into the man's jaw. Shannon pivoted and spun throwing another elbow strike into the face of the second deputy. Neither deputy could possibly know how lucky he was to still be alive. Each man was bloody with broken bones and broken teeth, but still alive, nevertheless.

Shannon heard the door open at the end of the hall and saw half a dozen or more deputies and security officers exit the stairway. The two lead deputies stopped and drew their weapons and at the same time began shouting verbal commands at Shannon.

Putting his hands into the air, Shannon slowly turned and faced the crowd of blue uniforms at the end of the hall. Focusing his attention on those two closest deputies, Shannon waited until he saw both men simultaneously take a deep breath to control the adrenaline rush they were experiencing. In that moment both deputies relaxed, took their eyes off of Shannon and glanced at each other. Using that split second of inattention to his advantage, Shannon dropped his hands, stepped over his latest two victims and walked into the elevator as the doors closed shut. Less than a heartbeat later the second elevator door opened pouring out a mixture of patrol and SWAT officers into the hallway where Father Richard Shannon had stood.

Interstate 35 North Bound

It's difficult to talk and hear with lights and sirens going full blast. Not to mention the fact that the driver is extremely preoccupied with controlling a motor vehicle travelling at speeds close to a hundred miles an hour. Knowing this, I kept my mouth shut and let Tex drive. The truth of the matter was, I was worried about how bad things could get at Parkland if Rick decided to resist arrest. I still wanted to believe that Rick, in spite of everything else, would never kill a police officer. If I was wrong then we were going to need an abundant supply of body bags.

Parkland Hospital
East Wing Elevator Shaft

After pushing the emergency stop button on the elevator between the fourth and fifth floors, Shannon moved into the far right corner of the elevator and began studying the seven foot ceiling and the service hatch right above his head. Making his decision, Shannon turned and faced out from the corner. Taking a few quick breaths he bent at the waist, spread his arms out and placed his palms just off the walls. Shannon exploded into a jump that put his feet onto the hand railing of the two perpendicular walls. At the same time he slapped his palms on the walls to maintain his position and catch his balance. Leaning back and making contact to the corner with his buttocks, Shannon was able to take his hands off the wall, reach up and open the service hatch. Knowing that it was only a matter of time before the police opened the elevator floor doors above and below his position; Shannon grabbed the lip of the hatch, pushed off the hand rails with his legs and pulled his body up through the hatch and onto the elevator roof.

Closing the service hatch, Shannon slowly stood up to survey his new position. He could hear deputies trying, without luck, to force open the elevator door. Turning in a quick circle, Shannon could see that to his right, there was shaft ladder imbedded into the cement wall. There were also heavily greased cables that hooked up to the elevator cabin/pulley system. "All in all, what one would expect to find in a dirty, nasty elevator shaft," mumbled Shannon.

His original plan was to avoid pursuit and head up to the roof by way of the stairs. With that in mind, several days earlier, Shannon had prepositioned equipment on the roof that he might need for an escape. Ropes, carabineers, knife, door wedges, pliers, gloves, energy bars and some water all packed neatly in a small backpack. Once on the roof, the plan called for him to jam the roof access door and then open a roof fire hatch that led back down into an electronics service room on the eighth floor.

After climbing into the service room, he would have three fair choices. Either exit the room to the eighth floor hallway and then head to the stairway at the far end of the building. This was a viable option unless officers were already searching that floor or had guards posted in the stairway.

The second choice in the electronics room was to pop open a very large air conditioning vent and use the duct system to move from room to room and floor to floor; however, unlike in Hollywood, there were several problems with using the duct systems as a mode of travel. It could be noisy like a bass drum, excessively dusty which would mark his location, if disturbed, and there was a very good chance the duct work would not hold his weight.

His third choice in the room was to re-open a roof hatch after laying a false trail in the electronics room and make good his escape from the roof.

Shannon glanced at his watch and thought: *It's only been two minutes since my first encounter with the deputies and three minutes since the news report started. That's not much time to get organized, seal off and search a building. But somehow that's what has happened. If officers were in place or on stand-by before coming up to the sixth floor, that would explain the rapid response and the number of officers I've encountered. It looks like someone was watching me and got the ball rolling when the warrant was issued, damn the luck.* With only another second's hesitation to assure that he had left no signs of his passing, Shannon began to climb the shaft ladder.

Parkland Hospital
Emergency-room parking lot

We made the trip in record time - only six minutes. Pulling into the emergency room parking lot, we got the word, via the radio, that six officers were injured and that Rick had gotten on an elevator, killed the power, and was now trapped between the floors with the doors to the elevator locked down.

Looking at me, Tex said, "Trapped? Somehow I seriously doubt that shit."

I agreed saying, "Figure that report is at least five maybe ten minutes old. Rick is not barricaded in that elevator. He was off the elevator within a minute of stopping it. They'd do better to search all the floors and the elevator shaft rather than focus on the elevator box itself."

Tex thought for a second and asked, "Ok. I agree, but why do you say that?"

I answered, "Because it's what I would do. Based on military 'Escape and Evasion' training, Rick knows that he can't stop moving for any length of time. He won't allow himself to become trapped or cornered. Tex, no matter where he goes in that building, he'll have an escape route already scouted and planned. Also, somewhere in that building he's pre-staged some equipment for an escape. Rick might have had to get on that elevator as his only choice but I guarantee you this, in that elevator he has plenty of options."

As we parked and got out of the car I said, "Holy shit, Tex, look at all the police."

Any direction you turned there were officers (Dallas County Sheriff's deputies and Dallas city cops) running hither and yon. This was strange because the 911 system aside, most agencies are not known for a fast response to crisis situations such as a barricaded person, hostage rescue or officers getting their collective asses kicked liked today. So, as we began walking, I wondered how the Sheriff's office had gotten a command post, our SWAT teams and so many other deputies and police officers on location so quickly.

Looking around for someone in charge, off in the distance we could see a short, fat, bald Hispanic guy in an ill-fitting Dallas County Sheriff's uniform issuing orders. Apparently no one could understand what the man wanted because his deputies were walking away looking disgusted while he was still talking. Growing frustrated, he began to yell and wave his hands like a high school cheerleader.

I glanced at Tex who was shaking his head in dismay (*or maybe it was absolute amazement*). "Leadership in law enforcement can be such a flaming joke sometimes," said Tex.

Never one to let something like this go (*I hope that isn't surprising by now*), I replied, "You know, the way he's waving his hands and gyrating his body, I think he's having a grand mal seizure."

Tex must have liked that one because he was still smiling as we approached the cheerleader.

Making our way up to the man, we could see that on his uniform he wore the stars of a Chief Deputy County Sheriff. "And just who are you two?" the Chief Deputy asked in an abrupt manner.

Tex replied, "Sir, I'm Detective Beers and this is my partner Detective LaFleet. We're from the city CAPERS division."

Snarling at us, he said, "Oh great, like we can't take care of our own business! Then they send us the two incompetent assholes that let this guy kill what, five or six people?"

I wanted to snatch up the little bastard and slap him into next week. Of course, this would have cost me my job and probably a criminal indictment, but I didn't really care. It had been that kind of a week.

Tex put a restraining hand on my shoulder (*just in case*) and said, "Let's get a few things straight, Chief. First, we don't work for you or the county of Dallas. So professionally speaking, and with all due respect to your exalted rank, *you* can kiss our asses."

To intimidate the little jerk, Tex stepped in close and towered over him. Raising his voice to a near shout, Tex said, "Second, the man you're after was a person of interest but not a suspect until today. Your allegation that we just 'let him kill people' is not only bogus, it's also insulting and I personally take offense at such an accusation."

Tex finished softly but with no less menace in his voice, "Now, sir, you need to go over to the command post, get some hot coffee, sit down and let your field commanders do their jobs. Am I clear on what *you're* going to do?"

With a terrified look on his face, the Chief Deputy nodded and quietly walked toward the command post. Watching the Chief Deputy waddle off, Tex said, "Bureaucrats and bullies are all the same; stand up to them and they cower. Let's find out who is really in charge of this circus."

Parkland Hospital
East Wing Eighth Floor Electronics Room

It was a quick and easy climb up into the electronics room on the eighth floor. Shannon gently closed the floor hatch, stood up and walked over to the entrance door. Because the door opened out into the hall a door wedge wouldn't work. To combat this problem, while scouting, Shannon had left a ten foot length of thin nylon rope hidden on a shelf in the corner of the room. Taking the rope in hand, Shannon quickly made a slip knot and draped it over the door knob. Yanking it down tight, he then took the running end of the rope and tied it off to the shelf that was bolted into the wall. Shannon knew this contraption wouldn't hold for very long should someone attempt to open the door; however, it *would* last long enough for him to either vacate the room or prepare for a fight.

Finishing with the door, Shannon moved next to the air conditioning duct, kneeled down and removed the cover grill. Taking off his overcoat, Shannon crawled inside the small opening. Maneuvering as quietly as he could, Shannon made his way twenty feet into the small sheet metal tunnel intentionally marring the heavy dust on the top and sides as he crawled. Stopping when he came to a T intersection, he turned around and crawled back to his entrance point. Exiting the ductwork, Shannon grabbed his overcoat and inspected his handy work. Satisfied that his false trail would temporarily fool his pursuers, he then mounted the wall ladder, climbed up to the roof hatch and gently opened it approximately a half inch.

Parkland Hospital
Emergency-room parking lot
Mobile Incident Command Post

The Mobile Incident Command Post (MICP) is a forty foot, triple slide-out Recreational Vehicle custom-designed for law enforcement. Inside were numerous desks, dry erase boards, chairs, phones, computers and even a large coffee pot (which in my humble opinion was the most important feature I'd seen so far). There were at least fifteen police officers and deputies talking all at once. Sitting quietly in the far back of the room (staring daggers at us) was the Chief Deputy we'd met in the parking lot. Smiling as I waved at him, I followed Tex into the middle of the crowd.

In a loud voice, Tex said, "Excuse me ladies and gentlemen, we need to speak with the Incident Commander and the Tactical Commander."

Looking around, I saw two men dressed in tactical uniforms stop what they were doing, glance at one another and then at us, obviously wondering why we were interrupting them. A look of recognition dawned on both men's faces and one said, "Over here, La Fleet."

I grabbed Tex by the arm and guided him toward the two men.

"Tex, this is my former SWAT commander Lieutenant Dale Argus and this gentleman is Captain Juan Rico. Captain Rico is in charge of the newly formed Dallas County SWAT team." Back in my SWAT days, I had met Rico, then a Sergeant doing narcotics investigations, when my team had been tasked to run dope warrants for the county. At the time, it had amazed me that a county the size of Dallas Texas didn't have its own SWAT team. It had only been within the last few years that the Sheriff had finally committed to organizing a tactical (SWAT) division. The new team had had some growing pains, but under Rico's strong leadership, things were slowly taking shape.

After the introductions were made, Tex said, "Lieutenant, Captain, we're not here to disrupt or interfere with your plans or your operation, but since both of us know the suspect, Chief Wong felt we might be of service to you."

Smiling Lieutenant Argus said, "As soon as things went to crap, I should have figured La Fleet was involved in all this. Anyway, things are about over. Our guys have him trapped in the elevator between the fourth and fifth floors. We pried open the doors on the sixth floor and have a visual on the service hatch on the roof of the box. We also have the doors opened on the third floor and guards posted at the ground level."

I said, "Sir, I seriously doubt that Father Shannon is still on the elevator."

Looking at me Captain Rico said, "We'll know for sure in a few minutes, Ren; but I have to ask, who is this guy? All we were told is that he was a Catholic priest wanted for murder. Then he cuts through one of my teams in hand to hand fighting like so much wheat. So who is he, *Father Rambo?*"

Answering his question, I said, "His name is Father Richard Shannon, formerly known as Lieutenant Richard Shannon, United States Navy, Seal Team 1. The difference between him and Rambo is that Shannon's the real thing."

Parkland Hospital
East Wing Roof

Standing on the wall ladder in the electronics room, Shannon peered through the small opening looking for deputies searching the roof. Seeing that the roof was clear – at least for the moment, Shannon pushed open the roof hatch and silently climbed out on to the roof. Quickly kneeling down, he did a second and third scan in case he had missed something *or someone.* Feeling secure that he was alone, Shannon bent at the waist to keep a low profile and swiftly ran to where he had stashed his small backpack filled with the tools that he would need for the last part of his escape.

Opening the pack, Shannon pulled out four wooden door wedges and then moved to the roof access door. At the door, Shannon began jamming the wedges tightly into place at the bottom, top and at each side of the door.

Once this was completed, Shannon went back to the roof hatch, climbed back down into the electronics room, turned off the room lights and slowly opened the floor hatch. Approximately forty feet below him in the elevator shaft he could see several SWAT officers kneeling on the roof of the elevator box; obviously trying figure out how to safely open the hatch. Shannon knew once they found that box empty the search for him would intensify. Intentionally leaving the floor hatch open, Shannon silently climbed the wall ladder back to the roof. Once there, he quietly shut the roof hatch and, using a small key lock he had purchased days before, locked the hatch shut.

Parkland Hospital
Emergency-room parking lot
Mobile Incident Command Post

Captain Rico stared at me for several long seconds and then said, "Well that explains a lot but that isn't what we were told by detectives Hill and Miller."

Now it was my turn to stare. Before I could explain, Tex said, "Ah, sir, I'm their supervisor. Hill and Miller were in a shootout Thursday night and haven't returned to duty yet."

Growing angry, I asked, "What did they look like and where are they?" I forgot to add the 'sir' at the end of my sentence but under the circumstances, I doubt that Rico or Argus even cared.

Argus answered saying, "Two fairly big guys. Both had black eyes and what looked to be recently broken noses. Kind of like you, Ren."

I reached up and gently rubbed my nose and stated, "It's part of this story, but too a long story for now. Anyway, where are they?"

Argus continued, "They're seated right over...... Well they were seated in the corner drinking coffee."

Rico suddenly turned around and pushed several buttons on a digital camcorder. On a shelf just above the camcorder a blank monitor screen came to life in real time. Pushing a rewind button Rico moved the footage back about ten minutes and then zoomed in on the corner where two men were seated talking.

Tex said, "Those worthless lopped eared jackasses. Gentlemen meet Thomas Nolan and James Garret, Special Investigators for the Chief of frigging Police."

Looking ready to explode, Argus asked, "Special what… for who?"

Before anyone could say more, the wall mounted radio speaker blared "870 to the command post, we have breached the elevator hatch and the box is empty. I say again, the – box – is – empty."

Parkland Hospital
East Wing Roof
Interlude – Friday afternoon (3 days past)

Over the last ten years, Parkland Hospital has been forced to expand to accommodate the drastic increase in the population of Dallas County. Construction projects – not to mention all the tools that come with such endeavors – are a constant characteristic of that expansion. In addition to the tools and materials sitting around, hundreds of workers can be seen combing the exterior and interior of the buildings every day of the week. That is, until Friday noon when there is a mass exodus of construction workers heading home for the weekend. By one o'clock on Friday afternoon, the foremen begin walking their areas of responsibility to make sure there are no safety issues left unattended.

To that end, the East Wing project foreman dutifully braved the cold February rain when he walked out on the roof to secure the crane cable. Bending down, he picked up the cable hook off the roof and walked over to the air conditioning unit. Taking the hook in his right hand he tossed it over the thick metal piping that encaged the unit. Once the hook had stopped swinging, the foreman grabbed it and then hooked it back into itself.

Checking to make sure the hook was well-set the foreman radioed the crane operator to slowly take in the slack on the cable. This would keep the cable from coming un-hooked, freely swinging, and smashing out windows should the winds kick up. Finishing this last bit of work, the foreman headed back down stairs to lock down the crane sitting between the main building and the Two East building.

Standing up after the foreman had departed, Father Shannon moved out from behind the stair house and walked over to the air conditioning unit to study the cable and hook. Two feet above his head, but still within his grasp, Shannon reached up and gently tugged on the cable making sure that he could dislodge the hook. Shannon then walked over to the three foot retaining wall at the edge of the building to scrutinize the building across from him. Shannon slowly leaned over the retaining wall and gazed at the wide expanse between the buildings. "It has to be forty feet across and about twenty feet lower than this building. Simply too far to jump even with the angle in my favor," Shannon mumbled.

Looking up at the crane arm, Shannon realized that it was slightly oriented toward his building with about forty-five feet of cable hanging down. To a novice, this would appear not to be a problem, but if someone should attempt to use the hook and cable to swing directly across they might find themselves hanging over an abyss almost a hundred feet off the ground. If the daring soul made it across (or at least momentarily over the other roof until the weight of the cable pulled them back across) there was still a respectable twenty-eight foot drop to the Two East roof.

Current Day, Parkland Hospital
Emergency-room parking lot
Mobile Incident Command Post

Hearing that the elevator box was empty, Tex, Argus and Rico looked at me. Before I began talking, I turned and looked at a sixty-inch monitor that displayed satellite pictures of the complex. Parkland had been expanded so many times that the hospital resembled a series of square building blocks – some taller than others – pressed up against one another.

After a second or two consideration, I said, "With all the police and deputies running around in this immediate area and up on the floors of this wing, Shannon won't stay in this building. He'll move as quickly as he can, working his way down to ground level. Once on the ground, he's out of here. But at this moment, Shannon is up on the roof."

Just as I finished talking the radio came back on and an anonymous voice said, "870 to the command post. My team is in the eighth floor electronics room that the elevator shaft leads to. The roof access hatch is locked from the outside so that rules out the roof. We believe the suspect is trapped in the air conditioning ducts on the eighth floor."

Turning to Captain Rico I said, "Sir, Shannon is *not* in those ducts. That's a false trail he placed to toss off pursuit. He's on the roof. More than likely, he locked that hatch himself."

Pausing for a moment, Rico keyed the handset and asked, "870, tell us what you found?"

Within seconds the team sergeant, element 870 answered, "Command post, we found the floor hatch open, the vent grill off and obvious signs of travel inside the duct work. The entrance door was also roped off to slow entrance. The roof hatch is secured and cannot be opened from inside this room. The only place he could have gone is into the duct work."

Glancing at Lieutenant Argus, who quickly nodded his approval (technically all of the city teams here were under his command), Rico replied, "870 send three of your smallest guys into the duct work after the suspect."

Stopping to consider the placement and availability of other teams, Rico continued, "880 and 860 relocate your teams to the eighth floor and begin searching. 850 move your team to the roof and search there. 840 split your team into two-man elements and send them to all the adjacent roof tops. If he's on the roof we need to get a visual."

Looking back at me, Rico asked "Satisfied, Ren?" All I could do at this point was say, "Yes sir, thank you."

Parkland Hospital
East Wing Roof

Knowing that the traditional black clothing of a Catholic Priest would silhouette him against the beige roof and building, Shannon picked up his backpack and moved into the shadows of a wall. Kneeling as he put his rolled up overcoat into the backpack, Shannon began preparing for the next and final stage of his escape from the hospital.

Moving over to where the crane cable was tied off, he knelt back down and removed fifty feet of rappel line from the backpack. Shannon created a small bowline knot at one end of the rope and then slid the running end back through the knot-loop. This formed a very strong sliding knot that would not only bite down on an object, it would also hold his weight. Approximately fifteen feet from the bowline/sliding knot, he tied another bowline knot with a ten inch loop and then ten feet below that, a series of single granny-knots close together five feet from the end of the rope. Finally, at the very end of the rope he tied a single granny knot. By the time he finished all his knots, his fifty foot rope had been shortened by almost twenty feet.

Cautious not to lose his grip on the cable, Shannon dislodged the hook and slowly un-wrapped the cable from the pipe. Once he had the eight inch cable hook in his hand, he placed the sliding knot over its mouth, worked it down to the lowest part of the hook and then pulled the knot tight. Shannon had intentionally left four feet of rope on the other side of the original bowline. Taking the end of this small amount rope, Shannon slid it through the cable eye that the hook was attached to and tied it off with a series of half hitches. Should the bowline come off the hook, these half hitches would be all that separated him from a near one hundred foot fall.

After donning a pair of climbing gloves that he had had stored in the backpack, Shannon tucked the knotted end of the rope under his belt and then slipped his left fingers into the second bowline loop. Moving away from the air conditioning unit, Shannon gathered his extra rope in his right hand as he pulled the cable tight with his looped left hand. Muttering to himself, "Don't try this at homes kids" Shannon took several deep breaths in rapid secession, leaned slightly forward and then burst into sprint heading toward the back left corner of the building.

Parkland Hospital
Emergency-room parking lot
Mobile Incident Command Post

"870 to the command post, my guys are approximately twenty feet in the vent and they report the trail has gone cold and............ Command post, the duct work has collapsed and I have officers injured!"

"850 to the command post, we cannot breach the roof door. The door is somehow barricaded. We will continue our attempts.

"Command post, 860 and 880 are pulling back to assist 870."

Keying the mike, Rico answered, "10-4 all teams. 870 let us know what medical support you need. 840 kick it in the ass and get your people up on the roof – use an explosive charge to breech that damn door."

"Captain Rico, we still have the teams 810, 820 and 830 on stand-by. I recommend that we have them start searching the grounds," suggested Lieutenant Argus.

Looking chagrinned, Rico nodded and said, "Yeah Dale, let's get them moving and what's left of my team, too. Ren, you were right – he's on the roof, but where?"

Pointing at the monitor, Rico said, "All these adjacent buildings butt-up against the east wing. The east wing is either higher or lower by fifteen to twenty feet or more. That's a hell-of-a jump or climb."

Looking at the monitor, I replied, "None of those jumps or climbs would deter him, sir." Putting my finger lightly on the monitor, I continued, saying, "Going up into those buildings would only take him deeper into the hospital – that would improve his situation; but not his escape. My guess is he'll move to this building, Two East."

Looking at where I pointed, Argus said, "Ren, this guy is a stud – he's proven that already. But that's at least a forty foot jump from roof top to roof top."

Before Argus could finish his thought I said, "Sir, if you look here, between the buildings, there's a crane. And where there's a crane there's sure to be a cable. Even without a cable, Shannon will have stored ropes for his escape – trust me, he'll get across… if he hasn't already."

Rico grabbed the mike again and said, "830 send a couple of your officers up to the roof of Two East." Smiling at me he said, "I didn't listen the first time, so…"

Parkland Hospital
East Wing Roof

At a full sprint, Shannon hurdle the retaining wall. Shannon hoped that the angle and speed of his jump would swing him out and form a wide arc that would take him back toward the Two East roof. Shannon knew this would put him over the new roof much longer than a direct swing across, but it also meant that he was gaining a great deal of velocity as he reached the apex of his arc and headed toward Two East.

Continuing to pick up speed, Shannon's legs were no longer directly under him, but out at a 100 degree angle. To slow his momentum, he spread his legs and right arm creating a minor degree of drag. As he approached the Two East roof, Shannon had slowed only enough to release his handhold on the loop and slide down the rope to the first set of knots. Just as he passed over the retaining wall on Two East, Shannon released his hold on the knots and at the same time pulled out the knotted rope tucked into his belt. Snapping his feet together and slightly bending at the knees, Shannon tilted his head forward chin down, pulled his elbows into his sides and with his hands up by his face went completely limp just before he slammed into the roof of Two East.

Parkland Hospital
Emergency-room parking lot
Mobile Incident Command Post

Before I could say anything, Tex asked, "Captain, since we got here, we have been curious about something. How did you get everyone here so quickly? Also, who is the short, fat Chief Deputy sulking in the corner? Just after we arrived we tried to talk to him but ended up having a less than professional discussion. As we approached him, he was issuing orders that seemed to confuse and tick people off."

Answering, Rico said, "As far as us being here, that was a stroke of luck. We just happened to be across the street at that old apartment complex doing a hostage rescue scenario with my new team and all the city teams. We got the call that the suspect was here and we thought it would be great to run a live warrant and then train searching the floors as if he had escaped. Little did we know just how shitty things would get."

Rico stopped talking, looked at the Chief Deputy and then continued saying, "That little bastard is a political hack that was forced on the Sheriff by the County Commissioners. His name is Raul Fuentes. The Sheriff can't get rid of him, so she buried him here at Parkland. He's in charge of security and law enforcement activities, which is to say nothing much at all. The line troops take care of everything here. If he was out there barking orders, no wonder we couldn't get things organized."

Suddenly a disgusted look passed across Rico's face and he said, "When we first pulled into the parking lot, Fuentes was talking to Hill and Miller... I mean Garret and Nolan." Looking back at us, Rico asked, "Detectives, I have a feeling that I haven't got the full story on this case or its particulars. Ya'll want to tell us exactly what *is* going on here?"

Several minutes later we ended our "Reader Digest" explanation of what had transpired over the last week. Argus just sat there stunned and Rico shook his head in disbelief, saying, "Jesus, Ren, this guy is like a brother to you and we're all out to capture him or kill him. More than likely kill him. I'm so sorry, my friend."

Parkland Hospital
Two East Roof

The calf of his right leg hit first, then the thigh muscles, buttocks and the back shoulder muscles of the right side quickly followed. Shannon's momentum scooted his body across the roof and then flipped his legs – still together and bent slightly at the knees – over his body forming an "L" as he came to a stop. To the casual observer, Shannon's landing technique would have seemed spectacular, especially because he had survived such a brutal impact. However, to the average Special Forces warrior trained in the art of a parachute landing fall, the show would have gone unappreciated. That is, except for swinging across a forty foot expanse by rope – *that* would have been considered really cool and worthy of notice, if not praise.

Quickly rolling over on to his back and then sitting up, Shannon was forced to take a few seconds to collect his thoughts and shake off the after affects of the bone jarring impact. Slowly getting to his feet, Shannon knew that his clothing was torn and that he was injured, but he also knew that he had no time to worry about it. Taking the rope still gripped in his hand, Shannon jogged over to the air conditioning unit to tie the rope/cable off, as he did so, he heard the roof access door open behind him.

Parkland Hospital
Emergency-room parking lot
Mobile Incident Command Post

"840 to the command post, I've lost contact with 841 and 842. They were supposed to report in when they reached the roof of Two East. I sent them over there almost fifteen minutes ago."

Rico started to reply but was interrupted by 850.

"850 to 840 and the command post, we breached the door to the east wing roof. We're clearing the roof and I'm moving over to the edge of the building to see if I can spot 841 and 84...... Command post you have two officers down by the roof door on Two East."

Without a second's pause, me, Tex and Argus bolted out the door leaving Captain Rico talking on the radio trying to coordinate an inner perimeter around Two East. It took us about three minutes to reach Two East, head up six flights of stairs and reach the door to the roof. In front of us a SWAT team was preparing to re-open the door and clear the roof (I have no idea how they had gotten in front of us and beat us up the stairs). I seriously doubted Rick was still there, but we couldn't take the chance.

Seconds later, the door flung open and the SWAT team began to sweep and clear the roof while the three of us began to access the condition of the unconscious officers.

From a distance, Father Richard Shannon watched as Ren, accompanied by Tex and another person, entered the building. Taking a deep slow breath, Shannon said, "Sorry little brother... I hope you can forgive me someday." As Shannon turned and walked away, the rain turned into sleet.

CHAPTER 22

Police Headquarters / CAPERS
7:30 PM

Lieutenant Saxen and Chief Wong were waiting for us when we returned from Parkland.

Feeling frustrated and angry, Tex and I said not a word as we walked over to our desks and plopped down in our seats. Our body language must've been sending up warning signals because Mom took charge and started the debriefing. Had Wong started talking in his normal caustic and abrupt manner, things could have gotten ugly fast. Especially when you have two men like Tex and I pretty much looking for a fight.

Defusing the tension in the room, Mom said, "All right guys we need to talk. So take a deep breath and try to relax a little. We listened to the… incident over the radio but I think we need a personal account."

I began speaking first by outlining everything that had occurred after we left the office. I gave special attention to the 'coincidence' of the SWAT teams training so close by, Garret and Nolan identifying themselves as Hill and Miller and the incompetence of Chief Deputy Fuentes adding to the confusion of the situation.

I finished by saying, "Chief, there's one other thing – Lieutenant Argus and Captain Rico are going to take a lot of heat over what happened but based on my experience in SWAT and in military special operations, I believe they both did a remarkable job. I think if they had not had Fuentes confusing people by countermanding orders and had they known what they were up against, things might have gone much better. I am not saying that they would have caught Shannon, but......"

Tex said, "Chief, Lieutenant, I think Ren has covered most of it. The downside is that Shannon got away and, counting the officers that fell through the duct work, we have eleven officers with numerous injuries including broken bones, concussions, cuts, bumps, bruises and one poor moron incapacitated by his own Taser. The up side is that Shannon opted not to kill anybody today even though he very well could have. I guess the bottom line is that there are, as it has been throughout this case, a lot of unanswered questions."

After several seconds of silence, Chief Wong asked, "Detectives, I want you to *think* before you answer this question. Based on what you saw and experienced with Fuentes, is it possible that it was not incompetence but an intentional attempt to confuse issues during the incident?"

As I leaned back in my chair to contemplate this question, I heard Tex mutter, "Good God Almighty, what next?"

Personally, I really hoped that God would not answer that question.

City of Dallas (Near Love Field)
2700 block of Mockingbird Lane.
8:55 PM

Tired, injured and wet, Father Shannon finally reached the abandoned pawn shop in the 2700 block of Mockingbird Lane. Even though *this* designated pick up point was only a mile and a half from Parkland Hospital, it had taken Shannon over two hours to walk it. There were just too many police and Sheriff's deputies out looking for him to run or jog the short distance. Several times over the last couple of hours, Shannon had had to hide in thick brush near the street, in the shadows of a building or inside an abandoned residence to avoid apprehension.

Walking around to the alley behind the shop, Shannon jerked open the back door and stepped inside out of the wind and rain. Slowly taking off his overcoat, Shannon considered his situation. At the moment, the search for him appeared to be piecemeal with no centralized command. Sooner or later, the police would become organized and abandoned buildings or closed businesses would be searched. With emotions running so high after the injuries he had caused to the police, it might be several days before the hunt was called off. Shannon knew that he should continue to exploit the current confusion; however, extreme fatigue and his own injuries were beginning to influence his ability to think clearly.

Moving deeper into the dark building, Shannon came to a backpack identical to the one he had used, and discarded, while escaping the hospital. That small backpack and its contents, with the exception of his overcoat, had been tossed into a dumpster less than a block from Parkland. Cached in this new pack were five bottles of water, duct tape, a homemade first aid kit (with pain killers and antibiotics), a small belt, antibacterial baby wipes, fighting knife, dry set of clothing, money, a disposable cell phone and a suppressed .22 caliber automatic handgun.

Opening the backpack, Shannon took out the cell phone and speed dialed a number preprogrammed into the phone. After just one ring he heard a voice say "Are you safe?"

Answering, Shannon said, "For now. I'm at the primary pick up point. I'm changing clothing – doing some first aid. I'll be ready for pickup soon."

Pausing for a few seconds, the voice responded saying, "It will be at least an hour before I'm there. Hunker down, I'll be there as fast as I can. If you must leave that location, contact me when you can."

Without saying anything else, Shannon closed the phone and set it down next to the backpack.

To watch Shannon move, the injuries he'd received when he hit the Two East roof might have appeared to be minor and of no consequence. Looking down at the amount of blood dripping from his hand, Shannon knew the opposite was true. First and foremost, there was a single painful laceration on his right arm between the shoulder and the elbow. Then there was the road rash that covered the right side of his buttocks, back, and shoulder. Knowing that he needed to take a look at the injuries, Shannon carefully removed his torn blood soaked garments and then walked over to an old mirror to assess the damage done to his body.

City of Dallas
West End Market, TGI Friday's
9:00 PM

"Listen you miserable little piece shit, *you* don't call a meeting with us! If we'd wanted to talk to your fat ass, we would've contacted you." Taking a deep breath, Nolan continued, "So, now that we're here, *what do you want?*"

Chief Deputy Raul Fuentes had rehearsed for this meeting for the last hour. Now that Nolan and Garret were actually standing next to him at the bar, the preparation seemed less than worthless. With a shaky voice, Fuentes replied, "I held up my end tonight – I confused the deputies… and Dallas SWAT. It's not my fault that the priest didn't kill someone or get killed himself. I think my debt to you is paid."

Looking out of the corner of his eyes at Garret and Nolan, Fuentes tried in vain to read their faces.

Leaning close to Fuentes's ear, Garret smiled and whispered, "Really, dip shit? Just like that, you *think* you're off the hook with us? Let me explain something to you, it was *our contacts* that got you the Chief's appointment. It was us that put pressure on the County Commissioners to force the Sheriff to take you. It was us that kept those pictures of you and that little pubescent hottie from surfacing. And it was us that cancelled your gambling debt, paid off your mortgages, back taxes, cars and credit cards. We have done it all for you… And now you want out?"

Staring at his reflection in the mirror behind the bar, Fuentes knew he was defeated. He had made a deal with the devil and, short of death, he would never be free of that ill conceived bargain. "Ok… But I don't think we should be seen talking. I mean in public. The media might have gotten footage of us together at the hospital" said Fuentes.

Rolling his eyes, Nolan replied, "Ya think? We're not worried about that. We have the means and capability to control all of that. Listen

Fuentes, if you behave and do what you're told, with our pull, you might end up as the next Sheriff of Dallas County. You'd like that wouldn't you?"

Glancing at Garret, Nolan knew he was laying it on thick by appealing to Fuentes's ego; but buying this fool had cost a great deal in favors and money. It wouldn't do to lose him now. Not with that frigging pseudo priest running around killing people by the numbers.

Sensing what Nolan was trying to do, Garret chimed in, saying, "Look Chief, we know that Shannon not getting shot and killed was a fluke. You did a masterful job of confusing the situation and raising tempers. We'd hoped for a better outcome, with that son of a bitch dead or at least wounded and arrested, but hey… that wasn't your fault. You did great!"

Walking to their car ten minutes later, Nolan said, "Jesus, what a fool. That fat little shit couldn't find his ass with both hands! Do you think that idiot will ever figure out that we took the pictures of him and that little girl?"

Garret smiled and said, "No, he's too arrogant. He thinks she came on to him because he's so handsome. Yeah, he's an idiot, but he's our idiot. Bought and paid for. I think as long as we keep him on a short leash, he'll be fine. If he gets to where we can't control him, he'll have a little accident. Good job by the way of smooching up to him. That bit about being the next sheriff really appealed to him. Did you see the way his eyes lit up with that?"

2700 block of Mockingbird Lane.
9:01 PM

Staring at the mirror, Shannon knew he had two choices. The first was to wait to clean his wounds knowing that he not only risked infections, but also the gravel embedded under his skin would slow him down. And worse, the deep laceration was bleeding profusely. His second choice was to take care of all this now.

Thinking out loud, Shannon said, "I don't think I'd be welcomed back at Parkland. And with my face plastered all over the TV, I can't go to a Doc-in-the-box for treatment, so I'm gonna have to do this myself."

Turning his attention first to the deep cut, Shannon knew this wound would require an extreme and painful effort to clean and bind it. The parachute landing fall technique had protected him from shattering bones and/or a severe concussion, but not from the effects of blunt trauma. Slamming into a roof with such momentum had compressed flesh and muscle between the humerus bone and the roof literally splitting open the flesh. The laceration was three or four inches long and approximately, at its worst, a half inch deep. While the bleeding was steady, it was not squirting out, which served as a good indicator that the brachial artery had not been damaged. The simple fact that he could still painfully move his arm meant that there were no broken bones; but with a wound that deep, there had to be some damage to the muscles of the shoulder, triceps and biceps. Regardless of the amount of injury, the wound would not stop bleeding and that had to be dealt with before blood loss took its toll on him.

After studying the cut, he opened a bottle of water and poured it over the wound to wash away what debris he could. Taking the small pants belt, Shannon placed it on his arm just under his armpit and cinched it down creating tourniquet effect. Shannon watched as the flowing blood decreased to a very slow drip and then came to a stop.

Father Shannon cleaned his hands with the wipes and put a small amount of antibiotic cream under his nails and on his finger tips. Taking a deep breath to steady his hand, Shannon began probing the wound with his fingers searching for gravel and bits of clothing. Grinding his teeth against the pain, Shannon pulled out several bits of debris from the gash. Following several goes at this and then using more bottled water to wash the wound out, Shannon was finally satisfied that the cut was clear for foreign objects.

Once the wound had air dried, Shannon gently placed a thin line of antibiotic cream as deep inside the wound as he possibly could. He then took the roll of duct tape and cut ten two inch strips of tape, sticking the very end of each on the edge of his chair. Taking a tube of super glue out of the first aid kit, Shannon put dabs of the substance on the sides of the flesh and then pinched the two sides together. Once he was sure that the glue had held; he took one of the strips of tape, smeared it with glue and placed it horizontal across the wound and again gently pinched the two sides together. Shannon repeated this process until the wound was completely closed off.

After wrapping his upper arm tightly with an ace bandage, Father Shannon opened another bottle of water and poured it over the wounds on the outside of right calf first, then at the thigh, and finally the back of the shoulder and upper arm. Waiting for the stinging to subside, Shannon took the second water bottle and drank it down to rehydrate. Feeling somewhat better, Shannon took several antibacterial wipes and made his fighting knife as sterile as he possibly could. Finishing with the knife, he used another tissue to wipe down each injury site scrubbing them with as much force as he could apply. Then, taking the edge of the blade, he pressed it to the outside of the calf muscle just above the road-rash and began scraping in a downward motion removing roof gravel from under his skin. Shannon repeated this process at the thigh and shoulder. Once the majority of gravel was gone at each injury site, Shannon rinsed the areas again, wiped them down and then applied a mass amount of antibiotic cream.

Satisfied that he had done as much first aid as he possible could, Shannon popped a fist full off antibiotic tablets and some pain killers into his mouth and then wearily began to get dressed.

Home
10:00 PM

I was cuddled up on the couch with Danner watching the ten o'clock news. It wasn't surprising that the televised news media had roasted the sheriff's office as well as the Dallas SWAT division over the fiasco at Parkland Hospital. Quite frankly, I was relieved that the coverage had not been much worse. One of the channels had alluded that the whole episode had resembled a Keystone Cops movie. I really hated to agree (especially with the media), but if the shoe fits… I lay there thinking about Wong's question concerning Fuentes and his conduct at Parkland. Was it asinine incompetence or brilliant subterfuge to screw up the entire operation? And what were Nolan and Garret doing there to begin with? And why lie about their identity? With the protection of the Chief's office they were Teflon coated (meaning no allegations of wrongdoing would stick to them). Jesus, none of this crap seemed to make sense!

With Danner nuzzled into the crook of my arm, I drifted off to sleep thinking about the investigation. I'm not sure what, if anything, I was dreaming about but I suddenly woke up with these thoughts in mind: More than once each member of our team (including me) had echoed what Tex had said about this entire investigation being riddled with questions – questions with no apparent or easy answers. But was that really correct? Could all of our questions actually have the same single answer? And was that answer staring us right in the face, but for whatever reasons we were being unintentionally blind? No, wait. We were not unintentionally blind, we were being *intentionally blind*! Is the answer to this investigation – the whodunit part – so bizarre that we have refused to acknowledge the obvious?

I sat up, looked at Danner and said, "Come on old buddy, we've got work to do." With that, Danner and I got up off the couch and headed to our home office.

2700 block of Mockingbird Lane.
11:05 PM

For about the one hundredth time, Father Shannon walked around the empty building. To stop for any length of time would mean that his wounds would stiffen and worse, he might succumb to the drowsing effects of blood loss and pain killers coupled with exhaustion and simply fall asleep.

Shannon was on the far side of the building when he heard three short taps of a car horn. Grabbing the backpack and overcoat, Shannon walked over to the back door, glanced at the car idling in the back alley, then at the alley in front and behind the car. Feeling secure that the alley was clear of pursuit, Shannon walked out to the car and got in on the passenger side.

"Father, I'm sorry you had to wait. It was a long drive from the safe house and then I had to dodge squad cars, road blocks and foot patrols."

Momentarily shutting his eyes and sitting back, Shannon said, "No worries, Detective Connor. Things went better… and in some cases worse, than even I had anticipated. How is Pastor Towers doing?"

Home
2:30 AM Monday Morning

On my office chalk board (yes, I said *chalk* board) I had written, erased and then re-written the names, occupations, addresses and previous addresses (if I knew them) of people involved in the case. Everyone including my team, Sergeant Smith's team, Chief Wong, Lieutenant Saxen, IAD, patrol officers guarding the crime scenes, the sphincter twins Nolan and Garret, witnesses, lawyers and victims. Anyone that had anything to do with the case made my list. Hells bells, I even included my own dear sweet mother and father, Pat Beers, Ian Webb and of course that sorry bastard from the FBI, Dr. Hershel Gaspar – poor Carmen!

As I made this rather lengthy list, a quote from Sherlock Holmes kept running through my head. Okay, look, I know that Sir Arthur Canon Doyle's Sherlock Holmes is a fictional character (so work with me on this); however, there's a quote made by Holmes in the book 'The Sign of the Four' which states "when you have eliminated the impossible, whatever remains, *however improbable, must be the truth.*"

It took several hours to draw lines through names that I knew I could justifiably eliminate, and then to draw lines to names that connected people. And then I started the process of elimination all over again. That is, until I had one single name left.

Danner and I sat staring at the board for almost another hour before I picked up the phone and called Tex.

Midlothian Texas
Safe House
3:00 AM

Father Shannon sat staring at the open road wishing he could take some more pain killers; however, he knew that until he was at the safe house that simply was not an option. He had to keep a clear head in case he had to bail out of the car and make a run for it. If that happened, Connor would have to convince everyone that he hadn't known that Shannon was wanted. And that he had seen Shannon walking down the street, recognized him as a friend of Detective LaFleet and picked him up. As a show of gratitude, Shannon had pulled a gun on him. That was the plan anyway. As to whether or not it would work became a moot point as Detective Connor avoided the last road block and turned the car on to I-35 south bound.

Connor said, "If getting into the area to pick up you up was difficult, getting out again has been a real bitch."

Shannon nodded saying, "Yeah. It looks like they finally got organized and have begun to tighten the noose. In the next hour they'll find my puddle of blood and the tracks leading to the attic of the pickup point. With any luck, SWAT will be called out and the search will be called off."

Slowly relaxing as he drove, Connor said, "When SWAT finds the attic empty they're gonna go ballistic!" Shaking his head, Connor continued, "Oh, I never answered your question about the good doctor. Glenda is fine. She's bored and restless but otherwise fine. When I left, she and Burt were playing chess. She'd beaten him four out of five times. Of course they were still on the fifth game and that wasn't looking very promising for Steve either. I obviously don't know her well but I sense that she's a real tough cookie, Father."

Quiet for a moment, Shannon said, "Yes Rocky, she is. She was a Navy chaplain. We met back when I was at Coronado Island with SEAL Team One. She's *very* special to me. Had I not become a Priest, we might have gotten married." Glancing over at Connor and seeing the shocked looked on his face, Shannon chuckled and said, "My son, outside of my work on the teams, I had a very normal life before I took my vows."

Forty-five minutes later, Connor pulled into the safe house driveway and killed the engine. Sitting in the car for a few extra seconds both men enjoyed the silence after what could only be construed as a very long and difficult day. Looking up, Shannon watched as Detective Steve Burt escorted Pastor Glenda Towers out the front door.

Home
4:30 AM

Walking into the house without knocking (it really wasn't necessary with Danner baying his head off in welcome), Pat came over to me, kissed me on the cheek, and said, "Ren, if this isn't good, I am going to personally geld you."

Looking at Tex and then Pat, I said, "I'm really sorry to have woken ya'll up, but what I have to show you is very important."

After I got everyone a cup of coffee we moved to the office where Pat, Tex and Danner sat down on an old sofa.

While I'd waited for Tex and Pat to arrive, I'd taken some old wrapping paper and taped it over parts of the chalk board that I didn't want them to see until I was ready. Absently scratching Danner's head and ears, Pat began to study the board. Tex must have been a little ahead of Pat because he said, "Ok, I see the information Ren, and I suspect that you're going to walk us through a process of elimination. You and I have already done this – several times over. Why is this going to be any different?"

Taking a moment to gather my thoughts, I replied, "Because I've plugged in some information like news paper articles, conversations and names that we didn't use before. Honestly, Tex, we should have used that information because it was so obvious, but for whatever reasons we didn't."

Slowly and methodically I walked them through my entire hypothesis. Both Tex and Pat grilled me over and over again as to why I had eliminated certain people, especially Rick, who was actually one of the easiest to remove. Rick is a killer – there's no doubt in my head that he did Redcliff down in Houston as well as the Interpol murders. All of those M.O's indicate that they were done professionally with no posing. All the victims were Catholic priests or Nuns and lay people that had turned pedophile and escaped secular justice. Yes, Rick is a killer, but not our serial killer.

I had just removed the last piece of wrapping paper exposing the conclusion to my theory when Tex, still studying the board, got to his feet and said, "Ren, you understand that if you... if *we* are wrong about this, our careers in Dallas are done? Even if we're right about this, the political repercussions will be nothing short of phenomenal."

Turning to Pat, Tex asked, "What say you, love?"

After several long seconds of silence as Pat continued to study the board she finally replied, "I see no flaws in Ren's logic... therefore his hypothesis is, in my professional opinion, sound."

Hearing this from Pat, Tex pulled out his cell phone and then stopped as if contemplating his actions. Looking up at me, Tex saw the concern in my eyes and said, "You've obviously had more time to consider the ramifications to all of this, Ren. I was going to call Wong and Saxen. But if we drag them into this and we're wrong, then we've potentially destroyed their careers along with ours. If they have knowledge, they have no plausible deniability. If we're right and we don't call them in, we are equally as screwed for violating procedures – especially if we have to kill this bastard. The media would paint us as two rogue cops doing their own thing."

Almost whispering, I replied, "I agree with everything you said, Tex. I've agonized over this exact problem for hours now – including whether or not I should call *you*. My only answer is that I personally would want to know if one of our other teammates had stumbled on to this. I don't think it's right withholding this information and taking away a person's ability to make his own choice."

Cuddled up on the old sofa with her head resting on top of Danner's back, Pat said, "Ren honey, you do realize if you're wrong, that you'll be sacrificing not only the career of somebody you're in love with, you'll also destroy that relationship, too? Also, you need to understand that if you're right, you could still lose her."

Slowly sitting down on the other side of Danner, I said, "Yeah, I have thought of how this could hurt Rachel. But I maintain it's all about having the choice... of being given the opportunity to decide for one's self. Besides, why should I put my emotional welfare in front of the safety of others I'm sworn to protect and serve?"

Taking a deep breath and slowly exhaling, Tex said, "Then I'll make the calls. We'll need to meet everyone here – not at the office."

I looked up at Tex and asked, "That's fine with me, but why?"

Tex answered saying, "Here's the deal. A confidential source informed me late last night that the investigation is being turned over to the FBI. After what happened at Parkland, both Chief Smyth and the Dallas County Sheriff are pushing for this. We have a meeting scheduled at two o'clock today with the Feds. Anything on this case still in the office gets turned over to them. I'm pretty certain Wong won't want this information to go to them. Ren, you might as well put that wrapping paper back up; you're going to have to walk everyone through this again."

6:30 AM

Chief Wong sat staring at the board without saying a word for almost thirty minutes. Finally standing up Chief Wong said, "Before we continue, I want to take a poll – are we right or are we wrong? If you think we're wrong, please tell me why."

Jon and Todd both nodded yes. Tex, Pat and I reaffirmed our positions.

All eyes turned to Lieutenant Saxen who was looking down at the carpet. Realizing she was being watched, Mom slowly lifted her head and said, "I agree. But I think proving it will be next to impossible; especially now with oversight from the Feds. He'll be there watching our every move......"

Wong replied, "I agree with LaFleet's hypothesis, especially when one considers how antagonistic he's been toward us. I also agree with Lieutenant Saxen. Even if we met with the Special Agents now, before they take over, I doubt we could convince them that Shannon isn't our serial killer. That goes double for all the chiefs on this department. With the help of Anne La Fleet, I might be able to convince the District Attorney and the City Manager. Unfortunately, that *will not* stop the Feds at this point."

Jon asked, "Sir, what if we show the Feds what we have here? It's hard to refute what Ren and Tex have outlined."

Shaking his head, Wong answered, "I will, of course, present some of this argument to the Special Agent In-Charge, however, I'm afraid that the FBI has already succumbed to tunnel vision. The circus at Parkland

Hospital added fuel to that perspective and I doubt very seriously if these facts would change their minds. This means that we're back to trying to catch him in the act, which also means we'll have to balance our actions against the desires of the FBI."

Looking directly at me Wong continued, saying, "LaFleet, we need a thorough list of all the victims – not just names – but the entire reports. So please pull out your unauthorized copies of all the investigative notes, files and M.E.'s findings, including the ones from Houston and present them for our use."

Seeing the look of dismay on my face, Wong smiled and said, "Come now Detective, I haven't always been a chief."

Midlothian Texas
9:00 AM, Safe House

Having slept fitfully, Father Shannon painfully made his way to the kitchen for a cup of morning coffee. Walking through the living room and into the kitchen Shannon saw that Connor, Burt and Pastor Towers were seated around the breakfast table reading the morning paper.

Glancing up as Shannon walked in, Burt said, "Good morning Sunshine. I'm proud of 'ya; you made the front page headlines! Looks like you were a big hit with the Sheriff's office, not to mention Dallas SWAT. You'll be pleased to know that all of the injured officers have been released from the hospital."

Sounding like a rock sliding across cement, Connor chuckled and said, "Maybe our SWAT teams will focus on training instead of filming that cheesy 'Inside Dallas SWAT' television show."

Snickering, Burt chimed in, "Yeah that show was pretty embarrassing. Anyway, as expected the media really raked law enforcement over the coals."

Studying Shannon, Pastor Towers asked, "Rick are you okay? You look like something the cat drug in and the dog wouldn't eat."

With a cup of coffee in hand, Shannon gently sat down and replied, "Smart dog. Yeah, I'm good. The arm is extremely painful, but I can still move it. I won't be winning any arm wrestling contest for a while. The road rash is scabbing over. No fever or chills so with any luck at all, the antibiotics I'm on will keep infections at bay."

Looking at each person seated at the table, Shannon continued, "Rocky, Steve, you two have put your careers on the line to help me. With Kothner injured we had little choice but to ask your help. The other members of our Order are on the way here, but it's doubtful they'll arrive before this thing is concluded. Also, getting into Chief Smyth's office and securing the other diaries Father Lanton wrote was a daring stroke of genius. So thank you both for everything you've done."

"Glenda, I know all this is very distressing and not just a little confusing but thank you for trusting me. We're not sure if you're a target but... I mean I just couldn't let you..."

Smiling sadly at Shannon, Towers started to reply, but then stopped, took the newspaper from Burt's hands and began reading out loud.

'Copy-Cat Killer Humiliates Police'
Deranged Catholic Priest man handles police/SWAT.
By Ian Web
Staff Writer

I can only describe it as comedy in action. Last night at around 6pm, members of the Dallas County Sheriff's SWAT unit accompanied by the much acclaimed Dallas Police department's SWAT team, attempted to arrest a Catholic priest by the name of Father Richard Shannon. Shannon is wanted for the murder of gay rights advocate, Episcopal Bishop, George St. John. The lone priest was able to not only beat the officers into submission; he was also able to cross a forty foot expanse between buildings, subdue more officers and make good his escape. Later in the evening tracking dogs found his blood trail and followed it to an abandoned pawn shop in the 2700 block of Mockingbird Lane. There, the SWAT teams from both departments surrounded the place, attempted to negotiate - failed and then put a great amount of chemical agents into the building trying to force Shannon out.

At approximately two in the morning, officers made entry only to find the building empty.

Little is known about Father Richard Shannon. All attempts to contact his immediate superior Father Michael Leopole have failed; however, a confidential source within the Dallas Police department informed me that Shannon has been, on more than one occasion, a consultant for the City.

Ironically, the murder of St. John occurred Friday morning just after an earlier attempt had been made on his life by the serial killer Rico Salavar. Behavioral Science expert Dr. Hershel Gaspar of the FBI stated that St. John's death, based on the similarities of other murders attributed to Salavar, is an obvious indication that Shannon and Salavar were working in concert with one another. "Shannon is the second half of a serial team. Until he met Salavar, Shannon was a want-to-be. He has no talent as a priest and certainly no expertise in killing. Salavar made him! This priest is a very sick man as are all the other criminals and perverts hiding beneath the guise of religion. I myself am a practicing Catholic. I personally knew Father Robert Lanton, Salavar and Shannon's first victim, and I…"

Home

We started with a single file and over the next few hours dissected each one in turn. I put up more wrapping paper over the walls so we could write out all the details of each murder. Times, dates, locations and other specifics about each case made our new list. We had done this at the office (several times over as Tex had previously alluded to) but it always helps to do it again, especially now that we'd a more viable suspect in mind. Eventually we all sat down and stared at what we had written about each victim. The problem was, absolutely nothing new jumped out at us.

Feeling frustrated and in desperate need of a stress break (not to mention about a four hour nap), I looked down at Danner and saw that his head was resting on a rolled up newspaper. Realizing that he must have brought it in a couple of hours ago, I reached down and taking the paper from under his chin, said, "Sorry dude, that was rude of me."

After scratching his ears for good measure, I unrolled the paper, looked at the headlines and cursed not so quietly to myself. This caused everyone in the room to stop what they were doing and look at me. Feeling rather chagrined I said, "Sorry, I just saw the headlines and Ian Webb is at it again. Not that I expected anything diff........"

Pat Beers cut me off in midsentence saying, "No way! It *cannot* be this easy."

After waiting almost a full minute for her to continue, Tex asked, "Ah Pat, what can't be this easy?"

Pat scrutinized our work one more time and then replied, "Starting with the Houston victims and working to the most recent killing of St. John, each murder took place almost immediately *after* the victim had finished doing a sermon, having a meeting, attending a conference or like the Houston attorney, Grayson Riggs, after he'd won the freedom of that pedophile priest Cedric Redcliff."

Rachel asked, "I understand what you're saying Pat, but what about Lanton and Whitehouse? Lanton didn't pursue his crush on Gonzales and Whitehouse was to be exonerated the very next day. Not disagreeing with your theory, Pat, but how do these two fit that pattern? Killing them just seems… illogical."

Now in her doctor mode, Pat quickly answered, "Rachel, we humans like things to be straight-forward and easily understood. The more something follows a rational progression, the more we're willing to accept it as fact or truth. And that's the greatest problem with trying to understand the mind of the serial killer. Based on *our* perspective, what these killers do makes little or no sense to us, but to the killer, his or her actions are *perfectly logical*. I do not believe that Lanton was killed because of his relationship with Maria Gonzales. There was something else that Lanton did, or was perceived to have done, that the killer felt was an affront to God. As far as Whitehouse is concerned, I doubt very seriously his innocence would have stopped his death."

Looking over at me and seeing the look of confusion on my face, Pat paused and then continued, "Look, it doesn't matter if it's voices in his head, the dog whispering words of encouragement or God telling him to kill someone. Once our boy locks on to a target, it's only a matter of time. Riggs got off lucky because his assailant was rushed but don't think for a minute that Riggs is safe. If our guy isn't stopped, he'll go after Riggs again. Also, there's something else we seem to have forgotten about what Riggs told us. The perpetrator spent time reading scripture after he thought he killed Riggs – I'm not sure how that helps but I think it might be important to remember."

Todd Miller, who had sat quietly for the last few hours, finally spoke up, saying, "Okay Pat, I understand what you just said. Based on your definitive conclusion we know that he strikes *only after* a perceived affront to God. If Ren's hypothesis is correct, we know who the killer is and we have pretty much always known our victims' profiles are fairly well known and/or controversial religious figures. Riggs is a bit different, but he can be associated loosely with Redcliff. We know all this, but we still don't know who his next victim is going to be. We tried to get in front of him with St. John and Pastor Towers – he dead and she's missing and assumed dead…"

Reaching down and snatching up the newspaper I had dropped on the floor, I said, "Actually ya'll, I think I know who his next target just might be." Suddenly all heads turned and looked at me as I opened the paper to a full page spread advertising a one night non-denominational Christian sermon and prayer meeting being held at the Cotton Bowl stadium tonight. "I think the next target is Doctor Christopher Beckham."

Midlothian Texas
9:30 AM, Safe House

Growing agitated, Pastor Towers asked, "Why would someone want to kill him, Rick? I don't think Doctor Beckham has an enemy in this world. His entire message is about God's love, acceptance and forgiveness. I mean geez, even the Mullahs in Iran say that Beckham is a good and Godly man."

Answering Tower's question Shannon replied, "It just makes sense, Glenda. You're right, he's a wonderful, divinely gifted person. Through Father Leopole, I've had the honor to meet him on several occasions. But I think the killer is going to see Beckham as a threat that must be eliminated. Remember, one of Beckham's core messages is that Christians need to let go of the hide-bound traditions that keep us apart in faith and as a people."

Conner asked, "So Father Shannon, you think our perp is going to take that concept as a personal insult on the Catholic Church? I don't understand how our killer could even go there. Beckham and the Pope are like fishing buddies!"

Nodding his head as he took a sip of coffee, Father Shannon said, "Rocky, you're right. Beckham and the Holy Father have been fast friends for years. But none of this matters to the killer. I think most serial killers see only what they want to see. Also, and I'm no psychologist, but isn't a major trait of a serial killer an egocentric – narcissistic personality? Killing Beckham would give him not just national attention, but also international notoriety."

Sitting back in his chair Burt asked, "If we're right about this, how is the perp going to separate Beckham from his security detail? When Rocky, Ren and I were SWAT we worked dignitary protection for Beckham to supplement his full time security staff. He's got better protection than most heads of state. On the same note, Father Shannon, how do we get you into the stadium unseen? No offense Father, you're injured *and* you're public enemy number one."

Shannon replied, "No offense taken, my son. As far as the injuries go, I'll load up on aspirin and cope with it. Infiltrating or ex-filtrating the stadium won't be a problem for me, especially if we get there and set up in the next couple of hours. Getting between Beckham, his security and the killer *will be* a problem – since his security will be at a heightened level with St. John's death. Steve, since you've been security for Beckham, would you please explain to us in detail his procedures? Then we'll dissect it and try to find weaknesses that our killer might try to exploit."

Home

I said, "Like all of Beckham's sermons and prayer meetings, this is a one night deal here in Dallas. If it follows his other sermons, there will be a sellout crowd of about 50 thousand people at the Cotton Bowl."

It had been several years since I'd last pulled a dignitary protection detail for Beckham, so I had to stop and think for a moment. Continuing, I said, "His security is really tight before and during the meeting. Afterwards, it loosens up some until he leaves for the hotel – then it tightens back up. After his sermon concludes, there will be a huge two or three hour reception in one of the new media/conference rooms at the stadium. Anybody who's somebody will be there – even if they skip the prayer meeting. That's when Beckham is the most vulnerable. He's known to leave the reception for short periods of time to walk and pray with mayors, city councilmen, business CEO's... really just about anybody that needs spiritual counseling."

Saxen asked, "Ren, does Beckham take security with him on these little jaunts? Surely he doesn't go it alone."

I answered, "Yes Ma'am, he takes his security team wherever he goes. Security will hang back however while Beckham counsels. The rest of his security staff stays in the reception center guarding his wife and kids."

Glancing at his watch Wong stood up and said, "All right, that's all we have time for now. We're supposed to meet with the FBI at 2:00 which means to show their superiority they won't show up until about 3:00. Let's meet at the office at 3:05. The other cities won't be at this first meeting so they won't be left cooling their heels waiting for us. One last thing; if we're right on all this, the political fallout is going to be very bad. Everyone is going to have serious egg on their faces." Pausing to look at each of us, he said, "I can, and I will protect each of you as best I can from the damage. Chief Winn at IAD has wanted to be the Chief of Police for years now. He'll use this incident to launch a purge to discredit the current administration – me included. Point being, I may not be on the Dallas Police department this time tomorrow."

I'd hoped to hang on to my IAD 'bigot' recording for personal use the next time I really screwed something up. With me, screwing something up is always just a matter of time. But here's the deal; Wong is my chief. In the military there's an old saying 'loyalty up / loyalty down.' This means that loyalty should be given by leaders and subordinates alike. Wong can be a real asshole from time to time and personally I dislike the guy. But in truth he's always been fiercely loyal and protective of us. In return could anything less be expected of me?

"Just a moment, Chief," I said. I walked over to my desk and took a small audio CD out of the drawer. I'd made several copies of the IAD conversation and now presented one to Chief Wong. "Sir, before we all go, I think you'll want to listen to this. You'll know how to use it better than I would."

With that, I popped the CD into my laptop and as it began to play a smile came across Chief Wong's face, Pat and Rachel started to chuckle. Jon and Todd were out right laughing, and Tex said, "You devious bastard. I am so proud of you I could almost cry."

CHAPTER 23

Police Headquarters / CAPERS
Monday 3:15 PM

Before going up to the office, we all gathered in the parking lot and waited for Chief Wong who was meeting with the City Manager, District Attorney and believe it or not, my mom. After only a minute or two Wong pulled up and parked. Getting out of his car and walking over to us I could see that Wong looked exhausted and maybe a little disappointed, too.

Wong said, "We did not present them with suspect information, so the meeting with the D.A. and the City Manager only went fairly well. Once this case is resolved, they're willing to open an investigation into Chief Smyth's conduct. Detective La Fleet, your mother presented an outstanding argument as to why we should remain in control of the investigation of these murders. However, they feel, and I must agree – as does your mother, that with all the media attention, it's too late to keep the case from being turned over to the FBI. Had St. John not been murdered, then we we'd had a fighting chance. Also, I *did not* – for obvious reasons – tell the D.A. or the City Manager our most recent hypothesis and who we think the next target will be." With that Wong stopped talking and we all headed up to our offices.

The special agents assigned to the case still had their jackets on when we walked in. Obviously, they hadn't been waiting long, but that wasn't the point. Their little dominance play of making us wait for *them* had failed. By the looks on their collective faces they were really upset about it, too.

Chief Wong headed directly to his small office, unlocked the door and, without acknowledging their presence, looked over his shoulder and said, "I need to see everyone in the conference room immediately."

This was not what the FBI was used to. As a rule, when the FBI decides to show up (if they decide to show up), they expect a certain degree of genuflecting and Wong was having no part of that.

As we entered the conference room, the senior Special Agent attempted to reassert his position. "I'm Special Agent A.H. Dixon. I'll be in charge of this operation hence forth." Looking straight at Tex, he said, "Get the working files for........."

Before Dixon could continue, Chief Wong yelled, "Stop!" He turned to Dixon and said, "In the future when *you* people call for a meeting, you will be punctual. We don't have time for your childish attempts to prove your agency's superiority. That's the first thing. The second thing is that our department has decided to turn this investigation over to the FBI; however, that does not mean my people are your hey-boys. You get your own goddamned coffee and carry your own goddamned books. The third thing is that you will never again order my people about. If you need something, you ask them, if not politely, then professionally. If they cannot or will not help you, then you go to Lieutenant Saxen. If she cannot or will not help you, then, and only then, you may come to me. Are you clear on these rules, Mister Dixon? Because if you're not, the next person I'll be talking to is the Director of the FBI."

From where I was standing, Dixon's face looked bright red. I could tell by looking at him that he was contemplating calling Wong's bluff. Maybe it was the way Wong had dressed him down or maybe he'd heard that Wong never made threats he couldn't back up *(I wouldn't be surprised to find out that Wong and the Director were on a first name basis)*; but suddenly the guy muttered that he understood the rules.

Wong replied, "Good, let's get everyone seated. We'll present all the information we have on this case in an orderly fashion."

Like I told you earlier, I personally don't have any ill feeling toward the FBI. That is, as long as they're working within the confines of their training, skill and experience. And by experience, I mean street experience of which most of them have none. The average Dallas homicide investigator has more contact with murders and murderers in a single month than most special agents have in a thirty year career.

Outside my own preferences, if it looks like our relationship with the FBI is strained, that's because it is. About fifteen or twenty years ago, the Chief of Police in Dallas had a major blow out with the Special Agent in-Charge of the Dallas FBI office. Accusations of improprieties and corruption flew in both directions. The FBI suddenly, and without provocation, opened up numerous federal civil rights investigations into the conduct of darn near every cop on the department.

The Chief bad mouthed the FBI for this and wrote numerous poison pen letters to the Director of the FBI, congressmen and senators. Both men ran their mouths to media whenever the opportunity presented itself. It kept escalating until the Chief was fired (for this and other scandals) and the local FBI guy was forced into retirement. Both men had acted like juveniles, damaging the reputations of their organizations. To this day there's still a great deal of animosity and mistrust between the FBI and the Dallas Police Department.

We'd been seated for a boring hour by the time we got to the subject of the perpetrator. As we'd expected, the FBI guys had locked onto Shannon as the only potential suspect. Despite Chief Wong's best efforts to subtly plant the idea of a different bad guy in the collective heads of the FBI team, Dixon would not consider any other possibility than Shannon. To be fair, we didn't lay out the charts and list to the FBI like we'd done at my house. Why? For starters we simply didn't have that much time – not with Beckham preaching in less than three hours. Also, there's an old Russian proverb that says, "Two people can keep a secret only if one of them is dead." Meaning that if we told the FBI our hypothesis (and they disagreed with us as they probably would), there was a very good chance it wouldn't be long before our killer had gotten the information, too. It's not that the

FBI couldn't keep their mouths shut. Actually they're pretty good at type of thing; however, since they weren't open to other possibilities, they might feel no compulsion to stay quiet.

"We'll be interviewing all of your witnesses and former suspects again; especially Kothner and Leopole. Our Behavioral Science team at Quantico, along with Doctor Gaspar here in Dallas, finds it very hard to believe that neither of those two men knew what Shannon was doing. Also, based on our latest profiles developed by Doctor Gaspar, we believe that Shannon is going to attempt to escape the country and therefore no longer poses a threat here in Dallas. Gaspar, as you may recall, did an outstanding job of profiling Shannon at the start of this investigation," said Dixon.

Before he could control his mouth, Todd Miller blurted out, "Oh bullshit! Gaspar changed his suspect and victim profiles, not once, but twice to cover his ass. Doesn't his flip-flopping raise any level of suspicion with the FBI? The guy is a lying, incompetent son of a bitch in cahoots with the media!"

This made Dixon furious. As if I'd made the comment, he looked directly at me and said, "Detective LaFleet, do you know that when a civilian department fails to catch a serial killer like Shannon, the Bureau does a profile on the detectives involved in the case? We want to know why you couldn't catch him. Gaspar believes that *you* personally have intentionally held back and at times, thwarted the investigation. It would amaze the public what we know about you. Such as, we know that you *live* with Shannon and that you have *known* him for many years. Met him in the military and forged a friendship under suspicious circumstances. And shortly after your meeting, both of you left the service. Gaspar thinks you both left the military in disgrace. Quite frankly, I see no reason to disagree since your military records are sealed and off limits to even the FBI."

At that moment, I'm not sure what got into me. I'm extremely self-conscious about the horrible battle-scars that riddle my body. At pool parties or at the lake, I always keep a t-shirt on. The one time I didn't, a young lady I wanted to date got really grossed out and never talked to me again. My last girlfriend, Carmen, a trained medical examiner, was squeamish and made a point to never touch the scars even when we were fooling around.

Anyway, I stood up and removed my suit coat and tie, then my dress shirt and finally my t-shirt. I heard several people mumbling profanity and then Rachel choked back a gasp. Staring Dixon in the face, I walked over to him and said, "You self-righteous little shit! Shannon and I met in combat. I saved his life and he saved mine – several times over. That's when I *earned* these scars that disgust you so much." Stepping close enough so that only Dixon could hear me, I said, "And if you ever again question my military service, I *will* kill you!"

Knowing that he'd crossed over a line, Dixon backed away from me and stammered, "I ah… I mean Gaspar said… the military – both your files are sealed and… the old don't ask - don't tell policy. We just thought that… I mean Gaspar is a doctor… and he said…"

I felt a hand on my shoulder and heard Tex whisper, "Renee, calm down. He's not worth your career, son… or a murder charge. Go put your shirt back on and sit down."

As I turned to go back to my seat I glanced at Rachel who was staring at me. I wasn't sure what she was thinking, but the look on her face was not the revulsion I'd learned to expect.

Clearing his throat first, Chief Wong said, "All right everyone, please be seated. We've obviously stepped on each other's professional toes enough for one day. Special Agent Dixon, I'm sure that you'll pursue this investigation as thoroughly as you possibly can. We believe our murderer's next target is Doctor Christopher Beckham, who is preaching tonight at the Cotton Bowl. To that end, we're going to be there to offer extra protection to Beckham."

Putting up his hand to forestall Dixon's protest, Wong continued, saying, "If you want to contribute a couple of agents to this, please do. But don't feel obligated. It's probably a wild goose chase anyway."

Sitting quiet for a few seconds, Dixon knew he had been suckered. If he failed to put some of his people at the Cotton Bowl and something happened, he'd be in serious trouble. But if he put agents on Beckham, it could be construed that he didn't fully trust Gaspar or the Behavioral Science division at Quantico. Sighing, Dixon said, "Thank you for the invitation, but my people are going to be very busy with interviews tomorrow and we have a ton of material to go over first."

With that declaration, everyone but me stood up to leave. I sat there trying to sort through my actions and wondering what it had cost me with Rachel. I vaguely watched as Jon Hill shoved an arm across Dixon's path at the door and said, "Dixon, if you were insinuating that Ren is gay or that he has an evil dark side, those are just rumors. I should know because I started most of them. The one thing you missed when profiling Ren is that his mother worked for the Attorney General of the United States. Her maiden name is Cross, as in Anne Cross. You might recall that she put several of *your* boys in federal prison for selling top secret information to the Communist Chinese. Methinks that if information detrimental to La Fleet's reputation and career leaks out from your office, your career in the FBI will come to a screeching halt."

Dixon had already had a very shitty day and I guess this news was the final straw for him because he went from smug and arrogant, to pale and nervous. What he didn't know was that my mother would faint from laughter if I whined about that kind of rumor. I could just hear her saying, 'For crying out loud, Ren, you're single, you dress well and you live with a priest! What did you think people were going to say?'

Watching Dixon cycle colors, Jon went in for the kill by saying, "Ya know, Special Agent Dixon, I'm curious about something. With everything we now know about the FBI's founding father: J. Edgar Hoover. Things like his cross dressing, wearing women's makeup, dancing around his office dressed as a ballerina and his propensity to diddle young men that worked for him. Well, my question is this: if I tell you to go get buggered, is that still an insult or a professional recommendation?"

CHAPTER 24

6:50 PM. The Cotton Bowl

Utility Closet, Near Gate D (North side of stadium)

Getting inside the Cotton Bowl stadium proved easier than Father Shannon had said it would. However, hiding in a small, cold, and damp utility closet on the second level for seven hours had grown beyond painful. There was just enough room for Shannon, Burt and Connor to sit on the cement floor but not enough room for any of them to stretch out. Shannon recognized that, as uncomfortable as the tiny closet was, it was an ideal hiding place because it was located at the far end of the stadium. By the time security swept that part of the Cotton Bowl, the officer's would be cold and tired wanting nothing more than to finish the job. That was what Shannon was hoping for; however, should they be discovered, Shannon knew that they'd be forced to neutralize and quite literally abduct the security officers. Of course, when the officers failed to check in by radio or in person, this could conceivably cause even greater problems. *'No'* thought Shannon, *'we don't want a repeat of Parkland Hospital. Besides, with this arm hurting so badly, I'm not sure I'd be much good in a fist fight right now'.* Somewhere around 5:30 Shannon's hopes were realized as the nearly numb with cold security team hurriedly by passed the closet and headed for warmer places.

Shifting his weight to one side in an attempt to find a comfortable position, Connor softly mumbled, "Note to self: Do not ever again allow yourself to hide in a small closet with two other people."

Smiling, Burt replied, "Ya know guys, there has be a joke in this somewhere. I mean, how's this for an opener? 'A giant, a skinny guy and a priest were hiding in a closet…' That's as far as I can take it. If Ren was here, I'm sure he'd find a suitable punch line." All three men quietly chuckled.

Shannon said, "I am sure he could." Pausing for a moment's reflection, Shannon continued, "I've been trying to think of how I can explain all this to him. I just don't know if I can."

Burt answered saying, "Father, you've known Ren a lot longer than we have. But like you, both Connor and I have been through some shit with Ren. Back in our SWAT days we three grew really close. He comes across like the class clown and I swear if there's a way to break something, Ren will find it; but there's not a more intelligent, resourceful and intuitive person than Renee La Fleet. Don't sell your brother short, Father. Once he has all the information, he'll come around."

Father Shannon glanced at his watch and said, "I hope so. All right, let's get out of here and hit a bathroom. I'm ready to explode from all the coffee we've drank. After that, we'll move down to section 25. With security walking around everywhere that's about as close as we can get to Beckham without fear of compromise. It's been sleeting and snowing all day so watch your footing, there's going to be patches of ice everywhere."

Cotton Bowl
7:30 PM

We were forced to wait for Beckham to start his sermon before we left the office. The wind was beginning to kick up and it had started sleeting and snowing like crazy; but that didn't seem to discourage the faithful. Based on traffic reports there were well over 75 thousand people in attendance at the Cotton Bowl.

As Tex drove, I sat next to him still thinking about my overly theatrical conduct in the conference room. Sensing my inner turmoil, Tex asked, "You okay, partner?"

Nodding my head, I flippantly replied, "Other than the fact that I really made a fool of myself today, yes I'm fine. Thank you for asking."

Chuckling, Tex replied, "Listen wise-ass, you didn't make a fool of yourself. In fact, it was what Chief Wong was hoping for – or at least something very close to it."

Seeing the confusion on my face, Tex continued, saying, "Ren, why do you think Wong acted the way *he* did? He wanted to keep the Fed's completely off balance and ticked off. With Dixon so infuriated, he'll make sure his team keeps its distance, which leaves us to pursue our own leads tonight."

I said, "That's great about explaining why Wong acted the way he did, but he's always an asshole. What has that got to do with me and my little show?"

Tex replied, "Your brilliant display of righteous indignation negated whatever dirt Dixon thought he had on you and therefore, vicariously, on us. That dirt would've gone straight to the media if the Feds screw up this case or can't solve it. Of course, Hill drove a stake in the bastard's heart by supplying that information about your mother."

I asked, "Jesus, Tex, what if I'd clobbered him or worse? I was so angry that I almost went postal on his ass."

As we pulled into the Fair Park complex (where the Cotton Bowl is actually located), Tex answered, "Never would have happened, Ren. When you started walking toward Dixon, both Todd and I were hot on your heels. Trust me partner, we had your six."

As we continued to drive, I looked around at the full parking lots wondering if Tex and Todd would have been able to stop me before I nailed Dixon. I guess it was a moot point and didn't really matter. Still, I'd been very surprised by my visceral reaction to having my service record doubted. It could have been because it was done in such a distasteful manner or maybe it was because it was Dixon who'd done it. I don't know, but somehow I felt like I had failed the team, Rachel, and myself.

Snapping me back to the present, Tex said, "Ren, we've got a serious bad guy to catch tonight, so please let it go for now. I need your game face on, partner."

Looking at Tex I said, "I agree and I'm good!"

Tex and I continued to drive at a snail's pace until we reached the Administration building on the south side of the stadium by gate K. As we pulled into the police parking area we could see Wong and Rachel standing outside the mobile command post trying to stay warm.

After we parked, Tex and I walked over to them. "Jesus, it's freezing out here, Chief! Are we not allowed into the Command Post?" I asked.

Rachel replied over the wind, "Too crowded! The Civil Unrest team is packed in there with all the other commanders."

I know it might sound strange that the department had deployed the forty-man Civil Unrest team for a religious function, but back in the early 1990's the City had learned its lesson by not planning properly for a Super Bowl victory parade for the Dallas Cowboys. The City Manager denied the overtime requests that the tactical division had made so they could better man the parade route. Idiotically, she convinced herself that only 50 thousand people (mostly adults) would attend the parade. Of course when close to 500 thousand people (mostly teenagers - there was 98% truancy rate in the school district that day) showed up, the police were sorely outmanned and outgunned. From what Tex said, it was a real bad day for the police. His exact words were, "We got our asses kicked."

Glancing at his watch, Wong stated, "Beckham's going be preaching another thirty to forty-five minutes. I've already sent Miller and Hill to the media room where the reception will be held. It's located above the locker rooms and the team field entrance here on the south end. Let's head there and warm up. We can discuss our next plan of action then."

The Cotton Bowl stadium had recently been renovated, expanding from 70 thousand seats to over 90 thousand. The entire two upper levels had been gutted and beautifully rebuilt. Unfortunately for us, because of the renovation, it took the four of us several long minutes to actually reach the media room. As we finally walked inside, we had to produce badges, police identification cards, and sign in with my old commander, Lieutenant Dale Argus of Dallas police Department's SWAT division.

Cotton Bowl
8:00 PM
Media Room

As I signed in, I looked at Argus and asked, "This is normally a sergeant's job, Dale. You being here, is this punishment for Parkland?"

Smiling, Argus looked around and then quietly said, "You better believe it, Ren. Smyth went ballistic – called us a disgrace to the uniform. Personally, I'm just glad to still be employed."

I said, "I really am sorry, Dale. No offense intended. But the SWAT teams were simply outclassed that day."

Stifling a laugh Argus replied, "Ya think? Shannon tore ass through us like a hot knife through butter. If he ever thinks about going on a rampage again – let me know, will ya? I'll call in sick and Smyth can kiss my malingering ass."

I replied, "I'll try to remember to let ya know. That is, providing he tells me first. Speaking of Chief Smyth, is he here yet?"

Taking the clipboard back from me Argus whispered, "Yep. And he's accompanied by his two goons, Nolan and Garret. Also, Dr. Hershel Gaspar of the FBI and that frigging reporter, Ian Webb, are here, too. They came in just behind the Chief."

Glancing at Tex, I said, "Great. That complicates things a bit."

At exactly 8:15 Beckham's lead security element walked into the media room, scanning for threats and counting heads. The senior officer took the clipboard from Argus, looked at it quickly, and then contacted Beckham's escort team by radio, saying, "Escort this is Lead, there are twenty– two, I say again twenty–two, Dallas Police officers in the room. Twelve stationed on security post dressed Class A uniforms, the Chief of Police and a small entourage of two – all in formal civilian attire and six suits (*that would be us*) logged in as additional free roaming security. There are approximately 200 guests awaiting Mr. Beckham's arrival. Go ahead and bring him in."

A moment later, Doctor Christopher Beckham entered the room to a resounding applause. Smiling, Beckham said, "Thank you! It is friends such as each of you that make this ministry so very special. I know it was bitter cold outside, so let's not stand on ceremony. There's food and hot coffee or tea. Please help yourself. I'll be roaming around the room after I visit with my family for a few minutes. I would dearly love to speak to each of you."

After a quick visit with his wife and kids, and much to the ire of members of the city government, Doctor Beckham began making his rounds by cutting a straight path over to the six of us.

Grabbing my hand Beckham said, "Hello, Renee La Fleet! I haven't seen you since I had dinner with your Mom and Dad, what, fifteen years ago? You were home on leave from the Marines."

Doctor Beckham was of average height but carried himself like the true spiritual warrior he was. Though he was a very good friend of my parents, I'd met him just that one time. Once in fifteen years, but that was one of his many gifts. You could meet the man and he'd remember you – and anything you told him, for life.

I answered saying, "I'm well, Doctor Beckham, as are both my parents. They send their regards and apologies for not being able to make it tonight. Dad asked that if you have time, to please call him before you leave town." Pausing for a moment, I continued saying, "Sir, may I please introduce Chief Harold Wong, Lieutenant Rachel Saxen, Detectives Danny Beers, Jon Hill and Todd Miller?"

Shaking hands with each of the men first, Beckham came back to Rachel and gently took her hand and said, "Rachel, what a beautiful name… and well assigned, I think." Still holding her hand, Beckham looked at me out of the corner of his eyes and then said to Rachel, "Dearest Rachel, you've got your work cut out for you, but I promise you this, it *will* be worth it!" And with that he kissed her on the cheek and let go of her hand.

I think Rachel and I could have competed for who was the deepest color of red. I looked at Wong who seemed amused, but Tex, Jon and Todd each had a shit eating grin on their faces.

Doctor Beckham then cleared his throat and grew serious, saying, "Ok… business now. Lieutenant Argus briefed my staff and I as to why you're here Chief Wong. I'll cooperate as well as I can, but I still must see to my flock. Also, Renee I don't believe that Father Richard Shannon is involved in these murders, but only time will tell us that. Now, I've got to make my rounds before someone – like the Mayor – gets upset."

True to his word, Doctor Beckham saw to those that needed prayer and counseling but he also made it easy on us. He never left the room without extra security (his own and ours) following behind him at a very discreet distance.

Chief Smyth and his 'Special Investigators' had left early after a brief but intense conversation with Doctor Beckham. Both Tex and I had been relieved outside by Jon and Todd and rotated in to warm up. From where we were standing we could hear Smyth and Beckham's conversation.

"Christopher, it's far too dangerous with a mad man running around killing people. Look, I myself have two security guards now. You should have a room dedicated to counseling here where it is safe… and warm!"

Beckham replied, "William, you know how important these little walks are to our congregation. For some, these walks represent the only time in their busy, daily lives when they hear the Word. I won't be deterred out of fear for my own life. Besides, I'm very well protected by Dallas SWAT, my own Security Specialists and by Chief Wong and his people." They continued to talk for a while longer then shook hands, hugged each other and then Chief Smyth left.

Tex and I had just returned from a bathroom break when I saw that Doctor Beckham was talking to Gaspar and Webb. All three were putting on their coats as they talked. Looking around the room I realized that it was practically empty except for Beckham's personal security detail and the caterers breaking down the tables and chairs. Chief Wong and Lieutenant Saxen had been called away to the mobile command post for a debriefing and by all appearances Lieutenant Argus and his guys had also left for the debrief.

Closing his cell phone, Tex grabbed my arm and, looking at a small map of the stadium, said, "Just talked to Jon and Todd. They're on the second concourse near section 16. That's on the northeast end of the stadium. Jon said because of the ice, they'll have to double back and head this way."

Looking at the map, I replied, "Jesus, that's the long route back. But I guess there's no helping it."

In the last two hours, the wind had increased to nearly forty miles an hour blowing rain, snow and then sleet over almost the entire west side of the Cotton Bowl. Sections 15 down to section 8 had become almost completely impassable. Sections 7 down to section 1 were fairly clear with some areas of treacherous footing. Unfortunately, for no rhyme or reason that we could discern, Doctor Beckham seemed to like that area for his walks. He'd leave the media room, take the back elevator down to the field, walk out to about the 50 yard line and then ascend the stairs between sections 6 and 7 to the second level concourse before heading back to the media room. Beckham had made this trip over a dozen times that night, never varying his route.

Watching as Beckham, Gaspar and Webb exited the room with a two man security detail following closely behind, Tex and I quickly re-donned our coats and headed for the door. Tex looked at me and said, "If it's going to happen tonight, this is it. We'll both do a quick radio check once we're on the ground floor. I'll stay on the command post tactical channel nine – you switch over to channel one. I'll call Wong and Saxen via my cell and they can start back-up."

Running out the door, we saw that Beckham had already boarded the elevator and was quite possibly on the ground level heading for the tunnel leading to the game field. Tex and I flew by the elevators to the stairs taking several steps at a time until we got to the ground level. We ran over to the field entrance tunnel where we could see Beckham walking slowly with Gaspar and Webb just past the southern goal post. After we cleared the tunnel we both stopped and attempted to make our radio checks.

Tex said, "Ren, I'm not picking anything up - my radio's dead!"

I checked the volume and then keyed my own radio mike saying, "CAPERS 133 to any element on this channel." Nothing but the small red light flashing when I keyed my radio meaning that it was functioning just fine!

"Tex the radios aren't dead, we're being jammed. Probably by an encrypted radio scanner cycling through departmental frequencies. Try your cell."

Tex hit redial several times for both Wong and Saxen. Looking at me, Tex said, "I'm not getting through to either of them." He then tried to call dispatch and 911 to no avail. I stood there just watching him and thinking that I've been through all this before. I had to fight back a wave of fear. I put my hand over his cell phone as Tex continued to try and call for help. Just like in Iraq our radios were jammed and there are men that need saving.

Shaking my head, I said, "Tex, let it be. We've got to catch up to Beckham and get him to safety." I scanned the field and realized that Beckham, Gaspar and Webb were already climbing the stairs between sections 6 and 7. All three men had reached the top of the stairs and then disappeared into the darkened concourse.

Beckham's two trailing security officers (who were still down on the field) stopped walking, looked at one another and then suddenly broke into a sprint, jetting toward the stairs in an effort to reach Beckham. It might have been my imagination, but even from this distance with the stadium lights slowly dimming, I thought I could see the worry on the faces of both men as they drew their handguns and ran.

CHAPTER 25

The Cotton Bowl
Section 25

Hidden from view, Father Shannon watched Beckham's security team peak the top of the stairs and disappear into the darkness on the other side. At the same time, he could see Ren and Tex leave the field entrance tunnel and sprint across the field heading toward the same stairs Beckham and his security team had taken. A second later he saw six flashes of light in rapid succession coming from the second level concourse where the security officers had gone.

Turning and facing Detectives Burt and Connor, Shannon stated, "It's started, gentlemen. We'll move down to the ground concourse, circle around and come out from the small tunnel at section 7. We've got a long way to go and we'll have to move quickly but stay tactical; we're hunting a very dangerous prey."

Upper Level Concourse
Section 14

After talking with Tex, Jon Hill and Todd Miller quickly realized that retracing their route back to the media room would take too long. It would be faster (though initially, much more dangerous) to go down the iced-over stairs at section 14. If they could negotiate those stairs, they could duck into the small tunnel that led to the ground concourse and then run like hell. With any luck, they'd link up with Ren and Tex somewhere along the way.

Section 7

Tex and I bolted across the field and began climbing the stairs as fast as we could. I watched as the security officers crested the top at full tilt, never stopping and never looking back. What they did was incredibly brave and a fierce display of loyalty to Beckham, but it was also tactically unsafe. A heart-beat later this thought manifested itself into reality when I saw brilliant flashes of light that could only be gunfire coming from the upper concourse. I wasn't sure if Tex had seen the flashes – most likely he had, but it didn't matter because you always sound off, letting your partner know what you've seen. The wind was blowing so hard I was forced to yell, "Gunfire!" and simultaneously we pulled our handguns from our holsters as we continued our climb.

Beginning to breathe heavy now, we stepped on the aisle landing at the small entrance tunnel for section 7 and then split apart to get up and around the tunnel without crowding one another. Just as I took the first step, there came several blinding flashes from the concourse and I dove behind the seats to my left for cover. In slow motion I saw Tex fall forward onto the lower steps right of the tunnel and slide back down to the landing. Until I saw the blood on his hands and lower left leg, I thought he'd slipped on a patch of ice and went down face first. Rolling over onto his back, Tex yelled, "Ren, I'm hit!"

Hearing that declaration of pain, panic, and fear, I fired half a dozen shots toward the concourse and then bolted from my position of cover. After only three steps, I slipped on the ice and fell hard to the ground as more bullets struck all around me. Not bothering to stand back up I crawled toward Tex, past the front of the tunnel opening and grabbed Tex's bloody, outstretched hand. Using the tunnel opening for cover, I yanked Tex to me and then pulled him down to the far end of the tunnel where I hoped we'd be shielded gunfire.

Safe or not, I kept my head on a swivel looking for threats that might come down the tunnel or from either direction of the concourse. Quickly glancing at his face I could see Tex's eyes start to glass over from pain and shock. I shouted, "Sergeant Daniel Beers, focus! Fight the shock – take several deep breaths, Jarhead, you know the Goddamned drill!"

Listening to me, Tex breathed deep several times then shook his head saying, "I'm good Ren… I'm good."

Knowing this, I ripped open his pants leg and looked at the wounds. There were two small bleeding holes an inch apart on the inside of the left calf muscle. "Tex, the wounds are bleeding but not seriously. Let me look at your arm and hand."

Against the pain, Tex pulled his left elbow in tight and turned his hand over palm up. The bullet wounds in his forearm and hand were, like the ones in his calf, bleeding, but not horrendously so. Also, none of the wounds were through and through. Meaning more than likely the bullets had lodged in bone.

I asked Tex, "Even in this wind we should have heard a weapons report echoing off these walls. I heard nothing, you?"

Tex shook his no and replied, "I heard nothing. It's a low caliber, suppressed weapon. You pegged it Ren, this is our boy."

Grinning, I responded, "Yeah, lucky us. Tex, Beckham is a goner if I don't keep moving. We don't have time to wait for Jon and Todd. For all we know, they've been ambushed and taken out, too."

I could see the look of despair in my partner's eyes as the realization of what I said hit home.

"Tex, we can't wait. If it gets too intense, I'll egress back to this position. Keep trying the radio or dial out on your cell. Where's your weapon?"

Tex replied, "Up there somewhere. Hand me my backup. It's in my shoulder holster on my right side."

Ground Concourse
Under Section 34

With weapons up at the low ready and Father Shannon on point, the three men moved in a small wedge formation as quickly and as tactically as they could. Setting a slow, measured pace, Shannon struggled to resist the temptation to speed up. In his heart of hearts, Shannon sensed that Ren was in danger, but he knew he couldn't afford to outrun his two wingmen or worse, blunder into an ambush. Every five or six steps, Shannon heard Connor turn around and check their rear to make sure they weren't being trailed.

Ground Concourse
Under Section 7

On a whim, I tried a wall-mounted payphone and found those lines to 911 not working either. I walked back over to Tex and, kneeling down, I extracted the used magazine from my weapon, reached into my magazine holder and grabbed a fresh magazine and reloaded my handgun. I wasn't out of ammunition, but I'd used heavy, suppressive fire when I went to help Tex (I'll probably catch shit from IAD about doing that) but that meant that I had only a half full magazine in my automatic. Changing it out was not only smart, it was also tactically correct. I picked up the used magazine and put it back into my magazine pouch. Unlike in the movies or TV, no real officer will just drop and leave a partially full magazine on the ground. God only knows if you might need that ammunition later.

I wanted to say a silent prayer (my first since Iraq), but I couldn't remember even the Lord's Prayer, so I asked Tex if he was okay.

Looking at me like I had three heads, Tex retorted, "No, you jackass, I've been shot! Pat's gonna kick your ass for letting this happen to me!"

Smiling as I stood up and put my hand out to Tex, "Fair enough, partner, Semper Fi!"

Staring me in the eyes Tex took my hand and replied, "Semper Fi, Marine. Try not to get yourself killed."

Thinking that I had heard those exact words in Iraq from Gunnery Sergeant Roberts, I nodded and whispered, "I always hear that just before I get the shit kicked out of me. See 'ya."

Walking to the end of the tunnel with my weapon up, I leaned out and quick-peeked up at the top lip of the tunnel entrance to make sure no one was standing there. Staying low, I moved to the end of the tunnel wall on the left side, quick-peeked again and then attempted to haul ass up the stairs. I could have moved slowly and tactically from one row of seats to another, but the stadium seats provide very poor cover (meaning I doubted that the plastic seats would stop a bullet) so reaching the top where there was a cement wall on each side of the stairway opening was my best option.

Of course, when I'd started my 'hauling ass,' I failed to consider the ice. More than once I slipped – sometimes catching myself, but most often I did a face plant into the steps. It would've been much faster to have carefully gone up the stairs tactically and slowly than trying to run them. Truthfully, I was just glad that none of my friends had seen me playing slip and slide.

I finally reached the cement wall, knelt down and began studying the concourse. Looking between the break in the wall where the row of stairs began, I started scanning objects closest to me. Immediately in front of the stairs were the bodies of Beckham's security team. The concourse was very poorly lit, so it was difficult to make out, but I was almost positive they were posed. Judging by the pool of blood under their heads, both men were dead.

On the other side of the concourse walkway was a row of a dozen or more rooms all with the doors shut. These were probably bathrooms, storage closets and concession stands that clutter a stadium. Even with the wind screeching through the concourse, I should be able to hear voices echoing in the bathrooms. From here the closets looked to be too small to hide grown men (or at least, that's what I believed), so, the concession stands would be the first rooms I searched.

To expedite things, I would have to move across the walkway and, starting at the right end, check each room door. If it was locked, I could move on to the next door working my way back this direction. I didn't think that the perp could have taken Beckham very far. I was really hoping that Jon and Todd would show up before I encountered anyone.

Thankful that there was very little ice in this part of the concourse, I brought my handgun up to the high ready position and moved across to the first door. Bending at the knees and dropping my left foot back, I brought my right elbow up and tucked my weapon into my side by my ribs, reached across with my left hand and tested the door knob.

Ground Concourse
Under Section 12

Helping his partner back to his feet, Jon Hill asked, "Todd, you okay?"

Hill and Miller had managed to come down the iced over stairs in section 13 without incident, but parts of the ground concourse had been just as precarious causing both men to slip and fall numerous times. Miller angrily replied, "Christ, Jon, at this rate we'll never get there!"

"Todd, the area ahead of us looks no better. We'll just have to slow down a little mo......" Abruptly Hill stopped talking drew his duty weapon yelling, "Suspect in the shadows on the right!"

As Hill yelled, the hidden suspect began to fire on the two detectives. Dropping down to a knee, Miller pulled his own handgun, sited on the suspect's muzzle flashes and began returning fire. Seeing the shadowed figure jerk back multiple times, Miller knew that he had scored hits. Coming to his feet, Miller continued to gently pull the trigger and walk slowly toward the now prone suspect. Finally standing over the twitching body, Miller scanned for more threats and then declared, "Suspect's down, Jon – I see no other threats."

Bending down, Miller yanked the Glock .40 caliber handgun from the assailant's fingers and then declared, "I can't identify this clown. He's got a hoodie pulled over his head and he's wearing a ski mask. This was a close one, Jon."

Hearing no reply from his partner, Miller turned around and saw Jon Hill lying on his back not moving.

Ground Concourse
Under Section 3

From somewhere up ahead, gunfire echoed through the cement corridors of the ground level concourse. Freezing and going to a knee, Father Shannon put up a closed fist with his left hand, signaling Connor and Burt to also stop moving and get down. Listening to the gunfire Shannon stated, "The shit's hit the fan for someone." Continuing to listen to the firefight, Shannon said, "A .40 caliber started it... a 9mm millimeter is answering. Listen! The 9's moving in for the kill." Pop – Pop – Pop – Pop. "He's firing every time his left foot hits the ground. That's *excellent* fire discipline!"

As quickly as it had started, the shooting ended. Glancing back over his shoulder, Shannon asked, "Burt, Dallas officers carry 9's, right?"

Scanning the area for threats, Burt replied, "Yeah Father, we do."

"Outstanding! I think we can chalk that engagement up to Dallas," exclaimed Shannon with a feral grin. "Let's keep moving but with that gunfire we'll have to slow down even more."

Upper Level Concourse
Under Section 107

I prepared to make entry and whispered to myself saying, "Of course it's unlocked, Ren. They've all been unlocked!"

By the time I had reached this, the sixth unlocked door, I was starting to get really pissed off and awfully tired. It violates every tactical entry technique written to clear a room without cover, but Jon and Todd had never shown and Tex was out of the fight. A few minutes earlier I'd heard a series of muffled gunshots coming from the bottom concourse and I couldn't help but fear the worse for Jon and Todd. Still, I had to keep going.

Forcing myself to again bend at the knees, tuck in my weapon, I pushed the door open and in a fluid motion stepped into a small single room filled with shelves and food stores. I started to immediately exit again when I noticed a green light coming from a large partially open drawer at the counter. I'm not sure why my curiosity got the best of me, but I reached down and fully opened the drawer and saw two small, lap-top computers activated and apparently running.

Picking up and opening the first lap-top, I studied the numbers 9-1-1 flashing on the screen over and over again. I know that with the right equipment, software, system codes and a litany of passwords it *was* possible to interrupt a 911 system. Hackers had done it several times in Dallas, causing a major disruption in our ability to respond to calls, but I never thought it could be done with a lap-top.

I set the computer on the counter and opened the second lap-top. There were seven phone numbers that constantly popped up on the screen and then disappeared again. The computer was apparently dialing the numbers, hanging up and redialing so quickly that the receiving phones could not answer or dial out. Looking at the phone numbers I immediately recognized the six that belonged to me and my team. The seventh number, I didn't know.

Seeing that both computers were plugged in to a wall socket and then hardwired into a wall phone jack, I reached up and started to yank the plugs and wires out… and then stopped. Shaking my head I mumbled quietly, "You tricky bastard!"

I didn't recognize that seventh number on the second lap-top but I could guess that it belonged to our killer. If I pulled the wires out of the phone jack, that would crash the block on our cell phones and the 911 system. It would also allow the suspect's phone to ring, telling him exactly where I was. The computers explained the phones, but not the radios. Somewhere around here was a very expensive piece of radio jamming equipment. Not that it mattered. I'd leave it running for the same reasons I wouldn't pull the wires on the computers.

Ground Concourse
Under Section 12

Moving as quickly as he could on the ice covered pavement, Miller reached his partners side and then dropped to his knees. Running his hands across Hill's head and body Miller looked for blood and injury. Finding none, Hill sat back on his heels feeling helpless and confused. Reaching down he gently took Hill's duty weapon from his hands and then began to gently shake Hill's shoulder calling his name, "Jon Hill, Jon Hill… come on partner, wake up. Come on, Jon, give me a break, will ya?"

Jon Hill's eyes suddenly snapped open, the last thing he could remember was a suspect coming out of the shadows, shooting. In that split second of realization, Hill's ingrained training took over. Flipping over onto his stomach and coming to his hands and knees, he began a frantic search for his handgun. Not immediately finding it, Hill reached for the backup gun he kept in an ankle holster. Somewhere in the distance, Hill heard a voice calling him and slowly the audio exclusion associated with a profound adrenaline rush began to subside.

"……… Jon, it's …here… I've got ……… partner. Jon Hill snap … of ……!" Miller said loudly. Stopping his movement, Hill stared at Miller as his body began to register the horrendous pain of being shot center mass while wearing soft body armor.

Collapsing to the ground and rolling onto his back, Hill cried, "This sucks! It's like getting wacked with a ball-peen hammer square in the chest."

Crawling over to where Hill now laid, Miller said, "Here this might help a little." Reaching over, Miller opened the front of his partner's ruined dress shirt and pulled out the now bent steel Shok plate from the ballistic vest. Looking at the plate, Miller said, "Still hot. Three hits in a nice tight little group. You're lucky there weren't more. The plate and vest might have begun to fail after these three. We've got to get you to a hospital for blunt trauma. If I help you, can you walk?"

Trying to slow his breathing, Hill said, "Yeah, I think so – really nauseated, though." Tears streaming down his face, he continued saying, "God bless number 33."

Confused, Miller asked, "God bless who, Jon?"

Hill replied, "When I was issued this vest last year, there was a little tag that stated 'This vest was inspected by number 33.' I don't know who number 33 is, but I'm gonna send that guy flowers and a thank-you card!"

Helping his partner to his feet, Detective Todd Miller said a silent prayer of thanks for the life of his partner and for the dedicated efforts of vest inspector number 33.

Upper Level Concourse
Under Section 107

I searched the last small room and stepped out in the concourse thinking that I must have missed something in one of the other rooms. Keeping my weapon at the low ready position, I leaned back on the wall and looked up and down the concourse contemplating my next move. I thought about going back to the room with the computers, yanking wires and calling for backup. That would help me, but it would possibly allow the suspect to escape or worse, get Beckham killed. I still believed that the killer could not have taken Beckham far. Based on what Jon had told Tex, to my left things were iced over and to my right the concourse went back to the media room. No, they had to be here in this row of rooms. Somehow as my exhaustion had grown, I must have missed another door inside one of the rooms.

In SWAT, where we routinely run dope raids on houses, fatigue is a noted cop killer. An officer can stay focused and tactical (meaning ready for anything) for only so long. Clearing a single house is a lot like playing four quarters of football in a single few minutes. It literally beats the living crap out of ya. Exhausted, I knew that I was getting increasingly sloppy in my entry and clearing techniques, but I couldn't help it.

With my non gun hand, I wiped the sweat from my face and got ready to start my search over. Trying to settle my nerves, I looked down and saw something that I had indeed missed: shoe prints! Don't get me wrong, it had been raining, sleeting and snowing and the stadium had been packed with thousands of people. So shoe prints were nothing special except that these broke off from the normal concourse path, they were wet, not frozen, and more importantly, they went past where I was standing to a door around the corner that I hadn't seen.

Pushing off the wall, I brought my weapon up to the high ready and moved to the door. Stopping just short of the opening I studied the door seeing that it stood ajar about an inch. Coming from the inside I could hear...... chanting?

As carefully as I could, I gently pushed the door slightly more open, trying to see without giving myself away. Straining to catch a glimpse of the inside, I could see that the room was dimly lit with flickering candles. Standing several feet away with his back to the door stood a man dressed in priestly garb. I could just make out Beckham who kneeled facing me, obviously with his hands tied behind his back. Next to him also on their knees were Webb and Gaspar.

The chanting stopped and in an almost giddy voice the priest declared, "Doctor Christopher Beckham, you have been found guilty of crimes against the Catholic church. Doctor Hershel Gaspar and Mr. Ian Webb because of your relationship with Doctor Christopher Beckham, you have also been found guilty of the same crimes. For these crimes and many, many others, you are here by sentenced to death! The sentence will be carried out immediately."

With the verdict passed, the priest turned to his right where, up against the wall closest to me sat an improvised altar. On the altar were more candles, statues of Christ and the Virgin Mary, a communion plate filled with the .22 caliber shell casings from each murder and a glass of wine. In the center of the altar I could see a large combat fighting knife and a .22 Caliber Auto Handgun with a suppression device attached to the end of it.

After lighting the candles on the altar, the priest knelt and began praying loudly. I didn't think I'd get a better chance to act so it was time to cowboy up and move. My entry would have to be dynamic with enough controlled power to knock the priest to the floor, putting myself between him and the gun and the knife. Dropping my left leg back and bending as best I could at the knees, I tucked my weapon into my side and with all the strength I could muster, I exploded toward the door. Shoving the door open as I moved, I stepped through and slammed into the priest sending him sprawling between the hostages and down to the floor. As quickly as he'd gone down, he rolled back up to his feet and looked at me.

I've seen malevolence in a thousand different ways – I've seen the horrors that people can to do one another in peace and in war but until this moment, as I looked at the demonic expression on the face of Chief William Smyth, I realized that I have never before been in the presence of true evil!

Ground Concourse
Under Section 7

Hearing the shots that echoed north from where he lay, Tex decided to move. With wounds still bleeding, he slowly dragged his body to the far side of the concourse where he concealed himself deep in the shadows. From this new vantage point, he could still see the tunnel where Ren had gone and, just as important, he could watch both directions of the concourse.

Upper Level Concourse
Under Section 107

"Keep your hands where I see them, Chief, it's over."

Out of my peripheral vision I could see Beckham, Webb and Gaspar struggling to break the plexi-cuffs that held their wrist and ankles. The trouble was, I couldn't do anything to help them *and* cover Smyth at the same time. Because of the confines of small room and even with the three hostages between us, I was already standing too close to Smyth. Granted I had the gun, but I'd learned the hard way that Smyth was lightning-quick in the attack. I might be able to crank out a few rounds should he make a move. But if I missed, the bullets could ricochet and kill a hostage. At this range it might be hard to miss, yet stranger things have happened. Especially where I am concerned.

Slowly raising his hands, Smyth smiled and said, "I'm very saddened that it's you confronting me. You're a very promising detective, Mr. La Fleet. I also think that you're a good man. Troubled and damaged, but good nevertheless. Please understand that it's nothing personal when I say that I'll enjoy killing you."

I didn't want to engage this murdering bastard in any type of discussion but as long as he was answering questions (or mouthing off) he was in the decision making process. It's an old hostage negotiator's trick to keep a suspect talking and out of the action mode. If I could delay him, help might arrive or one of the hostages might work his hands free. Picking my words very carefully, I said, "Chief, I understand why you sacrificed Joshua, Whitehouse, St. John and even why it was necessary to try to remove Riggs and the others in Houston, but we've never understood what Father Lanton did wrong. He never touched Maria Gonzalas – he was true to his vows, so why him?"

Shaking his head, Smyth said, 'You *are* wrong. Lanton broke his vows the moment he lusted after Maria Gonzalas. Does it not say in Matthew 5:28 'that everyone who looks on a woman with lust for her has committed adultery with her in his heart'?"

It struck me odd that I was having a theological discussion with a madman, but I didn't have time to contemplate this fact because the Chief was on a roll and I wanted him talking.

"But worse, so much more worse than the filthy lust in his heart was that he broke his sacred vows to keep what was said in confession a secret. He wrote about me in his diaries... I know because I read it! The fool left his diary out while I was visiting his house. He betrayed me and God. He claimed that I was losing my grip on reality... Oh, let me assure you, Detective La Fleet, that I know that I'm quite insane. I love torturing small animals, setting fires and killing people. I proudly fit the profile. I even collected the shell casings from each of my victims as trophies. But like the Apostle Paul, it doesn't matter because God has chosen me in spite of this weakness. I am charged by God to remove the evil from his one true Church!"

I think that I personally would have felt *much better* about all this if the Chief had denied being crazy. Instead this jackass had embraced his insanity. Besides, I'm no biblical scholar but I don't think the Apostle Paul was a nut-job like this guy.

Giggling now, he continued, "There are others out there fulfilling this anointed duty with me. I am not alone in this! That's how I learned what weapons I should use and what words to say."

It took me a full second to understand that he was talking about the Interpol reports. Most of those killings had been in poor third world countries. However, some had been in places like Argentina that had good police investigators and adequate forensic capabilities. That explained the .22 caliber he used and what he had said to Riggs before trying to kill him.

I was lost in this thought and almost missed what the Chief said next.

"And now, Detective La Fleet, enough of this discourse. You do remember your old academy mate Special Investigator James Garret, don't you?"

Tensing, I asked, "He's behind me isn't he?" Looking down at the hostages all three men were shaking their heads yes.

Shit and double shit!

Ground Concourse
Under Section 9

Detective Todd Miller fought to keep both he and Jon Hill on their feet. Looking back over his shoulder he felt dismayed that they'd only moved about a hundred feet since the shooting. Jon kept stopping to vomit and was in terrible pain from the blunt trauma. Looking at his partner, Miller couldn't fail to notice how pale Hill's face had become and that he was shivering uncontrollably and struggling to stay on his feet. Miller considered leaving Hill and moving on to help Ren but he knew if he did this, there was a very good chance that Jon might die from shock or the cold.

With eyes glassy, Hill mumbled in a slurred voice, "Todd, keep us moving... Ren and Tex are searching alone."

Upper Level Concourse
Under Section 107

Laughing rather manically, Smyth said, "James, please disarm Detective La Fleet. Remove his back up gun and his soft body armor, too."

Pressing his handgun into the base of my back, Garret replied, "Yes Father. La Fleet… The big war hero! I've hated your ass since the academy."

Reaching around, Garret grabbed my gun and tossed it to Smyth, who then pointed it at my face. Holstering his own gun, Garret continued to run his mouth as he frisked me. "La Fleet gets rookie of the year, Garret gets nothing. La Fleet gets a medal for valor, Garret get nothing. La Fleet gets promoted *twice* and Garret still gets nothing. I hate your guts, you little shit!"

Garret finally found my backup gun, a little six shot Smith and Wesson revolver, in my ankle holster. After quickly unloading the Smith, he tossed the backup to the far corner of the room. Reaching under my jacket and shirt Garret pulled the Velcro shoulder straps loose and yanked out my soft body armor. Stepping back and drawing his gun again, Garret asked, "What now, Father? La Fleet's partner is dead or wounded and I heard gunfire from where Brother Nolan set up his ambush. With a little blessings from God, Hill and Miller are dead too. But eventually this place is going to be crawling with cops."

Studying my handgun for a moment, Smyth unloaded it and then dropped it to the floor. "Yes, James, I agree. Please take Detective La Fleet to another room and kill him while I finish our Lord's business here."

As Smyth was talking I looked down and saw that Webb had worked his hands loose and was, as best he could, trying to make eye contact with me.

Ground Concourse
Under Section 7

Injured arm throbbing in pain and growing increasingly fatigued, Shannon allowed Burt to take point as he rotated back into Burt's former position. Within seconds of taking point, Burt could see two people slowly moving toward him out of the dimly lit concourse. One was obviously injured and being helped along by the other. Continuing to move forward, Burt brought his weapon up and shouted, "Stop! Hands – let me see your hands!"

So intent on helping his partner, Todd Miller had not seen Shannon, Burt and Connor moving toward him. Jerking his head up at the sound of Burt's voice, Miller dropped Hill to the ground, drew his gun and cried out, "Freeze, police!"

From the shadows near the concession stands a slurred voice loudly said, "Freeze! Dallas Police – do not move!"

With guns swinging in every direction trying to cover all the perceived threats, the men kept trying to yell over one another with challenges and orders to drop their weapons. As tensions grew, Jon Hill, who was lying on the ground at Miller's feet began to scream over his friends. "Burt, Connor, Tex – it's us, Miller and Hill!"

Slowly lowering his gun, Miller said, "Hill's hurt really bad."

From the shadows in a weakened tone, Tex said, "I'm afraid I am too, boys."

Recognizing the voices, Burt said, "All right, let's all lower our weapons gentlemen, shall we?"

Thinking that when Miller and Tex realized Shannon was there it might trigger another gun-fest, Connor said, "Tex, Jon, Todd, Shannon is with us. He's not the killer!"

Hearing no angry retorts at this statement, Shannon holstered his weapon and moved over to check on Tex. Burt and Connor ran to Hill, lifted him off the ground and carried him over to where Tex was lying.

Studying their faces and injuries, Shannon determined that while none of the wounds were fatal, both men were going into shock and quite possibly hypothermia. Either of which could kill them. Taking off his small backpack, Shannon pulled out two small silver warming blankets and disposable warming pads. As he began to treat Tex and Jon for hypothermia and shock, Shannon couldn't ignore the fact that every second spent helping these men were seconds that might cost Ren his life......

Upper Level Concourse
Under Section 107

Watching Webb out of the corner of my eye, I subtly made a clenched fist with my left hand hoping he would understand that I wanted him to wait for my move. Just before he searched me, Garret had pressed his handgun into the base of my back. That was a no-go all rookies are taught in the academy. Garret had never been a good cop or even a smart one. So all I had to do was to do something that would cause him to screw up.

My hopes of the cavalry arriving in time had already vanished and if Nolan showed up, it would be King's X and I'd be toast, as would the hostages. But, I needed a catalyst for Garret so, hoping to force the right moment I said, "I'm not going anywhere, Chief. If Garret is going to blow my brains out, he'll have to do it here. Of course that'll mess up your pretty little altar – not to mention, you'll get my blood and brains all over you and your sacrificial lambs. Besides, I don't think a sick asshole like you would be called by God to scrape up dog shit off the pavement."

The Chief just stood there smiling and then shrugged. Crap, not the reaction I had hoped for. I'm still quite the Marine and all good Marines live by the philosophy that if you push enough buttons (especially the *red* buttons) something is bound to happen. What I said next is offensive even to a faithless man like me. "So, Chief, before you kill me answer a question I've always had. Is the rumor true that Joseph got it from Mary three or four times before the 'virgin birth'?"

The words had just left my mouth when the Chief contorted his face and screamed, "Sacrilege! For that you will die by my hands!"

As the Chief began to move toward me I felt Garret press his handgun into my back.

I glanced down at Webb, nodded and then shifted my weight to my left foot and spun. Using my left hand, I pushed Garret's handgun away from me toward the wall. With my right hand closed into a tight fist, I struck Garret at the base of his neck stunning him and dropping him onto the altar. This caused the altar to collapse to the floor and Garret to fall unconscious with his body partly out the door.

At the same time I was moving, Webb, with feet still bound, stood up and then launched himself into Smyth, clawing at his face with his freed hands. Despite Webb's best efforts, the chief brushed him away and closed the distance between us as I stepped over Garret's body and backed out the door.

The Chief followed me out saying, "This is not what I had in mind for you, Detective La Fleet. In fact I wanted your death to be... quick and painless. But for your heresy, I am going to beat you to death very slowly."

As Smyth and I began to slowly circle one another, I said, "Really? Because all I see is you trying to talk me to death."

It was a bit of bluster on my behalf, but I had maneuvered the Chief so that his back was to the room with the hostages. Webb had freed his feet and, shoving Garret's body the rest of the way out the door, shut it and hopefully locked it.

Hearing the door shut, Smyth spun around and roared, "You sinful arrogant... You have interfered with God's work!" Turning back to me, he cried, "I will enjoy this!"

Smiling, I replied, "So will I."

Not waiting for more bantering, I suddenly attacked with a flurry of punches to Smyth's face. He managed to block my first few, but my fourth and fifth punches struck home breaking his nose and bloodying his lips. Smyth spun away, dropped low, and attempted to sweep my legs out from under me. Sensing what Smyth was doing, I quickly lowered my body into a near kneeling position, placed my right elbow just past my right knee and ducked my head down and to the outside. With my body set in such a position, it was like a rock; so when Smyth's leg smashed into my right side, he grunted in shock and pain. I used the momentum of his leg-sweep to help push me back up and into a fight stance.

Smyth rolled away and attempted to come to his own feet but I was all over him with low kicks to his shins and knees. I slammed a kick into his right knee and felt it as tendons and ligaments snapped with audible crack. Smyth squealed with pain and dropped to all fours. Stepping in, I brushed away an arm held up in a defensive manner and struck his upper scapula with a hammer blow punch. Lighting quick, I followed the hammer blow with an elbow to his face. The elbow missed my intended target of his nose (which could have been fatal) and hit his left eye shattering the eye socket.

I know it doesn't sound fair attacking a man on the ground, but I don't get paid to fight fair, just to win. The elbow strike slammed Smyth to the ground face first. Laying there, that pitiful piece of excrement began to scream, "I yield, I yield!"

I kicked Smyth in the ribs as hard as I could flipping him over on to his back where he gasped for breath past bruised or broken ribs. I grabbed the front of Smyth's priestly robes and pulled his face up to mine and said, "Now *you* know the difference between a chicken shit street fight and hand to hand combat!"

As I shoved Smyth back to the pavement, I stood up and looked at the room where the hostages were hidden. At the same moment, I realized Garret was not lying in front of the door I heard the distinctive sound of an expandable ASP (night stick) opening. Ducking low I turned, stepped back and gave ground as the ASP wielded by Garret struck the side of my face sending me to the cold pavement. I rolled three or four times to gain distance from him.

My rolls carried me over the dead security guards and smashed me into the cement retaining wall. Using the railing by the stairs that led down to section seven, I pulled my feet under me and stood up. Without any semblance of technique Garret attacked me swinging the ASP like a crazed swordsmen. I managed to block several of his wild strikes with my forearms and hands. With each block he seriously bruised, and then fractured my left hand and fingers. I knew that I had to end this fight before he could sneak in a head strike and put me down.

Garret suddenly stepped back and looked at me as I brought my hands up into a boxer's stance, intentionally leaving my ribs on my left side open. Garret took the bait and slammed the ASP into my unprotected ribs. Feeling excruciating pain as my ribs fractured, I dropped my left elbow down and trapped the ASP. At the same time I stepped into Garret and, with my right hand opened forming a *shutō-uchi,* I thrust my fingers into his exposed throat shattering Garret's wind pipe. For good measure I clenched a fist and crushed Garrets throat. Gurgling as he fell, Garret was dead before he hit the ground.

Bent at the waist, trying to catch my breath over the pain of the ribs, I saw one of the guns the security guards must have dropped when they died. As I picked it up, I heard someone laughing and talking.

"Very nicely done, Detective La Fleet" Smyth said as he pulled the trigger on what had to be the gun I had knocked from Garret's hands. I brought the guard's weapon up and fired at the same time missing Smyth's face by less than inch.

Ground Concourse
Under Section 7

After covering the men with the warming blankets and placing the warming pads at their groins, arm pits and abdomens, Shannon elevated their heads and feet to fight the shock. Looking at Tex, he asked, "Detective Beers, where did Ren go?"

Fighting to concentrate, Tex replied, "Up the stairs… into the fight."

As Shannon, Burt and Connor stood up they heard shots ring out like thunder.

Upper Level Concourse
Under Section 107

Smyth was severely hunched over, protecting his own broken ribs. With his eye swelling shut and his inability to right himself his aim was hampered as he rapid fired Garret's gun. The first bullet struck the wall next to me. The second round grazed my left bicep. The third bullet went through the flesh of my thigh on my left leg. Bullets four, five and six devastated the fibula, tibia (the shin bones) and the knee of my left leg.

Feeling the impact of the bullets as the bones of my leg broke and tore through my skin, I fell backward down the icy stairs. Increased by the ice, my momentum carried me down the stairs and brutally slammed me into the wall above tunnel that led to section seven. As my body spun and continued down the stairs, the guard's gun flew from my hand and came to rest by the wall. I finally came to a stop on the landing six feet from the tunnel entrance. I was more than just dazed, but I could see a steady stream of blood literally pumping out of the wounds in my leg. With my bruised and broken hands, I feebly grabbed at the wounds. Fortunately, I could exert just enough pressure to staunch the flow of warm blood squirting through my fingers.

I looked up and saw that at the top of the stairs Smyth stood giggling holding Garret's gun. After a moment's pause, he said, "My goodness, Detective La Fleet, what must one to do to kill you?" Carefully taking a step down, he continued saying, "You've been shot." Step.

Frantically I searched around me for anything that I could use as a weapon.

"You took such a horrible fall down these awful stairs." Step.

Just at the corner of the tunnel entrance I could see the vague outline of what had to be the handgun Tex had lost when he was hit. The gun was only six feet away – it might as well have been a thousand feet. If I reached for it I might be able to grab the gun, but I doubted I could bring it into play before he fired several times. Also, if I let go of the wounds I would quickly begin to bleed again. Critical wounds to arteries could bleed out in ninety seconds. I was already terribly thirsty, my vision was swimming and I was panting – all key indicators of rapid blood loss.

"You slammed into that nasty wall." Step.

I looked past the gun to the tunnel entrance and contemplated making a crawling dash down the tunnel; however, that led that bastard back to Tex. If Tex was still conscious (something I doubted) he could shoot Smyth. I might still bleed out and die, but at least Tex would kill him. If Tex was out and I was still functioning, I would take Tex's backup gun and pull the trigger as fast as I could once Smyth came into the tunnel. Spraying and praying with a handgun wasn't a great idea, but it was all I had.

"You lost that pretty gun you found." Step.

Preparing for my desperate dash to Tex, I looked at the tunnel and wondered if I could grab the handgun as I went by. Suddenly Rick was there kneeling down looking at me from just on the inside of the tunnel wall. In his hands was a suppressed .22 automatic handgun. Even as good as Rick was with a handgun, at more than five or ten feet, Smyth was out of pinpoint accurate range for a head shot with Rick's suppressed weapon.

"Slid down another flight of stairs and crashed into those hard seats." Step.

I wasn't sure if Rick could hear Smyth talking, but I knew that he couldn't see him. I released my grip on my leg with my right hand and, as the blood began to ooze out, I made a fist telling Rick to hold his position. I faintly reached up and wiped my cheek with three fingers. As I brought my hand down I made another fist and then put out four fingers – fist – and five fingers. I set my open hand flat on my leg with my fingers together at an odd angle to the right. Without saying a word I had told Rick that Smyth was at least thirty feet away, up at a 45 degree angle and slightly to the right of my body. Never taking his eyes off me, Rick nodded, holstered his own weapon and then reached down and picked up Tex's Beretta 92F 9mm handgun.

"And you are bleeding to death! No, Detective La Fleet, that simply will not do. I'm the one that will kill you today. Remember, I am God's instrument." Step.

I wanted Smyth closer but if he continued on too far, he'd be in position to see over the wall. Once he was able to do so, he was bound to spot Rick. Eye swollen shut, hunched over and dragging his leg, he reminded me of 'The Hunchback of Notre Dame' so I shouted, "Kiss my ass, Quasimodo. It's my choice! I *chose* the time and place of my death! *My choice psycho boy, not yours!*" I released my grip on my leg and held both hands in the air as my life's blood began to quickly gush out.

Smyth screamed, "Noooooo!" and, focused only on me, began taking several steps at a time.

Holding my right hand in a fist, I flashed up two fingers when Smyth was at twenty feet and then a few seconds later, when Smyth was at ten feet, I held up one finger. I turned and looked at Rick, smiled and gave him a thumbs up.

As I fell over, I watched as Rick stood up and, without sighting, fired three rounds into Smyth's chest. Without pausing, Rick stepped out of the tunnel, past me and began climbing the stairs closing the gap between him and Smyth. Looking confused Smyth dropped his weapon and fell to his knees. I guess it was the adrenaline because I could see and hear Smyth as he looked up at Rick and asked, "Why? I was doing God's work... Why?"

With the fury of an angered archangel in his voice, Rick replied, "Because no one fucks with my brother!" With that, Rick fired another three bullets into Smyth's face.

After that, I remember fighting to stay awake. I could see Rick was being pulled away by Steve Burt. A gun was pressed into my hands and then removed. Todd Miller thrust his hands directly into my wounds to stop the bleeding and then Rocky Connor scooped me up and began running with Todd matching him step for step. I was dumped into a squad car. Connor drove, Todd had a death grip on my leg and Rachel was in the front seat yelling at me, "Ren, please stay with me. Please, Ren!"

But the peace was so enticing.

CHAPTER 26

Southwestern University Medical Hospital
Dallas Texas

Confused, I slowly came awake from a dreamless sleep. My left leg hurt terribly, but as I looked down I saw the empty space where my left leg should have been. I wasn't very surprised to see it gone. Maybe I should have been, but I wasn't. I didn't remember all of what had happened, though I did remember how bad the wounds were. I would learn later just how close I had come to dying. The blood loss, the wounds, the shock and the infection had nearly done me in. I'd been delusional and in and out of consciousness for almost a week.

In fact, until I just woke up with a fairly clear mind, there was serious doubt that I ever would. Turning my head slowly to the right I saw my mother and Pat Beers sitting sandwiched tightly between Rocky Connor and Steve Burt. To my left stood Rachel, Dad, Todd and, though I had never met her, Pastor Glenda Towers. Next to them sat Tex and Jon in wheel chairs, looking like crap. At the foot of my bed Chief Wong, Doctor Beckham and Father Leopole stood holding hands praying. That explained why everyone had their heads down and their eyes shut (I thought that they were all asleep).

It came out like a dry cough, but I couldn't help laughing as I tried to say, "Is this a joke? A Catholic Priest, a Buddhist and a Protestant were in a room…"

Before I could finish everyone stood and began talking at once. Smiling, my Dad came to my side and, with tears in his eyes, bent over and gently kissed my forehead whispering "Sleep now, Sentinel. Let others take this watch." I heard the beep as the morphine pump activated and I drifted off thinking, *Crap and I probably won't remember my punch line either.*

10 Days later
Southwestern University Medical Hospital
Dallas Texas

Dear Granddad,

February 18th: Pat won't let me off the hook with this journal-writing business. She says I need it now more than ever. I'm not sure if it's helping or not; however, I must admit that I haven't had any serious nightmares since the fight with Smyth. Of course, I've been stoned out of my mind on morphine.

I was moved to a rehabilitation center where I'm to learn how to get along without my leg. I'll be fitted for a prosthesis in a few months. Until then, I'm expected to work out and regain my health. Just before they moved me, the doctors took my morphine pump away. Bastards – that was the one thing I was enjoying (probably why they took it away).

Though he's forced to still use a cane, Tex is recovering well from his injuries. He, Pat and Danner come to see me every day. When Danner is here, he refuses to leave my side until they have to take off for the night. Also, I've had a very steady stream of visitors from the department and the county sheriff's office. Not to mentions dozens of detectives from across Texas trying to solve other murders by tying their investigations in with Smyth. Conspicuously missing from my routine of visitors has been both Rick and Rachel. I've tried to call Rachel, but I always end up leaving a message. After the fifth or sixth time, I've quit calling.

Anyway, I guess there's only one last thing I need to write about tonight. I've felt Rick's absence since the moment I woke up ten days ago. Until today, I lacked the strength to ask where he is. I was honestly afraid that I'd be told that he has been arrested. Rick is wanted by the FBI (and probably Interpol too), not to mention Dallas City and Dallas County for the episode at Parkland Hospital. Houston PD will also want to talk to him over the death of Father Cedric Redcliff. I finally sucked it up and asked my mother where Rick was. Hesitantly she pulled out a letter from her handbag and gave it to me. As I opened it, I immediately recognized Rick's neat handwriting.

My Dearest Brother,

When you read this I will be many thousands of miles away on another assignment. By now you have guessed what my duties often include. I hope you believe me when I say that I have only taken human life when ordered to do so and only when secular justice has failed to protect the people. It is not what I had expected when I was called to serve Christ; yet I do it willingly. I do not ask for you to condone my action, only to understand that what I do is very important. I am so sorry that you had to find all this out through your investigative skills. Ren, I ask that you forgive me for not telling you sooner and for the pain, doubt and sorrow I have caused you.

My new assignment is deep in the mountains of Central America. Villagers and several Priests and Nuns have been brutally murdered and I am to investigate the circumstances and, of course, take corrective actions. I will be there for six months or more. If you wish to contact me, you may do so through Father Leopole. Also, Father Mike is the head of our small order and can answer questions, should you have any.

Ren, you have some very difficult choices to make. Forgiving me is one thing, choosing to ignore your duty is another. You know that I would never ask or expect you to turn a blind eye to the real or perceived crimes that I have committed. Should you decide that we must never again see one another, I will honor your decision. It's your choice brother.

God Bless you always
Your Brother,
Rick

Damn it! Every time I turn around, I am faced with lousy choices. In Iraq, I made the choice to lead my Marines to their deaths to help Rick's SEAL team. I do not regret that decision. But, I've paid for it a thousand times over. As a cop, I've killed men by choice, scarring my soul deeper and deeper each time. And then there was my choice to literally kill myself rather than let Smyth kill me. I did it to set the bastard up so Rick could take the shot. But does that absolve me of what is tantamount to an attempted suicide? A more perceptive person might say that I had made the wrong decision of suicide for all the right reasons. That no matter what I had to do to, Smyth had to be stopped. It's all so easy to rationalize if it isn't you on the hot seat.

Then there's the issue of who actually killed Smyth. People not there think it was me. I don't know who wiped Tex's Beretta clean after Rick used it, and then placed it in my hands for my prints, but it had worked. I'm a big hero. Granted I had beaten Smyth into submission and if it had not been for Garret (who I did kill) I would have arrested the Chief and brought him to justice. Still, I feel like I'm going to be living a lie if I don't fess up. But if I do fess up, I'll be destroying the careers of the people that had saved my life – including Rachel's.

And what about Rick? He is indeed a murderer. He's an assassin that works outside the established laws of man! I *have* no argument that the people he wasted needed killing in the worst way, but it goes against everything I believe in as a Texas Peace officer.

The bottom line is that all of my choices really suck!

Epilogue:

3 months later.

Pulling the car into the driveway of Father Mike Leopole's house, Tex turned and studied my face for several seconds, then said, "Ren, I'll be back in about an hour. Are you sure you're up to this?"

Nodding, I replied, "Yeah, Tex, I am." I opened the car door and got out. Still learning to walk with a prosthesis I slowly made my way to the door and knocked. Father Leopole answered it almost immediately.

Smiling, Father Mike said, "Hello Ren, you look much better than the last time I saw you."

Stammering, I blurted out, "Thank you for seeing me, Father. I ah… I need to get in touch with Rick. I want to talk to him. Can you help me with that, please?

Looking me in the eyes and searching my face, Leopole asked, "And about his job with the Church?"

Staring down at the ground, I replied, "Father Mike, I have made my choice. There's no difference between my life as a Marine or as a cop taking the life of an enemy of my country and Rick taking the life of an enemy of God and man. No difference at all."

Gently taking my arm and guiding me into his house, Father Michael Leopole said, "Please come in my son, we have much to talk about."

ABOUT THE AUTHOR

The son of a career military officer, Mike spent 12 years on active duty as a noncommissioned and commissioned officer. While in the military, Mike served in the Marine Corps elite Force Reconnaissance teams and then later as a commissioned officer in the U.S. Army Infantry and Military Police Corps. In 1988, after numerous deployments around the world, Mike left the military as a Captain and joined the Dallas Police Department. Mike served as a patrolman in south Dallas and as a member of a Tactical team (SWAT). Published in his field, Mike has written numerous articles for law enforcement magazines and has published eight tactical training manuals. Mikes career with Dallas ended after a severe line of duty injury forced him into early retirement. Currently, Mike is co-owner of Charlie-Mike Enterprises, Inc. Charlie-Mike Enterprises, Inc. specializes in teaching SWAT courses. Since its inception in 1998, Charlie-Mike Enterprises, Inc. has taught over 1500 officers from as many as 225 different agencies. Sentinel's Choice is his first novel. www.mikewitzgall.com

SENTINEL'S DILEMMA

Chapter One

3 Months Ago - October
Fort Benning, Georgia

In a black mood and drunk again, Staff Sergeant Cain Johnson staggered back to the barracks. Six months ago, he had been a Sergeant First Class up for promotion while serving as a Platoon Sergeant in Afghanistan. Now, he'd be lucky to regain his previous rank before retirement less than five years away.

Mumbling to himself, Johnson kept repeating how unfair the United States Army had been in its treatment of him. In his opinion, but no one else's, he had been made a scapegoat in the politically correct climate of the contemporary military. Because he had looked away when several of his troops were having a little fun with an inebriated female soldier, he had been busted in rank. He had also been given letters of reprimand and assigned to a dead end job, reviewing equipment inventories of units returning from overseas deployment. The Army had said he should have stopped his guys from getting the young medic intoxicated. Even though he had left hours before the gang rape, he was still responsible for the conduct of his soldiers.

What was missing in his self-pity was that he had indeed gotten off easy. He could have been kicked out of the Army for dereliction of duty. His troops had been charged under the Uniform Code of Military Justice, Articles 120, Rape, sexual assault, and other sexual misconduct. The victim, Corporal Melissa Ames, had had her life destroyed. To add insult to this grievous crime, because Ames had not immediately reported the attack, the eight perpetrators had been found not guilty of the rape. They had all been kicked out of the army for "Conduct Unbecoming", but there had been no justice for Melissa.

Coming to the barracks rear doors, Johnson began to search his pockets for his key. Hearing a noise behind him, Johnson turned around, "Who's there? If you want in, you'll have to wait until I find my key. Or go around to the front doors – those stay unlocked." Seeing no one, Johnson shrugged and continued rummaging his pockets for his key.

Close by someone quietly coughed. Spinning back toward the noise, Johnson this time demanded, "Who's there, God damn it?" Seeing nothing but a sudden blur from out of the shadows, Johnson felt a searing pain as a Grayman, 4-inch Suenami knife punctured his windpipe. While still in Johnson's throat, the blade turned to the right, and in one smooth motion, severed his carotid artery and then exited his neck. Johnson was dead before he hit the ground.

After wiping the knife clean on Johnson's shirt, his assailant reached down and pulled off the blood covered dog tags from around Johnson's neck. Standing back up and scanning the area, the murderer walked off and disappeared into the quiet night.

www.ingramcontent.com/pod-product-compliance
Lightning Source LLC
Chambersburg PA
CBHW061129200626
46817CB00016B/488